Divya's Dharma

By

Shaun Mehta

This book is a work of fiction. Places, events, and situations in this story are purely fictional. Any resemblance to actual persons, living or dead, is coincidental.

First published by AuthorHouse 05/12/04

ISBN: 1-4184-1480-8 (e-book)
ISBN: 1-4184-1481-6 (Paperback)

This book is printed on acid free paper.

Dedication

To Elaine, for always supporting my dreams and aspirations, no matter how farfetched they seemed.

In Memory Of

To Nilam, who dedicated her heart and life to her family.
You are terribly missed

Special thanks:

To the wonderful people of India, and the memorable friends I met at the Indian Institute of Management in Bangalore, and the Infosys Leadership Institute in Mysore.

Acknowledgements

There are so many people I would like to acknowledge and thank for their countless contributions for making my dream of publishing my novel a reality. These are:

For his invaluable assistance in substantive editing:
Sudhir K. Mehta

For their assistance in copy editing:
Kyla Hart
Sonal Sodha
Katie Willis

For their advice, support, and time:

Chirine Alamadine
Virginia Bannister
Jay Chai
Bhavana Chauhan
Thomas M. Dembie
Michael Fong
Marc Jumbert
Appi Khanna
Vivek Mehta
K U Nachappa

Marilena Macchia
Rakesh Majithia
Richie Mehta
Vishal Mehta
Aaloka Mehndiratta
Nick Patel
Michael Petersen
Diptarup Saha
Nina Sethi
Neeta Tandon

For their inspiration:
Kurran Mehta
Premlata Mehta (Biji)

Contents

Southern India

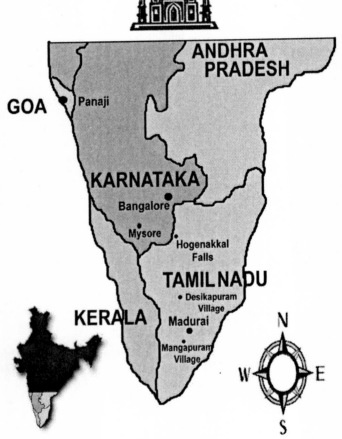

GOA • Panaji

ANDHRA
PRADESH

KARNATAKA

Bangalore •

Mysore •

• Hogenakkal
Falls

TAMIL NADU

• Desikapuram
Village

KERALA   Madurai
•

Mangapuram
Village

N
W   E
S

PROLOGUE

Mangapuram Village
Tamil Nadu, Southern India

Separations
July 1979

Perched on a thick, lower branch of the hundred-foot neem tree, Sedhu Mangalum stared at the letter apprehensively, torn with conflict. He did not know what to do. The grueling eighteen-hour days spent studying at Sourashtra College, and conducting research for Professor Jothi to pay for his prospective journey overseas, could have been for nothing. The piece of paper held between his sweating fingers contained his destiny. Sedhu felt nauseated, sick at how a few typed words could destroy years of sacrifice and ruin his dreams.

Every Monday for months Sedhu had anxiously waited outside the village for the post wallah to arrive with the weekly mail from Madurai—the second largest city in Tamil Nadu—where he had attended college. Finally, when Sedhu was on the brink of panic that somehow his letter and future had vanished into the abyss of the inefficient Indian postal system, the post wallah had arrived with the eagerly anticipated letter.

The post wallah had grinned broadly as Sedhu had snatched the letter and dashed out of the village. Sedhu had retreated to his favorite hideout, the seclusion of the sacred neem tree.

Situated beside the Gunnar River, the enormous neem was hundreds of years old, the oil from its seeds and extracts from it leaves used to cure a myriad of ailments for the community. Far before Sedhu was born, the villagers of Mangapuram had reverently named the neem 'Great Healer.'

But it was not its medical properties that attracted Sedhu to the sacred tree. The neem was a relief from the blazing sun, and the sound of rushing water from the nearby river often lulled him into a peaceful mid-afternoon slumber. Much to her distress, Sedhu's

2

mother often found her son nestled precariously like a lethargic monkey within the neem's wooden embrace. Sedhu never heeded his mother's concerns or reproaches. The neem was the perfect place for him to escape from the troubles and stresses of life. The neem was his sanctuary, and no ranting from his overly protective mother would alter that.

Sedhu nervously grinded his teeth as he stared at the letter, willing himself to read its contents and alleviate the torture he was inflicting upon himself. Conflicting thoughts filled his mind.

Perhaps I should tear this letter in half and stay in Mangapuram, he thought miserably. *What if I don't get admitted? Then I'll know I am a failure.*

Sedhu heard voices below and peered through the thick foliage, a welcome distraction. Two Untouchable women and a small girl walked past the tree and filled their clay pots with the muddy river water. They carefully placed the water-filled pots on ring-cushions on top of their heads. None of them used their hands to hold the clay pots, somehow balancing the heavy loads despite the uneven terrain of their two-kilometer trek back to the village.

Anger and helplessness filled Sedhu. The Untouchable caste was forbidden to use the fresh water wells located in the center of the village. The upper-castes, led by the Zamindars—the landlord caste—were afraid that the wells would be contaminated by contact with the Untouchables. Sedhu did not understand how the Zamindars could be so ruthless in their treatment of Untouchables. Mahatma Gandhi—a great inspiration for Sedhu—had called on eliminating Untouchability, fondly calling the Untouchables 'Harijans' or 'Children of God.' Worse, despite Untouchability being outlawed in the Indian Constitution—written after Independence by the great Untouchable leader, Dr. Ambedkar—it was still regularly practiced outside all the major cities. Dr. Ambedkar referred to his people as Dalits, the 'Oppressed' or 'Downtrodden,' a label that the Untouchables had enthusiastically embraced.

Sedhu was son of Selvam Mangalum, the most prominent Zamindar in the village. Sedhu despised his father's beliefs and values, which created much tension between father and son. Sedhu had explained to his father how wrong and oppressive the caste system was, using the same irrefutable logic as Gandhiji had to inspire millions. But Sedhu had failed to convince his father. Sedhu asked his father what was wrong with the upper-castes integrating with Untouchables. Why couldn't the Zamindars clean the latrines, dispose the dead, and make leather?

"Why are such terrible tasks forced upon the Dalits?" Sedhu had argued. "Why are Dalits treated so horribly because of the family they're born into? Zamindar or Dalit, are we not *all* 'Children of God'?"

Selvam often held his tongue and restrained his feelings regarding Sedhu's views, reasoning that his son was young and ignorant, and praying that this was a stage that Sedhu would outgrow. But Sedhu would not back down, believing that he had the ability to alter his father's thinking.

One day when he was fourteen, Sedhu had questioned why Kaddar, their Untouchable servant, was condemned to cleaning their latrines and garbage for a measly rupee a day. "All of us have two hands and are capable of cleaning ourselves," Sedhu had quarreled with his father. "What's Kaddar's crime that he's to be damned to a life of misery and tyranny?" Selvam had lost control from that remark, exploding into a fit of rage. Sedhu was nearly thrown out of the house. All of the volcanic anger and hostility that had been building up within Selvam was released that day. Sedhu was lashed on his back with his father's belt, but permitted to stay in the house only after his mother begged her husband. Selvam had reluctantly conceded with one condition: that Sedhu was forbidden to ever question him or raise the subject of Untouchability again.

For the love of his mother and for the sake of keeping peace in the house, Sedhu remained silent, but secretly vowed to do everything in his power to one day leave the village and the terrible hypocrisy of India forever. The barbaric oppression he witnessed daily was tearing him apart. He needed to escape.

He still had the scars on his back, and he could still remember the searing pain of the leather striking his flesh. But that had not been what had made him come to the decision on the fateful day. It had not even been the fact that his father had cursed and humiliated him in front of the entire household. What had convinced Sedhu that his father was beyond redemption was that

Selvam had beaten Kaddar with his belt as well, unjustly accusing him of manipulating his eldest son.

Despite all of Sedhu's efforts to escape Mangapuram, there was still one small voice in his heart that held him back—the obligation and responsibility he felt for his younger brother, Ramar.

Ramar was born four years after Sedhu. After the day Sedhu was whipped, Selvam, who felt personally responsible for the disgrace his eldest son had become, dedicated his attention to his ten-year old son, raising Ramar with disciplined fondness. Selvam spent nearly every moment with Ramar, teaching him everything he knew, including the prejudices towards the outcastes.

But Sedhu had also shown love and affection towards his younger brother throughout his life, and Ramar became increasingly distressed by the conflict between his elder brother and father. In the end, Ramar supported his father openly, but secretly continued to have a strong bond with Sedhu, despite their difference of opinion. Sedhu deeply loved his brother, and it pained him to see Ramar follow his father's footsteps. As Ramar grew into a young man, he inherited his father's uncontrollable anger and hatred towards the Untouchables. With Selvam's overpowering control in every aspect of Ramar's life, Sedhu became increasingly concerned that his brother's deep-rooted hatred would corrupt and consume him forever.

Until his marriage with Rani, Sedhu thought with a fond smile. *That certainly changed him.*

Although Ramar and Rani were promised to each other as toddlers, they had only met the previous year, a month before they were to be married. Ramar had been seventeen and Rani sixteen. Sedhu still remembered the first time he had seen Rani. She looked so young and innocent, and it had brought him much joy to see Ramar instantly fall in love.

Sedhu smiled as he thought about how nervous Ramar was moments before meeting his bride-to-be, and then how flabbergasted he became after he realized her beauty.

It was a defining moment for Ramar. Sedhu noticed a significant change for the better in his younger brother, especially when Ramar discovered his wife was pregnant three months after their wedding. Marriage and imminent fatherhood seemed to have brought peace to Ramar's restless soul.

Sedhu's brow creased with concern as he thought about the past few months, and how Rani had seemed distant and despondent. He had brought this to the attention of Ramar, who dismissed it, saying it was part of the pregnancy and that he should not concern himself with such womanly matters. Sedhu had never raised the topic again, but continued to worry about his sister-in-law.

Sedhu pushed the troubled thoughts from his mind and concentrated on his brother.

Perhaps when Ramar has a child of his own he'll change his ways and beliefs, Sedhu thought to himself. *He may be my younger brother, but he is also a husband and soon to be father. He no longer needs me to watch over him.*

Sedhu looked again at the envelope. He could not change the system here, but he could certainly begin a new life abroad. He had known for many years that he did not belong here. He was an anomaly. This was his golden ticket to leave Mangapuram and find a place where he belonged.

What if I don't get admission? What if this is a rejection letter?

Sedhu tried to push such negative thoughts from his mind.

You finished top of your class and are the youngest person to complete a Masters of Science in Microbiology at Sourashtra College, he reminded his skeptical half.

What if that isn't enough? What if...

Realizing he would drive himself insane with such thoughts, Sedhu said a quick prayer and tore open the envelope. The only way to find out was to confront his fears.

Sedhu pulled out the neatly typed letter written in English, a language that he had mastered by the time he was sixteen. The letter read:

June 19, 1979.

School of Graduate Studies
University of Toronto
65/63 St. George Street
Toronto, Ontario, M5S 2Z9
Canada

Dear Mr. Mangalum,

We are pleased to inform you that you have been accepted into the Ph.D program in Molecular and Medical Genetics at the University of Toronto with a full scholarship for the upcoming fall term. The deadline for accepting this opportunity is July 31. Once we have received your acceptance, we will send out a full information package regarding your academic and personal needs.

Congratulations and welcome to the University of Toronto.

Sincerely,

Dr. William Wallace
Admissions Co-ordinator

Sedhu's heart seemed to cease in mid-beat. He could not believe it. He read the letter three more times to make sure his eyes were not deceiving him.

I got in?

"I got in," he breathed. "I got in!" he shouted.

Forgetting he was in a tree, Sedhu stood up and began jumping.

Disturbed by the commotion, a band of crows sitting on branches near the top of the neem took flight, cawing with irritation, their great black wings flapping noisily in unison.

"I got in—whooooaaa!" Sedhu cried as he lost balance and plummeted to the ground.

He landed on the thick grass with a thud. Groaning, he sat up dazed, wondering where he was. He glanced at the letter clutched in his hand and began laughing, his aches forgotten.

He kissed the letter, read it, and kissed it again. He could not stop grinning. Everything he had wanted had come to fruition. His prayers were answered.

"I'm going to Canada!" he shouted jubilantly.

In the distance, a familiar voice called his name: "Sedhu! Sedhu!"

Sedhu stood up and saw his friend Alagu running towards him. "Oh my friend, you'll not believe the good news, I got into..." Sedhu stopped, noticing the grave expression on his friend's face. "What's wrong?"

"Ramar found Rani and Kaddar together in bed, undressed. He's gone into a mad rage, beating Kaddar into a bloody pulp. He has dragged him to the center of village, and is going to kill him!"

Oh my God, no!

Sedhu dropped the letter and ran towards to the center of village with Alagu in pursuit.

Like a bear being disturbed from hibernation, Sedhu knew Ramar would unleash a devastating wrath. He prayed that he would reach his brother before he did the unthinkable.

By the time Sedhu entered the village it was too late. The broken body of Kaddar hung from a top branch of a banyan tree. Ramar stood on a platform beside the body, dousing it with kerosene. Large crowds of the upper-caste community had gathered around the square, encouraging Ramar to set the body ablaze. Selvam handed his youngest son a torch. Ramar hesitated.

"Don't do it, Ramar," Sedhu whispered, his eyes urging his brother to stop.

Selvam sternly motioned Ramar to proceed. Nodding with encouragement, Selvam broke into a smug smile as Ramar lit the corpse ablaze.

Horrified, Sedhu watched as the crowd cheered wildly.

The stench of burning flesh wafted over the village. Sedhu lowered his head as he tried to overcome the urge to vomit. It was not the wretched smell that made him nauseous, but the realization that his family and community were murdering savages.

Sedhu's head snapped up as he heard screaming. It was Rani.

Two men dragged the naked woman onto the platform.

Sedhu desperately forced his way through the boisterous crowd.

Rani was thrown in front of Ramar. She desperately grabbed her husband's feet, pleading for help. Ramar spat on her with disgust and kicked her off him.

"Husband, I beg you to listen to me—"

"Silence, whore!" he screamed, beating her with a cane.

Rani shrieked with pain and curled into a fetal position, tucking her arms around her swollen belly to protect the baby.

Sedhu jumped onto the platform. He was appalled by the condition of his sister-in-law. Despite her largely pregnant frame, she had been beaten severely. Her eyes and lips were swollen and bruises covered her body.

But it was the rage and agony in his brother's eyes that tore Sedhu's soul. His brother had jumped into the abyss of deep hatred for the lower-castes. This incident would make Ramar far more dangerous and ruthless than his father had ever been. Selvam's monstrous creation was now unleashed.

Sedhu glanced frantically at his father, who was smiling as his younger son beat his daughter-in-law.

Ramar, oblivious to Sedhu, roared with frustration as the cane snapped in two from the impact on Rani's shoulder. Ramar tossed the broken cane aside and picked up the can of kerosene. He began to douse his moaning wife with the flammable fuel.

"Ramar, stop this!" Sedhu commanded sharply, his resonating voice silencing the rambunctious crowd.

It was the first time Sedhu had ever ordered his brother, and it made Ramar freeze with uncertainty. As if suddenly broken from a trance, he glanced uneasily at his brother. The look of disapproval and condemnation from Sedhu was unbearable. Ramar broke into tears.

"Ramar," Selvam said sternly, disgusted by his younger son's display of weakness.

Ramar glanced fearfully at his father.

"No, Ramar, no," Sedhu said, walking slowly towards his brother. "Listen to me. This is your wife and she carries your child. You will not kill her."

"She has ruined me!" Ramar cried with despair.

9

The crowd began to chant: "Burn the whore! Burn the whore!"

"There's no choice," Selvam interrupted coldly, his lined face full of hatred as he glared at his eldest son.

"And your unborn grandchild?" Sedhu demanded.

"Contaminated," Selvam deadpanned. "Impossible to salvage."

"Salvage? That child is innocent!"

"It's written that when two people from different castes commit such atrocious acts they must be killed."

"Where's it written?" Sedhu shouted angrily. "Where? Show me this law!"

The crowd fell silent, stunned.

Rage consumed Selvam at the outrageous defiance from his son. He had never been so humiliated in front of his peers and community. His body shook with fury.

"You deserve to burn like that animal did," Selvam seethed between clenched teeth, gesturing towards the charred body of Kaddar. "You are no son of mine."

Sedhu's mother, Nimi, burst into tears, and clutched her husband's leg, begging him to stop. "No, husband, please, don't say such things."

"Silence, woman!" Selvam roared. "Show some dignity." He turned back to his eldest son. "You've been a festering disease on my house ever since you were born. I should have buried you alive the first moment I saw your wretched face. The priests said you would bring me misfortune."

Sedhu flinched as if he had been slapped. But he did not back down. He had been silent far too long and his father's hatred only intensified his resolve. Glaring defiantly at his father, Sedhu took off his dhoti and covered Rani.

There were gasps from the crowd, accompanied with angry murmuring. Ramar continued to cry. As he fully comprehended what he had nearly done to his wife and child, he dropped the kerosene can and covered his face.

"What are you doing?" someone from the crowd cried. "Are you mad? She's polluted! She must be killed."

"Why must she be killed?" Sedhu demanded to the crowd. "She's a pregnant woman who made a mistake."

"Who will have her? Without a husband, who will support her child? She's an abomination," another man claimed.

"I'll have her!" Sedhu declared. "I'll take care of her. I will raise the child as my own. I'll leave this village with her forever so neither she nor the child will pollute any of you. I'll remove this abomination from you. She is now my responsibility, and no one shall lay a hand on her."

"Sedhu, no!" Alagu cried from the crowd. "You'll destroy your life! She deserves to be killed."

"Then kill me and spare her life," Sedhu said, appalled at the words coming from his friend. "Because the only way you'll kill her is by getting past me. I've claimed Rani as my obligation and now I bear this responsibility. You have punished Kaddar for this act, but I'll not let you kill an innocent, unborn child."

There was no sound other than Ramar's weeping and Rani's moaning. Both husband and wife were oblivious to what was happening, each lost in their own pain.

Sedhu picked up Rani.

"My son, no," Nimi cried, moving towards him.

"Let him go," Selvam hissed, holding his wife back. "Let these parasites fester elsewhere."

"I love you, Amma," Sedhu mouthed to his mother. "I'm sorry."

Nimi fell to her knees in tears, moaning.

Sedhu felt as if his heart was being ripped from his chest. He had never wanted to leave like this, so abruptly and without proper closure. He had imagined his departure a thousand times, the local pundit calling the Gods to bless him, and his family and village warmly wishing him a safe journey. But now that would never happen. Like an outcast, he was discarded from his home forever.

Suddenly realizing that he may never see his brother and mother again, Sedhu prayed to awake from this nightmare. He envisioned walking into the kitchen as he did every morning and embracing his mother and brother, and then smiling as she hunched over the burner cooking while Ramar impatiently banged on his metal plate complaining how famished he was.

Why did this happen? It's not supposed to be like this.

Everything was happening too fast, but at this moment such thoughts were dangerous. The time to mourn would be later. He held two lives in his arms, and knew that he would never be at peace if something happened to them. He had to act now otherwise Rani and her unborn child would be slaughtered.

Sedhu walked down the steps of the platform, and past the stunned crowd, his face reflecting stoned determination. Inside, he was terrified. If any member of the village tried to stop him, the rest would follow like a herd of bison. His false display of confidence was the only thing stopping him from being lynched and sharing a similar fate as Kaddar.

Without looking back, Sedhu walked out of the village.

* * *

The sky seemed to be covered by a red, silk shawl. It was late twilight, and Sedhu ran along the banks of the Gunnar and towards the familiar silhouette of the great neem tree.

Hitchhiking on the back of a diesel Tata truck, Sedhu had taken Rani to Sourashtra College where he had left her in the care of Professor Jothi and his wife. Then, he had quickly left Madurai and returned back to the outskirts of Mangapuram. He knew what he was doing was dangerous, but he had no choice. If he wanted to leave the country he needed money and his passport. All of his savings and essential documents were hidden in a box underground at the base of the neem tree, safe from his father.

Under the growing cover of darkness, Sedhu ran to the eight-foot wide trunk and dropped to his knees. He lifted a nearby rock that concealed a metal plate. Using the metal plate as a small shovel, Sedhu dug. Soon his makeshift shovel struck something metallic. Sedhu lifted the tin box out of the ground and wiped off the dirt. He opened it, and was stunned—it was empty.

Oh God, where's my money and papers? They were here yesterday!

Sedhu panicked. What was he going to do? Without money he could neither buy the airline tickets nor get the necessary forged papers to show that Rani was his wife. How was he going to leave India? His mind raced. He considered borrowing some money from Professor Jothi, but quickly dismissed the option. The wages of a professor were meager, and Sedhu doubted he could borrow more than five thousand rupees; barely enough to get him out of Tamil Nadu and find another place within India to settle with Rani.

Sedhu noticed a piece of paper by his feet and picked it up. It was the acceptance letter from the University of Toronto that he had dropped after Alagu had found him. As he stared at it tears filled his eyes.

What am I going to do? Sedhu thought miserably.

"Brother?"

Sedhu looked up in alarm to see Ramar standing before him. He was holding a plastic bag filled with money and documents. It was Sedhu's valuables.

Sedhu stood up warily. He was too surprised to say anything.

Ramar stepped forward and handed over the bag. "This belongs to you."

"How did you know about this?" Sedhu asked, relieved that he had found his voice.

"I followed you once," Ramar explained, staring at his brother's feet. "I watched you retrieve the box from the ground, put your money in it, and then bury it again." Ramar suddenly chuckled. It was a hollow and empty laugh. "Actually, I used to steal a few rupees here and there whenever I was annoyed at you. I used to buy cigarettes with the money I stole. I'm surprised that you never noticed."

"I never did," Sedhu admitted.

Ramar began crying.

Sedhu's heart ached for his brother's wretched condition. He dropped the bag and embraced him.

Ramar clutched him tightly, releasing his anguish.

"Oh brother, what have I done?" Ramar moaned with anguish. "What have I become? I love her *so* much. Don't take her away from me. She's all I am; but I can't bear to see her again. She has destroyed my honor; but I would do anything for her. She's my life; but I can't live with her. I love and despise her. What do I do?"

Sedhu felt something wet soaking through his shirt. He pulled away and stared at Ramar's hands. The sun had disappeared

13

behind the edge of the river, and the full moon illuminated the blood on his brother's hands.

"Whose blood is this?" Sedhu demanded, grabbing his brother. "Whose?"

"I'll kill them all!" Ramar erupted, pushing Sedhu away. "All of them for polluting my Rani. For taking her away from me."

"Is this the blood of a Dalit?" Sedhu asked, his face ashen. "Who'd you kill, brother? Who? Why?"

"Another parasite sucking the life of our country! What does it matter? The insolent animal dared to look directly at me, sneering, taunting me, that maggot! So I punished him. I didn't stop kicking him until his repulsive face caved in. I didn't stop striking him until my arms were too sore to lift. And then I severed his head and stuck it on a pike in front of the Untouchable settlement. They'll learn to respect our ways or they'll all suffer!"

Fury and hatred burned so intensely in Ramar's eyes that he appeared to be on the brink of madness.

"When did you do this Ramar? Were there witnesses?" Sedhu asked shakily, unable to fathom the truth.

"The whole village witnessed my actions. It was a symbol to deter all Untouchables for defying us! I'll crush them all like bugs!"

"You've ruined your life," Sedhu cried. "The police will arrest you for this crime. You had no right to commit such atrocities! You murdered an innocent man!"

"He is an Untouchable who deserved a death a thousands times worse. They all do," Ramar seethed. "And the police will not arrest me. Why would they? I bring order to the land. I enforce what they all believe. They'll respect and applaud me for this. I've done them a favor by exterminating one more rodent from this district."

"But you broke the law!"

"I *am* the law!" Ramar screamed.

Sedhu was too horrified to respond. He backed up slowly, shaking his head in disbelief. He picked up his documents and money, and ran.

He ran from the village and the madness that had encompassed it and his brother.

"Do you hear me?" Ramar's voice echoed in the distance. "I *am* the law! They all deserve to die!"

Sedhu wanted to keep running and never stop. He wanted to run out of the district, the state, and the country. He wanted to run until his heart would explode in his chest. But soon his lungs and legs would no longer co-operate, and he found himself standing a few hundred meters from the district police station in the nearby town of Kariyapatti, heaving for air and covered with sweat.

Sedhu suddenly knew what he had to do. It was the middle of the night and he could hear snoring from within the police station.

He quietly crept into the station. A police constable at the front desk was lying asleep on his desk, an empty bottle of whiskey clasped in his hands. A pool of drool had formed around his mouth. The ceiling fan was whirling rapidly. Music from the latest successful Hindi movie was playing from a battered radio. The rest of the stationhouse was empty.

Grabbing a confession document and pencil lying on the edge of the desk, Sedhu quickly scribbled that he was responsible for the brutal death of an Untouchable in the village of Mangapuram. He recounted the specific details that his brother had told him about the murder and then signed it with his full name.

Sedhu took off the shirt that his brother had stained with the Dalit's blood and left it on the desk. Despite the witnesses, he was confident that his testimony would provide enough evidence of his brother's innocence. The police would be reluctant to upset the local band of powerful landlords. Sedhu prayed that his act would give Ramar another chance at starting a new life. Despite everything that had happened, he still loved his brother dearly and wanted the best for him. Ramar now would not be held responsible for the terrible events that had happened.

Sedhu stuffed the confession in the police constable's shirt pocket, and disappeared into the humid night.

PART I

Goa to Bangalore Express Train
Karnataka, Southern India

Chapter 1
Planes, Trains, and Autorickshaws
Wednesday, September 5th, 2001

Divya Ambani stared with horror at the hole in the ground that was supposedly a toilet.

Everybody who had visited India told Divya the same thing—one day she would love it, and the next day she would despise it.

Staring at the filthy, mosquito infested stall on the train, she had to admit that this was one of those 'hate India days.'

A minute passed and she could not move. It was stifling hot, and sweat poured down her face, stinging her eyes. But still she was immobilized, trying to will herself to do the unthinkable. The only movement was the gentle rocking of the railway car as it sped southeast across the subcontinent.

Divya's eyes darted from the putrid hole to the countless black stains that covered the walls and floor.

God, I hope that's dirt, she thought, consumed with revulsion.

Divya began to wonder what insanity had possessed her to take a train journey from Goa to Bangalore. When planning the trip, it had sounded like an adventure, a great way to see the countryside and the 'real' India.

But not this real! Why didn't I just fly straight to Bangalore?

Upon arriving at the International Airport in Mumbai, Divya had felt the apprehensiveness common for most foreigners entering India for the first time. But, after she had passed through customs and begun to search for her baggage, those anxious feelings quickly turned to frustration and anger.

Divya had taken a KLM flight from Amsterdam on a Boeing 747 with nearly four hundred other passengers, and when she reached the baggage claim section, she was surprised to see a dozen Indian attendants casually tossing the luggage off the conveyer belt and onto the floor behind them. Hundreds of suitcases blocked access to the conveyer belt. Worse, most passengers had taken a trolley to help carry their bags, but there was no space to park them because of the blockade of baggage. With no space to move, and the ability to find a specific suitcase severely diminished, instant confusion and chaos was created.

After an hour of fruitlessly searching for her bags, Divya had waited impatiently by her trolley for other passengers to find their bags and leave. She hoped that in time only her bags would remain. After another hour, Divya was pleased to hear several Europeans screaming at the head luggage attendant. Non-confrontational, the man readily agreed with the disgruntled passengers and quickly gave orders to his subordinates, who shrugged, and began to toss suitcases from the largest of the five mounds of luggage back onto the conveyor belt.

"No!" cried several frustrated passengers, who had systematically been searching through each pile.

If her own suitcases had not been missing, Divya would have found the entire scene comical. But exhausted and irritable, her frustration was rapidly turning into open hostility.

The mounds of luggage seemed to be growing with time, and Divya abandoned her plan of waiting for her suitcases to appear. As she began to search, she noticed a suitcase lying on a platform surrounded by the conveyor belt. A black skirt, several pairs of colorful underwear and socks were sticking out of a tear in the familiar looking bag.

As she slowly squeezed her way through the groups of angry people and climbed over the walls of suitcases, she realized with mixed emotions that it was indeed her bag.

Who the hell would put a suitcase there? she thought incredulously. *How am I going to get it?*

The only way to access the bag was to climb onto the conveyer belt and cross it to the platform. Somehow maintaining her balance as she walked across the moving belt, Divya stepped onto the platform and examined her torn suitcase. She stuffed her clothes back into the tear, thankful that it was on the top of the suitcase. As Divya lifted the battered, weighty suitcase, she wondered how to cross the conveyor belt without falling.

"Excuse me, madam! You are not allowed to be there!" the head attendant shouted. "Please, come back down."

Divya glared at the head attendant, certain he was somehow responsible for putting her bag here.

As the head attendant grabbed Divya's suitcase and helped her cross the conveyor belt, she spotted her second suitcase at the edge of hill of baggage. She leapt over the conveyor belt and seized her second bag moments before the attendants could throw it back onto the conveyor belt. She examined it and was relieved to see that it was undamaged.

Divya had considered claiming her torn suitcase, but an enormous queue of enraged patrons at the counter made her reconsider. She was exhausted and would miss her train if she continued to waste any more time at the airport.

From the airport, Divya took a pre-paid taxi to the train station. Despite being pre-dawn in Mumbai—the time when most international flights arrived in the city—Divya was drenched with perspiration from the humidity. As the banged up black and yellow taxi drove towards the train station, she noticed countless bodies huddled along the side of the street and against tattered buildings, trying to get a few hours of rest before spending another wretched day begging for enough money to put food in their shrunken bellies. Divya thanked God for being blessed with so much, and her frustrations at the airport were forgotten.

The first leg of the journey from Mumbai to Goa had been quite pleasant. Divya had taken a first-class ticket. She even had a fascinating conversation with a kind Hindu woman with whom she shared the air-conditioned compartment. Divya had loved brushing up on her Hindi. Most importantly, she had slept soundly during the trip, and arrived in Goa refreshed and excited to explore the tropical surroundings of the former Portuguese colony.

Once reaching Goa, Divya started her adventure of India in luxury. After spending two days in a five star hotel in Panaji, relishing the beauty of the beaches and consuming countless tasty coconut and cashew spirits called Fenni, Divya decided to truly experience her parents' native country by taking a second-class sleeper to Bangalore. It was a sixteen-hour journey that had turned into an endless nightmare.

Just after midnight, she awoke from her bunk bed with a terrible stomachache. She had successfully avoided train latrines until now, and prayed that she had the strength and willpower to hold the urge to go for another ten hours.

Her prayers went unanswered, and another pang of cramps erupted from her abdomen. With dismay, Divya realized that even holding on for ten minutes was impossible. With little time, and her options limited, she entered the train latrine and gasped at the filthy conditions.

You have no choice. Do it as quickly as possible, and get out of her, Divya, she told herself. *Mind over matter, mind over matter...*

There was a sign on the wall written in English that read:

Please flush before and after use.

Divya searched for a flush, and was shocked to discover that none existed. The toilet was just a hole that led to the rushing railway tracks below.

Her urges were becoming too intense to ignore.

She took off her backpack and placed it down on the cleanest part of the dimly lit latrine stall. She unzipped the top of the bag and pulled out a roll of three-ply toilet paper. Divya paused and took a moment to admire the soft roll, her salvation. She glanced with disgust at the water faucet located beside the foul hole. The Indians used their left hand and water from a tap to clean themselves; the right hand was used for eating. Toilet paper was a luxury used by the upper-middle class, the wealthy, and foreigners.

Her mind raised another question: *What do left-handed Indians do?*

She shuddered at the thought and quickly pushed the question from her mind.

Divya knew that such habits were normal for the majority of the world's population, and many had preached that it was actually more sanitary. Her rational mind knew that she had been preconditioned, but her emotions and senses were far too ingrained and powerful to ignore, and feelings of repulsion swept through her. Then she realized that it was the stench emanating from the putrid hole in the floor that was the main culprit of her nausea.

Divya began breathing through her mouth and wondered if she had enough time to search for another latrine on another train car. This one was unbearably disgusting.

Another contraction struck her, and she doubled over in pain. Praying that the mosquito-repellent she had saturated her body with would continue to be effective, she quickly fumbled with her belt, dropped her shorts and panties, and squatted. She wobbled precariously as she positioned herself over the stinking pit.

Divya squeezed her eyes shut as her bowels expelled a rush of diarrhea. She dug her fingernails into her palms, momentarily wishing for death.

The contraction ended, and she exhaled heavily. Guilt swept over her for having such morbid thoughts. She had to be strong. She had survived the first battle. But she knew her stomach, and could hear it grumbling unpleasantly. She had no doubt that this war was going to be treacherous and brutal.

As Divya quickly wiped herself, she cursed her stupidity for eating the train food before retiring to sleep.

Why did I eat that samosa? Why am I so stupid?

She recalled her parents' dire warning of consuming street cooking and train foods until her body acclimatized. But, famished when she had reached the train station earlier that day, she had rationalized that one small samosa could not hurt her.

Divya stared at the stained metal floor. She realized with surprise that some of the black marks were moving and were actually thousands of tiny black insects. She shut her eyes again and tried to think of positive thoughts, focusing on her parents and her baby brother, Rahul. Her mind wandered to the immaculate bathroom back at home that she had taken for granted. She would give anything to be in that bathroom right now.

Her quadriceps began to shake from her uncomfortable position, and she tried to adjust her weight, but the tremors and pain intensified. Worse, she felt another urge quickly approaching. Sweat poured down her face as she struggled to maintain her position, trying to will herself to hold on for a few more seconds.

Divya heard the frantic buzzing of a mosquito in her ear. As she desperately swatted the little vampire, the train began to brake, further disrupting her shaky balance.

In a panic, she grabbed onto her backpack just in time to steady herself. She realized with dismay that she had dropped her precious toilet paper. It lay on the ground, soaked with black mud or feces. Near tears, she wondered how she was going to clean herself. She glanced apprehensively at the rusty tap.

What choice do I have?

She could not do it.

Divya opened the front pocket of her bag, and sighed with relief as she pulled out a pocket pack of two-ply Kleenex.

Thank you, Papa. God bless you for packing these.

Her relief was short-lived as she was bombarded by another series of cramps. She prayed that her ordeal would soon end. Divya grunted as she strained again, trying to force the samosa out of her.

* * *

Fumbling in the semi-darkness, Divya returned to her bunk bed.

It had been a difficult few hours but she felt better now, although dehydrated. She had run out of bottled water, and decided to avoid drinking the water on the train. She could tolerate her thirst until she arrived in Bangalore and bought properly sealed bottled water. Eating bad food may cause the runs, but drinking contaminated water could cause serious illness or death. It was a risk too dangerous to take. She had already learned a painful lesson after not listening to the sound advice of her parents.

Second class sleeper trains held seventy-two benches that were transformed into seventy-two bunk beds at night. There were a total of nine open compartments, each holding eight bunk beds per train car. Six of the bunk beds were perpendicular to the window, stacked in two pairs of three. Parallel to the other window of the compartment, two cots were stacked on top of one another. A small hallway dissected the nine compartments and led from one end of the car to the other.

Divya was grateful that she was on the upper bunk perpendicular to the window. It gave her a little more space and privacy. However, unlike first class, no pillow or sheets were provided, and she used her bulky backpack as her pillow. Her other bag—her torn suitcase—was secured to the metal leg of the bottom bunk by a chain and lock that she had purchased at the railway station in Goa.

Swindling crook! she angrily thought, recalling how the vendor at the kiosk had asked for two hundred rupees for the chain and lock. Divya had thought she had been very shrewd by negotiating the price down to one hundred and fifty rupees. Later on the train she had discovered from the local passengers that such a lock and chain was worth fifty rupees.

Divya felt a prick in her neck and grimaced. She used her rain jacket as a blanket and covered her face. The mosquitoes from the latrine had followed her, their thirst for blood unfulfilled. Soon the heat became suffocating, and she had to make a tough decision.

The mosquitoes or the heat?

The heat was unbearable. Her shirt was soaked with sweat and she felt close to passing out. Without water to hydrate, she decided to take a risk with the mosquitoes. She threw off her rain jacket, and flicked on a switch to turn on the overhead, caged fans. She lay on her back and stared at the light blue ceiling. The rocking of the train was hypnotizing, and she soon fell into a fitful sleep.

Divya awoke with a flashlight shining into her eyes. The powerful beam moved to the passenger in the bunk below her. She made out the shape of a police officer or soldier.

Studying his stern, wrinkly face, Divya guessed that the man had to be in his seventies. He wore a neatly pressed uniform partly covered by a thick, woolen sweater, and had a bushy, white mustache that curled upward at the ends. An enormous rifle hung over his shoulder and appeared more ancient than he did. She wondered if the guard was actually carrying a rifle or a musket.

How useful can such a weapon be in these congested quarters?

Divya wisely remained silent and did not move. Soon the aged soldier moved towards the next open compartment.

Her shirt was drenched with sweat again and she noticed that someone had turned off the fan. She angrily flicked the switch on and fell back asleep.

Divya awoke again to a baby wailing.

She noticed that half her clothes were soaking wet. She looked at the ceiling and saw drops of water dripping from a crack between the welding.

The train is leaking! she thought with disbelief.

Divya pulled out her plastic rain jacket from her backpack and used it to cover herself.

The screams from the baby seemed to reverberate within her skull and she yearned for the silence that she had taken advantage of back home. A man farted, and a woman somewhere in her compartment began hacking and spitting.

She clenched her teeth, feeling she would go insane by the end of the journey. She illuminated the display to her watch. There were still eight hours left before they reached Bangalore. Near the edge of utter despair, she covered her head with the jacket. She wished the plastic material was as effective in protecting her from the ruckus as it was from water. Divya imagined she was a mummified Pharaoh and that the plastic covering her was a sarcophagus. She smiled contently at the morbid thought of being buried in the bowels of the soundless Pyramid where she would not be disturbed by the screams of an infant, mosquitoes, or flatulence for hundreds of centuries.

Lost in her visions, the wails of the baby and the other irritating sounds seemed to diminish. The constant drumming of the rain eventually eased her back into sleep.

A few hours later, Divya was jerked out of sleep again when the train jolted to a stop with an ear-piercing screech. She almost rolled off the bed, but managed to grab onto the metal rod that held her bunk to the ceiling.

A woman was screaming and Divya stuck her head out into the hallway, searching for the source of the commotion. She looked over the dozens of black-haired heads towards the end of the car, near the latrines and the outer train doors, and gasped.

Blood poured from the ears of a hysterical Indian woman, her husband at her side yelled for a doctor. The door to the train was ajar, and Divya noticed that they were in some dense forest or jungle. It was too dark to tell.

"What happened?" Divya asked in her Canadian-accented Hindi to the man sitting cross-legged on the bunk bed across from her.

The man seemed unconcerned about the disturbance and was peering into a small mirror as he brushed his glistening mustache with a comb.

"Foolish woman opened the door to get some fresh air. As the train was slowing down at a crossing, a man jumped onto the train and stole her earrings. He disappeared into the bush," he said apathetically, as if such occurrences were common phenomena.

Divya's mouth fell open. She stared back at the hysteric Indian woman's blood soaked face. "The thief ripped them from her ears?" she asked the mustached man.

"How else would he steal them?"

Divya shook her head with astonishment, and watched the ancient guard make his way through the crowd, using his rifle to push people aside.

He took one look at the victim and then peered warily into the darkness of the jungle. He pulled out great cartridges from his pockets and began loading his rifle.

Divya watched with amusement as the old man extracted the hefty bullets that looked large enough to take out an elephant. She was surprised that he had not pulled out a bag of gunpowder to load his ancient weapon instead. She suddenly envisioned the soldier tearing a pouch of gunpowder and pouring it down the muzzle of the musket as the earring-stealing thief escaped through the jungle. She found herself smiling from the image.

Well, we're certainly in the right place for some good ol' fashioned elephant hunting, she thought, peering out of the window. All she could see was dense foliage that was illuminated from the lights of the train.

Divya rolled onto her back, and took off her fake diamond studs. It took three hours before the train was moving again, but by then she was asleep, happily dreaming of the decrepit soldier hunting the scoundrel vendor who had sold her the disagreeable samosa.

* * *

Although both her parents were Indian—born in Punjab after Partition—there was no doubt that Divya was a foreigner. With her baseball cap, shorts, T-shirt, sleek running shoes, and a Canadian emblem stitched on the back of her backpack, she knew that attaining obscurity among the masses that jammed the railway station of Bangalore was hopeless. Even if she had been in a sari, like the hundreds of women passing her, one word with her accent would betray her true origin.

Divya felt for her passport and wallet in her pockets and was relieved that they were still there. She glanced at her large suitcase as she had done so a thousand times in the past five minutes. It had not been stolen.

You're getting paranoid, Divya.

Despite being born and raised in Canada, Divya could understand Hindi from a childhood of watching a myriad of Hindi movies with her mother, an obsessive fan of Bollywood. All of the movies that her mother watched were subtitled in English, and spending three hours a day watching an Indian movie had given Divya the ability to understand most common phrases. Her ability to speak was another issue, and although she could put sentences together and be understood, any Indian would instantly realize that she was a NRI, a non-resident Indian.

The majority of the population in the region spoke Kannada, a language completely foreign to her. It boggled her that so many languages and dialects were spoken in India, with Hindi only prevalent in a handful of states in the northern part of the country. Divya was grateful that many people spoke and understood some English, a mark that reminded the nation of its former British Rulers. She found it ironic that English seemed to be the universal language in India, a key element that kept the culturally diverse states of the country united. Despite the brief time since her arrival, Divya had learned that India was more like two-dozen small countries under the banner of one name. She now understood why it was called the subcontinent.

"Excuse me?" Divya asked a vendor of a cart filled with exotic looking fruits. "How do I leave the train station and catch a taxi?"

"Take subway," the man said with a heavy accent, pointing to a staircase that disappeared underground.

This train station is that big? she thought with surprise.

"I have to take another train to get to the main entrance?" Divya asked the fruit wallah, seeking clarification.

A small boy in rags reaching for a coconut distracted the vendor. "Keep your stinking hands off my fruit, or I'll cut them off!" he screamed.

The boy darted off and vanished into the masses.

Divya tried to lift her suitcase, but it was heavy, and she still felt fatigued after the ordeal from the train ride. Before she could hire an attendant to take her suitcase, three coolies, or luggage wallahs, suddenly swarmed her.

It's like they read my mind, Divya thought, overwhelmed.

"Can I take your bags, madam?" asked one cheerfully.

"Come with me, miss. Cheapest rate," the second man said persistently.

The third coolie grabbed the suitcase out of her hand, and effortlessly heaved it onto his shoulder. The other two coolies complained angrily in Kannada. One vicious look from the coolie holding Divya's suitcase silenced them. The two coolies soon forgot about the incident as they noticed an elderly, foreign couple needing help with their bags, and ran towards them.

"Take me to a taxi, please," Divya said to the silent coolie.

The coolie walked rapidly through the crowd. The man was smaller than her five-foot five inches, but moved quickly, steadily holding the formidable suitcase with his hands and head. His strength and speed amazed her.

The coolie went down the staircase leading to the subway. Divya hurriedly followed him, sometimes having to jog to keep up. The subway was not an underground train as she had assumed, but instead a long, dark passageway that ran beneath the numerous train tracks to the main terminal.

Divya could not believe that she was in the central train station in Bangalore. The subway resembled a sewer system. It was humid and water was leaking everywhere. The walls were peeling and stained. She was astonished to see two men urinating along the side of the wall.

That would explain the smell, she thought with disgust, wrinkling her nose.

They reached a section of the tunnel flooded with water. The coolie walked through the ankle deep, muddy water without hesitation. Divya climbed onto a large sewage pipe that ran along the side of the wall, and used it as a bridge to cross the flooded portion of the tunnel.

Every twenty feet on the wall Divya noticed the same message painted in Hindi and English.

Watch out for baglifters, pickpocketers, and bombs.

Bombs?

Divya stopped and read the message again. She was struck by a moment of panic and despair.

Why the hell did I come to India? I could have gone on an exchange to Paris or Rome or Sydney. Am I mad?

Realizing the coolie had considerably widened the distance between them, Divya ran to catch up to him. At the end of the tunnel, she followed the coolie up a staircase and into the main foyer of the train terminal. The foyer was littered with sleeping bodies, stray dogs, and garbage. Divya carefully watched where she walked, afraid of stepping on an arm, leg, or a tail, and followed the coolie outside.

When she emerged from the train station and into the sun, she felt as if she had walked into a blast furnace. There was no wind and the heavy, humid air worsened the affect of the fumes from the excessive traffic.

At the nearby intersection across the parking lot, a smartly dressed police officer—wearing an air filter mask and an Australian style cowboy hat—directed traffic. A sickly looking cow was sitting beside the police officer, unperturbed by the stream of exhaust-choking vehicles racing past it.

The coolie walked towards a cluster of yellow and black painted autorickshaws parked nearby.

After surviving her train journey, Divya decided that she had had enough of traveling like the impoverished, and was willing to spend a little extra money for a taxi. She had no desire to endanger her life by taking an autorickshaw.

"No, I want a taxi," she shouted at the coolie.

The coolie ignored her, and kept moving away from the taxi stand and the traffic-directing police officer.

Divya quickly followed the coolie, suddenly afraid that he would run off with her belongings. Several autorickshaw drivers approached her, but were driven off by a malicious glare from the coolie.

The coolie walked up to the autorickshaw of a scruffy looking man who was absorbed in a local newspaper. The coolie placed Divya's bag in the back of the tiny vehicle. He spoke to the driver in rapid Kannada. Divya tried to listen to the conservation, hoping she could extract some key words that may be similar to Hindi, but she understood nothing.

The autorickshaw driver nodded and extracted a roll of rupees from his shirt pocket. He gave several bills to the coolie, who stuffed the money into his own dirty shirt pocket and walked away.

Not knowing what else to do, Divya climbed into the back of the pod-shaped three-wheeler.

"Where?" the driver asked harshly in English, his bloodshot eyes studying her.

The autorickshaw driver had dark brown skin, salt and pepper colored facial stubble, and wavy black hair. He wore a Metallica T-shirt.

"IIMB, please," Divya said anxiously.

The autorickshaw wallah continued to stare at her and lit a bidi, a brown-leafed, unfiltered cigarette. Divya was feeling increasingly uncomfortable. They both silently stared at each other for a few moments, and she wondered what she should do or say. She looked out of the idle autorickshaw and back at the police officer impatiently directing traffic two hundred feet away. She tried to wave at the police officer to notice her, but instead, the cow sitting in the middle of the intersection returned her gaze.

Stay calm, Divya. You can handle this.

"Indian Institute of Management in Bangalore," she elaborated. "On Bannerghatta Road."

The autorickshaw wallah forcefully sucked on his bidi and then flicked it away. He grabbed a large, black lever by his feet and pulled it forward with zeal, starting the tiny engine. The

Shaun Mehta

autorickshaw emanated a high-pitched buzzing sound, as if it was being operated by thousands of angry honeybees. Without glancing at the vehicles racing past him, he swerved madly into traffic.

Divya grabbed onto her suitcase and began praying.

No wonder they say you become more spiritual in India, she thought fearfully.

Within a few minutes, Divya was experiencing her first traffic jam. She instantly found herself preferring the reckless speeds to sitting idly in the poisonous haze of carbon monoxide and other toxic gases. She began coughing and feeling light headed from the suffocating traffic fumes. The autorickshaw driver lit another bidi.

Cars, buses, horses, dogs, trucks, bicycles, cows, autorickshaws, and innumerable scooters and motorcycles jammed the intersection. Each vehicle seemed to rumble with impatience, and the drivers revved their engines as they slowly inched forward, filling whatever little space remained, as if they were at the starting line of a Formula One race.

Divya found the persistent honking from the vehicles overwhelming, and she covered her ears in a futile effort to minimize the auditory assault.

The autorickshaw driver pulled out a newspaper and finished reading his article. He cursed in Hindi. Divya leaned forward. He was reading the previous night's lottery numbers.

I guess he didn't win, she thought smugly, pleased at his unhappiness.

The police officer standing in the center of the intersection motioned the traffic forward, and her smile transformed into a look of fear as the autorickshaw wallah took out his frustration by driving even more wildly.

The autorickshaw lurched forward and the driver somehow fit into spaces that Divya did not think existed. He drove so close to some vehicles that she could have pulled the hair off the other driver's arms.

By a sheer act of God, the autorickshaw avoided crashing into any vehicle, animal, or person, and clearing the intersection, raced down another pot-holed street.

The autorickshaw driver suddenly swerved into oncoming traffic, playing chicken with an enormous truck that was rumbling toward them.

Divya was too terrified to scream, certain her life was over.

The autorickshaw driver jerked his handlebars to the left, and pulled to the curb beside an irritable elephant being painted with intricate colors by a half-naked, malnourished looking man in a loincloth. The elephant trumpeted with displeasure.

It took her a moment to realize that she was alive and that they had not reached their destination.

"W-Why have we stopped?" she asked uneasily.

The autorickshaw driver jumped out of the front of the three-wheeler and reached towards her.

Oh my God, he's going to rape me in broad daylight? she thought, all sense of reason abandoning her.

The autorickshaw driver grabbed something behind her head and pulled it out. She noticed that it was a water bottle filled with fuel. He went to the back of the autorickshaw and opened the fuel tank.

"Oh shit, we're just out of gas," she sighed with relief, placing her hand over her racing heart.

The autorickshaw driver cursed and tossed the empty water bottle into the gutter. He impatiently motioned her to lift her feet. She complied, and the driver lifted the thin layer of carpet. Underneath was another bottle full of fuel.

Am I surrounded by bottles of petrol? she wondered in amazement.

Considering how many times she had nearly been in a serious accident in the past twenty minutes, Divya morbidly found solace that if she was going to die, the flames from the fuel concealed around her would quickly consume her.

The driver tossed the other bottle and jumped into the front seat. He pulled the black lever forward and the tiny engine shook with life. Within a moment, the restless elephant and his half-naked master were far behind them.

After a few more minutes of swerving and close encounters with death, Divya left her fate in God's hands and began to absorb the sights of the sprawling city.

31

She was amazed by the disparity between the wealth and poverty of the city, and how these two social extremes co-existed in relative harmony.

They passed a modern office building surrounded by slums and garbage filled gutters. They drove past a great Catholic cemetery with people defiantly urinating on the main bricked wall, which had the message: '*Do not pass urine here,*' painted in large, red letters. As they stopped at another intersection, Divya noticed a sleek, black Mercedes beside a wooden cart that was being dragged by two orange and pink painted bullocks, ribbons tied to the tips of their horns. It was a fascinating sight that she would never forget.

It's like every era of human history and technology have merged here, she thought as she watched an old man with a great white beard, and wearing only a dhoti, talking on a cell phone.

Before leaving Canada, she had read many articles on how Bangalore—known as the 'Garden City'—was considered the Silicon Valley of the East, a symbol of prosperity and progress of India, and a sign of the nation's entrance into the Age of Information Technology. But as Divya drove past six naked children begging a man in an expensive business suit for money, she did not see any of that. Instead, what she saw was a country trying to project itself one way to the world while desperately trying to mask its countless problems. It reminded her of the way she often saw married couples at parties pretending to be happy to conceal how miserable they were with each other and their lives.

As the autorickshaw drove over a bridge overlooking a stream, a foul stench of rot and human waste emanating from the greenish brown, sludge-like water burned her nostrils. The smell was so grotesque that Divya began breathing from her mouth. She was shocked to see several people washing their clothes and bathing in the filthy stream.

Past the bridge, the autorickshaw hit another traffic jam.

Divya was grateful that the fumes from the exhaust masked the stench of the open sewer. She preferred death by toxic fumes to the unbearable reek of decay and excrement.

As they entered the outskirts of Bangalore, the road was especially bad, filled with so many craters that Divya wondered whether the street had been bombed.

The autorickshaw suddenly stopped and the engine was shut off. Divya wondered if the tiny motor had consumed all its fuel again.

She looked across the street, and was relieved to see a gate and a golden sign that read: *Indian Institute of Management*.

She had made it!

Divya noticed that the sun had disappeared, and the sky was covered with black, menacing clouds.

"Could you please drive into the school?" she asked. "My bag is very heavy."

The driver turned around to face her. "No."

"No?" she echoed, warily studying his bloodshot eyes.

"Two-hundred and seventy-six rupees."

She looked at the meter. "It says seventy-six rupees."

"*Two-hundred* and seventy-six rupees."

"I don't have that much money," she lied.

"No money, no bag," the autorickshaw wallah sneered.

He extracted a bidi and a match. His eyes did not leave Divya as he struck the match with his thumb. The match flared to life, and he lit the barrel of the bidi.

She eyed the metallic divider that separated the driver from the passengers in the back of the autorickshaw. In white paint, a message had been scrawled on the black divider.

If the driver's demands exceed fare report to the nearest police station

Divya scanned her surroundings, but saw no police station or policeman. Even the guards protecting the main gate to the college were too far to help.

The driver had seen what she had read and extinguished his bidi on the white-painted sign. He shook his head, as if to apologize on behalf of the sign for getting her hopes up.

Divya knew she could not run with her bag. It was too heavy. Also, if she ran to the guards and asked for help, she knew that the driver would be long gone with her belongings. Upset at her inability to solve her predicament, she opened her purse and extracted three one-hundred rupee bills.

"Do you have change?" she asked.

33

"No change."

"But I don't have the change that you ask for."

"No money, no suitcase," the autorickshaw wallah said. He pulled the black lever, springing the three-wheeler to life.

"No, wait!" she cried, thrusting the money at him.

The driver snatched the bills and shoved them into his shirt pocket. He got out of the rickshaw, lifted the bag, and placed it across the street at the threshold of the driveway leading to the main gate of the campus. Divya climbed out of the autorickshaw and glanced uneasily at the black clouds. She hoped she would have a few minutes before it began to rain.

The sky suddenly released a deluge.

Standing in the downpour, Divya watched the driver cross the bustling street, get into his autorickshaw and drive off, the three-wheeler spewing thick, black smoke in its trail.

Soaked, frustrated, and exhausted, she sighed and lifted her bag. The handle snapped and the bag fell to the muddy ground.

Definitely one of those 'hate India' days, she thought with despair.

Chapter 2
Creature Comforts
Thursday, September 6th, 2001

"*B*awwwwwhhhooaaahhhhhhhhhhhhhhhh!!!*"

The terrible sound of someone vomiting reverberated through Divya's room, and startled her out of sleep.

"*Bawwwwwhhhooaaahhhhhhhhhhhhhhhh!!!*"

The retching sounded as if someone was violently ill.

It took Divya a moment to orient herself to the unfamiliar surroundings.

Where am I?

The entire trip from Goa to Bangalore flashed through her mind and she remembered that she was safely at IIMB.

Her stomach began to rumble noisily, and Divya wondered how long she had slept.

She looked at her wristwatch and was alarmed that it was six in the morning. She had planned to rest before dinner, but instead had fallen asleep for fourteen hours. She had not even changed her clothes.

"*Bawwwwwhhhooaaahhhhhhhhhhhhhhhh!!!*"

I better go see if that girl is okay.

With a lethargic groan, Divya got out of bed and grabbed an oversized brass padlock and key. She yanked aside the metal bar that sealed her room door, and walked outside into the brilliant sunshine.

What a gorgeous day!

The hostels were divided into ten blocks. Divya had been assigned to Block B. Block A and B were the only two female blocks, with the other eight blocks—C to J—housing men.

Each block consisted of a four-storied gray stone and concrete structure with sixteen bedrooms and two common bathrooms on each floor. Every dormitory-style room faced an inner courtyard, the center of the block.

When Divya had first seen the hostels, she felt that she was entering a prison. The scene of Tim Robbins walking into the penitentiary at the beginning of *Shawshank Redemption* had filled her mind.

The only difference is that I voluntarily checked into this.

Metal bars covered the windows and security personnel patrolled the halls with batons, whistles, and flashlights. There were even floodlights on the top of each hostel that resembled searchlights.

But that had been last night, when the wretched weather had matched Divya's foul mood. Rested, and now surrounded by sunshine and the cerulean sky, her impressions of the hostel improved considerably.

Divya's room was on the second floor. She used the padlock and key—issued to her by the hostel office—to lock her door. None of the doors on campus had locks, instead there were secured with heavy padlocks and large keys; items she suspected were constructed at the turn of the nineteenth century.

A crow sat atop an impressive tree that monopolized the courtyard. It stared back at her with its glittering, inky eyes. Its sharp glinting beak and talons seemed menacing, and Divya was first to break eye contact with the threatening looking black bird.

"Bawwwwwhhhooaaahhhhhhhhhhhhhhhhhh!!!"

Warily eyeing the bird to ensure it did not attack her, Divya walked along the open walkway to the source of the terrible retching—the closest bathroom. She entered the dingy bathroom to find a thin girl with a ponytail brushing her teeth. As far as she could see there was no one else in the bathroom.

Who was vomiting?

The girl began to brush the back of her tongue, triggering a retching reaction.

"Bawwwwwhhhooaaahhhhhhhhhhhhhhhhhh!!!"

"What are you doing?" Divya asked, alarmed.

The girl turned around, white toothpaste dripping from the corners of her smiling face. "Brushing my teeth," she replied cheerfully.

"Are you sick? Why are you making that noise?"

"Sick?" she echoed, confused. "What noise?"

"Bawwwwwhhhooaaahhhhhhhhhhhhhhhhhh!!!" Divya imitated.

The girl laughed, and toothpaste spilled out of her mouth and down her chin. "Clearing my throat."

"Doesn't such strain damage your throat?"

The girl laughed louder. "Rubbish! It's good for you."

"*Good* for you?" Divya repeated, frowning.

Nothing that sounds like that can possibly be good for you.

The girl continued to laugh, the remaining toothpaste landed on the floor and on her shirt. "Too funny." She turned back to the mirror, stuck out her tongue, and jammed her toothbrush in the back of her mouth, triggering another series of noisy heaves.

Shaking her head, Divya walked out of the bathroom. Fumbling with the padlock, she entered her room and waited for her eyes to adjust to the darkness. She had a headache and needed some coffee. She noticed that her machine was already set up. She remembered unpacking the coffee machine and turning it on for a cup to keep her awake until dinner, but had fallen asleep before the coffee had percolated.

Divya retrieved a new filter and a bag of specialty ground coffee. Although not a wealthy person, she never spared any expense for a good cup of java. Getting excited at the prospect of the rich aroma filling her room and the tasty hot coffee filling her belly, she opened the top of the machine to insert the new filter.

She screamed at the sight of thousands of ants swarming in the old filter.

"Hullo?"

Divya yelped with surprise, whirling around.

"Sorry, your door was open and I wanted to welcome you to IIMB," apologized a pudgy looking girl.

Divya did not say anything, but studied the stranger. Her face resembled a chipmunk with its cheeks full of nuts.

"I am Rekha Gupta. I am your buddy!" she said warmly, extending her hand.

Divya remained silent, eyeing the girl as if she was an alien.

"You are Divya Ambani, nah?" she asked, anxiously wondering if she had disturbed the wrong person.

"Yes, it's nice to meet you," Divya said, taking Rekha's hand. "I'm sorry for being so rude, but I have a dilemma." She pointed to the coffee machine.

Rekha took a quick glance at the coffee machine and smiled. "Oh, it is only ants. That is no problem. We will get some ant repellant and solve your little problem. But first, breakfast. You are hungry, nah?"

"Yeah, sure." Divya said, trying to ignore the movement within her coffee machine. She didn't think she would ever be able to have coffee again.

"I thought so. You are so thin that I azzumed for a moment that you are anorexic." Rekha laughed, and then looked seriously at her. "You are not anorexic, *are* you?"

"Pardon—"

"Why don't you get ready," Rekha interrupted, forgetting her question and oblivious that her comments had offended her buddy. "I will be back here in one hour. And oh, you have *wonderful* hair. I wish my hair looked as silky as yours. And it is *very* long," she gushed.

"Thanks, but—"

"My hair is useless, nah?" Rekha gave a heavy sigh as she wrapped her finger in her knotted dark hair. "But that is okay. At least my chin is not as large as yours."

"What?"

"Sorry I did not receive you earlier," Rekha continued, not hearing her. "I had my last exam yesterday. Financial Derivatives. A real bore, although the professor is *soooo* good looking." A dreamy expression crossed her face. She looked at Divya and beamed. "I am so happy to meet you. We are going to be like sisters, nah? I can feel it. If you need anything, let me know. I will see you in an hour. *Chhee!* You need to bathe," she said, grimacing and holding her nose. "Bye for now, buddy."

And then she was gone.

What just happened? Divya wondered. *Am I dreaming?* She glanced at her coffee machine and cringed. *More like a nightmare.*

* * *

"So how did you like your shower?" Rekha asked as they walked down the stairs and towards the school's mess.

"It was okay," Divya lied.

The shower had been a terrible experience. Divya had been given one large bucket and one small bucket when she had checked into the college the previous evening. With her buckets in one hand, and her other hand ensuring that the towel wrapped around her did not fall off, she had walked into the empty bathroom. Not distracted by any people retching, she had actually taken a moment to study her surroundings.

Although a tremendous improvement from the latrine on the train, Divya suddenly had a desire to avoid bathing. The bathroom consisted of two chipped sinks, one wall-sized, smudged mirror, two toilet stalls—one, which had an Indian squatting-style toilet, and one that was thankfully a Western toilet. The cracked, cement floor was covered in water, and she was glad to be wearing leather slippers. She had no desire to walk barefoot.

It was still early morning, and despite being in Southern India, it was cool, especially with no door leading into the bathroom. Shivering, Divya looked forward to having a hot shower. She slowly walked into the bathroom and studied the shower stall.

The shower stall was full of mosquitoes, and the walls and stall door were covered in mud and dirt. She took her plastic container, which held a bar of soap and a bottle of shampoo from her bucket, and placed it on the plastic shelf protruding from the wall.

Defying all laws of gravity, two green lizards sat on the ceiling of the wall, directly above her. Divya eyed them apprehensively for several minutes to make sure they posed no threat, before she reluctantly took off her towel, and put it on the metal rack. She had never felt more self-conscious about her nakedness and wished the lizards would stop staring at her. Realizing that the faster she bathed, the faster she could get out of the uncomfortable position, she turned on the shower.

"*Ewwwwww!*" Divya cried with disgust as she was covered by reddish-brown, tepid water.

She frantically turned off the flow of water and looked at the showerhead. It was covered with rust.

"Oh, *so* gross," she moaned, wiping the rusty water off her face.

A black dot flew past her and she viciously smashed her hands together. Blood, and the crushed remains of a mosquito, smeared her palms.

39

Die bastards, she breathed, flicking the remains off her palm.

She put her bucket underneath the tap and turned the handles. She filled the bucket with water, relieved to see that it was clear.

With her mini bucket, she scooped the water and poured it over her head.

"Shit, cold!" she gasped.

Divya felt the prick of a mosquito on her back. Another prick stung her leg. Apparently the mosquitoes were avenging the death of their comrade.

You want war? You got it.

She grimaced and tried to kill a few more mosquitoes. But there were too many. For every one she killed another two seemed to appear.

Retreat, Divya, retreat. Get your exposed, cold ass out of here, now!

Feeling an overwhelming sensation to bolt from the bathroom, Divya vigorously scrubbed her hair with shampoo, and her body with soap. She picked up the bucket of frigid water and dumped it over her head.

"Shit!" she gasped again, the icy water sending electric shocks through her body. "That'll wake you up in the morning."

She covered her body with her towel, threw everything into her bucket, and opened the stall door. A monkey sat by the sink drinking water from the dripping faucet.

Divya and the monkey both froze, staring at each other.

It was a thin, scrawny looking creature, with a pinkish face and gray fur. Its tail—longer than the rest of its body—curled upwards. Its large genitals clearly revealed that it was a male. His dark brown eyes sparkled with intelligence.

"Hello there," she said with awe.

The monkey turned back to the leaking faucet and began scooping water into his mouth.

She smiled, amazed by the animal's human-like behavior. Her smile vanished at the sight of something darting towards her from the corner of the bathroom with lightening speed. She felt something furry and cold rub against her ankle. It was a huge rat.

Divya screamed, dropped her bucket and ran towards the safety of her room.

My bathroom is a wildlife sanctuary, she realized with dismay. *I'm not going to bathe for another four months.*

"So you found the hot water tank, nah?" Rekha asked, snapping Divya's recollection of her unpleasant bathing experience.

"Huh? What?"

Rekha clicked her tongue impatiently. "You found the hot water tank, nah?"

"Hot water tank?"

"There is a separate tank by the main door that is used to get hot water. That is what we bathe with. The actual tap water is very cold. I forgot to tell you earlier."

"That's okay," Divya said, slightly irritated. "Who needs coffee when you can bathe in such cold water, right?"

"I am glad you think so since the ant poison will prevent you from using your coffee machine again. It is a powerful poison, and you do not want to accidentally drink some of it. And before I forget, do not use the shower. The water is red from rust."

"I'll remember that," Divya said darkly.

They walked past a staircase that led to A block. At the base of the staircase, against the gray-bricked wall, sat a metal cabinet and two large tables filled with neatly folded clothes. Lying directly underneath the staircase was the shape of a body underneath a thin sheet. The upper half of a black turban was sticking out from beneath the sheet.

"Who's that?" Divya asked Rekha.

"Oh, that is Pradeep, the laundry wallah. But everyone calls him Deep."

"He lives underneath the staircase?"

"Yes, for the past eight years. The college feeds him and allows him to use the bathroom and sleep underneath the staircase. In exchange, he does the washing and ironing of the students' clothing, and gives half his earnings to the college."

"How much does he charge?"

"Ummm, three rupees for each piece of clothing to be washed, dried, and ironed."

"That's ten cents Canadian!"

"Expensive, nah? But Pradeep is missing his left hand, and so we give him a little extra."

"No, that's not what I meant—"

41

"This is the ISD/STD phone booth!"

"What do 'ISD' and 'STD' stand for?"

"International Subscriber Dialing and Standard something Dialing, or something like that. You can make both local and international phone calls here. The phones by our rooms can only receive long distance calls."

Divya nodded, and then motioned towards the obese man sleeping on one of the two chairs in the booth.

"He is the phone wallah," Rekha explained. "Once you make the call, the machine will tell him how much to charge you."

"So his job is to read the machine and take the money?"

"Yes."

"That must be dull. How long is his shift?"

"The phone booth is open from eight in the morning until two the following morning. Can you believe he gets paid over four thousand rupees a month *and* has Sunday's off?

Divya calculated that four thousand rupees was only a hundred and thirty five dollars Canadian. "That sucks," she said, feeling terrible for the man.

"It is ridiculous, nah? He definitely gets overpaid, especially considering he always overcharges the students for calls and sleeps all day. He is like a hibernating bear."

"That's not what I meant, Rekh—"

"Come, the mess is right here and I am starving."

Frustrated, Divya followed her buddy into a separate building beside the hostels. The mess was an expansive room containing hundreds of tables and chairs. In the center of the dining hall was an island counter that had a stack of bread, metal bowls filled with cornflakes, baskets of eggs, and two thermoses filled with coffee and tea.

Rekha grabbed a metal plate and handed it to Divya.

A metal tray filled with boiling water was disinfecting a collection of forks and spoons.

That's good, Divya thought. *At least I know the utensils are safe to use.*

Divya put two pieces of bread on her plate and selected an egg. She wondered why the egg wasn't cooked and the bread not toasted. She looked around for a toaster but did not see any.

Perhaps the Indians here eat their breakfasts uncooked?

Not wanting to ask a stupid question, Divya silently followed Rekha into the enormous kitchen. As they walked past the several cooks who were busily preparing large vats of food for lunch, Divya began to appreciate the amount of effort that was required to feed six hundred students thrice a day.

A sign above a door said: *Vegetable room.* As Divya passed by it, she saw three men cutting huge piles of potatoes, onions, cabbage, coriander, tomatoes, green chilies, carrots, cauliflower, and cucumbers. There was also an impressive pile of pineapples. The skin from the fruits and vegetables were being tossed in the back of a wagon attached to a bicycle. The peelers hummed to the peaceful music of the sitar and tabla being played from an ancient looking radio in the corner of the room.

At the back of the kitchen a man stood by a natural gas stove. He was holding a black pan that was warped by excessive heat and use. A platter filled with chopped tomatoes, onions, green chili peppers, and Indian spices was in front of him.

Rekha handed him the egg and asked for an omelet. Divya did the same, and watched the man expertly create two fabulous looking omelets within a minute, constantly adjusting the hissing blue flame underneath the pan.

As Divya was entranced by the culinary creation, Rekha put the slices of bread in a nearby toaster oven that could easily hold a dozen pieces of bread. The coils glowed burning red. By the time the omelets were ready, the bread was toasted.

Above the toaster, a poster explained the steps needed to be taken when bitten by a poisonous snake.

Divya pointed to the poster. "Are there really poisonous snakes on campus?"

Rekha shook her head and closed her eyes, slightly tilting her head.

"No? Then why the poster?" Divya asked, perplexed.

"I said yes, nah? There *are* many snakes on campus. I have seen them."

"But you shook..." Divya caught herself, remembering being told by her father that when some Indians shook their head, they meant 'yes' or 'they understand.' He always referred to it as a 'circular nod'.

43

"Right, so what type of snake have you seen?" Divya asked, as Rekha led her back to the mess and took a seat at one of the many empty tables.

"A King Cobra," Rekha said nonchalantly, spreading butter on her toast.

"What? There are King Cobras on campus?"

"Yes. But they remain in the forests. As long as you stay on the paths and roads around campus you will most probably be fine."

Most probably? Divya suddenly lost her appetite.

"But if that's true then how did you see one? Were you frolicking in the forest?" Divya asked.

"Oh no, I was walking to Athica when..."

Divya gave Rekha a confused look.

"Oh, Athica is the convenience store located at one end of the campus. That is where you can get food, toiletries, and school supplies," Rekha explained, carefully piling her egg into a sandwich. She grabbed a slice of cheese and a bottle of ketchup sitting by the bread and eggs on the main counter.

"That's useful to know," Divya said. She would have to ask Rekha to show her exactly where it was located. "But finish your snake story."

"I was walking on the path and I saw this huge, black snake slither by me. It was about half a meter in front of me. I froze. It slithered into the bush on the other side of the path, ignoring me. I would guess it was eight to ten feet long, but I am not sure since it moved so fast."

"If it was moving so fast, how'd you know it was a King Cobra?"

"Its head is very easy to distinguish, nah?"

Wow! Divya thought as she took a bite of her omelet. It was delicious! She forgot about the snakes, rats, and her traumatizing bath as she took another bite.

There was a thunderous roar of a motorcycle. Divya dropped her toast with surprise as a formidable man with a curly, black mustache, and dressed in military camouflage fatigues, rode into the mess on a Honda motorcycle. He effortlessly maneuvered his motorcycle between the tables and drove into the kitchen.

Divya gave Rekha an astonished look.

"That is the head chef, nah?" Rekha explained. "He used to be a commander of the north Indian military in Kashmir before he retired a few years ago. He now is the head chef and in charge of campus security. A great man."

Divya nodded. She wondered what traces of chemicals from the motorcycle's fumes were embedded in the food.

She shrugged.

Better to accept than question, Divya, she told herself as she took another bite of her omelet. *Damn, this is good.*

"So what would you like to do today?" Rekha asked, admiring her beautifully constructed egg sandwich.

"What do you suggest?"

"Well there is an end of term party tonight. It will be so fantastic. But until then we can spend the day shopping on M.G. Road and Commercial Street. We have to get you out of those awful clothes and buy you some saris and shalwar kameezes'. With work, you may even begin to look like a respectable Indian girl."

Respectable? Divya looked at her blue jeans and white blouse and wondered what was so awful about her clothes.

"I don't know, Rekha. I'm not really in the mood for shopping."

"Oh, you must! I still have to find a sari for Diwali, nah?"

"Areé, *Motti!*" a lanky, tall guy called out to Rekha as he strolled past them and into the kitchen. "The sun's barely up, slow down with all that food, or like last time, you'll not be able to keep up at the dance tonight." He chuckled cruelly.

Divya was surprised by his audacity. She could see that Rekha was slightly overweight, but calling her 'fat' in Hindi was a gross exaggeration.

Rekha's face turned red and she put down her sandwich without taking a bite.

Indians are way too blunt, Divya observed.

After several moments of uncomfortable silence, Divya asked: "Who was that?"

"Oh, that is Chicken," Rekha said stiffly.

"Chicken? Strange name? Do you call him that cause he looks like a chicken?"

"No!" Rekha laughed. The uncomfortable moment was broken. "Chicken's father is a very wealthy man. He started a software company in Bangalore fifteen years ago. Two years back, Chicken persuaded his father to give him lakhs and lakhs of rupees to open a fast-food restaurant, which he called Fried Murgi. You know what 'murgi' is?"

"Yes, that's 'chicken' in Hindi."

"Very good. Chicken lost all of his father's investment in one year. His father was enraged and forced Chicken to go to business management school in order to refine his skills. Thus, Chicken's name stuck, although the restaurant did not."

"And does he like business school?"

Rekha giggled. "No, he absolutely despises it."

"Good," Divya said, returning her friend's smile.

"But, he does get some perks. As a reward for getting into IIMB, although it was not too difficult as his father is on the Board of Directors, his father gave him a servant to clean his room and clothes, and fetch him food."

"Really?" Divya said, her eyes widening with surprise.

"Oh yes. It is infuriating. He is very arrogant and flaunts his wealth in our faces. Just because he has money he believes he can say or do anything he pleases. It is terrible, nah?"

Divya nodded, her brow creased with sympathy.

"You will come shopping, nah?" Rekha asked, changing the subject and toying with her food.

Divya smiled gently. "Of course I will, buddy."

* * *

After breakfast, Rekha and Divya walked towards the main building where they would find an autorickshaw to go into Bangalore.

Although Divya did not feel like shopping, she wanted to cheer up Rekha and figured it would be a good opportunity to explore downtown. She also felt that she could learn a few things about negotiating with the autorickshaw drivers by staying close to an Indian. She wanted to witness how Rekha handled the rickshaw drivers, especially after the recent ordeal she had gone through.

As they entered the main building, Divya was amazed at how it resembled an exotic, ancient temple that Mother Nature had conquered over the centuries. Gaps in the ceilings enabled both sunlight and rain to reach the trees and bushes that surrounded the pathway. Interlacing vines grew up to the ceilings and masked the walls of gray stone.

Divya had the incredible feeling of being simultaneously inside and outside. She noticed that little holes drilled through the walls were part of an elaborate drainage system that had been meticulously constructed to control the flow of water that would otherwise flood the place during monsoon season. She realized that great planning and effort had been taken to construct the massive structure.

"Go through the front entrance of the building, and grab an auto, Divya. I just have to go to the loo," Rekha said.

"Sure."

Divya went outside and was pleased to see an autorickshaw parked nearby. A portly man was smoking a cigarette and gazing lazily at a black cloud of hornets, which were zipping in various directions at incredible speeds.

"M.G. Road, please," Divya said.

"I am engaged," the autorickshaw wallah said.

"Oh...okay...um, congratulations. But I'd still like to go to M.G. Road."

"Engaged," the driver repeated firmly.

"Divya, you got the auto, nah?" Rekha asked, emerging from the main entrance of the school.

"I don't think he understands English," Divya said. "I asked to go to M.G. Road but he keeps telling me that he's going to get married."

"What? Strange." Rekha turned to the man and began speaking rapid Hindi. "Boss, can you take us to M.G. Road?"

"I understand your friend perfectly and I am engaged," the rickshaw driver repeated with irritation. Although his accent was strong, he spoke flawless English.

"Chill, Boss," Rekha said, grabbing Divya's arm. Laughing, she led her from the rickshaw driver.

"What's so funny?" Divya asked, confused.

"You are, stupid! He is *not* getting married. His rickshaw is reserved, taken, *engaged*. That's what they say here, nah?"

"Oh, he's *that* engaged," Divya said, feeling foolish.

"You are too much, Divya. Come, I am sure there are a bunch of autos outside the main gates."

Divya smiled. She had a feeling that the culture shock she would endure would be a difficult and challenging experience. But that was one of the reasons she had decided to come to India—to learn and become stronger.

Divya followed Rekha out of the campus' gates and grabbed an unengaged autorickshaw to downtown Bangalore.

* * *

"The party is at midnight. You will be ready by then, nah?" Rekha asked, as the autorickshaw swerved around a diesel truck.

"I think I'll pass, Rekha. I'm dead tired," Divya said, yawning.

It had been a long and exhausting day. Rekha had taken Divya to a wide variety of sari stores ranging from shabby kiosks behind Brigade Road to elegant department stores on M.G. Road.

After three hours of haggling with rickshaw drivers and various storeowners without making a purchase, Divya was ready to give up and return back to campus. Although she had been impressed by Rekha's ability to haggle with each person, the heat of the day and fumes from the vehicles were giving her a dreadful headache. Worse, it would still take another thirty minutes before they reached campus.

But everything had changed when Rekha had led Divya into Sterling House on Commercial Street. Sterling House was an incredibly posh store, especially compared to the other dilapidated stores they had explored. As they had walked from the noisy congestion of Commercial Street, the glass doors leading into the store had automatically slid open, and Divya had felt that she had walked into a mahogany sanctuary.

The store was beautifully constructed with beige and salmon pink hued marble, thick glass tables and counters, full-length mirrors, and a funky steel staircase that wound up to the second floor. Even the sign next to the cash register made Divya smile.

Dear Customer
We can't spell
S _ccess without
U

After much fretting, Rekha found a lovely purple and white silk sari for Diwali.

"Yes, I know, Diwali is in November, and it is a little expensive, but you can never start shopping too soon, nah?" Rekha had said, justifying her purchase.

Once Rekha had found her dream sari, she became obsessed with finding something for Divya, despite much protest. Finally, and after much persuasion and approval from both Rekha and the store clerk, Divya purchased a saffron-colored silk sari. The four thousand rupees was steep for her budget, but the quality of the dress was exquisite, and would have been four times more costly in Canada.

"I got the right sari, nah?" Rekha asked, interrupting Divya's thoughts.

"Yes, Rekha," she said for the thousandth time. "It's perfect. The materials, colors, price, all perfect."

Rekha looked relieved for a moment, and then frowned. "Are you sure?"

Divya tensed as the autorickshaw wallah ignored the stop sign and drove past several braking cars.

"The party tonight is something special," Rekha said, oblivious to their brushes with death. "You can meet so many people there. Everyone will be there. And they will be serving *booze*. You *must* come, nah?" Rekha desperately grabbed Divya's hands.

"Well, maybe for an hour," Divya conceded reluctantly, unable to say no to her buddy's pleading eyes.

Rekha's face brightened. "Great! I will be at your room at midnight, sharp. Oh, it will be too much fun. And dress casually, nah? The party is in Main Square."

Divya saw the autorickshaw driver fiddle with the meter.

"Hey, Rekha, I think the driver tampered the meter."

"What?"

They both studied the meter. There was no doubt about it. The numbers were changing twice as fast as before.

"Boss, what did you do to the meter?" Rekha demanded in English.

The driver did not respond, his attention focused on the road.

"Areé, Boss! What's wrong with your meter?" Rekha asked, switching to Hindi.

The driver turned and smiled. It was an insincere smile. He turned back to driving, concentrating on cutting off a scooter.

Rekha gave Divya a look of disbelief and anger. "I hate autorickshaw drivers," she muttered. "All crooks." She harshly tapped the driver's shoulder. "Boss, stop the auto. Areé, don't ignore me, nah?"

The driver began speaking incoherently in Kannada, acting as if he did not understand anything Rekha was saying.

How stupid does he think we are? Divya thought. *He was speaking fluent Hindi when he agreed to drop us off to the campus.*

"Stop the autorickshaw," Rekha repeated in Hindi. The driver ignored her. "Stop it, now."

"*Stop!*" Divya roared in accented Hindi.

The autorickshaw driver turned, his expression filled with concern. "Chill, miss, chill," he said in English.

"There is no way you're getting more than fifty rupees no matter what your meter says, otherwise we'll go to the nearest police station and you can explain this meter to them," Divya said angrily.

The driver did not answer, speeding up the three-wheeler.

"Answer me! Do you understand?" Divya demanded, raising her voice again.

"Yes, miss, understand. Chill," he said with a circular nod.

Divya turned to Rekha, who was looking at her with admiration, and grinned triumphantly.

* * *

"Extra ten rupees?" the driver asked hopefully as Divya handed him a fifty rupee bill.

"Get out of here!" she growled, motioning for one of the security guards.

As the security guard neared, the autorickshaw driver cursed in Kannada. He turned on the three-wheeler's engine, made a U-turn, and drove down the tree-lined street towards the campus gate.

"Too amazing, Divya," Rekha said as they walked back towards the hostels.

"Wasn't it? That felt *so* good! And my headache is gone." Divya said excitedly.

As they reached the mess, Divya noticed a young man in a plain white kurta pajama sitting on the grass in a lotus position. His eyes were closed and he seemed to be meditating.

"That's Om," Rekha whispered to Divya. "He is a good friend, but a little strange."

"How so?" Divya asked curiously.

"I will show you." Rekha grabbed Divya's hand and led her up to Om. "Areé, Om, yaar, how are you?"

Om did not move.

Rekha poked Om on the forehead.

No response.

"Let him be, Rekha," Divya whispered. "He's obviously in a deep, meditative state."

"What?" Rekha snorted. "*Rubbish!* He can hear and feel everything we are doing. He is just trying to ignore us, nah?"

Rekha pinched Om's arm.

Om yelped, his eyes fluttering open. He glared at Rekha.

"See," Rekha said with a laugh, although Divya did not find her friend's actions very amusing.

"Nice to meet you, Om," Divya said guiltily. "I'm Divya."

Om ignored her. He exhaled loudly through his mouth and closed his eyes again.

The two girls walked away from Om and towards B-Block.

"Rekha, why'd you disturb him?" Divya asked, upset. "If he wants to meditate in peace then let him. He looked pissed. He didn't even acknowledge me."

"Oh, do not take things so personally, Divya. Today is Thursday, nah?"

"So?"

"So every Thursday and Friday, Om takes a vow of silence. He talks to no one. He believes that it will help clear and train his mind. Om believes that as the body needs to rest at night, the mind needs to rest as well. And the mind rests during meditation."

"Whatever his beliefs are, it looks like he takes them very seriously, and we shouldn't disrespect that, Rekha."

"Divya, I used to think like you, but you do not know Om. The whole point is that this vow of silence is a temporary phase, as everything spiritual Om does. No one takes him seriously. He keeps changing his habits and philosophies, sometimes on a weekly basis. Last year he was convinced that he had found his answers in Kali Ma."

"Is that a Hindu deity?"

"Something like that. Kali Ma is evil and means 'black mother,' nah?" Rekha scowled with disapproval. "We thought Om was kidding until we discovered that he had smuggled a goat onto campus and was going to sacrifice the poor creature in his room! Thank God we were able to stop him in time. Then there was that time when he became a Jain. He refused to kill any creatures, believing they all had a right to live as humans do, and that they all have souls. I wanted to remind him that he had been minutes away from sacrificing a goat a few months before, but wisely held my tongue."

Divya was impressed. In the short time she had known her, she didn't think her friend was capable of such a feat. Rekha had been talking incessantly since she had met her.

"I hoped this time Om would settle down and find peace," Rekha continued. "But he takes things to such extremes. He actually refused to bathe because he did not want to harm any bacteria growing on his body."

Divya burst into laughter. "Yeah, right!"

"I am serious, nah? After two weeks we could not stand his stench. *Chhee!* I get sick just talking about it. A bunch of guys grabbed him and threw buckets of hot water on him and scrubbed him with soap."

Divya laughed harder. "You're exaggerating!"

"I swear, Divya. Just wait and see. In the next week or so, Om will be practicing some other ritual in his pursuit to achieve Nirvana."

"By the way, what exactly does 'Om' mean? I know it has some sort of religious significance in Hinduism because my mother is often repeating it. Does it mean 'God'?"

"Infinite peace and love. The absolute. The super-conscious. Beyond the senses and intellect. It means to become one with a higher power, or something like that."

"Well, based on what you told me about Om, his parents certainly gave him an appropriate name."

They reached Divya's room, and she pulled out her key and unlocked the massive padlock.

"Thanks for the great day, Rekha," Divya said sincerely. "I'm going to take a nap and I'll see you tonight, buddy."

Rekha's face exuded happiness. "Okay, great, I will see you at midnight, nah?"

Divya watched Rekha walk away, and wondered whether to be grateful or apprehensive for drawing such a buddy.

Oh well, time will tell. She's eccentric, but seems nice enough.

Eyeing her coffee maker uneasily, Divya sighed and walked into her room.

Chapter 3
The Wizard of Oz
Friday, September 7th, 2001

It was early morning, and Aslam Khan waited impatiently for the traffic light to change green. He was at Infosys circle, one of the few intersections with a functioning traffic light that forced traffic to abide by the rules. As Aslam stared absentmindedly at the electronic counter—indicating how many seconds remained before the light changed—he thought of his new badminton racket tucked safely in his bag.

His old racket had cost only a hundred rupees, and he had got what he paid for. The heavy racket with cheap strings had snapped the second time he had played with it. Worse, when Aslam had returned to the sports store to get the racket re-strung the cost had been forty rupees. He got the racket re-strung because of his love for the game, and again the racket strings had snapped in the same place the second time he had used it. Frustrated, he spent even more money getting a better set of strings and a guard to ensure that that particular part of the racket was less vulnerable to breaking. After the strings broke a third time, Aslam had thrown his racket away in disgust. Without a racket to play with, Aslam begged his good friend Naveen to lend him his two-thousand rupee Yonex racket. With Aslam having a notorious reputation for destroying rackets, Naveen had only conceded once his friend had agreed to tutor him in economics and statistics.

This time I'll beat you, Chicken, Aslam thought confidently. *I am taking back the hostel title.*

"You!" someone barked in English. A mustached police officer, distinguished by an impressive hairy growth on his left cheek and a sizable paunch, swiftly approached Aslam.

"Me?" Aslam said, surprised at being singled out by the police officer.

"I am giving you a thousand rupee ticket."

"Why?" Aslam exclaimed. "I've done nothing wrong."

The police officer pointed to the road and smirked, revealing his blackish-red, betel leaf stained teeth. "Your motorcycle has crossed the white line. It is against the law to do this. You have violated section thirty-two of the Bangalore Municipal Traffic Act. Come with me, now."

Aslam's front motorcycle tire was a couple of inches over the line. He could not believe it, especially since there were several autorickshaws and cars far past the white line. But he knew how the police operated, and the worst thing he could do was to argue with the officer. That would certainly lead to a beating or prison time. He was just unlucky to be selected.

"Can't we talk about this?" Aslam asked.

"Come to the side first," the police officer ordered.

Feeling utterly helpless, Aslam drove to the curb and turned off the engine. He got off the motorcycle and waited for the police officer to ask for a bribe.

"This is a very serious offense, but I'm in a forgiving mood today," the police officer began.

"How much do you want?"

"I don't want anything," the police officer said with a greedy smile, his rotting teeth glistening. "But do you see that kiosk over there selling fruits, cold drinks, and magazines?" Aslam looked across the intersection and nodded. "Give the owner five hundred rupees and I will let you go this time. While you do that, I'll watch your motorcycle. Don't make it look too obvious. Take your time. I'll be watching."

Aslam nodded miserably, and crossed the busy intersection. It took him a week to earn that much money as a research assistant.

I've done nothing wrong. Why should I give him my hard-earned money? he thought with growing anger. *There's no way I'm going to allow that crook to screw my happiness!*

As he walked up to the booth, an idea began to form in his mind.

Before he could consider the consequences he asked the clerk in Kannada: "What is the most expensive item you have?"

"We have a foreign beer from Germany. Only one hundred rupees," the owner replied.

Aslam made some calculations in his head. "Give me two bottles of beer, and, um, four of those Dairy Milk chocolates, and... five, no, six packets of your most expensive cigarettes."

The owner put the items on the counter and grabbed a pen and paper. He scribbled the items down with their prices and added up the total. "Four hundred and eighty rupees, sir."

Aslam held up five one-hundred rupee bills in the air to make sure the police officer could clearly see him handing over the money. Across the intersection the police officer smiled and nodded.

Aslam handed the money to the kiosk owner. "Keep the change."

"Thank you," the owner said, pleased.

Aslam looked across the intersection again and saw that the police officer was harassing another innocent victim.

"Can I have a bag, please?" he asked the kiosk owner.

"Certainly."

Aslam took the bag and handed it to the first beggar he saw. "Sell this for the best price you can," he said.

"Oh, may God bless you, child!" the ragged old woman cried with gratitude.

He crossed the intersection and mounted his motorcycle.

"Can I go now?" Aslam asked.

Preoccupied with a harried, pretty woman in a violet sari, the police officer dismissed Aslam with a curt wave, as if he was brushing aside an irritating fly.

Aslam turned on his motorcycle and drove towards the campus. Although he had still lost five hundred rupees, he knew he would cause great friction between the kiosk owner and police officer when they tallied the money collected. He was certain the police officer kept his own tally to ensure the kiosk owner did not cheat him. He hoped their disagreement would destroy any partnership they shared, and prevent other innocent drivers from losing their hard earned money.

Aslam smiled with satisfaction as he roared towards campus.

* * *

Divya sat outside the mess basking in the morning sun and relishing her omelet. She was surprised at how alert and energetic she felt, especially since she had danced until four in the morning.

Ten feet from her, a crow landed and hopped onto the empty road that wrapped around the campus.

Are you the same crow I saw yesterday morning?

Three South Indian women wearing yellow flowers in their hair and colorful saris walked by, startling the black bird. The crow flew up to a tree across the road and landed on the lowest branch.

The three women held grass brooms in their hands. Divya wondered if they were the cleaning staff that tended to the grounds.

That'd explain how Main Square got cleaned up.

She smiled as she recollected the party.

As soon as Divya and Rekha had arrived, it began raining lightly. The drizzle not only kept them cool and invigorated as they danced, but with the flashing lights set up at each corner of Main Square, the falling drops had glimmered in red, blue, green, and silver. But the true magic occurred when the strobe lights were activated. The flailing arms, gyrating bodies, and raindrops all seemed to move in slow motion to the Indian and American music. Divya had nothing to drink, but still had felt intoxicated. It was delightfully surreal.

Divya continued to think of the evening as she tore off a corner of her toast and tossed it on the empty road. She watched the crow on the lower branch, hoping it would go for the bread.

The crow suddenly flew down to the street and landed two feet from the piece of bread. Its head quickly darted left and right, searching for danger. In a blink of an eye, the crow hopped over to the piece of toast, snatched it between its shiny, black beak, and flew to the safety of its branch. It lifted its head to the sky and the piece of bread disappeared down its throat.

Divya was delighted by the display. She tossed another couple of pieces of toast on the street.

Something soft landed on her head. Two crimson colored flower petals fluttered past her.

Is it raining flowers? she wondered with amazement.

A breeze had picked up, making the tree she was sitting underneath sway and release its flowers.

Divya sighed contently.

She decided to explore the lush campus with a jog. Not only would it help her burn off some energy, she reasoned, but it would also be a great way to start the day.

Returning to her room, Divya changed into her sports bra, T-shirt, shorts, and a pair of running shoes. She walked to the mess, stretched, and started down the tree-lined road in a relaxed run.

She was amazed at how lovely the campus was. Countless purple and yellow butterflies fluttered by her side as she ran. Every street was lined with mature trees; its canopy forming a tunnel of leaves for as far as the eye could see. The sight was magnificent and provided shade from the sun. Several trees were dotted with vibrant red, pink, yellow, and orange flowers, as if God had dabbed his paintbrush onto the leaves.

Divya ran along the main road that circled the perimeter of the campus, and ran past a water tower that resembled a giant concrete filter, the Management Development Center, the open amphitheater, and the library. Divya turned onto a side street and quickened her pace. She ran past rows of small homes that housed the school's faculty and their families. The side street looped back to the main campus road.

She approached two hump-backed, white bullocks yoked to a wooden cart filled with garbage. A boy walked beside them, clicking his tongue and whipping them casually with a piece of sugar cane to ensure they continued moving. The stench of rot was overwhelming. Bells attached around the bullock's necks rang pleasantly as the two animals slowly pulled the heavy load.

Is this the equivalent of a garbage truck? Divya wondered. *What a different world this is.*

There was one more side street to be explored that cut through a heavy forest. Remembering Rekha's accounts of the King Cobra, Divya sprinted the final two hundred meters. She stopped at the end of the street, gasping for air, her hands on her knees. She was drenched in sweat, her heart hammering painfully.

Divya surveyed her surroundings. In front of her were two concrete structures—a post office, and the convenience store Rekha had referred to, Athica. Between the two structures was a pathway that led to an imposing metal barn. After purchasing and draining a bottle of water from Athica, Divya followed the path to the barn.

She heard grunting and shouts coming from within the barn and wondered what the commotion was about.

Filled with curiosity, she walked past a motorcycle and black Mercedes that were parked by the entrance.

Divya opened the door and was surprised that the barn was a converted badminton court.

Two young men were playing an intense game. She recognized that one of the players was Chicken, the man who had made that terrible remark to Rekha about her weight. The other player, who she had never seen, was playing in his bare feet. A third person was standing on the middle of the three concrete benches that lined one side of the court, his hands on the top of the pole that secured the net.

"Twelve-Thirteen, Chicken's serve," he announced, acting as scorekeeper and judge.

The three were so focused on the match that they had not noticed Divya enter. She quietly took a seat on the closest concrete bench and examined the interior of the strange barn.

Thin, gray corrugated metal covered the frame of the barn. The structure was approximately sixty feet high, and was the perfect size for a badminton court. Although the barn prevented the wind and sun from obstructing the players, Divya was unsure how effective it was in keeping out rain.

From top to bottom, every metal wall and ceiling was covered with tiny holes, as if someone had sprayed the structure with machine gun fire. Like stars, dots of sunshine glittered through the punctured metal.

Although Divya was curious about the origin of the holes, she focused her attention back onto the badminton court.

The badminton lines were painted in white on top of the concrete surface. Two green poles were erected from the concrete foundation, and a torn but taut net was secured between them. Bars of phosphorescent lights were connected around the perimeter of the barn and provided ample illumination during all times of the day. Although it seemed crude, Divya could see that this was a well-maintained badminton court. Only a large stack of hay in one corner reminded her that she was in a barn.

"Fight!" Chicken fiercely said to himself. "Fight!"

Divya turned back to the game. Chicken's opponent was now serving. His sweat-soaked shirt clung to his defined body. Breathing heavily, his handsome face was filled with resolve.

Chicken, on the other hand, was bursting with frustration and anger. Cursing, he banged his racket against the side of his leg. Remembering the pain he had caused Rekha, Divya hoped he would lose.

Chicken's opponent served a drop shot. The shuttle flew an inch over the net and Chicken stepped back, thinking the shuttle would fall short. The shuttle landed just inside his server's box.

"In," said the judge.

"*No!*" Chicken screamed at himself, tossing his racket in disgust on the concrete floor.

"Thirteen - Fourteen, Oz serving," the judge said.

Come on, Oz, Divya thought, pleased by Chicken's grief. *Finish the bastard.*

Oz moved to the left serving box and waited for Chicken to retrieve his racket and indicate that he was ready.

Oz served the shuttle high and deep. Divya instantly recognized that it was a good serve. Chicken took three quick steps back, jumped and smashed the shuttle back at Oz. Divya barely saw it, and Oz blindly stuck his racket to the side and somehow made contact with the shuttle. There was the distinctive *twang* of a broken string.

The shuttle lazily drooped back over the net on Chicken's side. Divya watched with disbelief as Chicken ran forward and dove on the concrete.

Divya cringed at the sound of bone crashing against concrete. But Chicken made the shot. The shuttle trickled back over the net and Oz charged forward.

Come on, Oz! Divya urged him.

Oz's racket swung upwards and made contact with the shuttle. Everyone looked up to where the shuttle would have gone, but it was not there.

Where'd the shuttle go? Divya wondered.

Oz looked down at his racket in disbelief and frustration. The shuttle was wedged in the large space where the string had broken.

Oz angrily pulled the shuttle out of his racket and hit the shuttle back to Chicken. The shuttle flew wildly out. Oz shook his head and pulled the intact strings together to fill the gaping hole in the racket.

"Sorry, Oz, but under the Hostel Rules you must continue to play with your racket," the judge said grimly.

Oz nodded curtly and got into position to receive Chicken's serve.

"Come on!" Chicken urged himself, his adrenaline dulling any pain he was feeling from his dive. "You can do it! You're the best!"

Wow, they really take their badminton seriously, Divya thought.

"Fourteen-thirteen, Chicken's serve. Match point," the judge announced.

Chicken made a motion to serve deep but did a magnificent drop shot.

Oz took one step back and then lunged forward. He managed to return the shuttle with his broken racket, but the shot was far too high and clearly had not gone where he intended.

Chicken positioned himself underneath the descending shuttle and smashed it with a ferocious roar. The shuttle whizzed over the net striking Oz in the throat.

"Point and match, Chicken," said the judge despondently.

"Good game, Chicken," Oz sighed, angry and disappointed by the loss.

Chicken broke into a smirk, "Thanks, man. But next time you'll not be so fortunate. Shit, if Naveen hadn't given you some of those points that were *clearly* out, there's no way you would have won more than ten points."

Divya was astonished by the remark. Anger flashed across the judge's face. Oz remained silent, and tersely shook Chicken's hand.

"Sexy game, guys," Naveen, the judge, muttered. He extracted a cigarette and continued to glare at Chicken. "And those shots

I called were in, Chicken. It was a fair match and you're still the Hostel Champion, so drop it, okay?"

"Shit, don't get your panties all wound up, man. Chill. Hey, Oz, next time let's make the match more challenging and bet our rackets," Chicken laughed arrogantly. "But when I win, make sure that shitty racket of yours comes with the strings intact."

"I'll take that bet, Chicken," Divya said quietly.

The three men turned towards her with surprise. It was the first time they had even noticed her.

Chicken took one look at Divya and began laughing. "You're that new exchange student that I saw with Motti yesterday, aren't you?"

"Are you going to talk or play?" she demanded, giving him a threatening look.

Chicken stopped laughing and glared back with confidence. "I'd love to, but we only have two rackets, and one of the strings on Oz's racket is broken. I'd hate to put you in a further disadvantage. Perhaps some other time?"

"I'll play with the broken racket," Divya said calmly.

Chicken broke out into another fit of laughter. "You're not serious?" he asked between gasps for air.

"I'm always serious. We play for your racket."

"And if I win?"

"I'll buy you the same racket, whatever the cost."

"You do realize that my racket is worth three *thousand* rupees," Chicken sneered. "It's the top of the line."

"So?"

Divya approached Oz, who was staring at her with his mouth agape. "May I borrow this?"

He nodded dumbly, speechless.

She smiled warmly and walked onto the court, examining the racket.

"I don't have time to waste on a *girl*. Do you truly want to be embarrassed?" Chicken scoffed.

"What's the matter...chicken?" she mocked.

"I'll judge," Naveen announced enthusiastically, lighting his cigarette.

"Fine," Chicken said, his nostrils flaring with anger. "One match. First to fifteen points."

Divya nodded in agreement. "But give me a moment to stretch."

"I'm going to enjoy this," Chicken muttered, swinging his racket in the air.

As Divya took her time stretching her back, arms, and legs she thought about her game plan. She had watched Chicken and he was a strong player. If she had any chance on winning, she had to play smart. She needed to make Chicken run and needed to play on his weakness, which was his backhand clear. He had less control and ability to aim such a shot, especially when he was forced to the back of the court.

"You can serve first," Chicken said with a smirk.

"Hey, Chicken, at least let her warm up with some shots," Naveen suggested.

"Hey, man, she has taken enough of my time stretching. Shit, I've other things to do. Besides," he added with a superior smile, "you don't need to warm up, do you sweetie?"

"No." Divya said calmly, praying that she would be able to teach him a lesson in front of his colleagues. "Give me the shuttle, and never call me that again."

"Oh? What are you going to do about it, *sweetie?*" Chicken snickered, hitting the shuttle to her.

"Shut up and play," she said, catching the shuttle.

Divya stood in the upper-left corner of the right server's box, and hit a high, deep serve. Instead of going to Chicken's backhand as she had intended, the shuttle fell short and towards his forehand. Chicken smashed the shuttle with a quick snap of his wrist. Divya ducked, the shuttle whizzing past her, inches from her head.

"In," Naveen said, disappointed. "Love-Love. Chicken's serve."

Divya retrieved the shuttle and hit it to Chicken so he could serve, but the shuttle landed in the opposite corner of the court. With the broken racket, she had no control with her shots.

Shit, she thought, examining her damaged weapon. *It's completely ruined.*

"One minute," Divya asked the judge.

"Time out," Naveen said, taking his role seriously.

"What's the problem, man?" Chicken demanded. "Stalling already?"

Divya did not reply. She tied the remains of the broken string to the intact string beside it as tightly as she could, securing it with several knots. There was still a gap in the upper corner of the racket, but at least the rest of the strings were tight. Her game was still impaired but at least she would have some control of her shots.

"Okay," she said, examining her repaired racket with satisfaction. "Let's go."

Chicken served the shuttle as high as he could. The shuttle almost hit the lower rafter of the barn.

Divya positioned herself underneath the shuttle and smashed it back. The shuttle landed on the inner part of the sideline.

She smiled with satisfaction, and glanced at Naveen, Chicken, and Oz. Naveen was gawking at her open-mouthed, his cigarette hanging precariously from his lower lip; Chicken was staring at her thunderstruck; Oz's blank expression hadn't changed since he had first seen her.

Naveen was the first to gather his senses. "In. Still love-love. It's ah...um...your serve. Sorry, your name?"

"Divya."

"Divya's serve," Naveen said, a hint of admiration in his voice.

She took a deep breath, and served a drop shot that hit the top of the net, changing trajectory, and looped over Chicken's desperate swing.

"Lovely!" Naveen exclaimed. "One-Love, Divya's serve."

Divya's next serve was high and deep, this time to Chicken's backhand as she intended. Chicken returned the shot, but it was high and short. Divya leaped into the air and smashed the shuttle at Chicken. The shuttle struck him in the chest.

That's for aiming for my head, sweetie, she thought with an inward smile.

"*Ssexxxxy!*" Naveen exclaimed, clapping his hands.

"Are you a judge or a cheerleader?" Chicken snapped.

Naveen's smile vanished and he frowned at Chicken. "*Twwoo-love,* Divya," he said stiffly.

Chicken swore and aggressively thumped his racket against his leg.

With complete focus Divya prepared to serve her next shot.

* * *

"Fuck me!" Chicken screamed as his desperate smash struck the top of the net. "Fight, dammit, fight!"

"Thirteen – Four, Div—"

"I know the score, Naveen!" Chicken barked at the judge.

Sweat stinging her eyes, her hair completely slicked, Divya moved to the opposite server's court. Her face was void of all expression, her eyes burning with intensity.

Finish him, Divya. No mercy.

Divya served low and short, and Chicken dove and made the shot. The shuttle flew high and deep. She ran back and smashed the shuttle back to Chicken, who was back on his feet.

In a series of smashes, drop shots, and clears, the shuttle flew over the net a dozen times, both Divya and Chicken grunting with effort as they darted all over the court with jumps and lunges. With every good shot one player made, the other's shot was even better.

Chicken smashed the shuttle back at Divya's body. She managed to get her racket in front of her and returned a soft lob back to his side. Chicken jumped into the air and crushed the shuttle. She again managed to just return it. On the third smash, Divya instinctively swung her racket out of the way, correctly sensing that it was going out.

The shuttle landed two inches outside the back line.

"Out!" Naveen exclaimed, clapping his hands.

"In!" Chicken cried. "It landed on the line!"

"It was totally out," Divya replied, retrieving the shuttle.

"No way, man, that's in. Are you *blind?*"

"Chicken—"

"You shut up!" Chicken roared at the judge, throwing his racket against the floor. "You've been calling against me all day! *Fuck!*"

"Chicken, that's enough," Oz said, speaking for the first time since the match had begun. "Chill, man, chill. Naveen's right. It was just out. Relax."

Breathing heavily, eyes wild, fists clenched, Chicken gave him a venomous glare.

Oz fearlessly returned his gaze. "Chicken, pick up your racket and finish the match," he said sternly.

After what seemed like an eternity to Divya, Chicken broke eye contact with Oz, and picked up his racket.

"It was in," he muttered.

"Great judgment on that shot," Oz complemented her, his eyes filled with encouragement.

Divya nodded and refocused on the match.

Okay, Divya, stay calm and concentrate. You have the noose around his neck. Now it's time to hang him.

"Fourteen-four, Divya serving. Match point," Naveen said quickly, hoping that Chicken would not unleash his anger on him.

Divya served high and deep towards the back corner of Chicken's court. He returned the shot to her backcourt.

They exchanged several shots when Divya suddenly heard the sound of water splattering against the ground.

Is it raining? she wondered as she tapped the shuttle over the net.

Chicken roared as he lunged forward and struck the shuttle high and deep again, forcing Divya to take several steps backwards. She managed to get underneath the shuttle in time, and struck the shuttle as high and deep as she could. Her arm and wrist snapped over her head and she watched the shuttle sail towards Chicken's back line with satisfaction.

A stream of water falling from the rafters momentarily distracted her.

It is raining, and inside the barn.

Chicken ran backwards and planted himself underneath the shuttle. As he struck the shuttle back, his leg slipped in the growing puddle. He fell heavily on his front.

Divya heard Chicken striking the concrete, but her concentration was on the shuttle that was descending towards her. She tapped the shuttle back over the net and raised her arms with delight as it landed in the court in front of Chicken.

Divya glanced victoriously at Oz and Naveen who were both looking towards Chicken in stunned silence. Confused, she followed their gazes.

Chicken was slowly getting up from what appeared to be a pool of urine.

What the hell? she thought.

Divya looked up. Three monkeys were perched on the rafters, urinating. A snicker escaped from Naveen, and Divya used every ounce of willpower to suppress her laughter.

Savoring every word, Naveen slowly said with the most stoic face he could muster under the circumstances: "Point and match, Divya."

Chicken had still not realized what he had fallen in. He was staring at the shuttle as if it was the plague. With a mighty curse, he tossed his racket on the ground and stormed out of the barn. There was the sound of the Mercedes' door opening and slamming shut, and the powerful German engine roared to life. Chicken jammed the accelerator; the tires screeched as they caught the pavement.

As soon as they could no longer hear the car, the three of them broke into a hysterical fit of laughter. The monkey's bounced on the rafters sharing their merriment.

Divya retrieved Chicken's racket and gave it to Oz. "You can have this to replace your broken racket. I just wanted to deflate his ego a bit."

Oz accepted the racket, trying to find the words to express his gratitude. But any sort of sound he could muster was lodged in his throat and all the confidence he had shown towards Chicken during their brief standoff vanished.

"That was a sexy match!" Naveen said enthusiastically. "You certainly showed him. He'll never be able to live down what happened today, I'll make sure of that."

"I hope so," Divya said. "Now, I have to finish my run. It'll be a good way to end my workout. I'll see you both later."

"Where did you learn to play like that?" Oz blurted out, relieved that he was finally able to liberate his voice.

Divya smiled enigmatically and ran out of the barn.

"Because you are incredible," Oz whispered with awe to the space where she had just stood.

"You mean *were* incredible," Naveen corrected him.

"Huh?"

"The match is over. You meant that Divya *was* incredible, not *is*."

"Yeah right," Oz said, slapping his friend on the back. "That *was* incredible. Let's go, yaar, and share what just happened here."

"With whom?" Naveen asked.

Oz smiled devilishly, his eyes glinting. "Everyone."

* * *

After a hot water bucket bath and lunch, Divya decided to explore the library.

Upon entering the library, she was impressed by the enormous selection of books, journals, and magazines that were available to the students.

Discovering a stack of *India Today* magazines, Divya selected a few issues that seemed interesting. She knew that Canadian papers focused primarily on issues affecting the United States, and she wanted to see what perspectives were taken in India on world and domestic issues.

Divya found an empty table by the window overlooking the forested campus. She pulled out her portable CD player, inserted the headphones in her ears, and pressed play.

With Jennifer Lopez singing, Divya grabbed the top issue of *India Today*, dated September 1st 1997, and studied the cover. It displayed a picture of an Indian boy smartly dressed in a white kurta and standing in front of a huge Indian flag. It was entitled: *"If I were PM..."* She flipped to the cover story and read several accounts of Indian children's views on how they would better the country if they were leaders of the largest democracy in the world.

As she read about fourteen-year-old Sudarshan Govindrai Kamat, who complained that corruption was rotting the country and oppressing the poor, she noticed movement from the corner of her vision. She glanced up to see a sleazy looking man—with slicked hair, a thin mustache along his upper lip, a hooked nose, and wire-rimmed glasses—staring at her.

Am I imagining things? she wondered.

Divya focused on the magazine, hoping he would go away. When she finished reading about thirteen-year-old Manik Kumari, a Dalit, who was afraid that her rickshaw-pulling father would take a loan for her dowry and marry her off in the next few years, she looked up and flinched. The same man had moved closer. He held an open book in his hands, but was not reading it, instead staring intensely at her.

Feeling very uncomfortable, Divya decided to ignore him, and turned back to her magazine.

He'll eventually go away, Divya. Don't worry about it.

A few minutes passed and she began to relax and get absorbed in her reading. She read about thirteen-year-old Firdasua Akhtar from Kashmir, and how she had only known fear, bullets, and blood.

"Hullo, may I sit here?"

Oh my God, the creep is talking to me. What do I do now?

Divya did not answer, staring at the article, her heart beating in her ears and drowning out J Lo.

From the corner of her eyes, she watched the stalker sit down in front her and pretend to read. She had no idea how much time passed before he casually asked: "Are you the new exchange student?"

Divya remained silent, wondering why he had come to destroy the small bubble of contentment she had created. She increased the volume of the CD.

"You're very beautiful," he said, continuing to study her.

Does he have no shame? Doesn't he see that I'm not interested?

She flipped the page of her magazine loudly, trying to mentally form a plan to escape this situation.

"Hullo?"

Go away! she mentally urged him.

"Hullo, beautiful?" he said louder.

Fuck off!

From the edge of her vision, she watched him tear out the back page of his book, pull out a pen, and scribble a note. With a smile, he pushed the note in front of her so she was forced to read it.

I think you're sexy. Spend the weekend with me at the Taj West Hotel. I'll treat you to amazing dinners at its five star restaurant and then promise you the best fuck of your life. I guarantee <u>multiple</u> orgasms. Next week in classes, when you're thinking about the weekend we shared, I promise that you'll wet your seat. No girl has ever been dissatisfied by my performance. Please be my girlfriend.

Divya did not know how she managed not to drop her magazine, or mask the jolt of panic that coursed through her. She read the message again just to make sure she was not hallucinating. The combination of desperate pleading and disgusting forwardness appalled her.

Oh shit, how the hell am I going to get out of this?

Trying to remain stone-faced, Divya lowered her magazine, took off her headphones, and looked at the sadistic smile plastered on the young man in front of her.

Several voices screamed in her head. *Do something, Divya. Say something. Slap him. Run. Scream. Do anything!*

"Hey, Divya," said a familiar, cheerful voice.

A wave of relief washed over her as she saw Oz walking towards her. She released the breath that she had not even realized she was holding.

Oz subtly read the note in front of Divya and then looked at her. *Are you okay?* his eyes asked.

She did not say anything, her eyes pleading for help.

"Hey Tharki," Oz said, slapping the man's back. "Your group was looking for you in the C.C. They need your section for that large finance submission due tomorrow."

"I was doing research for it," Tharki said, giving a cold glare to Oz for interrupting him.

Oz read the title of Tharki's book: *The Life of Swami Vivekananda.*

"I see. Okay, well good luck," Oz said with a casual smile. He turned back to Divya. "Are you ready? Sorry that I'm late, but we have to go. Sanjay Kumar is a busy man and he won't wait for us forever."

"You have a meeting with the Director of the Institute?" Tharki asked skeptically, warily eyeing him.

"Of course. The Director is anxious to familiarize his newest exchange student with the campus. Ready?"

"Yeah," she said quickly, standing and collecting her belongings. The look of devastation on Tharki's face further disturbed her. "Let's go."

When they had walked out of the library, Divya sighed with relief. "Thanks. If you hadn't come, I don't know what I would've done."

"Are you okay?" Oz asked.

"Yes, but who was that sick pervert?"

"Yes, exactly, pervert."

"What?"

"That's his name. You were right on. I was calling him Tharki, which means 'pervert' in Hindi. That's what the students here have nicknamed him."

"You're kidding?" she laughed, much of the tension escaping her.

"No, I'm not. Sorry you had to go through that. Tharki can be quite..." He searched for the appropriate word. "Forward."

"Forward? That's an understatement. Did you see the vulgarity he wrote to me?"

"Yes, I did. But forget about him. He's all talk and harmless. He can be quite unsettling if you don't know him."

"And what's your name? I know they called you Oz at the badminton court, but that's not your *real* name, is it?"

"Aslam Khan, pleased to meet you, but call me Oz. That's what everyone calls me."

"Okay, sure...um...and why do they call you that?"

"Have you seen the film, *The Wizard of Oz?*"

"Oh, yeah, loved it."

"Well, I was in first year, on the first day of classes, and I was a little anxious."

71

"I remember my first day of class in University. I was so nervous since I had no idea what to expect and didn't know anyone."

"That wasn't why I was nervous. Actually, we had Professor Munde for marketing. That was what terrified me."

"I have Professor Munde for Marketing Communications on Monday," she said, a worried expression filling her face. "What's wrong with him?"

"I'll tell you, but on one condition."

"Oh really? This should be interesting."

"If you tell me how you learned to play badminton like that."

Her eyes sparkled playfully. "Okay, but you first tell me your story."

"Shake on it," he said, extending his hand, which she took. As their skin made contact, a small jolt of static electricity shocked them.

"Sorry about that," Divya said with an apologetic smile. "I tend to do that a lot."

"No, it's okay," he said, relishing the sensation that lingered in the palm of his hand.

They walked past the laundry wallah, Pradeep, who warmly greeted them as he ironed a shirt.

"So, you owe me a story," Divya said.

"Yes, of course. Well, it began on the first day of classes. We were supposed to have our cases pre-read. Professor Munde had sent us an e-mail telling us in advance, but it was orientation week, and all the students were partying and getting to know one another. So, most of us got up that first day of classes tired and hung over, and dragged ourselves out of bed. We barely made it to class on time. Naturally, none of us had even looked at the case.

"And that upset him?"

Aslam smiled at the memory. "You can say that. He walked into class at exactly eight a.m. and stared directly at me. He asked: 'Mr. Khan, have you read the case?' I was surprised by his bluntness, and the fact that he knew my name since this was the first time we had met. He caught me completely off guard, and I answered honestly: 'no.'"

"And then?" she asked, engrossed by the story.

"Ah, sorry, but we've reached your room," Aslam announced, smiling. "We'll have to finish this story some other time."

"What? No, no, no, finish it now. You can't just leave me hanging like that." Aslam smiled again and Divya could not help but return it. "Come on, Oz, don't make me beg."

"Okay, okay. Professor Munde then asked me: 'Mr. Khan, were you aware that you were supposed to have the case read for class?' to which I replied 'yes.' He then asked: 'Mr. Khan, are you aware that I am a demanding professor?' to which I truthfully answered 'yes.' He took off his glasses and came very close to me, and said: 'Mr. Khan, have you ever watched the movie, *The Wizard of Oz*?'"

"What? Why'd he ask that?"

"I'll tell you. He asked me whether I had seen the *Wizard of Oz*, to which I answered 'yes.' He then said: 'Mr. Khan, based on your one word answers, and the fact that you are completely unprepared for class, which you knew would be demanding, I would hypothesize that the scarecrow in the *Wizard of Oz* has more of a brain than you do.'"

"He didn't!"

"Oh, he did. He then told me to pack up my belongings and leave the classroom, as he had no patience or space in his class for a brainless *duffer* who did not prepare for class. I was so shocked, Divya," Aslam said, relishing how enraptured she was by his every word. "I was paralyzed. Professor Munde then leaned towards me, and coldly said: 'Mr. Khan, I know you have no brain, but you have legs so I suggest you use them and get out.' Still I did not move. I was having trouble registering what he was saying partially from the shock of his harsh words, and partially because I was suffering from the worst hangover in my life."

"Did you finally leave the class?"

Aslam nodded vigorously. "Oh, yes. After his leg remark, I still hadn't moved. He then shouted: 'Get the hell out of my class now, Mr. Khan, or I'll have you thrown out. And if you do not prepare for the next time, don't bother showing up!' I regained the use of my legs and bolted out of the room. And I was the lucky because he blasted the entire class for the rest of the lecture. From that point on, every student who hadn't dropped out of his class always came to class prepared and on time."

"And because of Professor Munde's comment everyone now calls you 'Oz'?"

"Yes, and I've never had a drink since then. I learned my lesson. His screaming left a lasting impression on me. I could hear those words bouncing around my throbbing head for days after."

"Amazing. So, do you suggest I drop out of that class and take something else?"

"Depends why you came here on exchange. If you're here to travel and for fun, then you better drop it. But, if you want to undergo a *phenomenal* learning experience, then I suggest you stay with him. He's tough and I worked my butt off in his class, but it was the best course I've taken at IIMB."

"Phenomenal, eh?"

"Definitely."

"Would you take another course he was teaching?"

"Hell, no!" Aslam exclaimed. "I'm never going through that torture again." Divya laughed. "And it's bad enough that I work for him."

"You work for him? No way!"

"Yes, ironic isn't it? I'm a teaching assistant. I conduct research, and mark papers and exams. The pay is barely enough to get by, especially since I send half my wages back home, but the work is fascinating. And I managed to save enough to buy and fix up a second-hand motorcycle...Divya, you okay? You're looking at me strangely."

"Huh?" Suddenly realizing that she was staring at him, she quickly said: "Yeah, sorry...so you mark papers, eh? If I stay in that class, can you help me out?" She smiled sweetly.

"Oh, that's not going to work on me, and I don't think you want me to mark your papers, Divya. There are a dozen students at this school who don't speak to me because I wouldn't help them out. Some even offered bribes, but one's conscience can be a powerful force."

She sighed and nodded. "Yes, you're right, I understand."

"But you can wait a week into the term before switching classes. Go to a couple of his classes next week and see what you think. If you don't like it, then you can always switch."

"Thanks for the advice. I'll do that. Well, I better go. Thanks for saving me from Tharki."

"It's the least I can do after you humiliated Chicken."

"He deserved it after what he did."

"Did he want to take you to the Taj West Hotel for the weekend as well," Aslam laughed. "What did he do to you?"

"It's his attitude, and the way he treated Rekha yesterday."

"You know Rekha? Rekha Gupta?"

"Yeah, she's my buddy, why?"

"Wonderful! She's one of my best friends...oh, I have a fantastic idea!" he exclaimed, snapping his fingers. "Rekha, Naveen, Om, and I are going to Mysore tomorrow for a day trip. All of us have been at school for over a year and have not seen it yet. It's supposed to be quite lovely. Interested?"

Divya paused for a moment, contemplating the question as she unlocked the padlock to her room. "Sure, it sounds like fun," she finally said, considering this was the last weekend before classes began, and she had no idea when she would have the opportunity to take such an excursion, especially if she decided to remain in Professor Munde's marketing class.

Aslam grinned. "Great, we're all meeting tomorrow at six in the morning in front of the mess. We've rented a jeep."

"Hey, by the way, how did you get Om to come? This doesn't sound like a very religious thing to do?"

"It isn't, but Om doesn't know that," Aslam said with a mischievous smile. "He thinks we'll be spending the day at the Nandi Temple, and once he discovers that we're not, it won't matter because he's currently on a vow of silence!"

"Ah, clever and cunning. I hope you save your tricks and deception only for Om, otherwise I may reconsider coming."

"You wouldn't do that."

"And why's that?"

He gave her a charming smile. "Because you find me too irresistible to decline."

"Is that so?"

"And, you won't have to pay a rupee. The day is on me. Consider it a thank you for getting me that racket."

"A girl cannot refuse such a generous offer. You really are an enchanting marketer. Professor Munde must have been impressed by your transformation after the first class."

"I think so. I did eventually marry his daughter."

Divya laughed at the remark, but Aslam remained serious.

"Y-You're married to Professor Munde's daughter?" she stammered, her face filled with disappointment.

He burst into laughter. "No, I was just kidding. Why, you jealous?"

"What? No, of course not!" Divya exclaimed, blushing fiercely. "I-I better go...I'll see you in the morning."

"Divya, don't be like that. I was only having fun."

"Ha, ha, very funny," she said crossly, closing the door on his smiling face.

"Hey, you didn't tell me how you learned to play badminton like that," he said, his voice muffled voice through the door. "Hello? Hey, you owe me a story. We shook on it."

She did not respond. She leaned against the door, closing her eyes as she tried to make sense of the confusing emotions that flooded through her.

Chapter 4
The Driver of Mysore
Saturday, September 8th, 2001

Divya met the others in front of the mess at six in the morning. A new, white Tata Jeep pulled up in front of them, glimmering in the sunshine. It was a beautiful vehicle, designed to comfortably seat six people.

They left before breakfast was served, and as the driver sped southbound through the empty streets of Bangalore, they all had cucumber and tomato sandwiches, cookies, and chilled water that Rekha had thoughtfully packed for them.

Divya offered Om some food but he ignored her. Since their departure Om had neither eaten nor spoken a word, angry with his friends for betraying him. After they had left campus, Aslam had admitted to Om that they were not going on a religious pilgrimage, but on a scenic tour of Mysore. Upon hearing the truth, Om had glared accusingly at Aslam, and turned his back to him, masking his sulking through prayers.

Divya felt bad for Om, understanding his anger. She would have been upset if her friends had deceived her, no matter how noble their intentions. In her view, there was no excuse for lying.

Aslam sat in the front of the jeep beside the driver since he had the tour book of Mysore, and was the only person in the vehicle who could converse with the driver in Kannada.

"I'm not fluent in the language, but I can tell him where we want to go," Aslam explained to Divya, trying to impress her. "Don't worry, with this jeep we have complete flexibility. We can do what we want, when we want, and how we want to," he finished with a reassuring smile.

Sitting on Divya's right, Rekha rolled her eyes, and Naveen on her left, snorted. Om sat cross-legged in the back of the jeep, his eyes closed as he mouthed his prayers.

The excitement of embarking on their adventure was quickly replaced by fatigue. Preparing for the trip and getting up so early had deprived all of them of sleep, and soon the passengers were asleep, except Om, who entered some type of spiritual trance.

Divya awoke an hour and a half later listening to Aslam having an animated conversation with the driver in the foreign tongue. Rekha and Naveen were still asleep. She could hear the soft murmuring of Om behind her.

Realizing Divya was awake, Aslam turned and smiled warmly at her. "Good sleep?"

She nodded, rubbing her eyes. Wedged between Naveen and Rekha, she stretched as much as she could in the limited space.

"I noticed in the *Lonely Planet* guide that there's this island on the river Kaveri. It used to be the capital of Tippu Sultan, a great ruler of southern India. The island has an ancient temple, mosque, and the Sultan's Summer Palace," Aslam said excitedly. "And since it's right on the way to Mysore, I thought we'd check it out."

"Sounds good," Divya said.

Divya turned to admire the verdant landscape of rice fields, forests of palm trees, and the distant rocky hills. It resembled an image from a tropical Caribbean island. She was speechless by the beauty of the countryside.

What a gorgeous country, she marveled. *If they could only take care of their cities...*

After thirty minutes of driving past small villages and the occasional cluster of huts along the tree-lined road, the jeep drove over a bridge that crossed the Kaveri River and through a narrow archway that led to the island of Srirangapatna.

Aslam spoke rapidly with the jeep driver, who continued to give circular nods.

"I've asked him to take us to Tippu Sultan's Summer Palace. It's supposed to be magnificent," Aslam explained. "Did you know, Divya, that Sultan Tippu was a great man and warrior?"

"But he lost his kingdom and got killed by the British insurgence, nah?" Rekha said, opening her eyes.

"Isn't that interesting, Om?" Aslam asked, trying to get him involved in their conversation.

Everyone turned to the back of the jeep. Even Naveen, who had slept through the entire journey, suddenly sprang to life to observe Om's reaction.

"Om, did you hear what I said?" Aslam said, feeling remorseful for upsetting his friend.

Om opened his eyes, and glared at them with defiance.

"Areé, Om, yaar, please don't be angry," Aslam pleaded. "I thought about you as well. Before we stop at the Summer Palace, the driver will take you to the ancient Ranganathaswamy Temple that was constructed during the ninth century. There's also a Krishna shrine inside its walls, and we'll be back in an hour so you have lots of time to explore and give your respects."

Om's hard lines softened and his eyes suddenly shined with benevolence. Divya was amazed how quickly the vibes emanating from Om had transformed into something so warm and positive. The tension pervading the jeep vanished.

Om was dropped off outside the exquisitely carved temple that resembled many southern temples Divya had seen in photographs and in *National Geographic*. The driver took the rest of them past a white marbled gravestone that claimed to be the final resting place of the Sultan, past a whitewashed mosque with two elegant towers, and to the opposite end of the island where the Summer Palace was located.

As they got out of the jeep in front of the entrance to the compound, Aslam turned to Divya and said: "Remember the agreement we made."

"Oz, no! I was only kidding. I could never let you pay."

"Well, I wasn't kidding. Please, it'll make me very happy and I'd be insulted if you protest any further."

Divya felt uncomfortable being treated, especially when she had the money and knew Aslam was a struggling student. But one look on his face made her reluctantly concede.

Aslam pulled out a ten-rupee note from his wallet. As he approached the main entrance, he noticed a large sign that was posted outside the ticket booth.

Foreigners: 225 rupees
Indians: 5 rupees

Aslam's brow creased with concern as he looked at his wallet. He did not know what to do. He could not afford to pay Divya as a foreigner if he wanted to treat her for the rest of the day.

Divya noticed Aslam's reaction and instantly understood his dilemma. Rather than offend him by insisting on paying the fee herself, she said: "Oz, I can't permit the government to capitalize on such blatant discrimination against foreigners. Just because I'm not born here, why should I pay fifty times the price? Huh?"

Rekha and Naveen nodded with agreement. Still holding his ten-rupee note, Aslam stared at her.

"Don't worry, I'll take care of this," Divya said, taking control of the situation. She marched up to the ticket booth with determination. The other three followed behind her.

"Four tickets," Divya said in her Canadian accented Hindi as she pulled out twenty rupees and slid it to the ticket attendant.

"Are you Indian?" the clerk asked suspiciously in Hindi, studying her.

"My parents were both born in Punjab, and I am studying at the Indian Institute of Management in Bangalore," Divya said in her best Hindi, concentrating to pronounce every word correctly. She pulled out her newly laminated IIMB student card that had been given to her on the day she had arrived, and showed it to the clerk.

The ticket attendant took his time studying the photo on the student card, and then conferred in Kannada with the security personnel guarding the main entrance.

The ticket attendant handed Divya back her student card and four tickets. Divya gave a striking smile, and handed a ticket to each of her friends.

"Where did she learn to speak Hindi like that?" Naveen whispered to Rekha.

"Indian movies," Divya replied with a broad smile.

"That was great, nah?" Rekha enthused. "Oz, was that not great?"

Aslam did not reply. He was still holding the ten-rupee note in one hand and the ticket Divya had given him in the other. He watched Divya walk down the steps and onto the manicured grounds that stretched towards the imposing Summer Palace.

How many more pleasant surprises are you going to give me, Divya? he wondered.

"Hey, stupid, wipe that idiotic smile off your face, nah? Let us go see this Palace of yours," Rekha said, waving her hands in front of Aslam.

Aslam followed her onto the sprawling grounds.

* * *

As the jeep entered the outskirts of Mysore, Naveen put his hand on his stomach. "Hey, Oz, tell the driver to take us somewhere for lunch. I'm starving!"

"What about you two ladies?" Aslam asked, turning around in his seat. "Ready for lunch?"

Divya nodded her head and Rekha gave a circular nod, both indicating they were hungry.

"What about you, Om, are you hungry for lunch?" Divya asked. Om did not reply. "Come on Om," she said, exasperated. "You're still not angry with us, are you? You must eat. You had nothing for breakfast."

"Divya, let it go," Naveen suggested. "He's not angry with us. Today is Friday, and Om always fasts on this day. He says that even one's stomach deserves a day to rest."

I wish he could speak so I could hear these profound statements myself! Divya thought with frustration. *He does not speak, does not eat, and spends all day praying. What a dynamic personality!*

"I know a great place to eat," Aslam said. "The guide here says that Lalitha Mahal Palace has good food and an amazing ambiance."

"Is it really a Palace?" Divya asked.

Aslam nodded with enthusiasm. "That's what the guide says."

"Sounds good to me," Rekha exclaimed.

"We'll be served as Maharanis in our Palace, Rekha," Divya laughed.

Aslam smiled, pleased, and spoke to the driver.

The jeep pulled up in front of a grand cathedral. Rekha, Naveen, and Divya gave Aslam a quizzical look.

Aslam shrugged in ignorance, and spoke with the driver.

"What's up, Oz?" Rekha asked.

"The driver says that the cathedral is on the way to the restaurant and out of the way to the other sites we wish to see. He said to take five minutes to see this cathedral and then we'll move on. Is that okay—"

The back door of the jeep slammed open and Om disappeared through the entrance of the cathedral.

Divya could not help but laugh. "I guess we don't have a choice."

"You two go without me," Naveen said. "I'm as interested in cathedrals as I'm in starving. I'm going to munch on this last package of biscuits otherwise I may lose control."

"Save a couple for us, nah?" Rekha said as Naveen tore open the package and began devouring the biscuits. Rekha snatched a couple and handed one to Divya, who gratefully accepted.

"Don't spoil your appetite," Aslam admonished, sounding motherly. "We'll soon be eating at a five star hotel."

As the three of them got out of the jeep, Divya realized that the courtyard and steps to the cathedral were covered with small children smartly dressed in white uniforms. The air was filled with the joyful ruckus of children.

"What's going on?" Divya wondered aloud.

"Catholic school must have finished," Rekha said, shoving her biscuit in her mouth.

Entering the cathedral, Divya admired the beautiful but simple structure, her footsteps echoing in the great chamber. She noticed with a smile that Om was at the front of the cathedral, lighting a candle and staring at the statue of the Virgin Mary.

"I wonder if this moment with Mary will convince him to embrace Catholicism?" Rekha whispered in Divya's ear.

When Divya, Aslam, and Rekha emerged from the church five minutes later, the number of children had reduced significantly. Divya watched with amazement as a dozen children somehow packed themselves into the back of an autorickshaw.

"How do they all fit in there?" Divya asked.

"I used to do the same thing when I was a child," Rekha mused. "It saves money and was fun, nah?"

"I hope Om hurries up. I'm also getting hungry," Aslam grumbled.

Om emerged with a peaceful smile fifteen minutes later, oblivious to the glares from his famished friends.

Everyone clamored into the jeep.

"Are there any more biscuits?" Rekha asked, her eyes pleading to Naveen.

Naveen handed her an empty wrapper with a smile.

Rekha sighed despondently. "You could have saved me one, nah?"

"Cheer up, Rekha, we're going for lunch now," Divya comforted.

Aslam and Naveen got into a discussion regarding the fifth term of school that would be beginning on Monday. Rekha stared out the window, her face nearly pressed against the glass, searching for the Palace. Divya watched Om, who seemed to have entered another meditative state.

How does a person become like that? Divya wondered, trying to understand the strange man. *I wish I could concentrate like that, but not if such eccentricity is the price.*

The jeep was now climbing the side of an enormous hill that overlooked the entire city.

Is the Palace on top of the summit? Divya wondered, her excitement growing. *The view must be spectacular.*

"Um, Oz," Rekha said. "The Lalitha Mahal Palace is a huge, gorgeous white building, nah?"

"Yes, do you see it?"

"Yes, way down there." Rekha said, pointing outside.

"What?" Aslam looked out of the window and gasped. "Why are we climbing Chamundi Hill?"

Hill? This seems more like a mountain, Divya thought.

Realizing he had asked the question in English, Aslam began speaking hurriedly at the driver in Kannada. The driver turned to him and said in English: "Yes. I from Mysore."

Divya looked at the driver with astonishment.

How is it that every driver in this country pretends to be ignorant in English? Divya wondered. *Do they enjoy surprising us?*

Realizing that Aslam had no control of the situation, she began to feel uneasy about the driver.

"What did you ask him, Oz?" Rekha inquired, exchanging an anxious look with Naveen.

"I asked if he was sure where he was going and you heard his response," Aslam said.

After five minutes, Aslam asked another question in Kannada, but the driver ignored him, accelerating up the narrow road that snaked along the side of the enormous hill.

As a truck roared past them at a reckless speed, making no effort to move out of the jeep's way, Divya's uneasiness escalated to fear. She had no idea how the two vehicles managed to pass each other at such speeds without the jeep being thrown off the cliff. Her only comfort was the two-foot stone wall that was built along the edge of the road. Although deep down she knew the little divider could never prevent the car from careening off the edge at the speed they were going, she still felt some degree of consolation that *something* was between them and imminent death.

As the jeep narrowly missed another car, Aslam began shouting at the driver.

"Oz, stop yelling and let him concentrate on the road," Divya said in a strained voice, trying to remain calm.

"I'm going to die hungry!" Rekha wailed.

"Shut up, Motti!" Naveen snapped. "There's enough meat on you to live for another fifty years."

Rekha was crushed by the harsh words, and Naveen immediately regretted uttering them. "I'm sorry, Rekha. I didn't mean it. I get very irritable when I'm hungry and this crazy driver is stressing me out. I didn't mean it."

Upset, Rekha did not say anything. Naveen's terrible words repeated in her mind. She turned, facing the rushing landscape, tears welling up in her eyes. She had thought Naveen liked her, and was angry and hurt knowing how he truly felt. She had always thought he respected her but now she knew the truth, and it stung dreadfully.

It took another fifteen minutes for the jeep to climb the three thousand-foot summit of Chamundi Hill, where Chamundeeswari Temple—which had an uncanny likeness to the temple they had earlier seen on the island—was situated.

The driver parked beside a group of kiosks and shacks. Before the engine had turned off, Om was out of the jeep and hurriedly walked past a narrow alley of stalls towards the temple.

The driver lowered the window of his door, spat, and said something to Aslam.

"He said that we should look around, and then he will take us to eat," Aslam interpreted.

"There's a restaurant up here, nah?" Rekha asked hopefully.

"I doubt it," Aslam said gloomily, getting out of the jeep. "Well, we better take a look. We have to wait for Om."

"Forget that," Naveen said, lighting a cigarette and inhaling deeply.

"That's a terrible habit, Naveen," Divya said with disapproval. "Have you ever considered quitting?"

"May I remind you that smoking *suppresses* hunger, which is of vital importance at this juncture in my life. Anyway, you three go ahead and enjoy the view. I need to conserve my energy. After my smoke, I'm going to sleep. Wake me when there's a plate of chicken curry and rice in front of me."

"I'm starving," Rekha moaned, suddenly envying the cigarette between Naveen's lips.

"There are two thousand stairs that lead down to the base of the hill," Aslam said. "You can start descending now, Rekha, or wait until Om returns."

"I could take an auto," Rekha snapped.

Aslam sighed. "Come on, girls. I know you're both hungry, and so am I, but let's not spoil the trip. We're already up here. We may as well see the view of the country. I'm sure it's breathtaking from this height."

Rekha was silent, hungry, and still upset by Naveen's remarks.

"Come on buddy, let's see the view," Divya said encouragingly, squeezing Rekha's arm in an effort to cheer her up. "This is part of the adventure. We can wait a little longer, can't we?"

Rekha nodded despondently.

Divya was grateful that the discussion was over. She had a tremendous urge to find a bathroom and relieve herself. As Divya, Rekha, and Aslam got out of the jeep, the driver lowered his seat and fell asleep.

"Look, our self-appointed guide is taking a nap," Rekha muttered angrily.

They walked along a stone wall that wrapped itself around the perimeter of the summit. Divya found an isolated corner behind the bushes to squat, and relieved herself. After purchasing a bottle of water to cool themselves from the oppressive heat, and several packages of biscuits to control their hunger, much of their irritation and discomfort was alleviated.

Divya and Rekha pulled out their cameras and snapped several photographs of the panoramic view of the city and distant countryside. They laughed as they shared embarrassing moments of their childhood as they sat on the wall, their legs recklessly dangling over the edge. Divya even found herself enjoying bargaining with the vendors who bombarded her with sandalwood carvings and other useless artifacts.

After a half an hour, they returned to the jeep, pleased to see Om waiting for them. Rekha smiled and nudged Divya with her shoulder as she noticed Om holding a book on Catholicism in his hands.

Aslam slammed his door shut to wake up the driver, who spat out the window again and turned on the jeep.

"Did you bring me any food or biscuits?" Naveen asked drowsily.

Rekha smiled smugly, and dropped the empty package of biscuits on his lap.

Naveen scowled. "Okay, I deserve that. Are you still mad at me or am I forgiven?" Rekha didn't say anything, frowning. "Look, it was a really stupid comment. I'm sorry, Rekha. I didn't mean it," he said sincerely.

Rekha glared at Naveen angrily. "You know what, you are *so* stupid."

"I know, sorry. *Please,* Rekha, I can't stand you being mad at me."

Her features softened to a smile. "Okay, yaar, forgiven."

"Great." Naveen said, returning her smile. "Now, Oz, can you tell our driver that we need to eat *now!*"

"No problem!" the driver exclaimed.

"Thank God," Naveen sighed.

The jeep rapidly descended Chamundi Hill. About a thousand feet from the peak, the road suddenly forked. The right road continued to head towards the city and the left road snaked back up the hill.

Take the road on the right! Take the road on the right! Divya mentally urged the driver.

The driver took the road on his left. Painted in white on the face of the cliff wall it read: *Nandi Temple.* As the jeep began to ascend up the side of the hill there was a collective groan. Only Om was pleased; he was actually smiling.

That bastard driver is smiling as well, Divya noticed with a flare of anger.

"I've realized that I have absolutely no control over this situation," Aslam admitted. "I suggest we make the best of wherever our driver takes us. Our fate is in his hands."

After a few minutes of depressed silence, the jeep pulled to the side of the narrow road, parking behind a tourist bus. The jeep had not completely braked when Om leaped out of the back.

The driver turned off the engine, spat out the window, and looked at all of them expectantly. Naveen, Rekha, Aslam, and Divya halfheartedly got out of the vehicle and crossed the street, following the crowd of people walking towards the base of a stone staircase that led to the temple.

The group took off their shoes at the base of the staircase, and climbed two flights of stairs to an enormous black statue of Shiva's bull. Far below, the city of Mysore could be seen sprawling across the horizontal landscape.

Although famished, Divya tried to push aside the hunger pangs and took out her camera. She backed up to ensure the fifteen-foot high, twenty-four foot long bull fit in her picture.

Oz is right, Divya thought, turning on the camera. *I may as well make the best of this.*

There was noisy rustling above, and Divya looked up. She was delighted to see numerous monkeys jumping from branch to branch. Suddenly, there seemed to be monkeys everywhere, up in the tree, sitting on the stone wall, and even running around the sacred bull statue.

Like the many children who found the acrobatic, furry creatures far more interesting then the Nandi statue, Divya focused her attention and lens on the monkeys. She snapped a dozen photos, amazed at how close she could get to the animals. They seemed completely unperturbed by humans.

After fifteen minutes of watching the children interacting with the monkeys, Divya searched for her companions.

They're probably in the jeep waiting, she thought with guilt.

Divya hurriedly made her way down the stairs, retrieved her shoes, and returned to the jeep. She frowned. The driver was fast asleep.

Remembering how Aslam had woken up the driver before, Divya slammed the door shut. The driver was startled out of sleep. Divya suppressed a smile.

Ten agonizing minutes passed sitting in hungry silence before the door to the jeep opened, and Aslam and Rekha climbed in.

"Where are the others?" Divya asked, thankful for their arrival.

"Om found some religious cave and wants to spend some time meditating, nah? We tried to coerce him back. Naveen is still trying to persuade him, threatening that we will abandon him if he does not come right now," Rekha said.

"Somehow I don't think that's not much of a threat for Om," Divya sighed.

The other two nodded despondently with agreement.

Naveen and Om returned twenty minutes later. Naveen was holding his friend by the arm and marched him towards the jeep, a determined expression on his face.

As Aslam nudged the driver awake again, Naveen opened the back of the jeep and motioned Om to get in. Om looked forlornly back towards the great black bull, whose majestic head could be barely seen from where they were parked.

Divya was feeling light-headed, and with her stomach beyond pain, felt no pity for Om. She almost began clapping when Naveen shoved him into the back of the jeep and slammed the door shut.

"Oz," Naveen growled with a menacing look, "you better tell that driver to take us to the restaurant, and he better listen, otherwise I'm going to tie you to the back of this jeep and drive it off this damn mountain!"

Aslam began speaking sternly to the driver in Kannada.

"Of course, sir!" the driver replied in English with an infuriating grin.

* * *

"Lunch here," the driver declared in English as he parked in front of the Viceroy Hotel.

Aslam was thunderstruck by the driver's audacity. His face contorted with pent up rage.

"I told you a dozen times to take us to the Lalitha Mahal Palace!" he shouted.

"Lunch here," the driver repeated.

"Why you—"

"Come on, Oz, it does not matter, nah?" Rekha said, pulling him out of the jeep.

"She's right, Oz. We're here and starving," Naveen said.

"Remember what you said, Oz, 'Our fates are in his hands'," Divya recited.

Aslam sighed, but continued to give the driver an ugly look.

The five students walked into the hotel and entered the posh restaurant. They were escorted by the finely dressed maître d' to a table in the corner, and gratefully accepted the menus.

As a waiter arrived and began pouring water into their glasses, Rekha begged them to order. It was already three-thirty in the afternoon and the restaurant was empty. Divya was confident that they would be served quickly.

The waiter took each of their orders and then turned to Om. To everyone's surprise, Om pointed at the items he wanted on the menu, and then walked out of the restaurant.

"Has Om broken his fast?" Naveen asked, his eyes wide.

"Where's he going?" Aslam wondered aloud.

"He's probably converted to Catholicism," Rekha said. "Divya, do you want to go to the bathroom and freshen up?"

"Yeah, good idea," Divya replied.

Becoming quite accustomed to his eccentricities, Divya had not given Om's actions a second thought. She felt tired and grungy, and was pleased to wash the dirt off her hands and face in the immaculate bathroom.

89

Sure the driver deceived us again, but this seems like a really nice place, Divya thought.

Re-entering the dining area, Rekha and Divya were surprised to find their driver sitting uncomfortably at their table beside Om, who was ignoring the glares from Naveen and Aslam.

"This'll be interesting," Divya observed.

The meals arrived moments later, and dishes of lentils, potatoes, and rice were served for the driver. Om sipped limewater, eating nothing.

Although Divya would have normally found the tension unbearable, she was too hungry to care, and attacked the dish of boneless chicken in cashew sauce and fresh pineapples that she had ordered with zeal. She tore a soft piece of warm, garlic naan bread, and dipped it into the steaming curry. She took a bite and grinned with pleasure. It was delicious. She told herself to chew slowly, and savor every moment.

Who am I kidding? she thought, and devoured the rest of her meal.

Divya pushed her empty plate away from her, the first to finish her meal. As she recovered from her gluttony, she noticed the driver take a quick, nervous glance at the maître d'. The driver seemed to be desperately searching for guidance. The maître d's face was expressionless, but Divya swore that his eyes seemed to be urging the driver to relax and eat the food.

So that's it! Divya realized. *The driver is taking us to all these places because he gets a commission. Why didn't I think of that earlier?*

The entire meal was eaten without a word spoken. Only the sound of cutlery scraping dishes and the sound of chewing was heard, although the tension was still high, especially between Naveen and Om.

The dishes were cleared and the bill arrived.

As Om pulled out two hundred rupees from his wallet to cover the bill for himself and the driver, Naveen exploded, unable to bear it any longer. "Om, how can you invite this man for lunch? He's been screwing our happiness all day, and now you're actually going to *pay* for him. Are you mad?"

Om ignored his friend and put the money on the bill.

"He's a criminal and he's swindling you, Om!" Naveen pressed.

Om stared at Naveen with a steady, piercing look. *He's my guest and I will do as I please,* his eyes explained.

Naveen angrily met Om's gaze. Time seemed to freeze. Rekha, Aslam, and Divya anxiously watched the standoff.

Naveen turned away and raised his hands in frustration. "Fine! It's your money. Waste it for all I care," he said, storming out of the restaurant.

There was a quiet uneasiness as the rest of them left the restaurant and hotel, but Divya's energy and spirits were up. She got into the jeep with newfound enthusiasm, the taste of the delicious food still lingering on her tongue. She looked forward to the rest of the trip. Divya was interested to see how the driver would try to manipulate or cheat them next. Now that she understood the driver's rationale, curiosity consumed her.

The driver navigated the jeep through several side streets to their next destination with no one bothering to inquire where they were going.

The jeep turned onto a narrow alley, the vehicle barely wide enough to pass between the buildings. Divya was lost in her own thoughts when the jeep jerked to a sudden stop. The driver began yelling at the obstruction in front of them.

Divya leaned forward to take a look and began laughing.

A brown cow had spread itself across the width of the alley and created a blockade. The driver pounded the jeep's horn, and the cow turned its massive head towards them, giving a look that Divya could have sworn was irritation.

The driver inched the jeep towards the revered animal, continuing to honk the horn.

The cow mooed with displeasure and slowly stood up. It gave another defiant look towards them before slowly ambling towards the end of the alley.

With the horn incessantly blaring, the jeep closely followed the cow.

Divya was fascinated as the cow took its time leaving the alley, as if it knew it would further anger the driver.

Even cows have a personality in this country, Divya thought with an amused smile.

She looked at Aslam, Rekha, and Naveen. All of them were smiling, quietly urging the cow to go as slowly as possible to further infuriate their driver. Divya noticed with relief that even Om was smiling at the spectacle. The tension was broken.

With a mournful moo, the cow ambled out of the alley.

The driver slammed onto the accelerator and drove recklessly to the next destination. After a few minutes, he parked the jeep in an obscure courtyard with three small stores. As the driver turned off the engine, Aslam gave him a questioning look, an expression that was becoming very familiar each time they reached a new destination.

"Shopping," the driver explained in English.

"Do you want to buy anything here?" Aslam reluctantly asked his friends.

Unwilling to increase the driver's commission, or be further cheated by purchasing some useless souvenir that would probably be sold far above its actual value, Divya firmly said: "I don't want to buy anything."

The others readily agreed, and Om did not seem to show any particular interest as none of the stores sold any religious paraphernalia. Pleased, Aslam told the driver in both English and Kannada that none of them wanted to go shopping. The driver was crestfallen.

"Go shopping," he repeated, the statement sounding more like a command than a request.

Divya did not like the tone of the driver and decided that she would rather sit in the jeep for the rest of the day than give the driver one extra rupee. The others seemed to share her sentiments, and no one moved from the jeep. She looked out of the jeep window and studied the contents within each of the stores, which were crammed with an assortment of things made from sandalwood—small boxes, letter openers, key chains, tables, chessboards, and carvings of animals.

"Mysore is obsessed with sandalwood," Rekha observed, staring at the shop and reading Divya's mind. "It is a very pleasant smelling wood, but this is too much!"

Divya looked at the expectant faces of the shopkeepers standing at the entrance of their stores, waiting to pounce on their prey.

Not this time, Divya thought smugly.

All the passengers were grinning when the driver finally conceded by turning on the engine. The jeep was back on the congested street, maneuvering through the swarm of people, animals, scooters, and autorickshaws.

To Divya's surprise, the driver took them to a tourist spot that they actually planned to see—the spectacular Maharaja's Palace in the center of Mysore.

Aggressive merchants swarmed them as they exited the jeep. The group shoved their way up to the ticket booth and paid the fare without incident. They walked through the archway and into a vast, cobblestone courtyard. In the distance, the spectacular Palace stood before them.

Divya was struck speechless by its beauty. The immense structure was a combination of red domes, lavish arches, and marble columns.

"Look, the entire Palace is covered with thousands of light bulbs!" Naveen exclaimed as they walked towards the elegant building.

"Yes, but according to the guide here, the Mysore Palace is only illuminated on Sunday evenings and on special holidays," Aslam said.

Divya was disappointed. She could imagine how breathtaking the Palace would be at night completely illuminated. Her disappointment was quickly forgotten as she walked mesmerized through the decadent corridors, halls, and chambers. The entire building dripped of wealth with colorful paintings, exquisite carvings, and gold.

At the end of the tour, Divya bought a postcard of the Palace lit up at night and decided she would send it to her family once she returned to IIMB.

Aslam gave a professional photographer forty rupees to take a Polaroid of them with the glorious Mysore Palace standing formidably behind them.

"You know I hate taking my photo, nah?" Rekha complained, worrying about how fat the photograph would make her look, especially since she had just had lunch.

"Come on, Oz, forget it," Naveen said. "This is a waste of money."

Om nodded with agreement.

"We already have plenty of postcards and pictures of the Palace," Divya added.

"I want a snap of *all* of us in it," Aslam said. "Come on, this won't hurt and it'll take a second." There was a collective groan and more protests. "This is important to me and I've already paid the photographer," Aslam persisted. "Besides, I don't want to forget this day. Now stop complaining and get close."

"Smile!" the photographer cried.

The large bulb atop the camera flashed, blinding them.

* * *

"Does this driver *want* to get us killed?" Rekha shrieked, staring at the growing headlights of the truck racing towards them.

"Shut up, Rekha!" Aslam hissed. "Don't further anger him."

The jeep continued to accelerate in the oncoming traffic lane until it overtook a van and swerved back into the proper lane seconds before an Ashok Layland lorry zoomed past them, its horn blaring.

The driver muttered angrily as he accelerated the jeep on the twisty one lane highway under the pitch darkness of night.

After leaving Mysore Palace, the driver and Aslam had wanted to go to the KRS dam and Brindavan Garden. The garden was filled with flowers and fountains that had been built at the base of the enormous three-kilometer wide dam.

"It's a great tourist attraction and only twenty minutes from here," Aslam had said, trying to persuade his friends. "Fifty years ago, this dam was a technical wonder, and the gardens are the highlight of any trip to Mysore."

"Very beautiful," the driver had agreed, dreaming of the additional commissions he would get for bringing the group to the dam.

"I want to go home," Rekha persisted stubbornly.

"So do I," Naveen grumbled. "After the ordeal we had getting lunch I don't suspect us getting dinner. B'lore is at least three hours away. We won't get home until nine if we leave right now."

"But there is a dancing fountain there!" Aslam said, exasperated. "The fountains dance to music. And they are all lit up at night. Come on! Om, do you want to go?"

Om responded with silent indifference and Aslam shook his head angrily. "Just because it doesn't have religious significance doesn't mean you won't like it." He sighed with frustration and turned to Divya. "Do you want to go?"

"It really sounds great, Oz," Divya began diplomatically, "but even if I did, the other three don't, so lets go home."

Aslam raised his hands in defeat. "Take us back to Bangalore," he told the driver.

To Divya's surprise, the driver complied without argument. But it soon became apparent that the driver had other means of demonstrating his anger for losing his commission. As he drove the jeep to its limits, the five of them crossed the path of death with every vehicle they came across on the isolated one lane highway to Bangalore.

Divya glanced at Aslam and Naveen, both of whom were quietly staring at the rushing landscape with fear in their eyes. Even the normal serenity on Oz's face had vanished, replaced with terror.

Realizing that saying anything to the driver would further endanger them, Divya resigned to leave her life in God's hand.

Whatever happens to me is out of my hands, she realized. *If I'm going to die tonight because of this maniac at the wheel, then let it be in peace as I sleep.*

Divya closed her eyes, a warm sense of peace swelling through her.

"Oz, tell him to chill, nah?" Rekha screamed.

"How? I'm powerless. He hasn't listened to me all day!" Aslam cried back. "Now, shut up!"

"We are going to die," Rekha moaned.

"Divya fell asleep!" Naveen exclaimed with disbelief.

"Are you mad, she's fainted, nah?" Rekha cried.

Despite the jeep bouncing as it drove over endless potholes, and despite Rekha squealing and clutching her as the driver aggressively overtook one vehicle after another by lurching into oncoming traffic, Divya allowed sleep to encompass her.

* * *

Divya awoke to discover that she was still alive and that the jeep was on Bannerghatta Road, a few minutes from campus.

"But I already bought the theater tickets!" Aslam argued.

"Sorry, but I want to go to my room and thank God that He has spared my life. I do not feel lucky enough to risk it another time in one day. Besides, I have seen the fil*lum* fifteen times. Aamir Khan is *soooo* good looking, nah?" Rekha gushed.

As a dreamy expression came across Rekha's face, Divya wondered whether her friend would forgo the praying in order to admire the Indian actor for a sixteenth time.

Aslam turned to Naveen who raised his hands. "Don't look at me, yaar! I'm famished. Hey, don't look so disappointed, Oz, I'll reimburse you for the ticket, okay?"

"We were supposed to bond as a group and who knows when we'll all find time together next term to go see this movie. I'm the only one who hasn't seen it."

"I think we've bonded enough for one day," Naveen said.

"You could always try to persuade Om, nah?" Rekha suggested, but averted her eyes when Aslam gave her a knowing look. Unless the movie was a biography on a religion or a religious leader, there was no way Om would waste his precious meditation time on the cinema.

"I'll go see the movie with you, Oz," Divya volunteered. She felt guilty for not supporting Aslam by going to Brindavan Garden and the KRS dam, and she felt well rested after her lengthy nap. "I've always wanted to see an Indian movie in India rather than just renting them in Toronto."

Aslam's face lit up and Divya smiled, any doubts of her spontaneous decision disappearing.

"Great!" Aslam exclaimed. "We'll drop these three off and then head to M.G. Road for dinner before we catch the movie. I know this great restaurant..." he stopped, remembering their recent ordeal with lunch.

"I'm sure it'll be wonderful," Divya said, laughing.

The jeep pulled up to the entrance of the campus, and as the security guards peered through the windows, Naveen and Rekha simultaneously cried: "Students!"

The guards waved the jeep through. The driver drove to the back of the campus and stopped the jeep in front of the mess and student hostels. Om, Naveen, and Rekha got out of the jeep and waved goodbye as Aslam asked the driver to take them to M.G. Road. The driver turned the jeep and drove off the campus towards downtown Bangalore.

Divya was amazed at the pollution that was visible by the headlights of oncoming vehicles. It appeared as if it was foggy, but the chemical stench and choking exhaust spewing from the hundreds of vehicles made it impossible to argue that the haze was a natural phenomenon.

Trying not to worry about what she was breathing, Divya turned back to Aslam. "What movie are we seeing, Oz?"

"*Dil Chahta Hai,*" he said with a grin, his eyes sparkling with anticipation.

'*The heart desires,*' Divya interpreted in her head.

Aslam's excitement was contagious and she could not help but return his smile. She looked forward to seeing her first movie in India.

Chapter 5
The Monsoons
Sunday, September 9th, 2001

"What did you think?" Aslam asked as they emerged from the movie theater.

Divya admired the star-splattered sky and studied the strange configuration of swirling clouds surrounding the full moon.

It's like a picture taken from a satellite of a hurricane raging over the ocean, she thought with fascination. *It's so beautiful. I've never seen anything like this before.*

As they approached the intersection of Brigade and M.G. Road, Aslam hailed an autorickshaw. He agreed to pay double the meter fare since it was so late at night and the school's campus was at the edge of the city.

They climbed into the autorickshaw and the small engine buzzed to life. Divya continued to eye the growing cloud cover.

"So? What'd you think of the movie, Divya?" Aslam asked.

"Hmmm...oh, it was okay," she said, facing him.

"Okay? Don't lie. I heard you laughing through the entire film!"

"Hardly. I don't know what you're talking about."

"Rubbish! You loved the picture. Deny it all you want, but I know the truth."

"Were you watching me or the movie?" Aslam did not reply, but smiled impishly. "Well?" she asked, poking him.

"You."

"Beast!" she laughed, punching his shoulder.

"Now, I've told the truth so it's your turn. Did you like the movie?"

"Yes, I loved it. It was well acted, the story was relatively original, and it even touched on a few serious issues."

"Like what?"

"Like how one of the three friends, that painter, what's his name?"

"Akshaye Khanna."

"Yeah, how he falls in love with the older divorced woman, the alcoholic. I'm surprised they address those types of themes in Indian movies."

"A lot of movies are like that today. You're still stuck in the early eighties when Amitabh Bachaan use to just kick everyone's ass and save the honor of his widowed mother."

"Don't make fun of Amitabh. He's a God, and practically taught me how to speak Hindi when I was a little girl. He was my guru."

"No wonder your Hindi is so atrocious," Aslam laughed, receiving a second punch from her.

To her astonishment, it suddenly began to rain heavily. She stuck her head out briefly and looked at the sky, all traces of the stars and the moon had vanished.

"At least we won't get too wet while we're in this auto," Divya said, wiping the water off her face.

"Speaking of wet, I remember someone looking a little teary-eyed near the end of the picture when Dimple Kapadia died from her alcoholism."

"Lies! I admit that scene was touching and surprising since I don't remember the last time a protagonist died in an Indian movie, but—"

"But?"

"But those tears you saw when you were *supposed* to be watching the movie was from laughter. I mean, come on, that next scene was *so* stupid. "

"What was stupid about the ending? They were all back in Goa like in the beginning and their friendship was re-established. I thought it was great."

"I'm not referring to that. I was laughing because Dimple's body is not even cold in her grave when the *supposedly* mourning Akshaye Khanna meets this gorgeous girl and falls in love! Is that his notion of love?"

"She was still in his heart," Aslam said defensively. "After all, she did tell him to move on with his life just before she died. And by the way, Hindu's get cremated."

"Okay, her ashes had not yet cooled when he found this other girl. But, it was a stupid ending."

"Hey, it's an Indian movie. There must be a happy ending to appease the masses, Divya. Remember, Indian movies help people temporarily escape their problems."

"Well, that's true," she admitted.

Divya turned towards the passing landscape, and was mesmerized by the number of dogs she saw. They seemed to be everywhere. For every one person she saw, there were at least a dozen dogs. It was as if canines ruled the city at night. There were dogs running in packs, dogs rummaging for food in the trash, dogs barking and fighting with one another, dogs fornicating, and dogs lying on the side of the road and watching the autorickshaw drive by. All of the dogs had one thing in common—they were large and looked sickly, with open sores, limps, and visible ribcages. She did not see any puppies, and wondered how high the survival rate for newborn pups was in such an environment. The entire scene was unsettling. She wondered if a similar scene had inspired Alfred Hitchcock to make the movie *The Birds*.

"And what'd you think about Aamir Khan?"

"He's okay, I guess," Divya said, happy to talk about the movie and push the canine infestation aside. "But I wouldn't see the movie fifteen times just for him. Rekha is mad."

"Absolutely," Aslam agreed.

"And there were too many coincidences in the movie."

"Name one?"

"When Aamir Khan is going to Australia and his first class seat is coincidentally beside the girl he's attracted to and tried to pursue earlier."

"The name of the actress is Preity Zinta, and that wasn't coincidence."

"Then what was it?"

"Fate, Divya, fate."

Divya snorted.

"Hey, what are the chances that you'd walk into the barn and save me from Chicken, and later, I'd save you from Tharki in the library," Aslam pointed out.

"Yeah, you sure did," Divya said, a shiver running down her spine at the unsettling thought. "And that's not the same thing. We're just friends."

So were they when they first met in the movie, he thought.

Aslam watched Divya shivering from the cold wind. He suddenly yearned to hold her, to not only protect her from the elements, but to also protect her from the world. He had never had such a powerful and strange feeling. He recalled how her beauty had stunned him when he first saw her. Her flawless skin; petite nose; soft, lush lips; prominent cheek bones; sparkling eyes the color of ebony; long, black hair; shapely yet athletic body; and her dazzling smile all accentuated her natural beauty. As he got to know her, her loveliness had only grown. Aslam found himself staring at the beautiful girl who had utterly captivated him.

"Divya?"

"Hmmmm."

"How did you learn to play badminton like that?"

"Oh, here and there," she said cryptically, smiling.

The rain intensified to the point that it was impossible to hear one another without shouting over the deafening noise of the raindrops smashing against the asphalt.

It's as if we're standing underneath a raging waterfall, she marveled.

The speed of the autorickshaw slowed considerably, and the driver suddenly shouted something in Kannada.

"What'd he say?" Divya shouted to Aslam.

"He said he loves when it rains as it washes all the sins from the city. He says the rains act like a spiritual bath."

"How many sins does this city have?" she asked as the rainfall further intensified.

"This is just the beginning. It rains like this virtually everyday until the end of October."

"That's bad."

"No, it is very good for the state's crops. The farmers' entire livelihood depends on the rain," Aslam shouted back.

The autorickshaw driver cursed as his three-wheeler splashed into a foot of muddy water that had once been a road. Divya and Aslam looked out and were shocked at what they saw.

They were ten minutes away from the campus, and Bannerghatta Road had been transformed into a vast, raging river. The driver shouted at Aslam who quickly responded.

"I've agreed to pay him triple to get us to campus since there is no way we can walk this," Aslam explained to Divya.

"We could swim," Divya joked uneasily, incredulously watching a cow swim past her. "Maybe not." She wrinkled her nose, realizing that sewage was overflowing onto the road. She tried not to think of what was floating in the muddy water.

A few cars and jeeps were barely managing to drive through the water. Divya watched with amazement as a man struggled to ride his bicycle through the river. Another man was suddenly swept off his motorcycle and disappeared underneath the water. Divya sighed with relief as he stood up, the water above his knees.

Divya yelped and lifted her feet as the brown water began to pour onto the floor of the autorickshaw.

The autorickshaw driver turned around and began shouting at Aslam.

"He's refuses to go any further," Aslam explained. "The water is getting deeper, and will destroy his engine if he continues. He says we can either get out now or he will drive us back to the city."

"What do you suggest, Oz?" Divya asked, feeling helpless.

"We won't make it to the campus unless we get a ride from a bus or jeep, and that is unlikely to happen at this time at night. We better go back and check into a hotel."

Divya nodded and Aslam conveyed their wishes to the driver.

The driver desperately tried to steer his autorickshaw back to solid surface when the engine suddenly spluttered and seized. He pulled the black handle but the engine refused to start. The driver jumped out of the rickshaw and motioned Aslam to join him.

"Shit, I have to get out and push," Aslam cried with dismay. "Wait here."

Divya nodded. "Be careful, Oz."

Holding onto the rickshaw so the rushing water would not sweep him off his feet, Aslam cautiously got out and pushed. With the flow of water against them, however, they were unable to move the three-wheeler.

"Divya, you have to come and help us!" Aslam cried.

Shit!

"Okay, coming!"

Divya sighed, opened her bag and pulled out her hair band, tying her hair into a ponytail. She gasped as two men dressed in undershirts and dhotis appeared out of the darkness. They offered their assistance to Aslam and the driver. With the crashing of the falling water she was barely able to hear Aslam gratefully accept their help.

With Aslam and the driver pushing from the back, and the two strangers holding each side of the autorickshaw, the four men shoved the three-wheeler until they could see the road beneath them.

The driver jumped into the front as Aslam thanked the two men profusely for their kindness. He joined Divya in the back of the autorickshaw, drenched.

"Wow, it's certainly raining outside," he said with a grin, wiping the water off his face.

Although Divya did not think it was possible, the rainfall further intensified. Never in her life had she witnessed such a downpour. The rain was falling so hard that it seemed to be forming walls and sheets of water.

Now I know how Noah felt, she thought.

"Who were those guys?" Divya asked, trying to distract her anxious thoughts.

The driver pulled the black handle, but the engine gave no signs of life.

"Some strangers that just offered to give a hand."

The driver pulled again, but to no avail.

"What did they want?" she asked.

"Want? Nothing," Aslam said. Divya did not look convinced. "Look, Divya, not everyone in India is a crook. There *are* people in India that genuinely help out of the kindness of their heart. In fact, for every one crook you meet, there are at least a thousand people who are warm-hearted and tremendously generous. That's what makes this country so incredible."

The driver shouted with frustration in Kannada and then pulled the black handle again. The engine roared to life.

Divya and Aslam cheered.

As the autorickshaw drove slowly back towards the center of Bangalore, Divya asked: "What did the driver say before the engine caught?"

"That he hates the rain."

* * *

Aslam paid the autorickshaw driver, and joined Divya underneath the awning of the Ramanashree Residency. The turbaned doorman smiled as he opened the door for them.

As soon as Divya left the rainy, humid night and walked into the bright, air-conditioned hotel, she sighed with happiness, and admired the quaint lobby. She followed Aslam to the granite front counter where an impeccably groomed man in a fine suit welcomed them with an amicable smile.

Divya could not help but return the smile of the gentle looking face in front of her.

"Good morning, sir and madam," he said with a trace of a British accent. "How may I be of service?"

"We would like one non-air conditioned, single room, please," Aslam said anxiously, surprised at the luxury of the hotel. He prayed that his remaining two hundred and fifty rupees would somehow cover the bill, and cursed himself for going to a hotel that Chicken had once recommended. Why did he ever think he would be able to afford such a place? His desire to impress Divya had seriously clouded his judgment.

It's that smile of hers. I can't help but want the best for her.

He looked at her and smiled pleasantly, wondering what she was thinking.

Did he ask for just one room? Divya thought, looking at Aslam with disbelief. *He must have, look at the way he's smiling at me. Oh God, this can't be happening.*

"I am terribly sorry, sir, but all of the rooms in this establishment are air-conditioned."

"Oh, I see, very well then, just a single, air-conditioned room," Aslam said, frowning.

Divya could not believe it. Just because they had had a good day did not imply that they were going to share a bed. Disturbing memories of Tharki in the library suddenly filled her mind.

"Very good, sir, we have a single room on the third floor," the front desk clerk said, typing into the computer.

"Actually, we'll take *two* single rooms," Divya said sharply.

Aslam gave Divya an incredulous look of his own.

Is she mad? he thought. *I'll have to work a month to repay this day. And all because of that smile of hers. Why am I such a fool?*

"Very good, madam," the counter clerk said, typing furiously on the computer as he checked for availability. He stopped typing, studied the screen, and then smiled apologetically. "I am sorry, madam, but we do not have two single rooms available." Divya frowned and Aslam smiled with relief. "However," the clerk continued, "we do have a double bed deluxe suite available on the top floor, with a balcony. And since it is so late, I will give you a regular double room rate."

Divya smiled gratefully and Aslam frowned.

"That is very kind of you," Divya said.

"How much is a regular double room rate?" Aslam asked, breaking into a sweat.

"Two thousand ninety five rupees, sir."

"I see," Aslam said slowly, having urges to bolt for the main entrance and drown himself back at Bannerghatta Road.

"Look, Aslam," Divya said, studying his anxious expression, "you've paid for everything for me tonight, including that wonderful dinner at Ebony's. You've been a wonderful host and I insist that I pay for the room tonight. It would be the least I could do to repay your kindness."

"I couldn't allow you to do that," Aslam said, cursing his ego for preventing him from escaping his predicament.

She sighed with frustration. "Look, Oz, I'm cold, I'm wet, I'm tired, and you can pay me back tomorrow if you have so much male pride, but *I am* staying here for the remainder of this night." Aslam was speechless and she turned to the desk clerk and tiredly asked: "Do you take credit cards?"

"Of course, madam," the man smiled. "We accept Master Card, Visa, and American Express."

"Excellent," Divya said, opening her bag and searching for her wallet.

Aslam and the desk clerk watched silently as she searched her bag with increasing urgency.

"What's wrong? You didn't lose your wallet, did you?" Aslam laughed hollowly, as she frantically began to pull everything out of her bag and place it on the counter. He stopped laughing. "Divya?

"I don't understand it. It was here!" Divya cried, turning her purse inside out.

"Divya, calm down and think carefully. Where did you last see it?"

"Um, in the autorickshaw. I opened my purse to get a hair band just before I was going to help you push the rickshaw and then..." she gasped. "Oh my God!"

"What?"

She glared accusingly at Aslam.

"Why are you looking at me like that? What did I do?"

"Remember those two men who *supposedly* helped us from the kindness of their hearts?"

"Impossible!" Aslam protested. "They couldn't have stolen it! There was no time."

"Excuse me, sir?" the front desk clerk said.

"Then where is it?" she demanded.

"Madam?"

"I don't know, maybe you left it in the rickshaw, or maybe it fell out?"

"Excuse me, sir and madam," the front desk clerk said sternly, raising his voice.

Divya and Aslam both turned towards him. She noticed he was no longer smiling.

"Do you have any money, madam?"

"No."

"And you, sir?"

"Is there anything available for two hundred and fifty rupees?" Aslam asked weakly.

The desk clerk was not impressed. "I'm sorry, sir. There are some hotels down the street that fit your price range."

Divya quickly put her belongings back into her purse, relieved to still have her passport.

"Look, sir, we'll take anything you have and give you two hundred and fifty rupees now and I promise to get the rest tomorrow. I'm a student at the Indian Institute of Management here in Bangalore and you can hold my student card until I return with more money," Aslam pleaded, pulling out his student I.D.

card and showing the desk clerk. "Or here, take my watch. It's worth at least a thousand rupees."

The desk clerk did not even glance at the card. "This is not a pawnshop, bank, or charity," he said coldly. "The guard will escort you out. Good evening." He snapped his fingers at a guard standing nearby.

The guard led Divya and Aslam through the quaint lobby and the turbaned doorman opened the door for them. As they walked back into the humidity and rain, Divya noticed that the doorman was only a few feet behind them, ensuring that they did not loiter underneath the awning. She noticed that he was no longer smiling at them either.

Aslam and Divya paused briefly at the front of the awning and glanced down each end of the street desperately searching for an autorickshaw, but there was nothing. The street was deserted.

Even the dogs have retired for the night, she thought miserably.

"At least it's not raining as hard," Aslam said feebly as they stepped into the street and were immediately soaked.

They walked quickly to the edge of the street and turned the corner. Everything was closed. After two blocks of walking in the rain, Divya nearly cheered with joy when she saw a lit opening between a cluster of dark shops at the far end of the street. From the dull, yellow glow of the streetlight she could barely read the painted sign above the opening: *Sunflower Hotel.*

Divya ran towards the hotel.

"Hey, where are you going?" Aslam called from behind. "Come back, it's too dangerous to be running out here on your own."

As she approached the front entrance of the hotel, Divya was surprised that the entire front wall of the first floor was missing, resembling an open garage. She entered a large room filled with two-dozen narrow tables, content to have escaped the rain and oblivious that she was dripping all over the shiny black-and-white checkered floor.

A dark-faced man emerged from a swinging door from the back, which led to a small kitchen.

"Do you have anything available?" Divya asked in Hindi.

"Yes, please have a seat." He gestured to a table. "I'll be right back."

Shaun Mehta

She smiled with gratitude and sat down as Aslam caught up to her.

"Divya, what are you doing?" he demanded.

"He says that he has something available."

"He did? Who?"

"Him," she said, as the man re-emerged from the kitchen, pleased that his customer base had doubled in the last few seconds.

"Divya, you don't understand—"

"Oz, I don't know what you're going to say, and frankly I don't care right now. I'm not going back into the rain. I'm staying here."

"But—"

"And by the way, you can find your own room."

The dark faced man smiled broadly as he handed Divya a menu. Confused, Divya took the menu and studied it, hoping that it was a list of available rooms. But to her dismay she only saw prices and listings for food.

"How much will it cost for a room for the night?" Divya asked in Hindi, putting the menu down and realizing that the man must have misunderstood what she had initially asked.

The man blinked with surprise. "Order something to eat," he urged.

"What? No, I just want a room," she said, smiling sweetly.

"No rooms. Only food. This is the Sunflower Hotel."

"I know, exactly, this is a hotel. And I want a room," she said, frustrated.

"Divya, that's what I'm trying to tell you—"

"Oz, you've done more than enough," she snapped. "I'll handle this."

"This should be interesting," Aslam muttered under his breath.

"Boss, I'm not hungry," she said to the young man in Hindi, certain that she had pronounced the words correctly.

"Oh I see," he said, his eyes filled with comprehension. He disappeared into the kitchen, and Divya smiled triumphantly to Aslam.

The dark faced man emerged from the kitchen and handed her a menu filled with drinks.

"I'm not thirsty either," Divya said, slamming the table with her fists. "I just want a room to sleep for the night."

"Then why are you here?" the man asked. "Go find a place to stay."

"But this is a hotel!"

"Yes, Sunflower Hotel. We serve excellent butter chicken. Would you like some?"

"No!" Divya cried.

"Dessert, then? We have the best rice pudding in Bangalore," he boasted proudly.

Realizing that communicating was a waste of time, she glared at the dark faced man, willing him to show her a room.

The man looked at Aslam for guidance.

Aslam began speaking rapidly in Kannada. After a few moments, the man's expression changed from confusion to amusement.

"You funny girl," he told Divya in English, laughing.

As the young South Indian walked back into the kitchen, Divya angrily turned to Aslam. "What'd you tell him that was so amusing? Is he getting the keys to our rooms?"

"Come on, Divya. You've made enough of a fool of yourself."

"Not before you telling me what is going on."

"This is a restaurant, Divya."

"Yes, I can see that, Oz," she said sarcastically, "but I don't understand why he won't let us stay in the hotel upstairs."

"You're ill-tempered when you are tired," he sighed. *Although still beautiful,* he thought. He pushed the thoughts from his mind. "Listen to me, Divya. Even though this place is called the Sunflower Hotel, it's not a hotel. It's only a restaurant, and the room upstairs is that man's apartment. He's the owner of this establishment and lives upstairs."

"But why the hell would he call this place a hotel?" Divya demanded, banging the table again with frustration.

"Ignorance, sheer ignorance."

"I don't understand."

"All the best restaurants in the city used to be in five or six star hotels like the Taj West Hotel and the Oberoy. So, these small establishments began naming their places 'hotel' assuming that it referred to superior restaurants. They have no idea what hotel actually means in English. They just copy success and are very superstitious. If it worked for the Taj West then they assume it will work for them. Why change something that works, right?"

She looked at him with bewilderment. She did not know whether to cry or laugh. It all seemed so foolish and unbelievable.

"Come, let's go," Aslam said, holding his hand out. "It's late and soon we'll not even need a place for the night."

"Can't I just sleep on this table?" she moaned.

"Look, Divya, it stopped raining. The owner of the Sunflower Hotel may not have a place for us, but he did tell me where to get a room for the night, and it's not too far away. The place is called the Laxmi Inn, it's still open, and best of all, fits our budget."

Divya groaned and nodded.

He gently helped Divya to her feet, and they walked back into the humid night.

After a ten-minute walk, they entered a narrow and flooded alley where a group of dogs were asleep on a mound of garbage. Divya and Aslam warily navigated around the snoring dogs, and apprehensively opened a dented, metal door that led into the dilapidated Laxmi Inn.

Covered with dust, mould, and spider webs, the battered lobby looked as if it had not been cleaned since India had declared Independence fifty-four years ago. A figure was slumped on the cracked, wooden counter.

Divya studied the unhygienic man sleeping on top of the customer registrar book. Unlike the immaculate desk counter clerk at the Ramanashree Residency, the snoring man in front of them had a mustache that seemed to be growing out of control and clothes that looked dirtier than the counter he slept on.

There was no one else in the little lobby, and Divya motioned Aslam to wake the man.

Aslam nudged him awake and stepped back.

The desk clerk grumbled and smacked the back of his neck, obliterating a mosquito and startling Aslam and Divya.

"Excuse me, sir?" Aslam said.

"What do you want?" he muttered in rough English with a heavy Indian accent, his eyes still closed as he wiped the remains of the mosquito on his filthy shirt.

Divya stared at the smear of blood on his shirt with disgust.

"A room with one..." Aslam winced as Divya angrily kicked him in the shin. "...I-I mean *two* beds, please."

"Four hundred rupees."

"Do you have air conditioning?" Divya asked.

The man smiled with amusement, his eyes still closed and his head still resting on the book. Divya was unsure if the man was smiling from her remark or from a dream.

"How much for a just one room with one bed?" Aslam asked.

Her eyes widened with disbelief, and he showed her the two hundred and fifty rupees he had remaining in his wallet.

"Two and fifty rupees," the man said.

Divya and Aslam turned with surprise. The filthy man was sitting erect, devoid of sleepiness as he alertly studied the bills in the wallet.

Aslam sighed, and emptied his wallet.

"Here is your key. It is room two-o-one, up the flight of stairs. It is the first door on your left. The bathroom is at the end of the hall."

"There is no bathroom in the room?" Divya asked.

"If you wish to have air conditioning or an adjoining bathroom, princess, then you can go to the Ramanashree Residency, which is three blocks from here," he said with irritation.

"No, this is fine, thank you," Aslam said quickly.

"And check out is at nine in the morning," the man said sharply. "Otherwise you pay for another night."

"But that's in five hours!" Divya exclaimed.

"And that is why I gave you a discount," the man said, revealing gray teeth as he smiled. He dangled the key in front of her. "Enjoy your stay at the Laxmi Inn."

Divya snatched the key and gave him an angry look. The man smiled again and lay back down on the counter.

Oh what's the point? she thought, suddenly feeling very tired. *Just go to bed and end this nightmare. Tomorrow is another day.*

Divya wearily followed Aslam up the rickety stairs to the second floor of the building. She tried to concentrate on climbing the stairs, her feet feeling so heavy that she was afraid she would trip. She shuffled across the soiled, carpeted hallway and up to

111

their room. She opened the door and was struck by a blast of hot air.

"I'm going to the loo," Aslam said. "I'll be back."

"Okay," she said, flicking on the light and entering the sweltering room.

The sixty-watt light bulb fizzled to life and washed a dull, yellow light over a room that was so small that she wondered how the staff had managed to wedge the only piece of furniture—the bed—into the room.

The bed was a thin mattress on a flimsy metal frame that looked so ragged that under normal circumstances she would not even have allowed a dog to sleep on it. But after what she had endured that night, the bed looked as tempting as sleeping on a pile of goose feathers.

Her eyes moved from the tiny bed to the drawn curtains.

It'd be funny if that window looked out on a brick wall, Divya thought dully.

She pulled the curtains open and stared at the windowless, brick wall. The curtains were cosmetic.

Beside the curtains, Divya saw the switch that activated the ceiling fan. She flicked it on, but the fan refused to spin. She flicked the switch on and off, but to no avail. Sighing, she quickly undressed before Aslam returned.

Divya took off her wet shoes, socks, jacket, bra, and pants and put them over the baseboard of the bed. In her damp shirt and underwear, she climbed underneath the thin blanket.

She worried about Aslam sharing the bed with her. She had never shared a bed with a man before, and the bed was so narrow that they would practically be on top of each other. Although a small part of her was curious and tempted by sleeping with Aslam, a larger and more reasonable part of her was terrified at the prospect. She had always known that she would eventually end up in bed with someone, but never like this. She had to admit that Aslam was handsome and charming, but she was not ready to share her bed with anyone.

Just tell him that you're uncomfortable with the situation, Divya, she thought to herself. *He seems very kind and reasonable. He'll understand, won't he?*

Her nervousness grew as she wondered what Aslam would do or say if he refused her request. It wasn't as if she could escape through the window.

The door to the bedroom opened. Divya closed her eyes, pretending to be asleep. She suddenly felt very vulnerable and naked in just her shirt and underwear, although the stifling heat made her wish she could discard the remaining clothing she was wearing.

Aslam moved quietly through the room. She held her breath, her heart frozen, as the blanket was lifted.

Is he checking me out? she wondered, petrified.

He grabbed one of the flimsy pillows and dropped the blanket.

Shit, he only wanted a pillow. She was stunned by her feelings of disappointment. *What the hell's wrong with me?* she thought, trying to sort the complex emotions swirling within her.

She heard rustling at one end of the room, but kept her eyes closed. She listened to him struggle to take his wet clothes off. She felt compelled to peak, but resisted.

Aslam flicked the light switch off, and whispered: "Good night, Divya." Too afraid to admit that she was awake, she remained silent. "Divya, honestly, how did you learn to play badminton like that?"

She smiled into her pillow but did not say a word.

After what seemed like an eternity, Divya opened her eyes and waited for them to adjust to the darkness. She noticed Aslam huddled on the floor by the front door. He had taken down the curtains and used one as a sheet and the other as a blanket. Their wet clothes were hanging on the metal rod that had held the curtains.

I didn't even hear him take those down. He must have worried that any sound would disturb me.

She was touched by his thoughtfulness and felt guilty for questioning his intentions. As she continued to study his peacefully sleeping face, she suddenly yearned for him to be in the bed, holding her within his arms. She was surprised by the images and the warm feelings they had stirred within her.

Realizing that she was smiling wistfully, Divya frowned. She felt as if she was losing control of her emotions, and it troubled

113

her. She closed her eyes and the exhaustion of the day overcame her. Within moments, she was fast asleep.

* * *

"Boss, IIMB on Bannerghatta Road," Aslam told the driver as he sat down beside Divya in the back of the autorickshaw.

As the three-wheeler began swerving through traffic, Divya reflected back on the hectic day they had endured.

At quarter to nine that morning, Aslam had nudged her awake and given her privacy to dress as he waited downstairs. Divya had stretched her aching muscles and envied Aslam for wisely sleeping on the floor rather than on the terrible bed. She quickly dressed in her dried clothes, determined to check out before nine rather than allow the desk clerk to charge them for another night. After taking a glance at the common bathroom, Divya had opted to use the bathroom at the nearby Pizza Hut on Brigade Road, despite her tremendous urge to relieve herself.

Without warning, the autorickshaw pulled to the side of the road. The driver jumped out and crossed the bustling street.

Divya gave Aslam a puzzled look. "This happens to me a lot," he said. "Don't worry."

The driver returned a few moments later with a package of chewing tobacco and a small box of cigarettes. The driver tore open the package of chewing tobacco and stuffed a large chunk into his mouth. Soon his crimson lips were dripping with blackish-red juice. As he pulled back onto the congested road, he enthusiastically spat onto the road to relieve the excess juice in his mouth.

Disgusted by the nasty habit, Divya returned back to her thoughts, reflecting on the day.

After leaving the Laxmi Inn and relieving herself at the Pizza Hut, Aslam had taken her to the local ISD/STD phone booth so she could contact American Express and Visa to cancel her credit cards. It was a relief to learn that no transactions had been made since the cards were stolen.

As they brainstormed how they were going to get home without any money, Aslam miraculously ran into some friends who had lent them enough rupees to last the day.

What were their names again? she wondered.

The autorickshaw turned the corner and screeched to a halt to avoid smashing into a cow ambling across the street. With his stained sleeve, the driver wiped off the black tobacco juice dripping onto his chin.

"Hey Oz, what were the name of those nice friends of yours?" Divya asked, unable to remember. "I want to treat them to dinner for their kindness...Oz?"

Aslam did not reply, fast asleep. She had a strong desire to lean on his shoulder and do the same, but resisted. Who knew how the driver would swindle them if they were both asleep.

Divya continued reminiscing.

After treating themselves to a steaming vegetarian pizza at Pizza Hut, Divya was exhausted, and had yearned for a bucket bath at the hostel, but decided to finish a few more errands before returning to campus. She had told Aslam that he could go home, but he refused, staying by her side. She was touched and grateful. His presence brought her much comfort.

"So, what now?" Aslam had asked.

"I should notify the police that my wallet was stolen."

"Are you mad? They'll interrogate you all day for disturbing them. It's not worth it, Divya, trust me."

"Okay, then I need to open a bank account so my father can send me funds directly from Canada."

"Do you have a particular bank in mind?"

"Yeah, Citibank. There's an ATM at the school, and there are a few branches in Toronto. It should make the entire transaction much easier."

"Okay, let's go. There's a Citibank on M.G. Road."

When they had entered the exquisite building and were escorted into the bank manager's office, Divya figured that the entire process of opening an account would be an efficient and painless procedure. Then, the bank manager began speaking. Divya was shocked to hear that no account at Citibank could be opened unless a minimum of one lakh was in the account at the beginning of every month.

"That's over three thousand Canadian dollars!" Divya exclaimed. "I don't even have that much money in Toronto. Why do you have such a policy and yet have a branch within IIMB where only a few students have that type of money?"

"I don't make the policies, madam," the bank manager said impassively, flicking a piece of offensive lint off his immaculately tailored three-piece suit.

"And do I have any other options if I wish to be a client at this bank?" Divya asked.

"No. But you can always go across the street to the State Bank of India. They may be more helpful as they cater to a segment of the market that fits your...profile." He stood up, signaling that the meeting was over. He escorted them out of his office. "Thank you for choosing Citibank. Good day."

Appalled by his coldness, Divya angrily stomped past the glimmering marble foyer and shoved open the glass doors. Aslam followed, relieved to be out of the posh environment.

"Hey, Boss, where are you going? Take a right turn here," Divya barked in Hindi at the autorickshaw driver, annoyed that he had tried to go straight and take the extended route back to campus. She was pleased that she now understood exactly how to get to campus from downtown, and had handled the matter without waking Aslam.

No more rickshaw drivers are going to cheat me!

The autorickshaw driver spat tobacco juice on the street, and reluctantly turned the vehicle onto the proper street.

Divya returned her mind to the past, reflecting back on her initial impression of the State Bank of India. As she had entered the enormous chamber, which housed the entire bank, she was astounded by the building's state of disrepair. The paint was peeling off the grimy walls, and there were cobwebs and thick layers of dirt all over the dimly lit building. A blackboard incredibly had the Indian/U.S. exchange rates from three years ago still scrawled in chalk. But the most startling thing was the lack of security. There were no cameras, and stacks and stacks of rupees were being counted or sitting on empty desks all over the branch. The only security was a decrepit looking guard who bore a remarkable resemblance to the elderly man patrolling the train she had taken to Bangalore. Even his great, white mustache, colossal gun cartridges strapped across his scrawny chest, and antique rifle he carried seemed to be identical replicas. She was certain that any thief would be able to rob the bank and vanish long before the fragile guard was able to load, aim, and fire his nineteenth century weapon.

While Aslam waited at the front of the bank, Divya was led to the NRI section where she had explained that she was a Non-Resident Indian studying in India who needed to open an account so her father could transfer funds from Canada. After explaining her situation, she was relieved when the balding banker had said: "No problem."

Divya spent the next hour filling out forms and answering his questions. She even found wallet-sized photographs of herself in her purse to attach to the documents as was requested. Her efforts to open a bank account were coming to fruition.

"I now need proof that you're indeed studying at the Indian Institute of Management in Bangalore," the balding banker said.

"Of course," Divya replied, extracting her passport.

"I am sorry, but this is not adequate proof. I need a certificate issued directly from the school."

"What's wrong with this? I have a student visa stamped by the Indian Consulate in Toronto that clearly states I am studying at the Indian Institute of Management in Bangalore. See?" Divya said, opening her passport and pointing to her student visa. "Look, I even have my student I.D. card as additional proof." She pulled out the student card and showed it to the banker.

"I'll need to talk to my superior," he said, frowning. "Our policy dictates that we need a stamped and signed certificate. This is most unusual."

"You do that." Divya said, irritated at the bureaucracy. She hoped that this had not been a waste of time.

He returned a few minutes later. "Very well, madam, we will open your account. But you must return with the school certificate tomorrow."

"Certainly, no problem, thank you," she said, relieved.

"Now, please fill out this form," he said, handing her a lengthy document.

After another half an hour of filling forms, the balding banker smiled broadly and said: "Finally, I need a signed and stamped certificate from your school as proof that you are a student studying at the Indian Institute of Management."

Divya was thunderstruck. Had she heard him properly?

"W-We just went through this conversation," she stammered, staring at him stupidly. "We agreed that I would bring proof tomorrow."

"I regret that I cannot help you until I receive that document. Thank you, come again."

He collected the documents, stamped them, and put them in a pile on one corner of his desk.

Anger quickly dissipated her shock. "I want to talk to your supervisor immediately," she demanded.

He smiled thinly. "So sorry, but he just left for the evening as the bank is now closed. Good day."

Before she could say anything else, he stood up and walked away to fetch a cup of tea.

Divya numbly walked out of the bank, rubbing her throbbing head and cursing the Indian banking system. Aslam, who had been waiting patiently, chased after her, asking whether she had managed to open the account.

It's like they don't want my money, she thought angrily. *No wonder most of the country hides their savings underneath their mattress.*

"Students!" Divya cried as the autorickshaw reached the front gate of the campus.

Aslam woke up as the school's security guard glanced in and waved the three-wheeler through.

"Good afternoon, sleepyhead," she said happily, ecstatic to be back in the sanctuary of the lush campus. "Do you know that Bannerghatta Road was completely dry? It was like yesterday was a dream."

"Or nightmare," he said, yawning.

The autorickshaw parked by the mess. Aslam handed the autorickshaw wallah the amount displayed on the meter.

"Twenty rupees more," the driver said rudely in Hindi.

"What? Why?" Aslam demanded. "I already gave you a tip above the meter price."

The driver and Aslam got into a heated discussion over the price of the fare. Divya listened aptly until the argument shifted into Kannada.

"Look, Oz, thank you so much for being with me today, but is it okay if I go while you settle this?" she asked.

"Boss, I'm not giving you another rupee!" Aslam said in English, raising his voice with every word.

The driver angrily started his autorickshaw, turned the three-wheeler around, and defiantly spat tobacco juice at Aslam's shoes as he drove by.

"Bastard!" Aslam cried, running after the autorickshaw who accelerated down the tree lined street.

Divya walked past the phone booth where she saw the phone attendant fast asleep.

She entered A Block and paused to admire Pradeep—whistling to the music blaring from his battered radio—expertly ironing a pair of trousers with his one and only hand. An impressive mound of clothes lay on the floor by his feet. In one fluid motion, the laundry wallah flipped the trousers over, ironed a perfect crease, and folded them on top of a neat pile on an adjoining table.

He looked up and beamed. "Hello, pretty lady," he said, gyrating to the beat of the music for a moment before saluting her and returning to his work.

Laughing, Divya made her way to the base of the stairs and ran into Rekha.

"Oh my gosh, Rekha, you won't believe what I've been throug—"

"Divya, what should I do?" Rekha interrupted, not hearing a word her friend had said. "I have had the worse luck since we got back from Mysore. At dinner last night Chicken called me Motti again."

Divya sighed. She climbed the stairs and walked towards her room with Rekha in pursuit.

"And someone took my wet clothes from the laundry machine and left them on the floor. People are so self-absorbed, nah?"

Divya pulled out her key and unlocked her padlock.

"Then I just noticed that I have a pimple growing on my nose! It is hideous, nah?"

Divya glanced at Rekha's nose and barely noticed a slight discoloration that could have been anything.

"*Chhee!* Why are you were wearing such dirty, smelly clothes?" Rekha asked as Divya entered the bedroom and turned to face her. "Areé, were you not wearing those yesterday?"

Divya slammed her bedroom door in her friend's face.

Chapter 6
The Roof
Monday, September 10th, 2001

Divya sat in the back of the classroom observing the class, and apprehensively waited for Professor Munde to arrive and begin the lecture. Some students were sleeping, some excitedly chatting with each other, while others were either reading the newspaper or sending electronic messages over their cell phones. She estimated that a third of the students had actually brought a pen and notebook. Everyone was sitting in the last three rows of the class. The first two rows of seats were empty except for one student who was reading the assigned textbook readings.

Recollecting what Aslam had told her about Professor Munde, Divya felt a stab of fear for not reading the assigned case. She had slept in again, and barely made it to class on time.

A short man with Elvis-like hair and bushy sideburns briskly walked into the room, and a hush fell across the class.

This is the infamous Professor Munde? Divya thought, imagining a far more imposing figure.

"Welcome to Marketing Communications," Professor Munde began with a booming voice which seemed to shake the room. "Can someone tell me what the four P's are?"

Product, Place, Promotion, and...and...shit, what's the fourth one? Divya thought, trying to recollect the knowledge she had accumulated from her first year marketing course.

The hand of the lone student sitting in the front of the class shot up.

"Yes, Mr. Ansari," Professor Munde said. "What are the four P's?"

"Product, Price, Place, and Promotion," Mr. Ansari said confidently.

Price, that's it.

"Wrong, wrong, wrong, and wrong," Professor Munde said, snatching the smile off Mr. Ansari's face.

Stunned, Mr. Ansari frantically flipped through the textbook searching for the correct answer.

"I am referring to *my* four P's, the four P's necessary to pass this course," the professor continued. "Mr. Ansari, you made an incorrect azzumption that I was referring to the four P's of marketing. Remember to always question your azzumptions. In fact, I challenge all of you to question everything, for I relish a good debate. Understood?" Professor Munde paused, scrutinizing each young face. "Now, *my* first P is *Problem Solving*. Life is not about theory. It is about being able to think expeditiously and intelligently, making tough decisions and doing so with a very limited amount of information. This is why I am here. Forget about the grades. Forget about your degree. Here, I will teach you how to think, and it will not be an easy process for either of us. I assure you that you will be challenged more than ever before. So, the question is: Are you brave enough to embrace this life enhancing challenge?"

A harried girl suddenly rushed into the room; hair in disarray and wearing flannels, she clearly had just awoken. "You, get out!" Professor Munde screamed at her. "You are eight minutes late for class!"

Terrified, the girl bolted out of the room.

Professor Munde slammed the door shut.

The class sat rigid, watching their professor with fear.

"The second P is *Punctuality*." Professor Munde said coolly, turning back to the class and smoothing his hair. "If you are even one minute late, do not dare consider coming. Class will begin on time. Respect time and deadlines. I promise you that I will never keep you a minute after class is scheduled to end. You and I both have other things to do. Life is too precious to waste and I will not allow one inconsiderate student to delay the rest of us. Think about it. If we, a class of sixty, collectively wait one minute for a classmate, we have effective wasted an hour. *An hour!* Nations have fallen in less time. Such a disregard of resources is absolutely unacceptable. Are we clear?"

There was not a cough or movement or even the sound of breathing. The only noise came from the spinning ceiling fans. The air of apprehension seemed to please Professor Munde.

"The third P is entirely up to you. I have been bold enough to give you a choice. The third P can be either *Pain* or *Pleasure*. Now, *listen*, and listen to me carefully," Professor Munde growled. "You will take my class seriously or you can get out. Either way I get paid, and I could not care less what you do. This is your first day of boot camp and I am your drill sergeant from hell. I will make you work to the point where you think the pain in intolerable, and then, I will make you work more. But, in time, as you grow stronger, you will yearn, crave, for more."

"He's mad with power," a girl behind Divya whispered.

Professor Munde shot a dangerous look in Divya's direction and the whispering behind her ceased.

"For most of you the third P will be a transition from Pain to Pleasure. I will take your minds to places you never thought possible. I will train that wasted, atrophied matter between your ears with practical and indispensable tools that can be universally applied to every marketing problem you encounter. As Albert Einstein once said: 'Only two things are infinite, the universe and human stupidity, and I am not sure about the former.' I hope together we can change his views."

There were a few chuckles throughout the room.

Divya relaxed. There was a cold harshness to the man, but he seemed to have a genuine desire to teach those students who wanted to learn.

"The more I make you work, the more you will enjoy it. I will transform your mind to such an extent that this course will provide more satisfaction than any lover could. I will give you the type of passion and ambition that drove such people as Carl Friedrich Gauss, whose words, when he was interrupted from his work to learn of his wife's imminent death, were: 'Ask her to wait a moment—I am almost done.'" Professor Munde smiled broadly.

"Does this man have no heart?" the same girl whispered to her friend behind Divya.

"Any questions so far?" Professor Munde asked, glaring at the guilty whisperer. "If anyone is unhappy with my expectations, I encourage, no, *dare* them to leave right now. Run, *hide*, from this challenge, and *embrace* mediocrity."

No one moved or spoke.

"Very well, then, let me talk about the fourth P—*Prepared*." Professor Munde walked to the back of the class. All eyes followed him except two, which were reading e-mail on her cell phone. "Miss. Singh, stop gossiping on the phone with your tardy friend who I just kicked out of my class, and tell me whether you read the case that was assigned today. Otherwise, I assure you that you will be soon gossiping with her in person."

* * *

After being blasted by Professor Munde for not having read her case, Divya was relieved that she only had one more class before lunch. She used the fifteen-minute break to go to the bathroom and the coffee shop to quench her need for caffeine. Although the ant repellant she bought had solved her ant problem, it had destroyed her portable coffee machine as Rekha had predicted.

Divya had heard much about the coffee shop from students around campus but had never visited it. As she followed a stream of students, she wondered what type of service she would get; the coffee shop had a monopoly on campus for snacks and drinks between meals.

The coffee shop turned out to be nothing like Divya had envisioned. Rather than being a separate building where one could sit at a table and relax over a cup of steaming java, the coffee shop was merely two tables filled with an assortment of packaged snacks, a mini-fridge filled with juices and pops, and a tea and coffee machine. It reminded her of an elaborate version of the lemonade stand that she had set-up one summer as a child.

Twenty students were shoving money and orders at the frazzled attendant. Refusing to wait even one minute, Divya aggressively pushed through the crowd. She grabbed a bottle of water from the mini-fridge, placed twelve rupees on the table, and emerged from the crowd of yelling students, unscathed. She took a swig of water; it had never tasted so good. She smiled, proud at how quickly she was adapting to the culture.

"Hey, Divya!"

Divya turned and smiled as Naveen emerged from the horde of students.

"Hi, Naveen. Is it always so crazy here between classes?"

"Oh, yes," he said, extracting a cigarette tucked behind his right ear and lighting it. "I heard you were having some banking problems."

Divya's face darkened. "I don't want to talk about that."

"Why don't you just open an account at the State Bank of Mysore, right here on campus?"

"What? There's a bank on campus?"

"Yeah, it's beside the amphitheatre. You just show them your student card to prove you are a student, and have a minimum of five hundred rupees to put into your account, and you are set. The whole process should take five minutes."

Divya was stunned. "That's it? I could kill Oz for not telling me. Why'd he drag me across B'lore?"

Naveen shrugged, eyes twinkling.

"Is there something you are not telling me?" she asked, narrowing her eyes. "Don't avoid the question, Naveen."

"Aren't you getting late for your next class?" he asked, tapping the dial of his wristwatch.

"Shit, we'll finish this conversation later," Divya said.

As she quickly walked to her next class, she hoped her professor would not reprimand her for being late. Entering the classroom, she was surprised to be the second person there. Mr. Ansari—the studious student that had incorrectly answered Professor Munde's four P's question—sat in the first row reading.

She checked the clock on the wall; it matched her watch. Class should have begun three minutes ago.

Am I in the wrong room?

Divya checked the room number and confirmed that she was in the right place.

Unless my schedule is wrong...

She cleared her throat to grab Mr. Ansari's attention. He looked up at her. "Excuse me, but is this Professor Bhagnani's class?"

"Yes," he said, returning to his text.

Feeling foolish, she cleared her throat again. "Um, where is everyone else, Mr...um, your name?"

"Tapan Ansari. And what is your good name?"

What the heck is a good name?

"Ambani, Divya Ambani," she said, sounding like James Bond.

"Ambani?" He looked up eagerly. "Are you related to the Reliance Ambani's?"

"No."

"Oh," he said, disappointed. "Too bad. Reliance is a great Indian conglomerate, and the Ambani family are great business leaders who have helped industrialize India."

"Uh huh," she said, not caring. "Are you sure we're in the right class?"

"Quite, and don't look so concerned. The other students will be here in a few minutes. This is a fart class, and everyone is still recovering from Marketing Communications."

Fart class, eh? Interesting term.

Divya looked at the clock. Class should have started five minutes ago, but not even the teacher had arrived.

Selecting a seat in the back of the class, Divya observed the empty classroom with growing apprehension. She looked back at her watch, sighed, calculated how many collective minutes had been lost, and wondered how Professor Munde would have reacted to such blatant tardiness.

He'd probably have had a vein burst in his head, she thought.

"Tapan, are you sure we're in the right class?" she asked again.

"Yes, of course," he said irritably.

"This is *Time Management* class?"

"*Yes,*" he said, not perturbed by the irony.

She shook her head with disbelief.

* * *

"Good afternoon, class, I am Professor Krishnamurthy, and welcome to Spirituality and Business."

"Areé, Divya, how many fart classes are you taking this term?" Rekha whispered with a snicker.

Divya ignored her, captivated by the little man in front of her with no hair on his shiny, brown scalp, and thick, black-rimmed glasses that were far too large for his little head. He reminded her of a Cabbage Patch Kid doll.

He must be at least eighty, Divya thought.

"Don't ignore me, nah?"

Divya focused on the professor's words, thankful that he had the attention of most of the class.

"The purpose of this class is to teach you various aspects on how to be a successful business executive *and* maintain your spirituality. Yes, ladies and gentlemen, although it may be impossible to believe, one can still keep their soul, be at peace with the world, and be successful in business." The teacher smiled serenely. "Now, the first lesson is to learn how to balance work with your passions. And that is why I am going to keep this class for only ten more minutes before letting you all go. Life is constantly changing, so let's change the class times for today, shall we?"

Divya was startled as everyone began banging the top of the tables. Confused, she turned to Rekha who was enthusiastically banging the desk.

"We always bang the desks whenever something pleases us," Rekha explained, noticing her friend's perplexed look. "If something amusing or surprising happens, we normally do this, like clapping, nah?"

Divya nodded, eager to participate in the next table banging session.

"However," Professor Krishnamurthy cautioned, "just because you're not in my class for the last hour doesn't mean you don't owe me this time." The banging stopped. "So, you'll spend this one hour doing a homework assignment for me." The class groaned. "And that assignment will be doing something that you love to do the most. Maybe it's writing, sleeping, watching movies, or even drinking! But doing anything academic is simply unacceptable, that is, unless, you love doing work."

The class pounded their desks again, and a few people even cheered in the back. Divya could not help but get caught up in the excitement, and pounded her desk until her palms were smarting.

When the class settled down, Professor Krishnamurthy continued. "Then, next class, I will call five students randomly.

They will give a fifteen minute presentation on why these activities are so special for their mind and soul. My only expectations are that you speak honestly and put some thought into it. Any nonsense or exaggeration will not be tolerated. Agreed?"

Professor Krishnamurthy smiled serenely as the class nodded with agreement.

"Good, now, before you all go, I want to *briefly* talk about the central essence of life according to Vedic scriptures. This essence focuses on our body, mind, intellect, and soul. It is also referred to as our Purusharthas—Artha, Kama, Dharma, and Moksha."

Divya leaned forward, listening with rapt attention.

Professor Krishnamurthy took a sip of water from the glass sitting on his desk, cleared his throat, and then to everyone's surprise, began reciting in Sanskrit. *"Hey ishvara dayā-nidhey bhavat-krypāā anenā japo-paasanā-dikarmnāā-dharmāā-arthāā-kaamāā-mokshāā-naam sadyah siddhiir-bhavennāh."* The class was silent, mesmerized by the old man. "O, Lord!" he began to translate, "May we, by Thy Grace, and by Thy energy, soon achieve Dharma—righteousness, Artha—material wealth, Kama—fulfillment of our desires, Moksha—salvation, by revering and adoring Thee."

Om, sitting in the front of the class, began pounding his desk, and soon the entire class followed.

"Thank you. My grandmother used to sing this to me before I went to bed," the professor said. "Now, the first Purusharta is Artha, something that I am sure all you future CFOs and CEOs will appreciate. Artha refers to accumulating material wealth and possessions. After all, if we all renounced the world and meditated our lives away in a cave then society, as we know it, would not have evolved. Artha helps achieve freedom and independence. So, at a certain stage in our lives Artha is necessary and encouraged. Artha is a means of securing enjoyments and comforts in life. The second Purushartha, Kama, refers to fulfilling our desires. It is common to all animals, and may refer to finding shelter, filling your belly with food, or copulating for the purpose of procreation or just pleasure. It is the experience of fulfillment, joy, and pleasure through the senses."

The little man paused to push his large glasses back up his nose.

"All humans are social beings. We live amongst our own kind, in groups, and those evolve as cultures. Dharma, the third Purushartha, provides the ground rules for how we interact and behave in those groups. Dharma defines a set of rules to regulate our ethical and societal code of conduct. It is fulfilling our social obligations as a husband, daughter, sister, student, executive, priest and so forth. And depending on what your place and role is in life, one has a set of duties that one is expected to abide to. Dharma is being sensitive and caring about others. It also implies conscientious, orderly, and holistic living. It is realizing that our choices are driven by that inner voice, our conscience. Dharma guides our behavior, and helps us choose between right and wrong."

He paused to take another sip of water.

"Presume many years from now you have acquired wealth, experienced many pleasures, and cared for the people around you. What more do you want? But, if you are constantly acquiring wealth and searching for pleasures, are you truly happy? True happiness begins when you no longer seek any self-centered desires. And this leads us to the fourth Purusartha, Moksha, which means 'liberation.' This is the ultimate purpose of life. Moksha is the pursuit of seeking liberation from bondage, not in death, but in *this* life. Moksha is seeking liberation from insecurity and fear, being free from all limitations of time and space. Turning our mind from external preoccupations, and focusing on deep introspection to realize our basic essence and true self is what Moksha is about. It is about finding happiness and peace from within. And Artha, Kama, and Dharma are the means to begin to understand Moksha. Oh, I see that my ten minutes are up, so I will talk about Moksha in more detail in another class. Are there any questions before I dismiss you?"

A hand rose in the front of the class.

"Yes?" Professor Krishnamurthy said, nodding towards Om.

"What are your views on death?"

Divya was thunderstruck. It was the first time she had heard Om speak, and like a mother waiting to hear the first words of her child, she had been curious to how he would sound. But never in her wildest imagination did she think his voice would be so deep and powerful.

Geez, he sounds like James Earl Jones.

"Hmmm, interesting question," Professor Krishnamurthy said, taking a moment to contemplate an appropriate answer. "This is definitely a question worthy of a full class discussion, and I am no means young enough to believe that I have all the answers in life. That's why I've surrounded myself by such youth and wisdom in the classroom for nearly fifty years. But, to quickly answer your question, I believe that death itself will be a very peaceful affair. It is the process of dying that I find distressing. Good day."

* * *

"Oz!" Divya called, running down the gray stone corridor that connected each hostel block. "I was looking for you."

Aslam turned and smiled brightly. "Hi, there! So?"

"So, what?"

"How was Marketing Communications?"

Divya frowned. "A *real* joy."

"I think Professor Munde likes you."

"Yeah, right. He yelled at me for five minutes for not reading my case."

"True, but he didn't kick you out of his class, did he?"

"No, he didn't. Although, a part of me wishes he did," she said dejectedly.

They walked past the ISD/STD phone booth where the phone attendant was sleeping.

Aslam snapped his fingers. "Hey, I know how to cheer you up. I have something I want to show you."

"What is it?"

"A surprise."

"I wish I could, Oz, but I have a group meeting."

"Really? When?"

"In ten minutes in the computer center, I mean C.C.," Divya sighed. "Geez, all these acronyms should be included in the manual you hand out during Orientation."

"Is this group meeting for Time Management class?"

"Yup."

"And you have Meena Chopra and Sachin Sharma in your group, correct?"

"Uh huh. How'd you know?"

"I just ran into a very distressed Sachin who told me."

"Distressed? What's wrong?"

"Did you know those two are dating?"

"Yeah, both Meena and Sachin told me in class. They assured me that it wouldn't be a problem."

"True, they work quite well together when they're a couple, but—"

"Don't tell me they broke up?" Her eyes widened as he nodded. "Oh, no. What happened?"

"Meena caught Sachin smiling at his ex-girlfriend, Anju, and broke up with him."

Divya sighed. "Well, maybe one of them will show up at the meeting."

Aslam chuckled. "There will be no one at the meeting."

"But this is *Time Management* class," she said, exasperated.

"Divya, I heard that even the teacher was late for class."

She frowned. "Yeah, by fifteen minutes. Ironic, eh?"

"See, this is the fifth term and no one does any work. Even most professors don't really care at this point, except for Professor Munde, of course."

"Care? That man is insane. And if I want to be spared from his wrath I better go and prepare for his class tomorrow. I have two chapters to read and a case to do. Actually, on second thought, first I better go see if Meena is alright."

"Whoa, chill. Those two argue and break up at least two or three times a month. I can bet that Meena is right now in her room crying and refusing to talk to Sachin, who is standing outside her door and begging to be forgiven."

"Are you sure?"

"Divya, their pattern of behavior is as certain as gravity. If they didn't break up every few weeks I would wonder what's *wrong* with their relationship."

She laughed. "Okay, I guess I'm off to the library."

"But what about the surprise I want to show you?"

"Not tonight, Oz. Can't it wait?"

"Yes," he said, disappointed. "By the way, you said you were looking for me?"

"I wanted to thank you for taking care of me the other night."

"You're very welcome. But, remind me never to take you out if there's a chance of rain. A *stormy* side of you seems to pour out."

Divya blushed with embarrassment. "Yeah, sorry about that. I was tired and irritable."

"No, it's understandable. It was a stressful situation," he said, wishing he could somehow think of an opportunity to persuade her to spend more time with him. He suddenly felt awkward as their eyes locked for a moment. "Well, have fun at the library. See you."

He began walking down the corridor.

"Oz, wait!"

He turned expectantly. "Yes?"

"Here are the three hundred rupees I owe you."

She pulled out the money from her bag.

"Oh...Divya, this is too much. You owe me only a hundred and twenty five rupees for the Laxmi Inn."

"I also owe you for the money I spent on those calls to the credit card companies, for lunch, and of course, for the autorickshaws."

Although Aslam needed the money, he could not take it. "It's alright. It was my pleasure." He placed the money back in her hands.

"Okay, fine," Divya said, frustrated by his stubbornness. "I'll see this surprise of yours if you swallow your infuriating male ego and *please* take these rupees." Aslam was silent, contemplating the offer. She held out the money. "Oh stop being such a stubborn mule, Oz! This is silly. Take it before I get angry."

"Okay," he said reluctantly, taking the money, and feeling terrible for doing so. "But you'll have to close your eyes."

"What for?"

"Hey, this is a surprise, right? You have to close your eyes." Divya frowned, reconsidering. "Come on, play along," he pressed. "It's nothing humiliating or painful. I promise."

"Fine," she said, closing her eyes. "But this better be worth it."

"Good. Now keep them shut."

Aslam grabbed her right hand and led her towards J block.

* * *

Divya peered over the edge of the hostel roof, four floors down. "Are we allowed to be up here?" she asked apprehensively.

"Not really, but it's not enforced and we'll be careful," Aslam said with a reassuring smile.

He climbed the metal rungs of a ladder, and pulled himself onto the small landing above the top staircase; she carefully followed.

"But the door leading up to the roof is supposed to be sealed shut, right? How'd it get broken open like that?" Divya asked, taking his outstretched hand.

"No idea," Aslam replied mischievously, pulling Divya to the top.

"Oz, did you—"

"Shhhh, look at that!" he exclaimed, pointing up.

A shooting star whizzed across the glittering sky.

"It's beautiful," she breathed, enraptured by the spectacle. "I've never seen one before."

"What? I thought you were from Canada. Isn't it all wilderness over there?"

"Yeah, most of it is, but I've rarely left Toronto. And the lights and pollution from the city prevent anyone from seeing most of the stars. Even on those clear nights when you think you've found a star, you usually find yourself watching an airplane." She sighed. "I can't remember seeing such a beautiful night."

They admired the scene in silence. Divya studied the skyline of Bangalore. The lights from the city emitted an orange aura over the horizon, giving the clouds in the distance a nuclear-like glow. Below them, the faint sound of laughter and music—being played over a myriad of radios and computers—failed to disrupt the peace she felt.

"This is a wonderful surprise, Oz," Divya said. "Thank you for bringing me here."

Aslam looked at her with a smile. "I'm glad. This place is very special to me."

His smile faded as he was drawn into her eyes. The intensity of his look set electric ripples down her spine. She was locked in his gaze, as if he was looking directly at her soul. She wanted to kiss him.

Uncertain and confused by the emotions bursting from her heart, Divya managed to break away from his coffee-brown eyes.

She looked down at the roof and studied how the crowns of the large trees jutted through of the center opening of each hostel block.

"Look at that, Oz, isn't that a strange sight? It looks as if bushes are growing right out of the concrete."

"Beautiful," he said, not taking his eyes off her.

"Tell me about your family, Oz?" she asked, trying to change the subject. "I know so little about you. Tell me about your mother and father."

A painful expression crossed his face. He looked at the sky.

"Oz?"

"My father and mother died during a Hindu Muslim riot in Bangalore just after I was born," he said, sounding distant.

"Oh my God! I'm sorry, Oz."

"It was a long time ago."

"I shouldn't have brought this up. We don't have to talk about it."

"No, I want to. You should know about my past, and I want to know about yours." Aslam paused and Divya remained silent, sensing he was trying to build the courage to start. When he began, he spoke with a quiet sadness.

"A mosque was desecrated by Hindus who declared that it was built on a sacred Hindu site. These were all lies, a farce concocted by the local Godfather who wanted to control the land for himself and drive out the Muslims. The tension escalated and a planned riot broke out. As I said, it was just after I was born. My father, a staunch Muslim, was protecting the mosque with many members of the Islamic community from the growing Hindu mob that demanded they leave the neighborhood. My father and his friends refused, waiting for the police to save them. But the police force—dominated by Hindus—were bribed by the Godfather not to interfere, and stood by as the Muslims got butchered."

His eyes filled with tears and she ached to hold him. The despair on his face was heart wrenching.

Aslam's next words were barely audible. "When the Hindus stormed the mosque, my father was killed, beaten with a stone to his head. My mother found out and committed suicide that night, unable to live without him."

"Oz, you don't have to do this."

"Please, it's okay. I don't even remember them," he said, wiping his tears. "And I was raised with much love."

"How'd you know all of this? Did your family tell you this?"

"Yes, but not in the sense you think. Any blood related family I had was killed that night."

"Then, who raised you?"

"I was raised by a Hindu family."

Divya was surprised. "What? How? You said Hindus killed your parents. How could you bear being raised in a Hindu home?"

"One of the men that stormed the mosque that night was a young Hindu activist who foolishly got caught up in religious propaganda, ignorant and too naïve to understand the consequences of his actions. This man had come from a small village to Bangalore to search for work so he could provide for his pregnant wife. Like hundreds of desperate people on the streets, he agreed to create a riot and tear down the mosque by the Godfather. After storming the mosque, he was devastated by the actions of his people. He had been lied to. He was told that they would only scare the Muslims out of the mosque, nothing more. Even then he felt terrible about causing trouble, but was desperate. His family needed money. But, as he stared at his celebrating comrades, and at the bloodied and broken bodies around him, he felt sick. With tears in his eyes, he took out those few rupees he had earned and tore them apart. He vowed that day to never defy his conscience, no matter how badly his family needed money."

"This man found your father?" she whispered.

"Yes, he crouched down to the closest body to him, which was my father. In my father's wallet he had found a home address where he went to beg for my mother's forgiveness. He found her the next day hanging from the ceiling fan. I was alone, screaming from hunger. This young Hindu took one look at me and knew what he had to do to atone for his sins. Once he was certain that no one would claim me, he embraced me as his own son, but raised

135

me as a Muslim. He took me to his home village where his entire family embraced me. And even though he was a Dalit and every upper-caste Hindu threatened him physically and emotionally to discard me, a Muslim, which they considered to be lower than a Dalit, he refused. He was confident that as long as he followed his heart, God would protect his family. So he became my Appa, and his wife, my Amma."

Aslam watched the orange clouds slowly cover the star splattered sky. Divya flinched as lightening flickered in the distance.

"You see," he continued with a fond smile. "I was raised to be proud of my culture and religion while still loving my adopted family. I was loved and nurtured, and worked twice as hard to make my parents proud of me and to prove to the village that I was worth something. When I got this scholarship to come to IIMB, and told my parents, the pride and happiness on their faces made me even more determined to succeed. I swear to you Divya that I will become a great man one day, and spoil my family with every luxury they deserve. Appa breaks his back every day in the sun drenched fields for the Zamindars—upper-caste landlords," he clarified, noticing her quizzical expression. "And I will make sure Appa never has to worry about money, food, or anything."

"What will you do for your family once you have become wealthy?" Divya asked with a smile.

"Ah, easy. Appa will have someone to massage his back for as long as he wishes. I'll provide such wealth that he will never have to worry about my sister's dowry, which keeps him awake many nights."

"And your mother?"

"Amma will never have to clean or cook again. She'll be draped with jewelry and the finest saris. And she'll watch with pride and joy as her children and grandchildren blossom."

"You have any siblings other than a sister?"

A proud smile filled his face. "I also have a younger brother. He's brave and far too wise for his age. He's like a man trapped in a boy's body. And another little one will soon be joining our family.

"Your mother's pregnant?"

There was the distinctive sound of someone whistling and climbing the staircase towards them

"Shhh, it's security," he whispered. "Lie down on your stomach, quickly, or he'll see us."

Divya apprehensively lay down beside Aslam on the small landing.

The whistling stopped and someone called out in Hindi if anyone was there. Divya held her breath as she saw the security guard emerge below her, scanning the roof, and this time calling out in Kannada. The pounding of her heart in her ear was deafening; she was certain it would betray her.

After a tense minute, the whistling resumed and the guard disappeared down the staircase. She sighed as the whistling and footsteps grew fainter.

"That was close," she said, sitting up.

"And exciting, right?" he asked, his eyes shining.

She grinned. "Yeah, it was."

"Tell me about your family, Divya?"

After hearing Aslam's tragic tale, she tried not to sound too appreciative of the loving, stable family she had. "Oh, I have a very mundane family, there's not much to tell. I have a father and mother who adore each another, and a baby brother."

"How old is he?"

"Three. A spoiled brat. Gosh, I miss him terribly."

"And your parents are from Gujarat, correct?"

"No, Punjab."

"Really? I thought Ambani was a Gujarati name?"

"It is, but my parents had a love marriage despite both of their families forbidding them to marry. They were shunned. They fled Punjab, got married in Ahmedabad, and my father changed his last name to Ambani."

"When did they move to Canada?"

"Papa got a scholarship to study in Canada. The University sponsored him and he brought my mother along. It was a very difficult time for them—foreign country, no friends or family to support them, my mother pregnant with me. I still don't know how they managed."

"I do. They had each other."

Remembering what Naveen had told her outside the coffee shop, she looked away from Aslam nervously. "Oz?"

"Yes, Divya?"

"There's something I want to ask you."

"Anything."

"Why didn't you tell me there was a bank on campus?"

Divya gasped as the entire city was suddenly cast into complete darkness. She could not even see her hands in front of her. Fear, isolation, and anxiety consumed her.

Two strong arms wrapped around her like a warm blanket, and the apprehension she felt from the blackout dissipated. She was surprised how comfortable she felt in his arms, as if she had always belonged in them. She suddenly understood why he had spent the entire day with her trying to open a bank account. No words needed to be spoken.

With the citywide blackout, the stars and the flickering lightening brightened dramatically. The occasional flicker from the clouds in the horizon added to the magical enchantment of the scene. Divya felt as if she was floating among the stars. Time and space ceased.

Without realizing it, she put her head on his shoulder. She did not want the moment to end.

She found it odd that despite the jagged bolts of electricity over them there was no thunder or any other sound. Like the darkness between the bolts of lightening, the silence was absolute, as if the entire world had simultaneously become blind and deaf.

The lights throughout the city returned, masking the few remaining stars that the clouds failed to conquer.

"We better go," Aslam said reluctantly.

"Not yet," Divya said softly. "Just a few more minutes."

The two remained silent and motionless, his arms around her, her head on his shoulder, until the first raindrops descended from the heavens.

Chapter 7
A Day of Birth and Death
Tuesday, September 11th, 2001

At the sound of someone banging on her bedroom door, Divya looked up from the Marketing Communications case, and sighed. She was used to the constant ruckus outside her room, but this was getting ridiculous.

"Coming, coming," she muttered, slamming the textbook shut.

The pounding increased in force and volume.

"Hold on!" she shouted.

The door was being struck so hard that her toiletries and trinkets on the shelf were shaking.

"What's your problem?" Divya demanded, unbolting the door and swinging it open.

"Surprise! Happy Birthday!" cried the crowd of fifty girls.

"What are you doing?" Divya laughed with surprise, amazed that every girl from her block was present. She turned to Rekha, who was standing in the front of the group. "How'd you find out?"

"I am your buddy, nah? It is my duty to find out. Now, let us go, we do not have much time."

"For what? I'm sorry, Rekha, but my birthday is tomorrow."

"Yes, and that is in four minutes. So, hurry up, nah?"

Divya looked at her watch and was shocked. She had been studying for hours and had completely lost track of time.

"Let me put on some jeans," Divya said.

"I wouldn't recommend that," said another girl whose name Divya could never remember. "What you're wearing is fine."

"But, I'm only in a T-shirt and flannels," Divya protested.

"Which is perfect. Come, nah?" Rekha said, grabbing her friend's hand and pulling her outside.

Divya felt like a prisoner as the girls surrounded her and marched her to Main Square for what she suspected would be less merciful than a hanging.

She noticed that Pradeep was still ironing.

He saluted and warmly wished her a happy birthday, and was rewarded with an appreciative smile.

The smile turned to one of amusement as she was escorted past the phone clerk, who was still asleep in the ISD/STD phone booth.

As they entered Main Square, Divya relaxed. Aslam and Naveen were placing a birthday cake on a table. She was also touched to see Om present among a dozen other guys.

"So what do I have to do?" Divya whispered to Rekha.

"Just cut the cake after the countdown and we will do the rest," Rekha said with a sinister smile.

"Rekha, what are you planning to do?"

"Just introduce you to a little Indian tradition, nah? Those clothes you are wearing do not have too much of a *senti* value to you, do they?"

"What?"

"Shhhh, it is time."

"Ten! Nine! Eight!" the crowd of students began shouting.

With a sympathetic smile, Aslam handed her a cake knife.

"Seven! Six! Five!"

"Why are you looking at me like that?" Divya whispered with growing apprehension.

"Four! Three! Two!"

"You'll see," Aslam said, stepping back.

Divya suddenly realized the girls had surrounded her.

"One! Happy birthday!"

Everyone cheered as Divya cut the cake.

Before she knew what was happening, the knife was snatched from her hand, and chocolate cake was smeared across her hair, face, and clothes. The female mob cheered and laughed as cake was shoved down her shirt and pants. Divya now understood why the boys were not allowed to participate in the pastry assault. She hated to think what Tharki would do with such an opportunity.

Divya gasped as something cold and slimy was poured over her head and down her back. She tried to open her eyes, but could not; they were covered with cake.

When she heard the distinctive sound of eggshells cracking, she knew that the worse was yet to come. She tried to make a blind run for safety, but realized with horror that several people were holding her.

"The more you fight, the more food we are going to cover you with," Rekha warned.

Divya stopped fighting, but cringed as cold egg yolks were smeared on her face and hair.

The bombardment stopped, and Divya silently thanked God that it was over. She yelped with surprise as she was lifted by her arms, legs, and back.

"Birthday bumps!" the crowd cheered.

Divya nearly cried out with pain as her block mates began kicking her buttocks with such ferocity that she was sure she would not be able to sit in comfort for a month.

"Beat her! Beat her!" she heard Rekha screaming with frenzied relish.

Divya covered her bottom with her hands, but realized that the force of the kicks could break her fingers. She removed her hands and clenched her teeth.

Just when she felt she could no longer endure the pain, she was put back onto her feet and handed a towel. She tried to wipe the layer of thick goo that encased her face. When she opened her eyes the chocolate cake, eggs, and noodles that stained the towel gave an indication of what she looked like. Like a dog, she shook her head and noodles flew in all directions.

"Ugh, this stuff is hardening. I'm never going to get this off," she complained with disgust.

"We can help with that!" Naveen exclaimed, dumping a large bucket of liquid over her.

"Oh shit, cold!" Divya exclaimed.

Divya applied the towel back to her face and was pleased to see the guck coming off. Her eyes widened with dismay as she looked at the towel; Naveen had not dumped water, but orange soda over her.

She glared at Naveen.

He smiled sheepishly. "Truce, Divya?"

"Sure, when's *your* birthday, Naveen?"

"In a few weeks," Aslam said. "And when it is a boy's birthday, *both* the boys and girls get to retaliate."

Divya rubbed her hands with glee. "Excellent."

Naveen frowned.

"By the way, happy birthday, Divya," Aslam said warmly. "Unfortunately, I must go. I have a really early start tomorrow morning. I have to do some research for Professor Munde."

Before she could ask him to stay, or even say goodbye, friends swarmed her and began warmly wishing her a happy birthday with handshakes, smiles, and hugs.

"Happy birthday, buddy," Rekha said, grinning.

"How's your foot?" Divya asked with a mock frown. "I hope you broke it when you were kicking my ass."

"Sore. I should have worn my steel-tipped boots because you certainly have a hard behind," Rekha laughed.

"I was impressed how you were able to kick my ass *and* urge the crowd like that. You're quite the multitasker."

"It is a gift, nah?"

"Uh huh, and since you're the only one I know who did this to me, I promise to get you back on your birthday." Divya wiped some chocolate off her face and smeared it across Rekha's cheek. "You are personally responsible for this."

"You can plan my revenge later, Divya," she said, handing her friend another clean towel. "Get cleaned up. We are going to have a party in B Block. I got some booze, so hurry, nah?"

Rekha and Naveen left to prepare for the party.

Divya walked up to Om, who had not yet congratulated her; he was leaning against the wall, engrossed in a book.

"Hello, Om," Divya said cheerfully.

The enigmatic man looked up from his book.

"You don't talk much, do you?" she asked.

"Knowledge speaks, but wisdom listens," he said, his deep voice rumbling. "Jimi Hendrix."

Divya didn't know what to say, and decided to take another approach. "I heard you're taking several financial and statistical courses this semester but are only planning to go to Spirituality and Business class. How will you pass all those courses without attending class?"

"I have never let my schooling interfere with my education. Mark Twain."

I'm talking to a living encyclopedia!

"Okay. Well, aren't you going to at least wish me a happy birthday? And please do not quote someone."

Om closed his book and seriously asked: "What's so happy about one's birthday?"

Divya was taken aback by the strange question. "Well, it signifies the day I was born, and if that hadn't happened, I'd never have had the pleasure of your acquaintance. Then who'd be there to be such a positive influence on you?"

Om was not amused. "There's nothing happy about being born. Does a newborn ever come into this world smiling? No, the baby is *always* crying. Life is nothing but suffering. Existence is sorrowful, and it's absurd that we celebrate it."

Divya read the cover of Om's book: *Theravada Buddhism: The Path to Nirvana*.

"Om, you are *way* too somber. You need to come to my party and dance. You can read that depressing book some other time."

Om turned back to his book. "No sane man will dance," he said. "Cicero."

"Okay, how about singing with me?"

"Anything that is too stupid to be spoken is sung. Voltaire."

I think I preferred his vow of silence.

"Divya!" Rekha called from the top of the staircase. "You have a long distance call."

"Om, I'd appreciate it if you could come to my party. I'll prove to you that there *is* joy in our existence," she said, trying to sound philosophical.

She studied Om for a moment, trying to decipher his emotionless face and wondering whether she had successfully convinced him.

"Divya! Phone, nah?"

Oh well, time will tell whether I got through to him.

Divya dashed up the stairs and ran to B block. Panting, she picked up the phone receiver.

"Hello?"

"Hello, Divya?"

"Hi, Mama!"

"Hello, beta. Happy birthday."

Divya was filled with the loving image of her mother. She loved how her mother called her beta, 'daughter' in Hindi.

143

"Thank you, Mama, but I can barely hear you."

"Strange, the connection is very clear at this end. You sound like you are in the next room, beta."

"Hold on a second, Mama."

Divya looked at the receiver and grimaced; chocolate and noodles covered it. She stuck her finger in her ear and pulled out as much food as she could, and then wiped the phone with her towel.

"Hello?"

"Hello?"

"Hi, Mama!"

"Oh, there you are. I thought I lost you for a moment. Can you still hear me?"

"Yes, much better. I can't tell you how great it is to hear from you. How is everybody?"

"We're good, beta. We are at Uncle Sebastian's house."

"In New York?" Divya asked, wistfully wishing she was with her family. She loved Uncle Sebastian, especially since he showered her and Rahul with gifts and affection whenever they visited, treating them as the children he never had.

"Yes, we just arrived. Your father has a conference and invited us to come along. I'm taking Rahul to the World Trade Center and Statue of Liberty tomorrow morning. Divya, he's so excited!"

"That's wonderful, Mama."

"Enough about us, beta. How are you? Have you been bitten by snakes? Had any life threatening case of the runs? Or have you been conscripted to join the Indian military at the Pakistani border yet?"

"Mama!" Divya laughed. "Actually, to be honest, I'm chocolately."

"Yes, that nice friend of yours, Rekha, told me what they did to you for your birthday. Trust me, beta, you got off easy compared to what my friends did to me when I was in school."

"You could have warned me, Mama. I may have taken an exchange in a country that celebrated my birthday by *not* kicking my ass!"

"Language, Divya, language," she admonished.

"Sorry, Mama."

"And don't forget that you must take them all out for dinner. It's tradition."

"Wait, I take *them* out for dinner? They kick my as...err... behind...and I treat *them* to a meal?"

"Yes, and make sure it is a nice restaurant, okay, beta?"

"Okay, I will. Thanks for the advice."

"And what about your health, beta?"

"I had some trouble with my stomach on the train, but I'm better now."

"You didn't have the train food, did you? Remember what your father and I warned you about? Avoid the street vendors and always drink bottled water."

"I'm fine, and I will, Mama," Divya said. "Oh, I can hear Rahul screaming in the background."

"Yes, beta, he misses you a lot and he's pulling the phone line because he wants to talk with you."

"Can I talk to him?"

"Of course. Hold on, beta. Take care of yourself and I love you."

"Love you too, Mama, and thanks for calling."

"Okay, hold on." Divya heard her mother talking to her little brother. "Rahul, talk to Divya didi. Come and take the phone and talk to your sister."

Divya smiled as she heard the receiver fumbling around and her mother chiding her son for not holding the phone properly. For some reason, Rahul loved to speak on the phone while lying on the floor.

Divya could hear the heavy breathing of her three-year old brother. Her mother coaxed him to say something.

"Hi, squirt! How are you?" Divya asked.

"Divi, Divi!" Rahul cried excitedly at the sound of his sister's voice.

"Rahul, your sister's name is Divya, not Divi," Divya heard Uncle Sebastian laugh in the background.

As he had learned to speak, Rahul had gotten the Hindi word for sister, 'didi', and Divya's name mixed up, and had begun to call her Divi, a strange combination of the two words. No amount of persuasion from his parents or sister could change his mind. To Rahul, Divya would always be known as Divi.

145

Hearing her brother call her Divi made Divya realize that she would take the hair pulling, temper tantrums, and constant need for attention to see him again for a few moments.

"Divi, Divi!"

"Is that all you can say, squirt?" she laughed.

"Divi, Divi!"

"How are you? I miss you so much."

"Divi, Divi!"

"Enough, Rahul. Mama says you are going to see the Statue of Liberty tomorrow. Are you excited?"

"Divi, Divi!"

"Rahul, that's enough," said a stern voice in the background. "Give me the phone."

"Nooooo!" Rahul screamed.

"Honey, can you take him, please," Divya heard her father ask his wife.

"I want *Divi!"*

"Bye, squirt. Love you," Diva said affectionately.

"Hello, Divya, beta?"

"Hi, Papa. Will he be alright?"

"Of course," he sighed tiredly. "How's my birthday girl?"

"Papa! I'm twenty-two years old. I'm a young woman now."

"Is that so? Listen, beta, I changed your diapers and fed you from a bottle and you will always be my little girl. Now, tell me, how are you?"

"Great, Papa. Everything is fine since I spoke to you from Goa. School started today and everyone is very nice. I'm quite comfortable, although I'm still trying to get used to the bathrooms."

"You'll come back twice as strong, beta. Then, I'll have to admit that you are a young woman."

"Papa, there is one thing," she said slowly, praying her father would not get too upset.

"Yes?"

"Please, don't get angry, but my wallet was stolen."

"What? Are you okay?"

"Oh yes, Papa, I'm not hurt and everything is fine. But, I cancelled the credit cards, and lost two thousand rupees."

"Thank God. And why'd you think I'd get angry, beta?"

"For not being careful, I guess. You told me to be wary when I was traveling."

"I'm just relieved you didn't get hurt. You must be careful, beta."

"I will, Papa."

"That's my girl. Listen, beta, I have to go for my conference, so we'll talk to you soon, okay?"

"Okay, Papa, love you."

"Take care of yourself, Divya. Study hard, have fun, and find some time to discover the beautiful culture and countryside. Hey, why don't you go to Mysore? It's close, and I heard it's lovely."

Divya smiled. "That's a good idea, Papa."

"Good. We're all missing you, beta."

"I miss you too, Papa."

"Bye and happy birthday."

The line disconnected and Divya put down the phone, her mind absorbed with her family that was thousands of miles across the continent and ocean.

"Areé, Divya, hurry up," Rekha cried, snapping Divya from her thoughts. "I am already half drunk and you have not even bathed yet. Get cleaned up, nah?"

* * *

"Unlike Christianity or Islam, Hinduism does not have a single founder, a single system of morality, or single deity," Professor Krishnamurthy lectured. "Hinduism consists of countless religions that have been mingled and evolved in India thousands of years before the birth of Christ. In fact, Hinduism is the third largest religion in the world, and is considered one of the most tolerant religions. That perception, however, has been diluted since the Hindu nationalistic party took power in India, and Hindu fundamentalism began rising dramatically," the old man added sadly.

Divya tuned out the lecture and looked at her watch. Every minute seemed to be dragging. Since awaking with a terrible hangover, and vowing to never drink again, the entire day had gone in slow motion.

Divya glanced at her watch for the umpteenth time and was relieved that there were only a couple of minutes before class ended.

"Finally, I have a question for you to ponder," Professor Krishnamurthy concluded. "Now, I suggest you write it down as you may be asked to submit a thousand word essay on it, or something like that." The class groaned and the old man smiled. "The question simply is: How do you explain what color is to one born blind? How would you describe what is, say, red or blue? Pleasant pondering."

"I'm *so* happy classes are over for today," Divya exclaimed, joining Om and Rekha at the front of the class.

They walked outside and followed the rest of the class towards the mess for dinner.

"Why, I thought the class was good," Rekha said. "And this essay will be interesting, although I have no idea what I am going to write."

"No, it's not the class. I just have the worst hangover. I'm *never* going to drink again," Divya said, rubbing her temples with her thumbs.

Rekha snickered. "I've heard that line before."

"I swear," Divya said seriously. "Drinking is trouble."

"The phone attendant did not seem to have any troubles. He invited himself over to your birthday party and drank the entire night away," Rekha pointed out.

"He's been sleeping in that phone booth all day to recover from his hangover while I've been in classes," Divya countered irritably. "And worse, you got him drunk so you could make long distance phone calls without paying."

"He drank two of my whiskey bottles. I had to get my investment back, nah? And who are *you* to talk? You monopolized the phone by calling your friend in Toronto."

"What? No, I didn't," Divya exclaimed, aghast at such an accusation.

"Oh my God, do not tell me you do not remember? Perhaps, you should stay off the booze after all, Divya. You are such a pathetic drunk," Rekha said.

"You're full of crap, Rekha."

"Is that so? Tell me if you remember this: 'Oh Tatyana, I love you. Why did I leave you? I love you, Tatyana. I am so sorry for leaving you to come here. Please, forgive me. I miss you so much,'" Rekha mocked.

Divya's eyes widened at the mention of her best friend back home. Deep in the recesses of her mind snippets of her drunken, overseas conversations began to emerge.

"Oh, shit, I *was* on the phone," Divya breathed. "Rekha, how long did I talk?"

"It was only an hour and a half before you passed out," Rekha laughed. "Four people had to carry you to your room."

"How embarrassing," Divya moaned. "I feel so guilty. I can't believe I did that. I have to pay the phone wallah back."

"Why? He will just manipulate the records. Trust me. He would take two bottles of whisky any day for the calls we made. This is a win-win situation for all of us, nah?"

"Are you sure?"

"If you do not believe me, you can pay those thousands of rupees to him, but he will only pocket the money himself. Either way the school will get nothing."

"Alright, but I'm definitely not going to drink anymore. It's terrifying to lose control like that. Who knows what else I did last night. Having such memory lapses is very unsettling."

As they walked past the library, Rekha asked: "Hey, how was your second class of Marketing Communications? I heard that half the class has already dropped out."

"If only I had been smart enough to do that," Divya sighed. "That class is going to be the death of me. Professor Munde asked me a question about the case we had in class, and I was actually prepared, or so I thought. He kept grilling me for ten minutes until he stumped me on the financials."

"I heard he enjoys going one-on-one with his students. You must have done really well if you lasted ten minutes. You must have really impressed him, nah?"

"I doubt it. When I failed to answer his last question, he said: 'Miss. Ambani, your ignorance seems to be encyclopedic,' and then the whole class began to pound their tables."

Divya frowned; Rekha's laughter intensified the throbbing in her head.

"Some cause happiness wherever they go; others, whenever they go. Oscar Wilde," Om said solemnly, his deep voice rebounding relentlessly within Divya's skull.

"That's a terrible thing to say, Om," Divya said.

"Terrible? Om has lightened up a lot. You should have heard what he used to quote when he had Professor Munde for marketing last year. Om, what did you say again?" Rekha asked.

"He would make a lovely corpse," Om said with a reminiscent smile. "Charles Dickens."

Divya and Rekha burst out laughing.

"Hey!"

Divya turned to see Naveen running up to them, his face filled with anxiety.

"What is it, Naveen?" Rekha asked.

"Did you hear the news?" he asked, gasping for air. "America is under attack!"

"What do you mean 'under attack'?" Om asked.

"Terrorists. They've highjacked several planes and are crashing them across the country. They've hit the Pentagon, and both of the World Trade Center towers."

Divya paled, her books falling from her hands. "Are you sure?" she demanded, grabbing him.

"Y-Yes, of course," Naveen stammered, troubled by her expression. "I just saw it on CNN in the rec room."

Divya bolted towards the recreation room.

"What's wrong?" Naveen asked Rekha. "I thought she was from Toronto."

"Her family is visiting New York," Rekha said, chasing after her.

As Divya ran towards the recreation room, she prayed Naveen was somehow mistaken. Entering the packed room, she saw black smoke pouring out of the burning north tower. She pushed her way past the students, her eyes never leaving the television. With growing panic she watched the replay of the second plane turning towards the World Trade Center, as if magnetically drawn. As the airliner rammed into the south tower and disintegrated into an explosive ball of fire, her eyes welled up with tears.

"Please don't be in there, please don't be in there," she repeated with a trembling voice, standing in front of the television.

She prayed this was fiction or an elaborate hoax. It could not be happening. It was as if she was watching a film.

This can't be real.

She watched people leaping from the burning buildings, a hundred floors up, to escape the raging fires. The scene changed to dozens of screaming and weeping people running away from the debris that showered them from the crippled skyscrapers. Divya desperately tried to examine every bloodied face being televised, but she failed to identify her mother or brother.

Maybe they didn't go there this morning, she implored fervently. *Oh God, let them be safe.*

The word 'Live' popped up in the top corner of the screen, and the south tower of the World Trade Center suddenly collapsed from the heat of the inferno.

Tears blurred her vision as each floor smashed into the one below, until the cascading superstructure was reduced to a pile of rubble. An enormous cloud of debris and dust enveloped lower Manhattan.

She could no longer see the screen clearly. She covered her face, crying uncontrollably as Rekha came to her side and wrapped her arms around her.

Although the room was filled with a hundred students all murmuring about what they saw, Divya could only hear the voices of the CNN correspondents.

"Come on Divya, let me take you to your room," Rekha softly pleaded.

Divya kept crying, unable to move. The next twenty minutes felt like an eternity. She stared at the ghastly images in front of her, praying she would suddenly see her mother and brother emerge from the panic-stricken crowds, shaken but safe.

And then she watched with horror as the north tower disintegrated. Like the World Trade Centers, her hope perished.

She wanted to wake up from this nightmare. She could no longer bear it.

Divya squeezed her eyes shut, wanting to forget what she had heard and seen. The voices of the somber correspondents replayed in her mind over and over again. *'No one within, or at the base of those buildings, could possibly survive that...'*

"*Shut up!*" Divya screamed, picking up a plastic chair and swinging it at the replay of the crumbling north tower.

The television screen shattered in a bright flash.

She dropped the chair and collapsed into a weeping heap.

* * *

"Divi, Divi!"

"Rahul!" Divya cried as she awoke in the darkness, panting and covered with perspiration.

She was afraid and disoriented.

Where am I?

She gasped as a figure stirred in a chair by the bed. Terrified, Divya did not move or breathe until her eyes adjusted to the darkness. She sighed with relief; she was in her room and Rekha was sleeping in the chair.

"Rekha?"

There was no response. Her friend was sound asleep. Divya looked at the clock. It was five thirty in the morning.

How'd I get here?

The haziness shrouding her mind lifted and everything came rushing back to her.

They have to be all right. They went to the Statue of Liberty first. And Rahul always has trouble getting up in the morning, especially with the jetlag. There's no way they reached the World Trade Center so early in the morning.

The terrible images she had witnessed on CNN flooded her mind. Divya fought to control her despair.

Crying won't solve anything. Get a hold of yourself. You don't know anything yet. Find out whether they're okay. Stop thinking and start moving.

She dressed quickly into a fresh shirt and a pair of old jeans, and silently made her way out of the room without disturbing Rekha.

The hostels were relatively silent. As Divya descended the staircase, she saw several students huddled around Pradeep's radio. The laundry wallah was still ironing but with less efficiency as he listened intently to the broadcast.

"And that was CNN National Security Correspondent David Ensor," said the radio announcer. "To recap, Mr. Ensor just reported that U.S. officials have good indications that Saudi militant Osama bin Laden may have been involved in what President George W. Bush called, cowardly acts, which have stunned the citizens of New York City, the United States of America, and the entire world."

Tears stained her new shirt, and Divya broke into a run so she would not have to listen to anymore.

All she cared about was the welfare of her family. Nothing else mattered.

She reached the ISD/STD booth and harshly shook the phone attendant awake. He glared at her, but activated the device. She picked up the phone and frantically dialed Uncle Sebastian's phone number.

She listened to the phone connect and begin to ring.

Pick up, pick up. Pick up the phone. Let me hear your voice and know that everything is all right. Please, pick up.

But the phone kept ringing. Tears streamed down her face, but she could not hang up. She kept listening to the phone ring, praying to hear her mother's voice only for a second so she would know everything was okay.

"Please, Mama, pick up the phone," Divya pleaded with despair. "Pick up. Pick up the phone, please. Pick up, *dammit!*"

The distinctive sound of someone picking up the phone froze her heart in mid-beat.

"Hello?"

Divya began sobbing. "Oh Mama, thank God you're okay."

"Divya?"

"Yes, Mama, it's me. Are you okay? I was so afraid that you were in the World Trade Center when the attacks happened. How's Rahul?"

There was no answer.

"Mama? Mama? Hello? Mama, why aren't you answering? It's me, Divya. What's wrong?" she asked desperately, a cold feeling of dread seizing her.

Her mother began weeping violently.

"Mama, what's wrong? Oh God, Mama? Mama? Why are you crying?"

Divya heard the phone receiver being placed on a table and the crying become fainter.

"No, don't go. Mama!"

"Who's this?" asked an angry voice.

"Papa? It's Divya."

"Oh, Divya," he said, his anger turning into relief and fatigue. "I was trying to reach you."

"Papa, what's wrong?"

"Come home immediately, beta."

"Papa, why is Mama crying?"

"I'll send you an electronic plane ticket immediately. Just come home."

"Where's Rahul, Papa? I don't hear him. Tell me he's okay," she begged.

"Everything will be explained to you once you return."

"What has happened? Is everything okay?"

"I just hope that the American airports open soon," he said more to himself.

"Papa, I can't bear this any longer. Why is Mama crying?"

"And I don't know how I am going to get your mother on a plane," he said with a hollow voice.

"Papa, talk to me. What's happened?"

There was no response.

"I want to talk to Rahul."

He did not reply.

"Put him on the phone. Papa, why aren't you answering me? Where's Rahul?"

Silence.

"*Answer me!*" she screamed.

"Your brother is gone. Come home."

The phone went dead.

PART II

Desikapuram Village
Tamil Nadu, Southern India

Chapter 8
The Zamindars
Tuesday, November 13th, 2001

Ladha Karai traced the mole on the corner of her newborn baby's mouth with her finger. Karuppan instinctively reached for his mother's finger and tried to suck it. He whimpered with displeasure as he failed to draw milk. Ladha smiled in the darkness as she held her newborn baby to her swollen breast. Eyes closed, the small mouth found the nipple and began sucking the nourishing milk.

Although the Karai Hut had no electricity, and all the candles had been extinguished many hours before, it was a cloudless night, and the moon shining through the hollow window provided ample illumination for Ladha. She smiled with pride at the sight of her seven-year old daughter, Vasantha, and nine-year old son, Vellaiyan, curled on each side of the mat beside their snoring father.

Raja works too hard, Ladha thought, admiring her husband lovingly. *Tomorrow I'll ask him to come home early for dinner. No one should work the fields so late, especially on the eve of Diwali.*

Ladha adjusted Karuppan gently in her arms, wiped the milk that dripped from his tiny chin, and continued to think.

Asking him to come early will solve nothing, another voice within her reasoned. *He'll not listen. He's as stubborn as a mule.*

"And that is why I love you so, husband," she whispered quietly in the darkness.

It was the end of harvest, and still much work needed to be done on the ripe, golden fields on the nearby farms. It was a good time of the year for her family. Raja often made enough money in these three months to provide food for half a year. With another mouth to feed, Raja had been working twice as hard, leaving before dawn and returning well after dusk.

It pained Ladha to see her husband so exhausted, and she was amazed that he never complained when he returned from a grueling day in the sun-baked fields. Instead, Raja always came home with love shining in his eyes and a gentle smile. Ladha knew many other Dalit women in the village that were married into far more oppressive households, and she thanked God for being blessed with such a caring husband.

Raja was also a wonderful father. Unlike other Dalits who were resigned to fate, Raja was determined to create his family's destiny, especially when it concerned his children.

One of the upper-caste farmers taught a group of the Dalit boys underneath the large banyan tree in the center of a neighboring village, but was often unavailable to give lessons, especially during the harvest. Worse, Vasantha was prohibited to attend school, as female children were expected to help tend the household with their mothers.

Unsatisfied with the quality of education his son was receiving, and angered that his daughter was forbidden to learn, Raja made it his priority to teach the children himself.

At first, Ladha had pleaded with her husband to reconsider. She was horrified at what the other villagers would think and what the repercussions of challenging the norm would be. What if a member of the upper-caste found out? The thought of her daughter learning how to read and write was unthinkable. Ladha agreed with the schoolmaster, and vividly recalled the first and last argument she had had with her husband two years ago.

"Only Dalit males should learn how to read and write. That's the way it has been for thousands of years. What right do you have to change God's ways, husband?" she had asked.

"Who says it's God's ways?" Raja returned hotly. "You've been deceived with everyone else. Are my children not a miracle from God just as the children of the upper-caste farmers? Why should their sons and daughters be educated while mine continue to live in ignorance? I will not allow it! Don't you see that this is how they control us? It's our duty to make a better future for our children."

"Who tells you these things, husband? Who has put such dangerous thoughts in your mind? This is our karma and we cannot alter our fate."

"No, I can't believe it. I *will* not accept it."

"Who'll educate them then? We barely have enough money for food. Where will you get the money to find a tutor?"

"I'll teach them myself," Raja said after much thought.

"You! How? Have you've gone mad? You can't even read or write yourself?"

Out of the two hundred Dalits that made up the entire village, only a handful could read and write.

Raja snapped his fingers. "Murthy will help us. He's a kind and educated man. He even worked in Pondicherry for several years as a private tutor. If I ask, he will help us get started. And I will learn with my children. We'll support and teach each other."

"Murthy has a good heart and *was* wise many years ago, but now he is old and feeble."

"Feeble? Ladha, stop it. He's as sharp as your tongue."

"We can't afford it."

"Murthy has never asked for anything whenever he has read or written letters for us."

"Then when? You work all day. You barely have the strength to eat dinner! Please, my husband, think about what you are saying."

"I'll *make* time, wife!" he shouted, pounding his fist on the wooden table. Raja rubbed his throbbing temples. He regained control of his emotions. "Please, try to understand," he said softly, yearning for his wife's support and understanding. "I'll not burden my children to grow up to endure the hardships I suffer daily. They deserve better."

"Is your life so terrible?" she sobbed. "Do you consider me to be a burden? I would feel blessed if my daughter grows up to have as wonderful a family as I do."

"This is not about you, wife," he reasoned gently. "This is about our children and Dalits everywhere. We deserve to be treated as equals because we are all God's creatures."

Ladha fell to her knees and grabbed her husband's feet. "Husband, I beg you to not speak such words in public. The Zamindars will kill you for such blasphemy."

"*Stand up!*" Raja roared with frustration. "I'll not argue about this anymore, especially in my own home. If I cannot improve the future of my children then they will have *no* future! And then I am as good as dead already."

Hearing such terrible utterances from her husband's mouth was too unbearable for Ladha, and she had agreed to the education of her daughter. But secretly, Ladha believed Raja would drop such radical ideas. She was convinced his fatigue would dull his convictions.

Who has the strength to work all day and then learn such a difficult thing? Ladha had asked herself. *He'll certainly be too tired to learn how to read and write with the children once he returns from the fields.*

But she had underestimated her husband.

Instead of smoking and conversing with his friends after dinner—a routine he had followed for as long as she could remember—Raja had stayed true to his word. Murthy had happily taught Raja the basics, and even lent him some old books and a chalkboard, further strengthening his resolve. After much confusion, frustration, and struggles, he and the children had learned how to read and write.

Despite the criticisms and teasing by the villagers, the disapproval of his wife, and resistance from his children, Raja never yielded. With time and much patience, his convictions changed his own children's resistance into enthusiasm, and his wife's disapproval into admiration. The townsfolk soon stopped teasing him, and eventually began to ask him to teach their children for a small fee. Raja had agreed, but had done so without payment, further enhancing his reputation within the village. Within two years, Raja was teaching over a two-dozen Dalit children for two hours every night.

Despite her initial fear and resistance, her children had even taught her how to read. A whole new world had opened up for Ladha. She had first begun reading simple children's books, enthralled by the stories. She soon moved to more challenging magazines and books, voraciously devouring every word. She had even forgotten to prepare dinner for Raja the other night, as she had been so absorbed in the book she was reading.

Ladha silently praised her husband's determination. She could think of no happier time than when Raja would borrow another book from Murthy and read to his children aloud about far away and exotic places. Ladha learned about the injustices done to her people by the upper-castes, and the freedom of America, a place that she doubted could possibly exist. But despite such fiction, Ladha loved contemplating such radical thoughts of equality and endless opportunity.

There was movement among the shadows, and she smiled. "Are you awake too, Manu?"

Manu emerged from the shadows, her tail wagging furiously.

Manu was the family dog. She was a large, black stray that had one day followed Raja home from the fields. Raja had tried to get the mangy dog to leave him, but Manu had stubbornly refused. For three days, Manu had stayed in front of the Karai hut, hungry and cold, but never begging for food. After much pressure from the children, Raja had accepted the dog, and Manu had become a member of the family.

Manu's ears perked up and she went rigid. The dog made her way slowly up to the main door and began sniffing. She whined softly.

"Hold on, Manu, be patient," Ladha whispered because Karuppan had fallen asleep.

She lowered her shirt and stood up, still cradling her infant son. She opened the door to the hut, and Manu disappeared into a nearby bush.

Ladha was about to close the door when she noticed several dark shapes moving near the edge of a nearby forest, which surrounded half the Dalit village.

Manu began barking furiously. There was a sickening sounding thud, a heart-wrenching whimper, and then silence. Even the insects and creatures of the night grew quiet.

It's the Zamindars, she realized with horror.

Nine years earlier, the Zamindars—powerful upper-caste landlords—had killed her parents and siblings in the upper-caste dominated village where she and Raja had been born and raised. As her family was beaten and burned to death, Raja and Ladha escaped. The newlyweds had spent four days trekking at night and hiding in the hills during the day. Ladha was six months pregnant with Vellaiyan at the time, but never complained about her exhaustion, hunger, or fear. She obediently followed her husband, the only person she had left in this world. Finally, Raja and Ladha had come across several Dalit families also running from the Zamindars. Together, they founded Desikapuram Village on a lush piece of land that had an abundant river flowing through the adjoining forest. It was government land at the time, but the Dalits were later granted it as compensation for the atrocities they had endured. Despite half the village still depending on the upper-castes for income, the Dalits of Desikapuram experienced a freedom never thought possible. United, the dozen Dalit families vowed to protect and look after each other. With larger numbers, they felt safe. As the village swelled to over two hundred Dalits through the years, Ladha's fears of facing the wrath of the Zamindars again had faded—until now.

Ladha ran up to her husband and vigorously shook him awake. "Zamindars!" she whispered, her eyes wide with terror.

Raja bolted up. He grabbed a rusty scythe that he used to harvest the fields. Ladha awoke her children and motioned them to be silent.

No words were exchanged. Each member of the family knew that any noise could mean death. Their only chance was to escape into the woods undetected. Even if the children were caught, they would be brutally murdered. The Zamindars were incapable of mercy.

As the Karai family quietly ran out of their mud and straw hut, the forest was suddenly ablaze with hundreds of torches lit simultaneously. The Karai hut was near the edge of the forest and the entire family was completely exposed by the flickering light.

Like rabid animals, a terrifying roar erupted from the Zamindars as they charged the village.

"Run into the forest behind the hut!" Raja screamed, running towards the torches, his scythe held in the air.

"*Raaajaaa!!!*" Ladha screamed. "Don't leave us!"

Vellaiyan grabbed his mother's arm, and urged her to follow.

Clutching Karuppan protectively, Ladha ran with her children behind the hut and into the remaining dark section of the forest. She was oblivious to the branches and stones that cut her bare feet, her fear consuming her.

161

She heard gunshots and the clashing of metal behind her. Women were screaming and children crying, but Ladha did not look back. She kept running behind her children.

Ladha tripped, and cried out in alarm. She instinctively fell onto her side, protecting her wailing infant from being crushed beneath her. She opened her eyes and cringed at the sight of a masked man towering over her, a vicious machete clutched in his right hand.

He grabbed her hair with his left hand and pulled her up. Ladha cried out with pain and dismay at the sight of her captured children.

Vellaiyan and Vasantha were feebly trying to break free of the two men that held them. A fourth man was holding Punduthai, a young, Dalit woman eight months pregnant with her first child. Ladha had shared tea with her mother earlier that afternoon; they had discussed possible names for Punduthai's baby.

Ladha stared at the terrified young woman. Punduthai's face was covered with tears and bruises, but she did not struggle or make any noise, resigned to the grim fate of her and her unborn child.

The masked man studied Ladha for a moment; his eyes glittered menacingly through the mask. "Take this one," he said to his men. "Her face is bearable."

"Please spare my children," Ladha begged. "They're innocent."

"Innocent? They're despicable creatures!"

"They've done nothing, *please.*"

"All Untouchables will be butchered in their mother's womb!" the masked man snarled, slashing his machete across Punduthai's belly.

Punduthai screamed as the severed fetus poured out of her. The masked man cut Punduthai's throat to silence her screams.

"*No!*" Vasantha shrieked.

"Shut up!" The masked man dropped the machete, pulled out a revolver and shot Vasantha in the face. Ladha's daughter slumped to the ground.

"*Bastard!*" Vellaiyan screamed, struggling to break free from the man who held him, oblivious to the warm blood of his sister that covered his face.

"No, enough, *please!*" Ladha cried. "Take me! He's young and knows no better."

The masked man began laughing. "Oh, we will take you, whore, but first I'm going to teach this dog brat some manners." He aimed the gun at Vellaiyan.

Vellaiyan stopped struggling and stared defiantly at him.

"What did you call me, boy?" the masked man asked harshly.

Vellaiyan did not move or reply. He continued to stare defiantly at the masked man.

The masked man jammed the barrel of the gun against the side of the boy's head. "Say that your sister was a whoring bitch that deserved to suffer a death far worse than I gave her. Say it, and I'll spare you and your mother!"

Vellaiyan looked at his mother for a moment and smiled, reassuring her that everything would be all right.

Her vision blurring with tears, Ladha thanked God for her son's bravery.

"Say it!" the masked man demanded, pistol-whipping Vellaiyan across the face.

Ladha whimpered at the sickening sound of metal striking her son's bone and flesh. Vellaiyan slumped, on the verge on unconsciousness. The two men held him back up.

"Say it, *dog!*" the masked man shouted, his eyes wide with rage.

Vellaiyan spat blood and broken teeth on the masked man.

Ladha shut her eyes as the masked man emptied his revolver into her son. "All Untouchables are animals," he muttered. "No respect."

The sound of Karuppan's wails made him turn towards Ladha.

Ladha fell to the masked man's feet, desperately clutching her baby. "Please, not my last child. He's all I have. I'll do anything you want, *anything!* Just let him live!"

The masked man motioned two men to hold Ladha. He snatched the wailing baby from her arms and studied the child. Ladha feebly struggled and screamed. She was kicked and punched until she collapsed onto the ground.

"Take her," Ladha heard the masked man say before she lost consciousness.

Ladha regained consciousness as she was being dragged across the forest.

"Where's my baby?" she cried, noticing that the masked man and her baby were gone.

"His head exploded like a watermelon when we smashed it against the side of tree," snickered one of the men who was missing his two front teeth.

Ladha prayed for death. There was nothing worth living for, and she looked forward to meeting her children in the next life.

She was dragged into a clearing and her clothes were torn off. Two men pinned her arms and the other two spread her legs apart. The man missing his front teeth pulled off his pants and forcefully jammed himself into her.

Ladha cried out in pain, and he punched her across the face. "One more sound out of you and I will cut you from the inside," he snarled.

He withdrew and ruthlessly penetrated again. Ladha held her cries, biting her lower lip. She tried to ignore the pain, but it was unbearable. She felt as if she was being torn from within, and silently pleaded for death.

One of the men holding Ladha's legs began laughing. "This is one way to wipe out the Untouchables—we'll breed them out!"

"Shut up!" the toothless man barked.

The toothless man suddenly shuddered and emptied himself in her. He withdrew with a smug smile. "Whose wants her next?" he asked.

There was a cry of outrage from behind. The toothless man's smile vanished in a spray of blood; a flash of a blade sliced through his neck.

Ladha wept with relief as her husband appeared. She did not notice his bloody scythe or that her assailants were hacked into pieces. All she knew was that her Raja was alive.

He covered her with his shirt and slowly helped her to her feet. She grimaced from the pain shooting between her legs.

"The children?" he asked.

Ladha did not answer. Her crying intensified.

"Where are they?" Raja cried. He shook her frantically, unwilling to accept the truth he saw in her eyes. "Tell me!"

"Dead!" Ladha screamed. "They're all dead!"

Raja eyes were wild with fury. His body shook with rage, his grip on his weapon tightening. He slowly turned towards the distant village, which was ablaze. Even the edge of the forest was engulfed in flames.

Shrieking, Raja ran towards the raging inferno.

"*Noooooooooo!!!*" Ladha cried, taking a few steps towards her husband before collapsing.

* * *

Ladha regained consciousness as the rays of the early morning sun warmed her face. She winced from the pain covering her body, and unsteadily got to her feet, holding onto a tree for support. Black smoke billowed above the trees from the direction of the village.

She walked slowly, painfully, towards the village. Her mind was devoid of thought or emotion; she ignored the bodies intermittently scattered throughout the forest.

Reaching the stream, Ladha methodically began to wash herself in the frigid water, a task she religiously did every morning before her family awoke. She was oblivious to the mud and blood she scrubbed off her body, trying to make herself believe that once she returned to the village she would make breakfast for her husband and children, like she had done for the past nine years.

She made her way from the stream towards the village. Tears emerged at the growing sounds of women and children crying; any illusions she had been creating shattered.

There would be no one to cook breakfast for.

Her entire family was dead.

Stop it! she thought, angrily wiping her tears. *Raja still could be alive. Then why didn't he come back for you?* asked another voice. *Because he could be hurt,* Ladha reasoned desperately. *That's it! He's injured, waiting for me to help him.*

The idea of her husband wounded but still alive made her quicken her pace.

He'll never leave me alone, she thought. *I must find him.*

With a growing sense of determination, Ladha emerged from the forest and surveyed the destruction before her with dismay.

No more than a third of villagers had survived the massacre, the majority of which were women and the elderly. Most of the children and men seemed to be dead or missing. The Zamindars had been meticulous in eliminating the strong and young to minimize the chance of retribution.

As Ladha walked past the rubble of what had once been a thriving village, she eagerly searched the faces of the living, and apprehensively examined each body of the dead, trying to find her husband.

He must have escaped the Zamindars and is hiding in the hills, she thought with growing optimism. *He'll return at dusk.*

Ladha deciding that she would begin rummaging through the wreckage of her hut for anything she could salvage and use. She had to be ready for Raja once he returned. He would want to leave the village before nightfall; the Zamindars were notorious for returning to finish their work.

She walked past the smoking remains of her neighbor's hut, where her friend, Guran, was piling the carcass of her pregnant daughter, Punduthai, and her other family members on a crudely constructed pyre. The umbilical cord of the unborn baby was still attached to Punduthai. Ladha felt a hint of comfort that mother and child had died united, their bond unbroken despite the ruthless actions of the masked man.

Although Guran was only a few years older than Ladha, she seemed to have aged ten years over night. Ladha did not even want to think of what she looked like.

Ladha walked past the pyre towards the smoldering pile of ash where her hut once stood. There was something erected in front of the rubble that she could not clearly make out. She fell to her knees when she realized what the object was. A hollow, miserable moan erupted from within her. She covered her eyes, but the horrifying image remained imprinted in her tortured mind—her husband's head impaled on an erected spear.

I have nothing.

Ladha did not know how much time passed before she had no more tears to shed, but when she opened her eyes and stared at the charred ground, something caught her eye. The sun was reflecting off something metallic embedded in the ash. It was her husband's scythe.

I don't want to live anymore.

She picked up the blood-encrusted weapon.

I can't endure being in this world alone.

She raised the scythe into the air.

Soon the pain will be over.

Closing her eyes, Ladha swung the blade towards her chest.

Someone grabbed her wrist.

Ladha opened her eyes and defiantly glared at the woman.

"Let me be, Guran! I'll finish what the Zamindars started."

"There'll be no more death today, child."

"No! I wish to die. Let me be with my family. I have nothing to live for."

"But you do, child, you do," Guran said, still firmly grasping Ladha's wrist.

"They took my parents and siblings, Guran! And then they took my husband and children. I have nothing. *Nothing!* Let me be, Guran. Oh, God, let me die."

"You still have a child that lives."

Ladha dropped the scythe with surprise. "What did you say?" she whispered fiercely, yearning for her neighbor's words to be true. She shook her head, crying. "No, impossible. My son and daughter were shot in front of me. And my Karuppan's head was smashed against the tree."

"No, your baby still lives. I saw him."

"No, this can't be true."

"Did you see Karuppan die?"

"Lies!" Ladha cried. "The Zamindars are incapable of mercy."

"No, my child, I don't lie. I was hiding in the bushes when you fell unconscious and they cut my unborn grandchild from my daughter, my beautiful Punduthai," she said, tears streaming down her face. "Out of fear I did nothing, and watched my children get slaughtered. It should be me that takes my life, Ladha, not you. You did everything in your power to save your children. But I can still atone for my sins by saving your Karuppan. I swear to you that the masked man took the child to his jeep and drove off. I watched it all. If you don't believe me, search for your little boy's body. I promise that you'll not find it. Look into my eyes and you'll know I speak the truth."

Ladha stared deeply into Guran's kind, tormented eyes and could see no deception. If there was a remote chance that Karuppan still lived...

Oh, God, what do I do? I can't do this by myself. Please, help me.

"My child, you still have a purpose in this world. You must find your baby, and God will give you the strength," Guran said with fervor. "First cremate your loved ones properly and mourn for their loss. Then, begin your search for your baby. You'll find him again, and I'll do everything in my power to help you. You're not alone."

Guran had enough strength and confidence for the both of them, and after they had cremated Guran's family, they spent the rest of the day searching the forest to find the bodies of Ladha's children.

By dusk, another pyre was assembled. Brother and sister were laid beside their father just as they had been sleeping together moments before the massacre had begun. As her family was reduced to ashes, Ladha vowed she would not rest until her baby was found and the death of her family avenged.

* * *

Ladha awoke to the sound of several vehicles approaching the village. She began panicking; it was night. She and Guran had wanted to rest for only a moment. But now it was too late. The Zamindars had returned.

But they always attack by surprise. They'd never make such noise if they were coming, Ladha realized as she stood up in front of the smoking remnants of the pyre.

The main paved road was eight kilometers away, and was connected by a dirt road that led to the village. The villagers were not used to vehicles coming towards the village, especially during monsoon season when the road was transformed into a muddy river. In fact, only a handful of prosperous villagers owned two wheelers such as scooters and motorcycles. No one owned a car or a truck.

If it isn't the Zamindars then who is coming? Ladha wondered with growing apprehension.

The rumbling intensified far faster than Ladha would have liked. She shielded her eyes from the headlights of the first lorry that appeared over the crest. Ladha saw from the powerful beams of lights that several dozen villagers remained in the village, all mesmerized by the entourage of heavy vehicles that pulled up in front of them.

Could it be the military?

Ladha counted five trucks and two jeeps, but it was too dark to tell whether it was the military or the...

It's the police! she realized with alarm.

If there was one thing more terrifying than the Zamindars it was the district police force. The police—funded and supported by the Zamindars—manipulated the law for their own benefit and were just as ruthless as their masters.

"Guran, wake up," she whispered urgently. "The police are here."

As she helped Guran to her feet, Ladha heard the sound of hundreds of police officers jumping off the back of the lorries and marching into position. The police formed a line around the front of the village and pulled out their nightsticks.

"They're going to do a lathi charge!"

"Why? Why would they charge a small group of women and the elderly?" Guran asked anxiously.

"Come on, Guran, there's no time to explain. We must reach the safety of the woods before they find us."

Grabbing Guran's hand, Ladha ran into the woods. They hid behind the trees in terrified silence, and watched as several villagers approached the line of police, begging for assistance. An order was barked over a loud speaker and the police charged, beating and arresting anyone they could find.

"Why are they doing this?" Guran whispered, her voice trembling with fear. "Haven't the Zamindars done enough?"

"The police are funded and controlled by the Zamindars, Guran. They are finishing us off. The police will claim that they came to the village to file a report on a disturbance, but were attacked by us, and forced to respond with force."

"But how would they get away with this? Who'd believe that it took a hundred policemen to file one report?"

"Don't you see? No one cares about us. This is the police's way of appeasing the government, public, and especially the Zamindars. As long as the people believe that some justice has been done, nothing will be questioned. Raja always talked about this." A pained expression came over Ladha's face as she spoke her beloved husband's name.

The two women watched as the police rounded up the villagers and set the remaining huts on fire. During the entire episode, the silhouette of the stout Superintendent of Police could be seen standing in the center of the square as he barked orders to his subordinates. Ladha and Guran watched with horror as the police began urinating on the deceased, and gang raping Dalit teenagers, who futilely screamed first for help, then mercy, and finally from pain.

Ladha dug her fingernails into her palm, drawing blood. The pain between her legs seemed sharper as she helplessly watched the atrocities being committed to girls her daughter's age. Unable to endure another moment of the brutality, Ladha motioned Guran to move deeper into the forest.

There was rustling behind them.

Ladha looked up just as the butt of a rifle came smashing down on her face.

* * *

Sedhu felt something wet soaking through his shirt. He pulled away and stared at Ramar's hands. The sun had disappeared behind the edge of the river, and the full moon illuminated the blood on his brother's hands.

"Whose blood is this?" Sedhu demanded, grabbing his brother. "Whose?"

"I'll kill them all!" Ramar erupted, pushing Sedhu away. "All of them for polluting my Rani. For taking her away from me."

"Is this the blood of a Dalit?" Sedhu asked, his face ashen. "Who'd you kill, brother? Who? Why?"

"Another parasite sucking the life of our country! What does it matter? The insolent animal dared to look directly at me, sneering, taunting me, that maggot! So I punished him. I didn't stop kicking him until his repulsive face caved in. I didn't stop striking him until my arms were too sore to lift. And then I severed his head and stuck it on a pike in front of the Untouchable settlement. They'll learn to respect our ways or they'll all suffer!"

Fury and hatred burned so intensely in Ramar's eyes that he appeared to be on the brink of madness.

"But you broke the law!"

"I *am* the law!" Ramar screamed.

Sedhu was too horrified to respond. He backed up slowly shaking his head in disbelief. He picked up his documents and money, and ran.

He ran from the village and the madness that had encompassed it and his brother.

"Do you hear me?" Ramar's voice echoed in the distance. "I *am* the law! They all deserve to die!"

Sedhu wanted to keep running and never stop. He wanted to run out of the district, the state, and the country. He wanted to run until he could run no longer. But soon his lungs and legs would no longer co-operate, and he found himself standing in front of a pike with a severed head impaled on it.

Sedhu was drawn towards the head. He slowly moved forward. Although the face was too far to see clearly, Sedhu had an eerie feeling of familiarity. He felt as if his heart was pounding in his throat. His entire body was drenched with sweat despite the cool night breeze.

A cloud masked the moon, and the landscape was suddenly shrouded in a blanket of darkness.

Sedhu stopped a few feet in front of the shadowed head. His breathing was nearing the edge of hyperventilation. Although he did not know how it was possible, he suddenly knew whose face was on the pike.

The moon emerged from behind the cloud.

The shadow slowly moved off the decapitated head.

He screamed at his own image.

Sedhu gasped as he awoke from his nightmare.

With shaking hands he leaned forward in the wooden chair and reached for the glass of water on the table beside him. He drank heavily until he emptied the glass.

His body still trembled and his face was covered with perspiration. Sedhu wondered why he had dreamt of his brother's atrocities the night he had taken the blame for the murder of the Dalit and escaped with Rani.

Sedhu shuddered again as the images of the nightmare clung to him.

I haven't had that dream in fifteen years. Why now? What does it mean?

Sunlight was streaming through the half-open, horizontal blinds, creating alternating rows of shadow and light across the hospital room.

Why was my face on the severed head?

His wife made a soft noise and shifted in the bed. Sedhu pushed the macabre thoughts out of his mind, and gazed lovingly at his sleeping wife. He brushed a strand of hair that had fallen in front of her oval face, and put her limp hand into his. He studied her face, a face that became lovelier with age, and searched for some answers.

The hospital television was on mute and Sedhu glanced at the flickering images of the Allied troops capturing the capital of Kabul. Although the Taliban continued to control the southern third of Afghanistan, Sedhu knew that the Taliban regime had ultimately come to an end.

If only that day hadn't happened. I would sacrifice my life in a heartbeat to alter that day.

The images on the television changed to live shots of the American Airlines airbus that had crashed in a residential area in New York.

Sedhu turned off the television and looked back at his wife. She was still asleep, and he was grateful she had not seen the burning remains of the plane scattered throughout the quaint neighborhood in Queens. The wounds were far too raw to bear watching the coverage of the crash.

He put her hand against his face and began crying, wishing she would come back to him. The psychiatrist's optimism on the electroshock therapy had dissipated after several rounds of treatment, and Sedhu wondered what alternatives were left.

Should I call him and ask for help? Is that why I dreamt of him?

The idea he had been contemplating for several weeks was risky and illegal, but after every other alternative had proved to be unsuccessful, what choice did he have?

Even if it means bringing that monster back into our lives?

He leaned forward in his chair and apprehensively eyed the telephone.

But what life is worth living if she remains in this state?

Throughout the years, Sedhu had heard snippets of information about what his brother was doing back in India, and it chilled his blood. But if there was a chance to alleviate his wife's chronic depression...

Sedhu put Rani's hand back down and extracted a sealed letter from the pocket of his suit jacket.

Like every day since September eleventh, his mind was with his wife, and he would go directly to the hospital after work. He had become accustomed to sleeping in his suits. Only on his way to work the following morning would he stop home to shave, shower, and change, spending no more than fifteen minutes in the empty house.

Filled with indecisiveness, Sedhu examined the yellowing envelope—the only communication he had received from his family since that fateful day twenty-two years ago. Sedhu had never opened it, but he knew that the letter contained information on how to contact them. For the past two weeks he had been carrying the envelope everywhere he went, trying to summon the courage to open it.

He glanced uneasily at his wife to gain strength for what he was about to do.

I'll bring you back to me, Rani. I swear it. We'll have our lives back no matter what the consequences.

Sedhu tore open the envelope that had been sealed for over fifteen years. He read the message scrawled in Tamil.

February 28, 1986
Call 011 404 258 6982. It is urgent.

There was no signature, but there was no doubt that the familiar handwriting belonged to Ramar. He memorized the phone number and stuffed the note into the envelope.

Sedhu glanced at Rani, who was still asleep. He crept into the adjoining bathroom, locked the door, and pulled out his cell phone. Beads of perspiration formed along his hairline. Hands trembling, he slowly dialed the phone number. He was dripping with perspiration, near the brink of panic by the time the international call connected.

"Hullo? Who's this?"

"Ramar?" Sedhu said with surprise, recognizing the voice that he assumed would forever remain in his past. He suddenly realized he was not prepared to deal with his brother. A part of him had hoped that the phone number would belong to someone else, or no longer be in service.

"Who's this?" Ramar demanded again, this time in Tamil.

Sedhu clutched his cell phone tightly and sat down on the toilet. He had an impulse to hang up the phone and throw up.

"Hullo? Hullo?"

It's not too late to change your mind, Sedhu.

"If someone is there then answer me!" Ramar said angrily.

Do it for Rani...

"You don't recognize your own brother's voice?" Sedhu asked in English, trying to sound casual. There was a long silence on the phone. "Ramar?"

"I have no brother," he said, slamming down the phone.

Chapter 9
The Festival of Lights
Wednesday, November 14th, 2001

"Divya, I have to go," Meena Chopra said. "Sachin is taking me to a party at the Taj West hotel, and I have to get ready."

"But, we haven't finished the PowerPoint presentation or edited the final report," Divya protested.

"We can finish it tomorrow morning."

"It's *due* tomorrow morning."

"We'll meet early. I'll stop by your room."

"Our class is at eight-thirty, and you'll be out all night. How early can we possibly meet?"

"We can submit the project the following day then."

"Meena, don't you think we could hand in *one* project for our *Time* Management class on time?" Divya asked, exasperated.

"Chill, Divya. It'll get done." Meena said, flashing a brilliant smile.

How, by magic? Divya wanted to scream.

"Forget it," Divya sighed. "I'll finish things up tonight."

"Are you mad? It's Diwali! This is the largest festival in the country."

"Yeah, so you better go and get ready," she mumbled, turning back to the computer screen.

"How many times are you going to be in India during Diwali? Come on, Divya, you can't work *all* the time." Meena swept her hand across the empty computer room. "Except for Om, there's no one even here."

Divya began typing furiously on the keyboard.

Meena shrugged, and left her in the vast computer center.

"Those two should be lynched for how useless they are," Divya muttered underneath her breath, fuming at her incompetent and lazy group members. "How am I going to finish this on time?"

"When a man knows he is to be hanged in a fortnight, it concentrates his mind wonderfully. Samuel Johnson."

Divya turned to respond, but Om had walked out of the computer lab.

She glanced across the deserted room, and sighed.

You have work to do.

"Right."

Divya cracked her knuckles and turned back to the computer. She worked for the next forty minutes on the PowerPoint presentation, filling each slide with graphics and bullet points. She smiled with satisfaction as she looked over the finished product. It was professional and well researched, and she was confident the professor would be impressed.

If he bothers to show up to class, she thought with a flash of irritation.

Although it had taken nearly half the day to work on the project—with Meena and Sachin being more of a distraction than help—it had been well worth it.

Divya held down the *crtl* and *s* button simultaneously to save her document, and frowned when an error message popped up indicating that the computer was out of memory. She clicked on the *cancel* button, and tried saving the file again. There was no response. The entire system was frozen.

"No!" she shouted, pounding the keyboard with dismay.

It's okay, Divya, she thought, trying to calm herself. *The computer will automatically retrieve the file once you re-enter the program.*

She reluctantly shut down the program and went back into Microsoft PowerPoint. No file was automatically restored. She clicked on the open file icon and began searching her directory for the file, but the entire directory was empty. With growing apprehension, she did a search of the entire hard drive for any PowerPoint file. Nothing appeared.

"Fuck!"

Divya threw her notes on the ground in anger and buried her face in her arms, using every ounce of willpower to resist crying. She knew it was not her work that made her so upset. This was the catalyst for something else that had been building within her for some time.

What am I doing? she despaired. *What's wrong with me?*

Since returning to India from Rahul's cremation, she had lost all desire to interact with anyone. She had ignored and rejected any offers of comfort and friendship from her schoolmates. Instead, she dedicated virtually every waking moment to her studies. Over the past two months, she had not once gone out or done anything social. Her routine consisted of eating alone, sleeping sporadically and studying. Her only luxury was her daily run at dawn, a time when the heat was bearable and the least number of people on campus were awake.

In time, those who had offered sympathy and friendship now avoided her. Any student who tried to speak to her on topics outside the classroom would receive a countenance of dismissive irritation, or indifference. Unless a conversation was related to her studies, she was not interested.

After weeks of solitude and loneliness, Divya yearned for human contact. But she had closed her heart with such success that she did not know how to reveal anything other than hostility, apathy, or coldness to anyone who crossed her path. She knew she had no one to blame but herself.

Why did this happen? she wondered miserably. *Because there is no one else to be strong for you,* came the reply in her mind.

When Divya had seen the state of her parents after flying home, she realized it was her duty to take over. Her mother was an emotional wreck, and her father's energies were completely focused on tending to his wife. It was *she* who had organized the funeral arrangements and who was stoic during the entire ceremony, allowing her parents to lean on *her* for support. Divya had not shed a tear for her brother; there had been no time. She had not stopped moving for one moment, refusing to give herself the opportunity to reflect on or comprehend what had happened.

Upon arrival back at the Indian Institute of Management, she forced herself to work harder than ever. She discovered that as long as she remained insanely busy to the brink of exhaustion she could avoid or tolerate the pain within her. But, by avoiding her grief for the past two months, the pain had neither subsided nor grown. Like a malignant tumor being bombarded under chemotherapy, her cancer of pain remained temporarily contained.

A little envelope icon on the corner of the computer screen began flashing indicating she had e-mail. Divya clicked on the icon and was surprised that the message was from Om. He had never written to her before. She read the e-mail:

The walls we build around us to keep out the sadness also keep out the joy—Jim Rohn.

She read the message several times until her sight blurred from tears.

Om's right, this is not living. Everything is empty and meaningless.

She suddenly regretted all the time she had wasted ignoring her friends. She thought about Om and Naveen. She even missed the disgusting advances of Tharki, who had given up trying to seduce her since the arrival of a new exchange student from Sweden. But most of all, she missed Aslam.

No matter how hard she had tried to get Aslam out of her mind, she was unsuccessful. Her last thoughts before she fell into a fitful sleep, and her first thoughts when she woke up were of him. She knew he cared for her—he had made that abundantly clear when she had returned from Toronto—but she could not deal with the emotions she felt for him. The thought of loving again after having one so dear snatched ruthlessly from her was unbearable. Instead, she had neither wanted to love nor be loved. In her mind, losing love was far more painful than experiencing it, and she had done everything in her power to push Aslam away.

She remembered that moment she had climbed out of the autorickshaw upon her arrival in Bangalore, and how she had stood there stiffly as he had tried to hug her. She had wanted to return his affection, but instead dismissed him. She had coldly ignored every effort he made for the next week until she finally exploded and told him how she loathed him and wanted nothing to do with him. Although it had killed her to do it, she had shown no remorse at his devastated expression. She knew she had hurt him badly, but believed it was for the best. From that moment, Aslam had followed her wishes, avoiding her at every possibility. But, instead of feeling better about his absence, she became more miserable.

"Areé, Divya, there you are."

Divya looked up to see Rekha walking towards her, a large smile on her face.

Rekha was the only person Divya had not completely pushed away. Although Divya had made little effort to be close to her, Rekha had stubbornly stuck by her buddy. She often visited Divya without invitation so she could complain about the latest catastrophe affecting her life. Divya always listened, secretly cherishing the time they spent together.

One of the reasons Divya had grown so fond of Rekha was that her friend never asked how she felt or whether she wanted to talk about what had happened. Rekha understood Divya was suffering and had accurately assessed that she would talk when she was ready. Rekha had selflessly given her own time and presence without asking for anything in return, and Divya had thanked God numerous times for having such an understanding friend.

"Do you know what time it is?" Rekha asked. "You have to help decorate B Block and get ready. Come, nah?"

"I have to finish this Time Management project. It's worth a third of our final grade."

"I do not see anyone else working on it. This place is dead."

"So? A deadline is a deadline."

"Divya, I have some friends who took that course last term. You can copy their papers, nah?"

"What? I'd never do that and you know it."

"Areé, yaar, what do I have to do to get you to come and celebrate Diwali with me?"

"Nothing. I had finished the presentation and the paper just needed to be edited, but then the computer crashed, and I lost everything," Divya said gloomily. "Now, I have to start all over again."

"Let me try to retrieve it. I am good at this."

"Forget it, Rekha. I searched the computer. It's gone."

"What is the name of the file, nah?"

"I tried. It won't work."

"What do you have to lose? Tell me, nah?"

"Fine," Divya sighed. "TMfinal.ppt."

As Rekha began searching for the file, Divya stretched and yawned, accepting the fact that she was going to be spending a long evening trapped in the computer center.

"This is it, nah?" Rekha asked with a triumphant smile.

Divya turned back to the computer screen, her eyes widening with surprise. "Yeah, how did you—"

"Have faith, buddy. There is a backup directory that stores all files automatically when the computer crashes. If the lost files are not claimed after a week, they are automatically deleted by the computer department."

"Oh, I could kiss you!" Divya exclaimed. She pulled out a floppy disk and saved the file in several places to ensure she would not lose it again. "You've saved me many hours, Rekha."

"Yes, I did. And now those hours belong to me. So, no more excuses of working in this dreary hole, okay? You are coming with me, and we are going to win the hostel decoration contest, and then celebrate Diwali."

"But, I still need to edit my paper."

Rekha frowned. "Divya, either you come with me now, or I am going to drag you out."

Divya could see she fully intended carrying out her threat. Rekha had the will and the strength.

And I do owe her for retrieving my file...

"I will teach you dandia," Rekha pressed. "It is such a wonderful dance. Imagine the entire school dancing at the same time. It is *so* much fun. It will be great. Come on, yaar."

Divya sighed. "Okay, but only for a few hours."

Rekha grinned. She grabbed Divya's hand and pulled her out of the computer center.

* * *

Divya cursed with frustration as she studied herself in the mirror.

She had spent what felt like an eternity trying to figure out how to put on her saffron sari, and it still did not look right.

Hearing excited conversations, laughter, and music outside her room, Divya forgot about her losing struggle with her sari. She was filled with anxiety at the prospect of facing her schoolmates. She did not know what she would do or say, especially since she had been so reclusive the past few months. What would they think of her dressed up in traditional clothing? Would they laugh or scorn? Would she be forgiven and accepted as one of them?

Why do I suddenly care what they think?

Divya turned back to her sari and took it off until she was just in her blouse and waist petticoat. Remembering how she had been instructed, she tried putting on the sari. She tucked the fabric into the waist petticoat just below her navel, and wrapped the silk around herself. Then, she made pleats in the sari, concentrating on making them straight and even.

Divya studied herself in the mirror and threw her arms up in defeat. She looked mummified.

Who am I kidding? she sighed. *This won't work.*

She began taking off her sari again when Rekha walked in.

"Rekha, you look so beautiful," Divya breathed, admiring her friend's purple and white silk sari. Rekha was dripping with jewelry and her black hair was tied up in the shape of a lotus.

"Thank you." Rekha beamed. "Areé, why are you taking off your sari?"

"I can't do this. I'm going back to the computer lab to finish my project."

"I will break your legs if you do. I may never look this good again. You cannot do this to me."

"I'm sorry."

"Divya, stop this, nah? I do not care what you say. You *are* coming out tonight. Come on, just for an hour, nah?"

Divya studied her friend's face for some time, filled with indecisiveness. She sighed. "Fine, *one* hour. But, you have to help me with this sari. I don't even now how to put it on properly, and I feel like an idiot."

"Show me what you did, and I will tell you what you are doing wrong."

Divya went through the motions again, and frowned when Rekha began laughing at the mess she made with the fabric.

"It's not funny, Rekha. You should be helping rather than mocking."

"I am sorry, but you should be making the pleats five inches thick and there should be no more than seven to ten pleats all together, nah? Then, you should use a safety pin to fasten the pleats together."

"A safety pin? No wonder the pleats never stay in one place. The store clerk never told me that."

"Do not concern yourself. For your first try, you did great," Rekha smiled as she deftly made crisp pleats with Divya's sari. "It took me years to learn how to wear a sari."

"Really?"

"Yes." Rekha pulled a safety pin from her purse and inserted it into the silk.

"When'd you begin putting on saris for yourself?"

"Seven."

"Great, thanks for making me feel *so* much better," Divya laughed.

Rekha stepped back to study her friend, and clicked her tongue disapprovingly, her brow crinkled. "Hmmm, something is still missing,"

"What?"

"Oh, I know," Rekha exclaimed, her eyes sparkling. "Now, just let me do this. If you do not like it you can always change it, okay?"

Rekha applied a little make-up, and untied and brushed Divya's long hair to a glistening shine. She stepped back and smiled at her handiwork.

"How do I look?" Divya asked nervously.

"See for yourself," Rekha said, positioning her friend in front of the mirror.

Divya gaped at the sight of her own reflection. She could not believe she was looking at herself. For the first time since she had come to India, she felt Indian.

"Rekha, you're an artist, *no*, a genius! I look like a movie star," she said, smiling glamorously. "I know this sounds vain, but I feel beautiful. Thank you for doing this for me, and..." she paused, filled with emotion, a lump forming in her throat, "thank you for always being there for me, my friend. I couldn't have got through these past few months without you."

Touched, Rekha smiled with pleasure and warmly embraced her buddy. "I'll kill if you if you cry and ruin your make-up that I slogged over."

Divya smiled and nodded, wiping away her tears.

"Well, the two most beautiful women cannot stay hidden in this room all night. It is time for us to reveal ourselves to the world, nah?" Rekha said, brushing aside her own tears.

Divya took a deep breath. "Okay, let's do it."

Walking into the tepid night, Divya was astonished by the transformation of B-block. Hundreds of tiny, twinkling candles were placed all over the block. Huge patterns of colored powder were painted on the concrete floor, and blinking Christmas lights were strung on every column, banister, and rafter. It was magical.

"Rekha, this is amazing."

"What did you expect?" Rekha asked, her eyes dancing. "After all, this is the festival of lights, nah?"

Several girls dressed in exquisite saris and shalwar kameezes approached them excitedly.

"You two look so pretty," gushed one girl, who was wearing an elegant, black shalwar kameez.

"I'm very jealous," said another girl in a bluish-gray sari with gold trimmings.

"You've done a phenomenal job decorating this place. Is there any way I can help?" Divya asked.

"The girls lighting the candles have to go get ready, so you can help with that," a third girl in a silvery-white shalwar kameez suggested.

"I'd love to," Divya said.

"I will help too, but first can one of you take a snap of my buddy and I?" Rekha asked, pulling out her camera from her purse, and handing it to the fourth girl in a reddish-bronze cotton sari.

After the photograph was taken, Divya and Rekha spent the next hour pouring cooking oil in tiny clay dishes and molding pieces of cotton into wicks. Divya could not remember the last time she had felt such peace, and once again was thankful for having such a loyal and genuine friend.

"Rekha, what's the significance of Diwali?" Divya asked.

"Well, in Sanskrit Diwali means: 'row of lights,' and lasts for five days," Rekha explained, lighting each candle. "On this particular day, we celebrate the return of Lord Rama, who is an incarnation of Lord Vishnu—"

"Lord Vishnu is the preserver and protector of the universe, right?"

"Yes, and as Lord Rama, he returns to his capital of Ayodhya after an exile of fourteen years, and after killing the demon king, Ravan."

"Why?"

"Oh, Ravan kidnapped Lord Rama's beautiful wife, Sita. Diwali is celebrated for the return of Lord Rama and Sita. Diwali represents the victory of good over evil."

"Okay, but why is Diwali referred to as the 'Festival of Lights?'"

"Diwali also marks the beginning of the Hindu calendar year, and every Hindu home across the country lights diyas...um, oil, earthen lamps," Rekha clarified, seeing her friend's questioning look. "We light them to provide enough illumination to welcome Lakshmi, the goddess of wealth and prosperity, who incidentally is also the wife of Vishnu."

Divya was silent for some time, trying to digest all the information. "And the purpose of these colored patterns on the floor?"

"That is called rangoli, and like diyas or fireworks, it is also used to attract Lakshmi. In fact, see those little painted foot prints on the staircase?"

"Yes," Divya said, looking at small white markings on the stairs.

"Those are Lakshmi's foot prints."

Divya smiled. "There are so small and cute, like a baby ran by with flour on his feet."

Once the candles were lit, the two girls explored the other nine hostels to see how they were decorated. Although each was unique and beautiful in its own way, they both agreed that their block was the best decorated and would surely win the contest.

"The way Block H hung all those lanterns from the center tree in the courtyard was incredible. And the fog machine made everything look so ethereal," Divya marveled.

"Yes, but ours is still the best, nah?" Rekha said for the umpteenth time.

"And what about Om? Can you believe how he was dressed?" Divya laughed, visualizing the bright orange kurta pajama he was wearing. "It looked like a prison uniform."

"He's a fool! He probably wore it because it looks exactly like something Sai Baba would wear."

"Isn't he that spiritual leader with the super afro?" Divya asked.

"Yes, he is revered by millions who believe he can perform miracles."

"I remember now. Some even think he's a deity. Do you think Om has become a Sai Baba disciple?"

"I hope not, but anything is possible with that duffer. What did you think about Chicken's suit?"

"His kurta pajama looks like something a Maharaja would wear," Divya chuckled. "And that silk turban covered with pieces of colored glass was too much."

Rekha looked at her wristwatch. "Areé, it is nearly time to do the pooja. We pray to Lakshmi to drive away the shadows of the evil spirits."

"When does the pooja begin?" Divya asked.

"The worshipping should begin in ten minutes, if the pundit arrives on time. Last year he was nearly an hour late for the pooja."

"Even priests come late to such an auspicious occasion?"

"Do you not know by now that everything here runs on IST?"

"IST?"

"Indian Standard Time."

Divya smiled. "Well, that's true. So, where's the pooja taking place?"

"In the rec room."

Divya paled. The last time she was in there had been during the September eleventh terrorist attacks. She had avoided the room the entire semester.

I can't go back in there.

As they reached the mass of students gathered in front of the recreation room, Divya searched for a way to escape. She felt overwhelmed and nauseous. She had to get away.

"Hi, Divya, you look beautiful tonight," Naveen said, emerging from the crowd.

185

Divya admired his beige kurta pajama and black vest.

"And you look ravishing too, Rekha," he added with a warm smile.

Rekha blushed. "I love those gold patterns stitched in your vest, Naveen."

"Thanks. Are you going to sing a bhajan tonight?"

"I don't know," she said shyly.

"Rekha, I didn't know you could sing?" Divya said with surprise, momentarily distracted from escaping.

"Divya, you have to hear Rekha sing a devotional song to praise Lakshmi during the pooja," Naveen said, still looking at Rekha. "Her voice is so lovely that it will bring tears to your eyes."

Rekha gave a dazzling smile, her eyes locked with his.

A bald, shirtless man with a magnificent paunch, a loincloth, and markings on his forehead opened the doors to the converted recreation room. The pundit motioned the crowd to enter, and stepped aside as the congregation of students took off their shoes and sandals, and filed into the worshipping area.

Making sure Rekha and Naveen were still distracted by each another, Divya slipped away from the crowd and went to the one place she was sure to find solitude.

* * *

Divya stood on the roof, mesmerized.

The entire city was lit with a ceaseless eruption of popping and snapping fireworks. But unlike the collection of clustered blooms of colorful light she had witnessed in Toronto, these fireworks were very different and far noisier.

Divya felt as if she was in the middle of a war. The scene strangely resembled that of a city under attack. The explosions sounded like bombs being dropped from supersonic military jets, and the streaks of light shooting into the sky resembled anti-aircraft fire. Smoke from the cluster crackers that poured between buildings and trees made it feel as if the entire city was ablaze. She wondered if this was what the people of Kabul had experienced when the U.S. had bombed Taliban positions in Afghanistan.

She would not have been surprised if a BBC or CNN crew began setting up on a rooftop to film the exciting coverage to a world starved to witness destruction and human suffering. But, as the deafening booms and blinding flashes of light overwhelmed her, she reminded herself that these were fireworks. The sound of laughter below reminded her that this was a time of happiness, not war. This was the most celebrated festival in the country. There was nothing to fear.

Despite the mild breeze of the Bangalore night, Divya shivered.

She remembered the last time she was on the roof; she had felt so frightened of the approaching lightening storm and the sudden citywide blackout. Aslam had wrapped his arms around her in the darkness. She smiled, remembering the warm feelings of solace, comfort, and absolute happiness she had felt in his embrace. She closed her eyes and wrapped her arms around her in an effort to make the memory linger.

Why'd I throw that away when there was nothing more I wanted?

To avoid the pain of losing another loved one, argued another voice in her head. *If you do not love, you can't get hurt.*

But I am still so sad and lonely.

Perhaps, but at least you are functioning, living, unlike your broken-hearted mother. Do you want to end up like her, forever lost, a vegetable?

But, what type of life is this, to merely function? Oh God, what do I do? Is it too late? Did I throw it all away for nothing? Oh, I miss him so much, but how can I be happy after what happened? How can I be happy when Rahul is...? No, don't think about it.

Her memories of Aslam and that magical night dissipated. She opened her eyes, hoping Aslam would be standing in front of her. No one was there. She was alone.

Divya sighed despondently and wondered how long she could keep going like this.

She looked at her watch. An hour had passed, and she guessed the pooja would soon be over. She wondered if Rekha had sung, and suddenly regretted skipping out on her. Rekha had done so much for her, and she had abandoned her. Feeling guilty, she promised she would make it up to her friend during dinner.

She spent a few more minutes admiring the spectacle across the Bangalore skyline.

Okay, Divya, time to go back and mingle. You can do this, no problem. Be strong.

Turning, she gasped at the silhouetted figure standing by the staircase.

Tharki!

"S-Stay back," she stammered apprehensively. "I am warning you."

"Divya, it's okay. It's me, Oz."

She sighed with relief. As he stepped forward, she regained her composure and raised her defenses.

"What were you doing?" she asked warily, her voice filled with the icy harshness.

"Watching you."

"How long have you been there?"

"I don't know. I lost track of time."

"Why are you here, Oz?"

"I couldn't stay away any longer."

"Oz, I told you before—"

"Divya, I saw you tonight, just before the pooja. You looked so ravishing I had trouble breathing. I had to talk to you, just to hear your voice or catch a glimpse of your smile. I know what you asked me to do, and I've tried, but I couldn't keep away any longer, no matter how you feel about me."

"Oz, go," she said unconvincingly, her ability to resist him quickly diminishing.

How long can you maintain this charade, Divya?

"I will, if you tell me why you're doing this? Why are you avoiding me?" he said. "What have I done wrong to make you so cold and distant?"

"I can't."

"I deserve an explanation. You owe me at least that. Please, Divya, I can't stop thinking about you. It's driving me insane."

She bit her lower lip. "Leave."

"Divya, I know you're hurting. Let me help you. Talk to me!"

"Don't make me beg, Oz."

"Fine," Aslam said, swallowing hard. "But there's something I wish to say."

"Oz—"

"*Please.*"

"Okay," she whispered, nodding.

Aslam moved even closer until Divya could see him clearly. He was wearing a simple cream-colored kurta pajama that accentuated his coffee-brown eyes.

"My heart hasn't stopped aching since you left, Divya. I feel lost without you. Do you know how many nights I lay in bed thinking about you? Do you know that I would rather stay awake, and have you in my mind, than risk losing your beautiful image in sleep? You consume me, Divya. I need you in my life."

She did not respond, lost in the eyes that had filled her thoughts for so many days. She moved closer to him.

"Divya?" Aslam whispered.

"Yes, Oz."

"I love you."

"I know."

"I've never loved someone so much. There, I've finally had the courage to say it. I love you."

"Shhhh," Divya whispered, closing her eyes.

Just as their lips met, she pulled back as if she had been electrocuted. She backed away, guilty thoughts of her brother and suffering parents consuming her.

"What's wrong?" Aslam asked gently.

"I can't."

"Wait, please."

"I have to go," she whispered miserably, unable to look at him.

"Divya, listen to me—"

"Rekha is waiting for me."

"Let me in, *please*."

"She promised to teach me dandia."

"Div—"

She ran past him and disappeared down the stairs.

Chapter 10
Pleas for Help
Thursday, November 15th 2001

Leaning against the concrete wall, her arms wrapped around her knees to keep her naked body warm, Ladha wondered how much longer she could hold on. Since her captivity, three of the eight prisoners she shared the cell with had perished.

Ladha gingerly touched her temple; she was relieved that the swelling had decreased and the wound was healing. She thought about what she had suffered through, and wondered whether God would give her the strength to further endure.

When Ladha had regained consciousness two days earlier, she found herself lying on the dirty concrete floor, her face sticky with blood oozing from her gashed temple. Once she realized where she was, she wished she had never awoken. She had stood up woozily and approached the prison bars, calling out for assistance.

A guard eventually appeared, glaring at her with disgust as if she was a diseased animal.

"Please, help me. There's been a mistake," Ladha pleaded.

"Shut up, whore."

"But I'm innocent. I've done nothing wrong."

"One more word out of you and I'll smash your face with my lathi," he warned, reaching for his nightstick.

"Please, I mean no disrespect. Just tell me what my charges are and I won't be any more trouble."

"That's it," the guard growled, pulling out his keys and unlocking the steel door.

"What's going on here?"

A stout man entered the prison block with an air of authority.

Ladha froze as she recognized the man as the Superintendent of Police that had led the attack on her village. A wiry, uniformed man with a thin mustache followed the Superintendent.

The guard snapped to attention. "Nothing that I can't deal with, sir."

"What are my charges?" Ladha demanded.

"My, what a bold whore," the Superintendent said, chuckling with amusement.

"I asked you a question. What are my charges?"

"You dare speak to the Superintendent with such disrespect?" the mustached man said angrily.

"That's enough, Sub-Inspector Rao." The Superintendent motioned him to step back. He turned back to Ladha. "You're charged for burning your own home and bringing false charges on others."

"Lies. These are lies."

"Oh, is that so? I have several witnesses sharing this very cell who have signed written testimonies accusing you of these crimes."

Ladha was thunderstruck by betrayal. She turned to her cellmates; they hung their heads with shame. Only Guran proudly maintained eye contact.

"You beat them until they signed false testimonies," Ladha said.

"I don't know what you're talking about," the Superintendent said, his lips curling into a malicious smile.

Sub-Inspector Rao and the prison guard were also smirking.

Her anger evaporated as reality of the situation struck her. She realized where she was, and with whom she was speaking with. Hostility with such people was foolish and dangerous. She suddenly felt very vulnerable, alone, and afraid.

"I-I misspoke, sir, please forgive me." Ladha placed her palms together in an apologetic gesture.

"Oh?" said the Superintendent, his right eyebrow rising.

"I was upset because there has been a terrible mistake. Please, I need your help. My son has been kidnapped and is still alive. I must find him. He's all I have. I would be eternally grateful if you'd grant me some mercy. I beg you, sir, please let me go, and I'll never cause you any trouble."

The Superintendent stared at her for what seemed like an eternity. He then nodded and turned to his subordinate. "Sub-Inspector Rao."

"Sir?" he said, fiddling with a large ring on his index finger. Ladha noticed that the ring had an image of the Hindu deity Ganesh carved in its gold.

191

"Take this Untouchable whore, and beat her and all of her companions until she learns to speak and act with respect. I'll have peace and order in my police station."

"No!" Ladha cried.

The sub-inspector smiled. "Yes, sir!"

"And sub-inspector?"

"Sir?"

"Use any means at your disposal, but no markings on the face, arms, neck, and stomach."

For the first day of her imprisonment, Ladha and the six other women prisoners suffered every indignity imaginable. They were stripped, beaten, urinated on, and raped.

On several occasions, Ladha was ordered to sign a statement that the sub-inspector claimed would expedite her release. But they had mistakenly assumed that she was illiterate like the other women. Staring at the document with a lost expression of confusion, Ladha had quickly scanned the document. She was horrified to discover that they wanted her to sign a document not only claiming she was guilty for destroying property, but also that stated the district police were innocent of all wrongdoings against her and the villagers. Each of the other women had signed on the premise they would be spared from further torment, but Ladha refused and suffered the worst of the beatings.

The police did everything to coerce Ladha to sign, including breaking their word and beating all of the other women again. When the police had dragged Guran back into the cell after a session of beating during the second night, Ladha had cursed her stubbornness. She wondered whether she should just sign the document and spare her friend any further suffering.

Ladha gently lay Guran's head on her lap and tried to tend to her multiple wounds with a rag and some ointment—the only medical supplies the police had given her. But unlike Ladha, Guran no longer had the will to live, and her last words reminded Ladha to always have faith that she would one day be reunited with her child.

"I'm sorry, Ladha. I signed the testimony against you. I couldn't bear the pain anymore. They still beat me after I signed. I'm so sorry, my friend."

"Shhhh, Guran, don't speak. Please, rest," Ladha wept.

"Never give up, Ladha. Do everything to find your boy. Do not let my death be in vain."

After the police dragged the body out of the cell, Guran's words continued to remain locked in Ladha's mind, giving her another surge of confidence and defiance. She would not lose her will in front of her captors no matter what the consequences. After the death of the third women, however, Ladha began to wonder if the only way to escape from this hellish prison was by having your corpse hauled out.

Heavy footsteps approaching the cell broke Ladha's morbid thoughts. She looked up as two guards unlocked the prison door and stepped aside as the smartly dressed sub-inspector walked in. He studied the women with repulsion, as if they were maggots.

All of the women sat curled against the wall, cowering with fear from their tormentor.

"Get up, all of you! Fall into line against the wall," he ordered.

Each woman hesitated, abhorred by the thought of fully exposing her nudity to the police officers. But when the sub-inspector threateningly pulled out his lathi, the women complied, grimacing silently in fear of receiving more beatings.

"Hose," the sub-inspector ordered to one of the guards.

A hose was brought in and handed to the sub-inspector.

As the high-pressured, frigid water hit Ladha with full force, she felt as if she had been punched with a block of ice. She cried out with distress as the water threw her against the wall. Every time she tried to gasp for air, she swallowed water. She blindly stumbled into another woman and fell to the concrete floor, unable to escape the liquid assault.

The hose was disengaged, and the sub-inspector handed it to the guard and tossed five cheap saris at the battered, drenched prisoners.

"Get dressed," he commanded.

Panting, the women began to put on the saris, turning their backs to the probing eyes of the shameless police officers.

The sub-inspector checked his watch and frowned.

"Cover all your bruises with your saris," he shouted, agitatedly toying with his Ganesh ring. "Hurry!"

193

Ladha tried to move as quickly as possible, but her body refused to co-operate. Her body ached and her head spun, and the simple task of putting on a sari was proving to be too great a challenge. She felt as if she was moving in slow motion.

"Faster!" the sub-inspector barked, punching Ladha on the hip.

Half-dressed, Ladha grimaced and fell to her knees. Without a word, she got up and finished dressing.

After the women were dressed, their wrists and ankles were shackled, and they were led out of the Madurai central police station. Ladha used her chained hands to shield her eyes from the brilliant sunlight.

The five female prisoners were put into the back of a police van. The sub-inspector sat across them. The rear doors were slammed shut and the van sped off, its siren wailing.

During the fifteen-minute ride, Ladha was mesmerized by the sub-inspector absentmindedly playing with his ring. She could not believe that a thing of such beauty could have caused her so much pain. She still felt the sting of the ring striking her flesh. She flinched as the sub-inspector slammed his fist impatiently into his palm when the van stopped.

Ladha waited for the doors to open, but nothing happened. There was a metallic click. Her eyes widened and she began trembling; the sub-inspector had extracted a switchblade.

"You're outside the Siviputur magistrate court," he said, admiring how the light glinted off the menacing blade. "In a few minutes you'll be called to make a court appearance for sentencing. I'll be watching the entire procedure, and if any of you say one word, and I mean one word at all, I'll slowly carve you up. I don't even want to hear a cough coming from your direction. Don't dare reveal any of your wounds, otherwise I'll hunt down every member of your family and slaughter them in front of you. You'll do nothing other than stand there silently. Do I make myself clear?"

As the sub-inspector spoke, his quiet words pierced Ladha like venom. He fondled the razor edge of the blade until the tip of his index finger drew blood.

"Answer me! Are we understood?" He glared at the five women with such malice that Ladha flinched.

The women nodded fearfully.

Sub-Inspector Rao smiled thinly and pounded the side of the van. The rear doors opened.

Ladha once again shielded her eyes from the blinding sun, and shuffled her way with the police escort into the side entrance of the courthouse.

The prisoners sat on a bench in a small room beside an inner door. No words were spoken as their chains were removed.

Rubbing her wrists, Ladha searched for escape, but there was nothing she could do. There were a dozen guards in the room and the sub-inspector never took his eyes off them.

After a few minutes, the inner door opened and a court guard appeared.

"Ladha Karai," he called out.

Ladha stood up and was escorted by four guards into a packed courtroom. She was motioned to stand in the prisoner's box.

Ladha had never been in a courtroom, much less a trial. She felt overwhelmed, but soon began listening to the proceedings, aware that any chance of finding her son rested on what happened in the next few minutes. Her only source of hope was that the judge was a female. An interpreter stood beside her, and translated the English into Tamil so she could understand the proceedings.

Ladha turned towards the audience, and cringed at the sight of the sub-inspector swiping his hand across his throat in a slashing gesture, and then signaling silence by placing his index finger over his mouth. He smiled cruelly at her.

"The defendant has been charged under the Tamil Nadu Properties Destruction Act for allegedly burning her hut, and conspiring to falsely accuse others. Is this correct?" the judge asked, casting a steely look over her half-mooned spectacles at the prosecution.

"It is, your honor," the prosecution said, standing.

"And how does the defendant plea?" the judge asked, turning to the defense attorney, a man that Ladha had never seen before, and who had never consulted her.

"Guilty, your honor," he said, standing.

"No, I'm innocent!" Ladha cried.

Ladha anxiously eyed the sub-inspector whose face was filled with fury.

"Defense, I suggest you control your client," the judge said coldly, eyeing the accused warily.

Ladha was awestruck by the judge. She had never seen a woman in a position of authority, and the men seemed to be following *her* commands! Ladha realized that this woman could help her. It was the only chance she had to escape certain death from the enraged sub-inspector. Now that she had blurted her innocence to the court, she had nothing to lose. She had to be brave and speak out. It was the only chance to secure her freedom and find her son.

"Please, your honor, I beg you to give me a moment of your time in private," Ladha pleaded. "I have something vital to share with you, and if you feel I have wasted your time, you can imprison me for as long as you wish. *Please.*"

The crowd murmured with surprise at the unusual request. The judge repeatedly smashed her gavel in an attempt to restore order in her courtroom.

"Your honor, I must apologize for this *outrageous* request made by my client," said the defense lawyer, giving Ladha a look nearly as malicious as the sub-inspector.

The judge stared long and hard at the imploring defendant.

"*Please,* your honor." Ladha bowed her head and pressed her hands together in front of her face in a gesture of respect. "I swear on my children you'll not regret such a decision. If you have any mercy give me a moment of your time in private."

The entire courtroom was silent, all eyes on the judge.

Sub-Inspector Rao glowered with hatred from the back of the courtroom, vowing to inflict excruciating pain to the Untouchable bitch for so boldly defying him.

"You have two minutes of my time, young woman," the judge finally said. "Guard, take her to my private chambers."

"Your honor, I must protest!" cried the prosecution.

"I agree with the prosecution, your honor," the defense lawyer said.

"Court is in recess," the judge barked, slamming her gavel down to signal the finality of her decision.

The two lawyers began walking towards the judge's private chambers, but the judge held up her hand. "Alone, gentlemen. Just the defendant and I."

"But, your safety!" cried the prosecutor.

"I must represent my client!" cried the defense.

The judge glared at the two lawyers; they both sulked back to their tables.

Ladha was re-shackled and followed the judge into her private chambers. The judge sat down behind her desk, and studied the woman before her for several moments.

"Speak," she said coolly in Tamil. "And you better not have wasted my time."

Ladha was grateful that she could speak freely without the need of an interpreter. She took a large breath and began speaking as calmly as she could, sensing that any emotion would obscure her ability to convince the judge.

"Your honor, I am an innocent victim of police brutality and hatred because I am a Dalit. My entire village of Desikapuram was destroyed and its people butchered first by the Zamindars, and then the district police. My husband, daughter, and son were slaughtered. Please, your honor, you must believe me," Ladha said, breaking into tears.

"What brutality did the district police commit?"

"They beat, raped, and burned the rest of the village the day after the Zamindars attacked. This was two days ago. They arrested me and seven other women. They beat and raped us for two straight days. Three of the eight women prisoners were killed from the beatings."

"Who in the police department beat and raped you?"

"The Superintendent of Police led the attack on the village, and Sub-Inspector Rao, the man with the mustache sitting in the back of the courtroom, is responsible for the abuse we suffered over the past two days. He even threatened to kill me if I spoke a word in your court today."

The judge's expression went cold at the mention of the sub-inspector. "Do you have any proof of this?" she demanded.

"P-Proof?" Ladha stammered, surprised by the judge's harsh tone and sudden change in demeanor.

"I've risked my reputation by seeing you like this. I'm normally very good at judging character. I thought I saw something in you. It was a mistake. I assure you that you'll be punished severely for turning my court into a mockery."

"No, I speak the truth!"

"The sub-inspector is my nephew and an outstanding member of this community. He is incapable of the things you claim."

"No, no!" Ladha said wildly.

"I've seen hundreds of cases like yours. When I go back out into that courtroom I am certain the prosecution will give me a signed witness testimony verifying you destroyed your own property, and if I check my files the police will have recorded arresting *five*, not eight prisoners that night at your village."

"No, the sub-inspector beat and raped the women until they were forced to sign those testimonies, and he changed the records to hide the three murdered Dalits."

"You're a liar and I've heard enough," the judge said, standing.

"Check your signed testimonies then! If the police claimed to have arrested five, then why are there *seven* signatures that state I am guilty?"

The judge froze, and studied Ladha as she contemplated her point.

Have I misjudged this young woman?

The judge's face became devoid of emotion as she thought about her nephew, the pride of her older brother.

No, it can't be so.

"Your time's up," the judge said sternly.

Ladha desperately looked around, searching for something or someone to help her. She did not know what else to do or say. In a moment she would be back in the court, and the judge would be sentencing her to certain death. Ladha noticed a wooden carving of the elephant-headed deity, Ganesh, in the corner of the judge's chambers.

"I have proof that your nephew is involved!" Ladha cried, falling to her knees in front of the judge.

The judge stopped at the door and turned.

"Please, give me two more minutes. I'll show you the proof you need," Ladha begged.

"You have wasted enough of my time," the judge said, opening the door.

"You won't take two more minutes to clear any doubt of your nephew's innocence?"

The judge hesitated. "I have no doubts."

"Don't you?"

The judge closed the door and crossed her arms across her chest. "Show me."

"I can't show you in my chains."

"Do you have this proof on you?"

"Yes."

The judge eyed her suspiciously, and then summoned the court guard.

"Undo the shackles on the prisoner's wrists," the judge ordered. The court guard gave a look of surprise. "*Now*, and then get out!"

The court guard complied quickly, and left the private chambers.

"Show me," the judge said.

Ladha began taking off her sari.

"What are you doing?" the judge demanded.

"The police beat us where we normally cover ourselves," Ladha explained as she continued to undress. "If we reveal our wounds to anyone they threaten to kill us. But, usually the threats aren't even necessary because most women are too modest to reveal themselves to others."

"And what about the bruise on your temple?"

"That was when they arrested me at the village. It is nearly three days old."

When Ladha was undressed, the judge grimaced at the enormous welts and lacerations that marked her body from her chest to her knees.

"Even if you were recently beaten, it doesn't prove that my nephew was involved, or the police. These wounds could be self-inflicted."

"No, no, wait."

"I've seen enough, and I am not convinced. Cover yourself," the judge said, turning.

"Then why is the mark of the Ganesh ring he wears imprinted all over my body?"

"What did you say?" the judge asked, whirling around, her eyes wide.

Ladha pointed to the most recent imprint on her hip.

199

The judge came closer and carefully examined the wound. When she saw the familiar mark, her impassive face was filled with the pain of betrayal and regret.

How could I be so blind? the judge thought, sitting back down behind her desk, her hands trembling. *For so many years the signs had been there, but I dismissed them, unable to believe that my beloved nephew could be so cruel. And when the whispers and hearsay grew to a point that I could not ignore, he swore to me with tears in his eyes that these were lies. How many people did I condemn to protect him? How many innocent people did I wrongly accuse that he arrested? I became a judge to bring justice and change the system, and the system instead manipulated me. What have I done? What have I become?* she despaired, looking up at the young, trembling woman in front of her. *How do I make things right?*

"Get dressed, Ladha," the judge said softly. "I gave him that ring when he became a police officer. I was so proud that my nephew would be in law enforcement like his auntie, and look what he has become." The judge sighed with a weary sadness. "Ladha, I believe you, and I'm going to help you."

Ladha wept with relief.

"Ladha, I can't take back all the atrocities that you and your friends have suffered, but I promise that I'll do the best I can to free you."

Ladha nodded vigorously, tears of gratitude streaming down her face. She quickly glanced at the wooden statue of Ganesh that had inspired her, and silently thanked the deity.

"Have the police fed you anything?"

"Yes, one meal a day. It is some watery mixture of rice and curd."

"Well, all that will change once you return to jail," the judge said. Ladha's eyes widened with terror. "Ladha, it'll only be for two days."

"No, your honor, please. They'll kill me."

"Listen to me, Ladha. First, call me Seetha. Second, you have to spend a few days in jail otherwise they'll get too suspicious. You have no real proof that you're innocent, and I need time to get matters sorted out for your release and make the necessary inquiries. I'm sorry, but I have to find you guilty and sentence you otherwise I'll not be able to help you at all. Can you understand that?"

"My life, and the life of my child, is in your hands."

"I promise nothing will happen to you," Judge Seetha vowed. "I'm sending you to another jail where I have some influence, and will have officers loyal to me protecting you at all times. I'll also visit you every day until you're released. You've been very brave to expose the truth, and now, must trust me."

Ladha was speechless, consumed with emotion.

There was a knock at the door and the court officer appeared. "Your honor, the court counselors are becoming anxious. They respectfully point out that two minutes have passed, and that there are still several cases to go through."

"Let them wait," the judge growled.

The court officer gave a circular nod and closed the door.

"Now, Ladha, I need to ask you some questions. Did you sign any confessions?"

"No, I know how to read, and no matter how much they beat me I didn't sign anything claiming that I was guilty, or that the police were innocent."

Seetha smiled as a plan of action formed in her mind. "Excellent. That should make things easier. Can you tell me the names and background of the women from your village imprisoned and beaten to death?"

"Yes, the village was very small and I knew them all well."

Ladha recited the names with a brief history of who they were.

The judge wrote the information down. "Good, now, listen carefully. I do not want you to say a word in court, understand? Everything will be fine. Remember, trust me."

Five minutes later, the judge was behind her bench and Ladha in the defendant's box. The judge called the court back into session.

"How does the defendant plea?" the judge asked the defense attorney.

"Not guilty, your honor," the defense attorney said with reluctance.

"Very well, prosecution may state its case," the judge said.

Shaun Mehta

"Your honor, I have seven signed statements from other members of the Desikapuram village. They all claim that Ladha Karai burned several huts in the village with the intent of blaming these atrocities on a *supposed* attack by upper-caste landlords. I would like to submit this as exhibit A." The prosecutor handed the documents to the court guard who handed them to the judge.

The judge scanned the documents. "I see one of these witnesses is a Guruswamy Guruammal. I'd like to hear her personal accounts. Would you kindly call her to the court?"

The color drained from the prosecution's face. "I-I am not familiar with that name, your honor."

"You're not familiar with one of the witnesses who signed this testimony?" the judge asked with a raised eyebrow. "Let me help you remember. This witness was in her late forties, and was known by her friends and family as 'Guran.'"

The prosecutor flipped quickly through his notes for several tense moments. "Yes, of course. Forgive me, your honor, but she...ah...unexpectedly expired."

"Is that so? Tragic timing." The judge scanned her documents again. "And what of Irulayee Jayaram? I'd like to hear from her then."

The prosecutor did not respond, beads of sweat appearing on his forehead.

"Don't tell me she's dead as well?" the judge asked, looking over her spectacles.

"I believe she may have returned to her village, your honor," the prosecutor lied. "But of those seven testimonies, four can be immediately summoned if your honor desires."

"No, that's quite alright," the judge said, relishing the moment. "The prosecution may continue his case."

"Thank you, your honor," the prosecutor said uneasily ."When the police came to investigate the 'so called' crime scene, they discovered that the accused, and her band of social misfits, had caused considerable damage to the village themselves. Once the accused learned that the police had discovered the truth, she became enraged and attempted to assault several officers."

"According to my records the accused was not formally charged for attempting to assault the police, prosecutor. Please stick to the facts of the crime in question," the judge said sternly.

"Of course, your honor." The prosecutor nervously shuffled some papers on his desk, buying time to collect his thoughts. "I also have signed testimony from several police officers that Ladha Karai resisted arrest and—"

"Does the prosecution have any further evidence linked to the accused destroying property, which is the charge on record?" the judge interrupted.

There was a long, uncomfortable silence. "No, your honor," he finally admitted.

"No signed confession from the defendant?"

"No, your honor," the prosecutor said, wondering what Ladha could possibly have said to win the judge's favor.

"Very well, sit down, then. Defense may begin their case."

The defense attorney stood up slowly, and waited until everyone in the court had his attention. He cleared his throat, and loudly said: "Other than the defendant's own words of innocence, the defense has nothing to add, your honor. The defense rests."

Why am I not surprised, Ladha thought, fighting to control her anger.

The judge turned to Ladha, stone-faced. "Very well, then. Based on the evidence I find the defendant guilty and fine her two thousand rupees. If she is unable to pay the amount, she is sentenced to two days in Nillakoti Jail."

"But your honor, two days is not..." began the prosecution, looking at the defense attorney for support.

With one quick look at the judge, the defense attorney wisely remained silent.

"And may I add that if I discover that this woman is mistreated physically or emotionally in any way during her incarceration, I'll use the full power of the law to punish every person responsible," the judge said coldly, staring directly across the court room at her nephew.

The judge banged her gavel and called for the next case.

Stunned by the look of accusation and disappointment from his aunt, Sub-Inspector Rao stormed out of the courtroom, promising that this Untouchable woman would suffer immensely for his humiliation.

* * *

Divya felt as if she was going insane. For an hour she had been unable to register a word she had read in her Marketing Communication textbook, stuck on the same page. She sighed with frustration as her mind kept returning to Diwali, and the moment she had shared with Aslam on the roof.

Why did I back away from his kiss? What am I afraid of?

After she had run from Aslam, she found Rekha and Naveen eating together outside the mess. Rekha was not angry with her friend for abandoning her during the pooja; being absorbed with Naveen, she had been oblivious to Divya's disappearance.

Divya had quietly eaten her dinner beside the pair, listening to the two of them giggle and flirt with each other. Feeling very uncomfortable, she muttered a good night and returned to her room. She was happy for Rekha, but also upset; she desperately needed a friend to confide in with what had happened on the roof. It made her realize how much she had relied on Rekha over the past few months. With Rekha busy with Naveen, Divya turned to the one thing she was confident would distract her—her textbooks.

But even that failed her. Despite having two exams the following morning, Divya was unable to concentrate. Her mind kept returning to the roof and Aslam.

Divya felt so torn. Aslam had been honest with her, expressing his true feelings, and she had discarded them. She yearned to tell him that he was also in her dreams, and that she wanted nothing else but to be with him. But, how could she be so selfish? The guilt was unbearable, but being lonely and miserable was also destroying her. What could she do? How could she be happy knowing her parents were suffering and her brother was...?

She squeezed her eyes shut. *Dead. He's dead. Oh God, Rahul is dead. But you're not, Divya,* reasoned a small part of her. *You must keep living. Only you can bring happiness and peace to your soul, and only your mother and father can help themselves. It's not your fault that Rahul is gone and your parents suffer. Listen to your heart, Divya. You can't deny your feelings.*

I can't do this, she thought, shaking her head vehemently. *It's too much. I have to get out of this room and clear my head.*

Divya quickly got up from her desk. She had to distract herself from her mind, and the best way to do this was to work her body to the brink of utter exhaustion. She had been locked up in her room the entire day, justifying that she needed to study for her exams tomorrow. She had not even left her room to eat—snacking on stashed packages of biscuits and juice boxes—telling herself that she could not afford to waste time by going to the mess. But, after studying for hours and retaining nothing, she could no longer deny the truth that she was hiding from Aslam. If she saw him again, she was afraid of what would happen.

She changed, laced up her running shoes, and checked the time; dinner had ended, and the night canteen had not yet opened. The area around the mess would be empty, and she could go for her run with little chance of bumping into anyone. She wanted to be alone.

She locked her room with the padlock, and saluted Pradeep with a smile as she walked past the laundry wallah. Pradeep was one of the only people that still brought a smile to her face; he would always dance in front of her, synchronizing and gyrating his hip and arm movements to whatever Indian music was blaring from his radio.

Divya found it ironic how she had sympathized and pitied Pradeep when she first saw him. The man living underneath the staircase of A Block had an existence that seemed so miserable, subjected to washing, ironing, and folding clothes for mere rupees until he died, with no chance to improve his living conditions. He had lost his left hand as a child, but still had persevered over his handicap and learned to master his trade. Pradeep was content with so little, and she found herself envying the simple yet peaceful life he led. He was always smiling and dancing, blessing God for how fortunate he was compared to the millions of others, while she was miserable despite the countless opportunities she had.

What's wrong with me? she thought dejectedly, looking at her hands. *I can do so much, yet I do nothing but wallow in my misery.*

Divya reached the front of the mess, and broke into a fast-paced jog. It was a cool, cloudy night, and her body was soon covered in a film of sweat. She continued to think of what Aslam had said to her on the roof.

'*My heart hasn't stopped aching since you left, Divya. I feel lost without you.*'

She quickened her pace into a run.

'*Do you know how many nights I lay in bed thinking about you? Do you know that I would rather stay awake, and have you in my mind, than risk losing your beautiful image in sleep?*'

She broke into a sprint.

'*You consume me, Divya. I need you in my life. I've never loved someone so much. There, I've finally had the courage to say it. I love you.*'

Without warning, the sky released a furious downpour. Divya barely noticed the weight of the water soaking her clothes, or the rain blurring her vision. Her shoes slapped against the wet pavement and splashed in the puddles that had materialized, but she was oblivious to her surroundings. Aslam's words repeated over and over again in her mind, filling her with desire and guilt.

Searching for shelter, she ran past the post office and the convenience store, and into the metal barn that held the college's badminton court.

She flicked on the lights; the barn was empty. As she regained her breath, she looked out the window at the heavy rainfall, and listened to the water drumming against the metal roof and splattering against the concrete.

Divya turned towards the badminton court. Small pools of water were forming across the badminton court from the numerous bullet-like holes throughout the building. She remembered the first time she had discovered the place and watched Aslam play against Chicken. A smile crept onto her face. God, she yearned to hold him.

A new surge of guilt swept through her as she thought about Rahul. Alone in the barn, and trapped from the downpour, there was nothing to distract her mind from her baby brother.

Why had she lived while her brother had died? He was such a beacon of life, and before having a chance to grow and experience—to live—God had ruthlessly snatched him away from her. Why? *Why?*

These were questions she could not answer, but by asking them she unleashed a surge of buried emotions. Suddenly, the dull lump of pain locked within her flared up. Divya felt overwhelmed and lost. She struggled to control her emotions, but she was mentally exhausted. She no longer wanted to pretend she didn't care and that nothing mattered. She no longer wanted to keep running and acting as if nothing had happened and everything was okay. She no longer wanted to act strong while inside she was an emotional wreck.

For the first time since her brother's death, Divya confronted the emotions and memories that she had hidden within her.

Image after image flooded her mind. She remembered how she had marveled at Rahul's innocence and beauty when she first saw him in the maternity ward immediately after his birth, and she remembered how during the first year of his life, she would rock his cradle in the dead of the night until his crying ceased. She recalled his mischievous two-year old grin when she would catch him stealing a biscuit from the cookie jar, and how he would sneak into her bed during a thunderstorm because he was frightened.

The image in her mind's eye changed, and she saw her mother collapse in front of the tiny casket during the pundit's Sanskrit benediction. Then, she was descending the metal steps to the bottom of the Crematorium. She didn't want to go—was terrified to go—but had to be strong for her parents. Divya whimpered as she remembered her mother breaking into hysterics. She had to push the button; she had no choice. Her father was desperately trying to comfort and restrain her mother, and shouting at Divya to quickly do it. Her arm reached out and she pressed the cold, red plastic with a trembling hand, sending Rahul's casket into the crematory for incineration.

Hearing her mother's screams reverberate in her tormented mind as Rahul and his tiny casket were reduced to ashes, Divya covered her ears and fell to her knees in the barn.

For the first time since she had learned of her brother's death, she wept.

Like a bursting dam, the emotions poured out of Divya and she prayed to be spared from the pain she felt. She realized that for the past few months she had been neither dead nor alive. She had numbly gone through the motions, and now begged God to remove the pain so she could live.

I don't want to be alone anymore, she despaired. *Please, help me. I don't want to feel like this. I want the pain to go away. I can't take it. Please, give me strength to move on. Please help me overcome this. Help me. Oh God, help me.*

"Divya?"

She gasped. Aslam was standing by the entrance of the barn.

"I'm sorry I followed you but—"

Divya embraced him and buried her face in his shirt, unleashing another surge of uncontrollable tears.

Aslam held her tightly, stroking her hair as she wept.

When the sobbing subsided, he smiled tenderly and brushed away her tears.

"We'll get through this together," he whispered, gently kissing her.

Warmth encompassed Divya and began to melt the ball of ice that had encased her heart. She had revealed her sorrow to this man, and as he kissed her, she realized that she there was no one else on this world that she would rather be with.

She sobbed as she passionately returned his kiss.

"Spend the night with me, Oz. Make me feel better, make the pain go away," she whispered hoarsely. "Never leave me, Oz. Promise me." She led him to the dry corner of the barn.

He nodded, and lay down beside her on top of the hay. "I promise, Divya, never."

As the rain continued to rhythmically strike the barn, they undressed each other. First nervously, then with growing fascination and passion, they slowly explored each other.

Although she could not describe or understand these new emotions that filled her, she knew that she did not want the moment to end.

She pulled him closer and gasped.

He hesitated, afraid that he had hurt her.

Are you sure? his eyes asked, filled with love and concern.

She nodded and gently drew him back towards her, never more sure in her life.

As they tenderly made love, they stared deeply into each other's eyes. Divya felt as if she was staring straight into his soul. She had never felt more happy and sad at the same time, and later, as she lay in his arms, she cried again for the loss of her brother.

Like the landscape outside the barn, her mind and heart were cleansed, and as the edges of light brushed across the horizon, she fell into an untroubled sleep for the first time since her brother's death.

* * *

"Hullo?" said the cold, familiar voice.

"Please don't hang up, Ramar," Sedhu blurted out. "Your daughter is in trouble."

Sedhu silently cursed himself as he listened to his brother's breathing. Despite rehearsing what he was going to say for the past two days, his opening line had sounded desperate.

"One minute," Ramar finally said in Tamil.

"Thank you, Ramar, thank you. You see—"

"Have you dismissed your culture and people for so long that you've forgotten how to speak in your native tongue?" Ramar asked harshly in Tamil.

Sedhu had barely spoken Tamil in years, and had never spoken the language in front of his children. Now, his mind raced to find the words to express himself. "No, of course not," he said, wincing at how broken his Tamil sounded. "How are you?"

"Spare me with your attempts to pretend that you care about me. What do you want? You've already taken my wife and my daughter, Professor *Ambani*. Do you want my blood too?"

Sedhu froze.

What else does he know about my life and alias? he wondered.

"Do you want my life, money, what? Speak, dammit!"

"We lost our child in the September eleventh attacks," Sedhu said quietly.

"My child is dead?" Ramar asked, his confident voice cracking for a moment. "You said she needed me!"

"No." Sedhu was relieved that Ramar did not know everything about him, and actually seemed concerned about the welfare of Divya. "Your daughter still lives. Rahul, my three-year-old son, was killed in the attacks."

"All Muslims should die," Ramar spat angrily. "Like Untouchables, they're a plague, first destroying India, and now slowly spreading their poison across the rest of the world."

"Will you help me, Ramar?"

"How?"

"I heard you run an adoption home in Madurai."

"You want to adopt a child?"

"Yes, for Rani. I'm convinced it is the only thing that will bring her back. Since Rahul's death she has become clinically depressed and has been hospitalized. Ramar, she's on a suicide watch."

"Then let her take her life, I don't care. That whore should be blessed for having such a painless demise."

"Don't dare speak of her that way!" Sedhu cried, aghast by the hatred that still burned so fiercely in Ramar.

"My, my, how bold!" Ramar chuckled. "You're not as weak as I suspected."

"You may not care about Rani, but you care about the well-being of your daughter, and I am certain you would not want to deprive her of her mother."

"Why don't you adopt through the regular channels, or simply have another child? Why contact me?"

"She almost died giving birth to Rahul. Rani can never have children again, and adoption takes years. Rani can't last that long, and no adoption agency will give us a child while she is in this state. Please, Ramar, I love her and you owe me."

"*What* did you say?"

"You owe me. I made a confession for the crime of that Dalit's mur..." Sedhu caught himself, suddenly paranoid that the phone conversation was being recorded. "I saved your life."

"I owe you nothing," Ramar seethed. "I never asked for your help, and I can take care of my own battles."

"I can pay you. Please, brother."

"Call me that again and I'll have you slaughtered like a swine. My brother died a long time ago. Now, listen to me, Sedhu, and listen carefully because I'm only going to tell you this once. After you called two days ago, I began an investigation to learn everything about the illustrious Professor of Molecular and Medical Genetics at the University of Toronto. I can have you killed anytime and anywhere. You can't run from me, Sedhu. You may change your name again, or run to another city, it won't make a difference. I have more contacts and resources then you can possibly fathom, and don't think I won't hesitate to eliminate you. Do you understand me?"

"Yes," Sedhu whispered, cursing himself for bringing such a dangerous man back into his life.

"Good. Now, I'll help you, but this is for Divya and no one else, understand?"

"Oh, Ramar—"

"*Understand?*"

"I-I understand, yes."

"What type of child do you want?"

Sedhu described what he was looking for.

"I may have something that fits that profile," Ramar said after a moment, as if Sedhu was ordering merchandise. "Fax me a description, or any photo that resembles those characteristics at this number."

Sedhu wrote down the fax number. "And what about documentation?"

"All documentation you'll require will be taken care of. By the way, since I don't expect you to be entering this country, how do you expect to claim the child?"

Sedhu hesitated for a moment. "I'll have someone come to your adoption home in two days. Is that enough time for you?"

"It should be. One more question."

"Yes, anything."

"How did you find me?"

"I read the letter you wrote to me. I was surprised the phone number is still active."

Ramar laughed. Sedhu shuddered at the hollow and humorless sound. "You only *now* read the letter I sent you fifteen years ago? I told Amma there was no point to send that, but she would not listen."

"How are Amma and Appa?"

"Why do you care?"

Sedhu sighed sadly, hanging his head with shame. "I deserve that, Ramar, but not a day has passed when I didn't think of them. They are still my parents. Tell me, how are they?"

"Dead."

Sedhu squeezed his eyes shut "I didn't know. I'm sorry."

"Appa died first in nineteen-eighty four, never once mentioning your name after you left. But, Amma never stopped asking for you, even on her deathbed. She died three weeks after I sent you that letter, three years after Appa. I lost track of how many times she asked for her eldest child to share her last moments, and begged me to find you. I finally found your home address, but you never responded. When Amma's soul was finally put to rest, I knew that I'd lost both my parents *and* my brother forever."

"We'll always be broth—"

"Say it, Sedhu. *Say it!*" Ramar shouted into the phone.

"I'll fax you that information by the end of today," Sedhu said shakily, pressing the end button on his cell phone.

With trembling hands, Sedhu slowly put the phone beside the bathroom sink.

What have I done?

He fell to his knees, and vomited into the toilet.

Chapter 11
Requests
Friday, November 16th, 2001

Divya awoke with a lazy smile of contentment.

The beat of Aslam's heart, and the warmth of his body, gave a sense of security and love she had never expected to experience again. She kept her eyes closed, afraid that if she opened them she would discover this to be a dream.

And if it is, may I never awake.

To her delight, he began to gently stroke her hair. It was such a soothing feeling that she began to drift back into a blissful sleep.

"If you live to be a hundred, I want to live to be a hundred minus one day, so I never have to live without you," he murmured.

Divya lifted her head.

"Good morning," he said.

She kissed him softly.

"What's that for?" he asked with a smile.

"For saying such a romantic thing."

"Actually, it's not mine. It's a quote."

"Don't tell me you are turning into Om?"

"No, no, nothing like that. I was so caught up with the moment that it just came out."

"So who said that?"

"Winnie the Pooh."

"Cute."

"Me or the quote?" Divya smiled slyly and kissed him again. "Oh no, Divya, you can't avoid the issue with a kiss."

"Oh, really?" she said, her eyebrow rising with surprise.

"Divya, do you love me?" he asked, his face tender yet serious.

Divya looked at him for a long time, searching her feelings. She nodded. "I do."

"Then, will you do something for me?"

"Anything."

"Tell me how you learned to play badminton? How did you beat Chicken that day I first saw your beautiful face?"

Divya smiled, and shook her head ruefully. "I can't. Anything but that."

Aslam mocked a frown. "I'll find out, you know."

"I wish you luck. Now, is there anything *else* I can do for you," she asked seductively, nuzzling her face into his neck.

"Hmmmm, as a matter of fact there is."

"Name it."

"Brush your teeth. You have terrible morning breath."

"Bastard," Divya exclaimed, striking his chest. "I was being serious."

"So am I," Aslam said, laughing.

She pounded his chest again, and he playfully grabbed her arm. They began wrestling in the hay. He locked her in his arms, and kissed her passionately. Divya shuddered with pleasure.

They froze from the sound of children's laughter. They popped their heads out of the hay to find two young boys—sons of professors living on campus—standing by the barn window, giggling and pointing at them.

Divya ducked underneath the hay as Aslam cried in Kannada: "Get out of here!"

The boys bolted from the window, still giggling.

"Are they gone?" Divya asked, her voice muffled.

"Yes. You can come out now."

"How embarrassing," she moaned, cautiously emerging from the stack. "What are people doing up so early?"

"Early? It's nearly eight in the morning."

She paled. "Oh my God, I have an exam in fifteen minutes."

She frantically searched for her clothes with one hand; the other kept a clump of hay covering her at all times in case someone else passed the barn. As soon as she tied her shoelaces, she was out the door running towards the hostels.

"Goodbye," Aslam said to the empty barn.

He sighed, and slowly began dressing himself.

As he was buttoning his jeans, Divya ran into the barn and embraced him.

"I'll always be with you for as long as you live," she said, breathless. "I'll see you tonight, love."

214

Aslam smiled as she disappeared through the barn door.

* * *

After sprinting to her room to change and retrieve her textbooks, Divya made it to the exam hall five minutes after the examination had begun. She had not even had time to use the washroom. For her tardiness she was awarded a stern frown of disapproval from Professor Munde, and a snicker from Tapan Ansari—her greatest rival for finishing first in the class. Sweaty and grungy, she pushed Aslam, the previous night, and all other thoughts except for Marketing Communications from her mind. For the next three hours she sat in the uncomfortable plastic chair, and relied on all of the preparations and hard work she had put into the course over the past two months. Ignoring her urges to relieve herself, she wrote furiously without pause until Professor Munde snatched her paper from her hand. It was then that Divya noticed she was the only student left in the exam hall. The man feared by so many had generously given her an additional five minutes.

Frustrated that she had not articulated her ideas as clearly as she had wanted, Divya slowly stood up and stretched. Each answer she had written lingered in her mind, and she sighed as she remembered several elements of theory and practical examples that she had wanted to include but had eluded her during the exam.

Suddenly feeling exhausted, she turned and was dismayed to find Professor Munde reading her exam paper, his frown deepening with each passing moment. Her heart sank, and she wondered how she could escape his imminent wrath. She wondered if staying with Aslam all night was worth sacrificing all the work she had put in.

Definitely, she thought with an inward smile.

Professor Munde looked up from the paper, and glared at her. "Miss. Ambani, do you realize what you have written?"

"Yes, sir, I'm sorry, but I can explain—"

"An apology under these circumstances is unacceptable, Miss. Ambani."

"But sir—"

Professor Munde raised his hand to silence her. "That will be enough, Miss. Ambani. Frankly...what is this?" He tilted his head, and plucked a piece of hay from her hair, which after a moment of scrutiny, tossed on the ground. Divya blushed furiously with embarrassment, wishing she had the power to disappear. Professor Munde cleared his throat. "As I was saying, frankly, I am surprised by this," he said, shaking her exam paper. "I must admit that during those first few weeks of class I incorrectly azzumed, and *grossly* underestimated, your capabilities."

Divya could not believe her ears. She looked up to see the hint of a smile appear on his face. "If you ever need a job, I will gladly hire you as my personal assistant. It is these rare moments that relinquish any doubts I had in choosing a career in education. Well done, and good day, Miss. Ambani."

Stunned, she watched the professor turn sharply and walk out of the examination hall. By the time his words had sunk in, and she had gathered her senses, the next stream of students were entering the examination hall for the Time Management exam. Once again, she had no time to relieve herself.

As she sat back down in the orange chair, and locked the wooden tablet across her lap, she worried about the last exam of her business degree. She had not studied at all for her Time Management final.

"You may begin your exam," announced the examination proctor.

She shifted uncomfortably in her small, plastic chair, realizing for the first time how similar the piece of furniture resembled a high chair for babies.

Divya sighed, and flipped over her exam. She smiled with disbelief.

I should have known.

The exam was the complete opposite of the difficult exam she had just written for Professor Munde. The entire Time Management final examination was one question, and she was certain it had taken the famously tardy and slothful Professor Bhagnani one minute to compose.

So, this is his notion of Time Management.

Divya chuckled as she read the exam question again:

*Succinctly explain how this course has
helped you manage your time.
Give concise examples.
Do not write more than two pages.*

Taking a few minutes to structure how she wanted to answer the question, Divya began writing quickly, trying to ignore the growing discomfort and pressure in her bladder.

* * *

"Chance favors the prepared mind," Om said, his powerful, deep voice causing several people at nearby tables to turn in their direction. "Louis Pasteur."

"What's he talking about?" Divya asked, putting her dinner tray down beside Rekha and Naveen.

"I was just complaining how Om rarely shows up to class, and I have never seen him holding anything but a religious book, and he *still* gets phenomenal marks," Rekha explained. "He is too lucky, nah?"

"So, how'd you find your two exams today, Divya?" Naveen asked.

"Better than I expected."

"You are done all your exams, nah?" Rekha asked.

"Yes, thank God. Not only that, but I'm officially done my business degree," Divya said.

"We should celebrate," Rekha exclaimed.

"What about your Spirituality in Business class?" Naveen asked.

"You do not listen to a word I say," Rekha snapped at him. "I already told you how Professor Krishnamurthy gave us a take home exam, nah?"

"No, you didn't!"

"It was only yesterday, Naveen. We walked together to his office and slipped the exam underneath the door. You remember, nah?"

"That was for *his* class?" he asked, lighting a cigarette.

Rekha shook her head and raised her arms in the air with frustration. "Too much, Naveen!" she exclaimed, snatching his cigarette. "And you promised to quit."

"Stop harassing me, Rekha. This is the last one, I promise," he said, extracting another cigarette from his pack and lighting it.

"Kill yourself, see what I care!" Rekha said angrily. "See Divya, how he treats me, ignoring my feelings?"

"Come on, Rekha, it's not like that," Naveen objected.

Those two are sounding more and more like an old married couple with each passing day, Divya thought, smiling.

Divya listened to Naveen and Rekha bicker for several moments with amusement.

"Where's Oz?" she asked at the first moment of silence, trying to sound casual.

"He went to the mosque, and then the local Islamic orphanage. He goes there twice a month for fundraising or to spend time with the children," Rekha explained. "But he should be back any moment."

"You're kidding?" Divya said, frowning as Om drowned the white rice on his plate with ketchup, and began to mix it with his right hand into a gooey mush. Whenever he was not fasting, this was the only thing Divya had ever seen him eat. She still had not gathered the nerve to ask him why he ate such a strange concoction.

"If a society cannot help the many that are poor, it cannot help the few that are rich," Om intoned. "John F. Kennedy."

"Do you have to quote everyone, Om?" Naveen sighed.

Om did not respond; too busy eating the reddish slop of gruel with his hands.

"What did you three do this afternoon?" Divya asked, changing the subject.

"We went and saw *Ashoka*, starring Shahrukh Khan," Rekha said dreamily.

"Oh, isn't that movie about King Ashoka spreading peace and Buddhism across India after he surveyed the death and destruction he caused on the battlefield?" Divya asked.

"That is the one," Rekha confirmed. "Om actually persuaded *us* to see it because the fil*u*m was *supposedly* about Buddhism.

The grand opening of the fil*lum* was even viewed by the Dalai Lama, nah?"

"Supposedly?" Divya echoed. "What, you didn't like it?"

"Ask Om that question," Naveen said, smiling.

Om's face darkened. "There is more stupidity than hydrogen in the universe, and it has a longer shelf life," he said with disgust. "Frank Zappa."

"That bad, eh?" Divya said.

"Divya, the fil*lum* was a very bad romance, and the *only* reference to Buddhism was a paragraph written before the credits that stated how King Ashoka spread Buddhism around India after his transformation on the battlefield," Rekha said.

"I've lost my appetite," Om said, standing.

"Where are you going, Om?" Rekha asked.

"I've had a wonderful time, but this wasn't it. Groucho Marx." Om turned, and walked out of the bustling mess.

"Is he okay?" Divya asked, concerned.

"Oh yes, he is probably going to the meditative room to repent his sins for watching such rubbish," Rekha laughed.

"What was your opinion of the movie, Naveen?" Divya asked. "I'm not sure if I trust Om's judgment."

"Oh, it was okay," Naveen ventured, avoiding the dirty look from Rekha.

"He just liked Kareena Kapoor dancing half-naked throughout the entire stupid fil*lum*. Divya, even when they were walking across parched, desert like canyons, her hair was soaking wet. It was very blatantly sexual and despicable, nah?"

Divya burst out laughing, clearly visualizing Rekha's description.

"I thought the battle scene was well done," Naveen said, instantly regretting uttering the words.

"Well done? *Well done?*" Rekha shrilled, glaring at him. "How the hell did Kareena Kapoor survive being impaled by that sword in the midst of that ferocious battle? Divya, I swear, at the end, Sharukh Khan is walking among the carnage where there are bloody body parts everywhere, and she suddenly gets up from the massacre unharmed. And her hair was *still* dripping wet! After that battle she looked better than we did during Diwali. How? How? How is that possible?"

Shaun Mehta

"Please, no more," Divya begged.

"What's so funny?" Aslam asked.

Divya stood up and embraced him. "Hey stranger, it's good to see you."

"And you," he said, smiling. "Have you already eaten?"

"No. These two cribbing about *Ashoka* made me forget about my food."

"Is that the film with Kareena Kapoor?" he asked, his eyes lighting up.

Naveen nodded vigorously with an enthusiastic smile, and Rekha slapped him across his arm.

"Not you too?" Divya asked, with a mock frown.

"No, no. I have my girl," Aslam said, pecking her on the cheek. "Are you hungry?

"Famished."

"Great. We have a reservation at Guru Gardens."

"What? Really?" she said, excited at the thought of being spared of the insipid mess food for one evening. "Are we going to take your motorcycle?"

"No, it's close by, and a beautiful night. We can walk."

"I don't want to be rude and just abandon you two," Divya said reluctantly, remembering Rekha and Naveen.

"No, no, go!" Rekha enthused, ecstatic that her two best friends were finally together. Divya had told her everything in the afternoon, and Rekha had been so excited that she forgot Chicken had called her Motti again.

"Are you sure?" Divya asked.

"I will kick your ass if you do not go. Areé, *go*, nah?"

"Okay, thanks," Divya said, smiling with excitement, and taking Aslam's hand.

"And check out the movie if you get a chance," Naveen called out to them. "Rekha, no*ooo*!" he whined as she angrily snatched the cigarette from his mouth, and snapped it in half.

* * *

"I've heard so much about this place, and now I can't believe I'm here only *after* I've completed my term at IIMB," Divya said, admiring the quaint, outdoor restaurant.

220

"You've never been here before?" Aslam asked, surprised. "I assumed you would have come here with the exchange students at least a few times."

"No. But I've heard that the Swedish exchange student eats and studies here all the time to avoid Tharki's probing eyes and shameless advances."

Aslam laughed. "*This* is where she hides! Tharki was harassing me the other day of whether I'd seen her."

"It's so peaceful here," she sighed, appreciating the mini-waterfalls and candle-lit tables that were placed around the lovely gardens.

"Yes, and I can't believe I'm sharing this with you," he said, holding her hands.

"Oh, Oz."

"Divya, there's something I want to ask you."

"Yes?"

"Well, um—"

There was an electrical explosion from a transformer on the wooden pole outside the restaurant. Sparks showered the street, and the block was suddenly smothered in darkness.

"That was scary," Divya breathed.

"But at least the atmosphere is a little more romantic," Aslam said.

They both watched the waiters rushing around lighting more candles.

"As I was saying—" Aslam began.

"Sorry to interrupt, Oz, but is there anything the waiters can do about these mosquitoes? I'm being eaten alive."

"Of course."

Aslam called over a waiter and explained the situation in Kannada. The waiter nodded and disappeared into the kitchen. A moment later the waiter returned with a mosquito coil, which he lit and placed on a hook underneath the table. A strange, pleasing scent came from the mosquito repellent.

"Is that better?" Aslam asked after a few minutes.

"Yeah, thanks," Divya said, smiling with gratitude. "Now, what were you saying?"

"This is much more difficult than I thought."

"That's okay. There's nothing you need to keep from me. I love you."

He smiled. "I love you too, Divya. More than you'll ever know."

"So what is it?"

"Well, I was wondering, hoping in fact, if you would—"

"Are you ready to order, sir?" asked the waiter.

Aslam looked incredulously at the waiter. "No, we need a few more minutes." His glare urged him to disappear.

"Very good, sir," the waiter said, failing to catch Aslam's tone or look.

Aslam brushed his hands through his hair, and sighed heavily.

"Oz?"

"Marry me."

"What?"

"Will you marry me?"

It took Divya several moments to find her voice. "You're seriously proposing to me?"

"Yes," he said, getting off his chair and falling to his knee. He pulled out a tiny, black box, and opened it to reveal a ring of white gold. "Divya Ambani," he said, holding her hand and putting the ring on her finger, "will you make me the happiest man in the world by agreeing to be my wife?"

"But we only had one amazing night," she whispered, stunned.

"And I want to make every night with you amazing until I die. I never want to sleep alone again."

She was speechless.

"Divya, say something, please?"

"This is too fast, Oz. What happened to getting to know each other, and having a normal boyfriend girlfriend relationship?"

"Divya, you're leaving India in a week."

"I see, so this is your way of stopping me from leaving?"

"Yes."

"Oz, we can't make the most important decision of our lives based on the premise of keeping me in India."

"Why not?"

"There are so many more things to consider."

"Do you love me?"

"Yes, you know I do."

"And, I love you. What else is there to consider?"

"Oz, what about our families getting to know one another?"

"You'll instantly be embraced by my parents as their daughter. You'll see how much warmth and love they have. Amma and Appa will adore you."

I wish I could say the same about my father, Divya thought unhappily.

"And what country will we live in, or how will we live? I can barely take care of myself. I mean, neither of us has any money. Have you considered any of these things, Oz?"

"Divya, we have our entire lives to figure all of these things out. That's the beauty of life. We'll never have a dull moment. Sure things may get challenging from time to time, but together we'll get through it. Besides, I'll take care of you. And our families will provide us with the support we need until we're self-sufficient."

"And religion?"

He sighed wearily.

"So it *is* a problem, *isn't* it?" she persisted.

"Divya, I want you to know something. I went to the mosque today to inquire if there was some way that a Muslim man could marry a Hindu woman. I know of interracial marriages between Muslims and Christians or Jews, but even those are strongly discouraged, and are only accepted once the woman eventually converts to Islam."

"I would never—"

"I know, and I would never ask you to. The mullah, my Islamic teacher, a man I love and respect, was furious at me for even considering marrying a Hindu woman, even though I told him that you weren't that religious. But, he wouldn't listen. And you know what? It didn't matter to me. The mullah said that even though our marriage may be legal in India or Canada, it's unlawful in the eyes of Allah. I think he's wrong, and that he misunderstands the Qur'an, as Allah only preaches love. You see, nothing, including the Islamic community, can stop me from loving you and spending my life with you."

Divya was touched, her eyes glistening from his love. But to be shunned by the community and religion he cared deeply for was too great a sacrifice for her to accept. She remembered him telling her the obstacles and challenges his Hindu surrogate father had endured raising him to embrace his religion and people. She could not accept the responsibility of him discarding the hardships he and his father had suffered through just for her. What if Aslam began to resent her later for such a sacrifice?

"I can't allow you to abandon your faith," she said firmly.

"You're wrong, Divya. I'm *embracing* my faith and what I believe in. I don't care what anyone says as I know there's no truer voice than what is spoken from my heart. My Hindu parents taught me this."

"And children? How would they be raised?"

"With an open mind. They'll be taught all religions of the world, and be encouraged to follow whatever they believe. As long as we teach them how to be good people with good ethics and values, how can we go wrong as parents?"

"Oh, Oz—"

"Divya, we've wasted too much time trying to resist our feelings for each other. Why are you still running away from me? There's nothing to be afraid of."

"I'm not." She sighed sadly and shook her head. "Oz, I can't."

"Can't or won't?" he asked, a pained expression on his face. Suddenly feeling like a naïve fool, he got off his knees and sat back down across from her. "This was stupid. I'm such a *duffer*."

"No, it was lovely, and I'm *so* flattered, Oz....but...I'm sorry, it's just *way* too soon, too fast." she said, pulling the ring off. "I don't want to hurt you—"

"Just promise me that you'll take a few days to think about it."

"Oz, I must say—"

"*Please*," he pleaded. "That's all I'm asking. Think about it, and if you're still certain about this then I'll take back the ring without objection. Think about it, okay?"

Divya studied Aslam for some time, and reluctantly put the ring back on her finger.

"Congratulations!" said the waiter, materializing in front of them. From a distance he had watched the young man get on his knee and put the ring on the lady's finger. He would definitely be receiving a large gratuity tonight.

The power was restored throughout the block, and there was a collective cheer throughout the restaurant.

"We're ready to order," Aslam told the waiter sullenly, looking at his menu.

"Oz, don't let this ruin our evening."

"I'll have the butter chicken and fresh naan," he said impassively, ignoring Divya.

"And for you madam?" the waiter asked, smiling at her.

"Oz, please—"

"The same for her," Aslam said, slamming the menu shut, unmoved by her tears.

"Very good, sir," the waiter said, pleased that the young woman was weeping with happiness because of her engagement. He hoped his gratuity would be large enough so he could afford to see *Ashoka* with his friends that weekend. He smiled dreamily at the thought of watching Kareena Kapoor dancing in those provocative clothes for three hours.

After a silent and uncomfortable dinner, Aslam bitterly paid the bill leaving no gratuity, and walked Divya back to her room without a word.

* * *

Divya fiddled with her ring as she stared at her bedroom wall. She was extremely upset by Aslam's behavior but could hardly blame him. After all, she had avoided him for the past two months and now that they were finally together, she was leaving him again in a week.

I should feel blessed for being so loved, she thought, looking down at the ring for the umpteenth time.

Divya's mind turned towards her parents back home. Her mother was already in such a precarious mental state, and she doubted her father was doing much better. How would they react if they suddenly discovered their daughter was engaged to a man she had never once mentioned to them, and that she had decided to stay in India?

She remembered how her parents would not sleep until she came home, even if they knew she was with her best friend, Tatyana. Only last year had she been permitted to date, and her

225

parents had reluctantly conceded after much negotiation and under strict guidelines. The only reason they had even allowed her to go on an exchange program was because she was traveling to their homeland. They wanted her to love the people and traditions as they did, to become more cultured in order to make a better Indian wife when they found her an appropriate match.

If she agreed to Aslam's proposal, she was certain her parents would do everything in their power to stop her, especially her father. If she could barely fathom how quickly things had transpired, this would be beyond their comprehension. And breaking their hearts by such an announcement was unbearable.

At the same time, thinking about returning to Canada without Aslam was equally unbearable. She could understand Aslam's motives, and was torn at the prospect of being apart from him. For the past two months she had cursed herself daily for pushing the man she loved away, and now when they were finally united, she was making the same tragic mistake.

Divya smiled at the thought of Aslam being her husband. She realized that she too wanted to spend every waking moment with him, but what was more important—accepting his proposal for her own selfish happiness and breaking her parents' hearts, or returning to Canada and becoming as depressed as her father and mother? She had already spent the last two months grieving and basking in solitude and loneliness. It had driven her to a state of utter despair. How could she subject herself to such misery again, especially after she had finally discovered happiness and love?

What am I going to do? Oh God, what?

There was a knock on the door. Divya wiped her tears, and opened the door.

"Hi, Rekha, what's up?" she asked, trying to sound cheerful.

"You have a long distance phone call," Rekha said, scrutinizing her friend. "I think it is your father."

Does he know what happened? Divya panicked for a brief instant, before dismissing such a ridiculous thought.

"Thanks."

Rekha blocked the doorway. "Areé, what's wrong? I can get him to call you back, nah?"

"I'm fine."

"Never deceive your friends, nah? It is pointless. I know you better then you know yourself."

"I'm *fine*, Rekha. But thanks for caring."

Rekha frowned, but stepped aside and let her pass.

Divya walked to the opposite end of the floor with Rekha marching behind her.

"Hello?" Divya said into the receiver.

"Divya? It's Papa."

"Hi, Papa, it's good to hear from you."

"And you, beta."

"How are you?"

"Fine, just fine."

"And Mama? Is she feeling better since we last spoke?"

"No, beta, she isn't. Actually, that's why I'm calling."

Divya clutched the phone tightly. "Papa, what is it? You're scaring me."

"Beta, your mother's condition has worsened. The anti-depressants are not working, and the psychiatrist has put her through several electric-convulsive therapy sessions."

"Oh God...Papa, is she okay? Honestly, please tell me."

"It was awful, beta, and unsuccessful," he said, his voice distant and melancholy. "A side effect of the ECT has been significant memory loss, and she's now in the hospital under a suicide watch. The doctor wants to try another combination of anti-depressants, something new and more powerful, but the physical side effects are even more terrible."

Divya began crying.

Although Rekha could not hear what was being said on the other end of the line, she could piece the gist of the conversation, and sympathetically put her arm around Divya.

"I didn't want to tell you earlier, beta. I wanted you to finish your degree without worrying about her. But now that your finals are finished, I thought you deserved to know."

"Is there nothing we can do?"

"Don't cry, beta. Listen to me. I don't think another combination of drugs is the answer. There's another solution. And it is something *we* can do. I need your help."

"What is it, Papa? I'll do anything."

"There's a strong possibility that your mother may come out of her state if…"

"If? If what, Papa?"

"If she has another son."

Divya was startled, wondering if she had heard correctly. "Did you say another son?"

"Yes, beta, I did."

"Papa, I don't understand…how can *I* help with that?"

"As you know, your mother can no longer have children, and the adoption process here is lengthy, and even then there are no assurances. I've made arrangements with a…um…an old school friend. I want you to go to Madurai this Sunday and bring your new brother back home."

Divya was thunderstruck.

"Hello, hello? Hello, Divya?"

"I-I'm here Papa," she stammered.

"Did you hear what I said, beta?"

"Yes."

"Can you make it to Madurai by Sunday?"

"That's in Tamil Nadu, right?"

"Yes, I'll tell you how to get there. Write this down."

"Give me a sec," Divya said, motioning Rekha to get her a pen and paper.

Rekha pulled out a pen from her jeans, but had nothing to write on. Divya tore off the directory listing posted by the phone and flipped it over.

"Okay, Papa," she said, wondering if her father was thinking rationally.

"There are several buses and trains running from Bangalore to Madurai daily. Once you are in Madurai, you need to go to the Priceless Child Adoption Home. Got it?"

"Yes, the Priceless Child Adoption Home."

"Madurai is a sprawling city, so it's very easy to get lost. From the bus or train station take Vilachery Main Road up the slope of Pasumalai Hill to Sourashtra College, which is about six kilometers away. From there, you can see the Meenakashi Temple and the Vaigai River."

"Papa, you talk like you've been there before."

"No, no, no, don't be silly. My friend, the adoption home director, gave me good directions. Priceless Child is located near Sourashtra College. Do you have all that?"

Rekha impatiently leaned over Divya, trying to read what her friend was scribbling.

"Yes, Papa," Divya said, nudging Rekha aside. "And what is the director's name and phone number?"

Sedhu recited the information and added: "When you call, ask for Ramar, and arrange for a time to meet him."

"Yes, Papa."

Rekha poked Divya on the shoulder to show her what was written on the directory.

Divya handed the paper to Rekha, and motioned her away.

"Beta, be careful. We're counting on you. I'll call you on Monday once you've returned to the campus with the baby."

"Papa, what about documentation and immigration? I can't just take a baby out of the country like this, can I?"

"Don't worry, everything has been arranged."

"It just seems like a strange way of doing things," she said, uneasy about the entire situation.

"I know, beta. But you have to remember that things in India are done very differently than in Canada, as I am sure you've noticed. If you have any doubts or questions you can always call me."

"Okay, Papa."

"Thank you, Divya. I'm confident this will bring our family back together. Your mother and I love you very much. Never forget that."

Feelings of guilt consumed her as she thought about Aslam and her other predicament. Although she wanted to, this was not the appropriate time to tell him. Besides, she had not made a decision yet. What was the point of unnecessarily getting her father upset? He had enough things on his mind.

"Okay, bye, Papa,"

"See you next week, beta."

Divya hung up, and looked at Rekha's concerned face.

"This is madness, nah? You are actually going to do this?"

"Yeah, I think so."

"You will be alright, nah?" Rekha asked, giving her a hug.

229

"I hope so," Divya sighed, returning the embrace.

* * *

Divya awoke from troubled dreams of adoptions and proposals at the sound of knocking on her door. She was surprised that it was not even midnight. She had been asleep for less than an hour.

She got out of bed, and after making sure her T-shirt sufficiently covered her, warily opened the door. She warmly hugged the man standing outside.

"Oh, Divya, I am so sorry," Aslam spluttered. "I've been such an inconsiderate fool! We've lost so much time together, and I just want to make the most of the time we have left."

"Shhhh."

"If you have to return to Canada, so be it. I was being very selfish, and you were right. I was rushing you into something you're not ready for. Go back to Canada and be with your family, there's nothing more important. I'll work hard and follow you there. I don't care how long it takes. Please, forgive me. I made a promise that I would never leave you, and I won't. I'll never forgive myself for my behavior. I ruined our dinner. Even if we are thousands of miles apart, I'll always be with you, whether or not you're my wife."

She kissed him gently. "You don't have to say another word."

She closed the door, held his hand, and led him to her bed. He watched mesmerized as she took off her shirt. As he slowly kissed her, she undressed him and pulled a sheet over them. She sighed as he pressed his warm body against her.

He was about to kiss her again when he noticed the troubled look in her eyes. "Divya, what is it? Are you still upset at me?"

"No, that's not it."

"Then what?"

"Oz, I have to go to Madurai."

"What? Why?"

Divya told him about her father's request.

"I'm not sure of the adoption laws in India, but you're right, it does sound strange," Aslam said.

"Well, I have no choice, I must go. But I'm sure everything will be fine, won't it? I know Papa would never do anything dishonest or wrong."

"How could he if he raised such a wonderful daughter as you?" he said.

Divya felt more reassured, and rested her head against his chest.

"So, when do you have to be there?" he asked, stroking her hair.

"Sunday."

"Oh."

"I was hoping that you'd come with me."

"Really?"

"And I want to meet your parents as I believe their village is on the way."

He smiled and embraced her. "Nothing would make me happier."

"Good."

"Now, let me see...if we leave tomorrow morning by train then we can spend most of the day at the village, and leave for Madurai Sunday morning. You can meet my entire family. My younger sister will especially love you."

"I can't wait to see them. But, there is one problem."

"What's that?"

"You said we would leave tomorrow by *train?*" Divya said, anxiously recalling the last time she had traveled by Indian rail.

"Yes, why?"

She smiled sweetly at him. "Well...um...Oz, *honey*, about taking the train..."

Chapter 12
A Morning of Mourning
Saturday, November 17ᵗʰ, 2001

Divya was jolted awake and lurched forward as the bus braked with a piercing screech. The bus' diesel engine roared as the driver released the brake and slammed back onto the accelerator, the force tossing her back against the cushioned seat.

She groaned and opened her eyes, cursing her stupidity for taking the bus.

Why didn't I listen to Oz? she thought, turning towards the sleeping figure beside her. She was amazed that he had still not awoken.

He could sleep through a nuclear war.

Glancing at the moonlit landscape that rushed past her, she recalled how she had vehemently refused to take a second-class train to Madurai.

"Why are you so against taking the train, Divya?" Aslam had asked her.

"Oz, the last time I took the train was when I came to B'lore from Goa, and it was one of the worst and most traumatizing experiences in my life. It was hot, congested, and the bathrooms were disgusting. I mean, a thief ripped a woman's gold earrings out of her ears and jumped off the train! Out of her *ears*, Oz! I never want to endure anything like that again."

"What do you suggest we do? I don't have the money to fly or rent a car, and taking my motorcycle such a distance isn't feasible."

"We can take a luxury bus. I overheard two guys talking about it at the mess. The seats recline, are cushioned, and you don't have to share it with a dozen other people. You actually get your *own* seat. Besides, the price is comparable to the train."

"Yes, but it'll take several more hours to reach our destination, and the bus leaves at three in the morning, which means we'd have to get ready and leave now."

"Please, Oz."

"But we're in bed, warm, happy, and *naked*," he groaned.

She kissed him, and seductively rubbed his back and shoulders. "I'll give you back massages for the rest of the week."

"Ahhhhh," Aslam sighed as her hands moved down his back. "Okay, fine, but those naughty hands, and that sad, puppy dog look of yours won't work forever."

"Thanks, Oz. Let's go."

"We still have a few more minutes," he said, seductively tracing his finger along the side of her breast.

Divya grinned and tossed him his shirt.

"I should have agreed *after* the massage was over," he grumbled.

With little time to spare, both quickly packed and reached the bus station by autorickshaw; Aslam was unwilling to leave his motorcycle at the bus station over the weekend. The autorickshaw wallah had demanded three times the metered fare to take them to the bus station, and being so late at night, and with little alternatives, he reluctantly agreed. Even Divya felt slighted, and questioned whether the rewards of taking a luxury bus were worth the trouble. Her doubts vanquished the moment she had stepped onto the air-conditioned bus. She was ecstatic at how comfortable the cushioned seats appeared. An adorable boy—no older than seven or eight—sat in the front of the bus, and smiled sweetly at her. She had warmly returned the smile, feeling as if she belonged there.

As the vast majority of the passengers crammed themselves in the front and middle of the bus, Divya had moved to the empty back rows. With visions of spreading out across the back of the bus, and sleeping soundly through the entire trip, she took a seat in the rear without consulting Aslam.

"Divya, let's sit in the middle of the bus," he suggested.

"Come on, Oz. Let's sit in the back row. There's far more space there."

"But if we sit over there you'll—"

"*Please*," she said, giving him the puppy dog look again.

Aslam shrugged, and joined her in the back.

Reclining her seat and resting her head on the cushion, Divya sighed contently, and gave Aslam a dazzling smile.

This is how people should travel through India!
Divya had pulled out her novel and began to read.
"What are you reading, Divya?" Aslam asked.
"It's a new novel by Shaun Mehta."
"Oh, I've heard about it. How is it?"
"I've read better."

Patrons continued to fill the bus, and by the time the bus driver boarded the bus, every row was occupied except for the rows immediately in front of Divya. Dressed in his brown uniform, the bus driver took a seat behind his oversized steering wheel, and started the bus.

As the great diesel engine rumbled to life, the bus had shook so badly that Divya could not read a word of her book. When the bus left Bangalore and got onto the southbound highway—that seemed to have more craters than Berlin after the end of the Second World War—her entire body jerked as if she was being electrocuted.

With atrocious suspensions, and the rear wheels built near the middle of the bus, she understood why the other passengers had avoided sitting in the back of the bus. Gyrating like a frenzied marionette, she had turned to Aslam in dismay only to find him fast asleep, an expression of peace on his face.

For five hours she had tried to fall asleep, but the combination of reckless driving and terrible road conditions made it virtually impossible. As each agonizing hour passed, she promised God she would never ridicule the Indian railway system again. She would have done anything to have the gentle rocking of the train put her into sleep. Finally, blessedly, she had dozed off until the driver had awoken her with his foot indecisively switching from brake to accelerator.

Divya activated the blue indigo light of her Timex; she had miraculously slept for forty minutes. Like Aslam, the majority of the passengers were still asleep. Two rows ahead of her, a small girl was sleeping peacefully across her parent's laps. It was a touching scene, and she briefly considered sleeping on Aslam's shoulder. As the bus sped over several potholes she changed her mind, afraid she would end up breaking her jaw against his shoulder.

With her head continuously bouncing off the back of her seat, Divya wondered if the bus company had installed cushioned seats to prevent the passengers from cracking open their skulls.

Her thoughts were knocked out of her mind, and she grunted with irritation and pain as her teeth slammed together from the impact of the bus driving over a series of deep potholes.

I feel like I've been on a six-hour roller-coaster, she thought. *No, it's like I'm trapped on an out of control vibrating bed during an earthquake.*

She smiled and closed her eyes, continuing to think of other similes related to the brutal shaking that rattled her.

It's like a single engine plane caught in ferocious turbulence. No, a cowboy on the back of a wild stallion during a rodeo.

Divya felt something brush against her ankle.

Startled, she opened her eyes and looked down at two arms extending from underneath the seat in front of her. From the moonlight she could barely make out the face of the adorable little boy who had smiled at her when she had first boarded the bus.

The little scoundrel is trying to steal my bag!

She loudly cleared her throat.

The boy looked up, his eyes widening with fear at the sight of Divya staring down at him. She smiled grimly, shook her head with disapproval, and motioned the boy to retreat. He nodded, and disappeared into the shadows underneath the seat, crawling up the bus to loot other treasures.

She closed her eyes and returned to her mental game.

I feel like I'm a raft caught in a great stormy sea. Like dice in a tense game of backgammon. No, it's as if my head is locked in a paint-shaking machine, she pondered sleepily.

At full speed, the bus struck a large speed bump that marked the entrance of a small town. Divya's eyes fluttered open; a scream trapped in her throat. As the bus hit the speed bump and soared into the air, she prayed for a painless demise.

When the bus crashed back down to the road, half the passengers were projected off their seats. The wind was knocked out of Divya so badly that she thought she had cracked a rib. The young couple two rows ahead struck their heads on the overhead baggage compartments, their child tossed off their laps and onto the floor like a sack of potatoes. The little girl began crying.

The passengers cursed and groaned. The bus driver continued to drive dangerously—switching between brake and accelerator—unsympathetic for the suffering he had caused his passengers.

"What happened?" Aslam muttered, half-asleep.

"We nearly died!" Divya cried. He did not respond. "Oz? *Oz?* Are you alright?"

She received a snore in response.

After two more hours of sleepless mind games, Divya shook Aslam awake as they reached the town of Vadippatti. They retrieved their backpacks and disembarked.

"What a glorious morning!" Aslam exclaimed, admiring the sphere of orange fire blazing through the palm trees in the horizon.

Divya had a splitting headache, and her anger was amplified by his cheerfulness. As the bus drove off and blanketed them in a huge cloud of black smoke, he beamed at her, oblivious to the deep creases of irritation across her forehead.

"You're right, Divya, the bus wasn't bad at all. What did you think of it?"

"Like a James Bond martini," she grumbled.

* * *

Ladha sat up from her metal bench as the door to her cell opened.

A girl walked in with a tray of food, and the cell door slammed shut behind her. She put the tray down without a word, her eyes on the floor.

"Suma?"

The girl looked up fearfully, her face covered with fresh bruises.

"Oh God, what happened?" Ladha gasped, reaching for the girl.

Suma stepped back, and put a trembling finger to her swollen, cut lips.

"If you speak, will they hurt you again?" Ladha asked.

The little girl trembled and fought back her tears.

"Did they touch you, Suma?"

The girl turned away from Ladha, sobbing.

"Suma?"

The prison door opened, and a female guard harshly beckoned for the child.

Acknowledging Ladha's questions with the slightest movement of her head and a flash of her teary eyes, Suma submissively lowered her head, and hurried out of the cell.

"I'm entitled an hour with her," Ladha protested angrily to the guard.

The door slammed shut with a thunderous, metallic echo.

The guard roughly grabbed the girl, and escorted her down the hall.

Furious and appalled, Ladha promised to tell everything that had happened to Mr. Kumar as soon as he arrived.

With nothing else to do, she picked up the tray, and fingered the revolting food with disgust. Roots and wild grass were thrown into the soup of rotten, watery rice. She forced the slimy gruel into her mouth, and swallowed with difficulty.

Ladha put the tray back down, and after a moment of hesitation, emptied the glass of water. She peered into the bottom of the glass where half an inch of mud sat. She knew the water was unsafe and contaminated, but she had little choice. The cell was suffocating, and her thirst was far too overwhelming to ignore.

She sighed, and reflected back at her time in the penitentiary. Although she would be released tomorrow, she could not believe that she had only been in Nillakoti Jail for nearly two days. She felt as if years had passed.

Despite the little time she had been incarcerated, she had quickly adjusted to the routine. Twice a day she was marched with the other prisoners to the common latrines. Hundreds would line up and wait up to an hour to use one of the fetid, open stalls. The guards promptly beat any prisoner that defecated or urinated before their turn, or took too long to use the loo.

These opportunities were the only time Ladha was able to interact with the prison population. Although she spoke little, and was always in line with unfamiliar faces, she absorbed every word she heard and every sight she saw, later trying to sort the information during her periods of solitude back in her cell. It was one of many ways Ladha had learned to occupy her mind, and prevent it from going mad with boredom or worrying excessively about her kidnapped baby.

On her first morning in prison, standing in the queue for the loo, Ladha had discovered that at least half a dozen prisoners were dying a week from a tuberculosis epidemic plaguing the prison. She had also overheard that a new batch of young children were coming into the prison later that day to be auctioned off as slaves.

"What are you staring at?" asked a severe looking woman to whom Ladha had been listening.

"Don't talk to her, she's an 'A' prisoner," the woman's shorthaired friend said bitterly.

Ladha noticed that the two women had the letter B emblazoned on their prison uniforms while she had an A on hers.

"So?" Ladha said, a little too defiantly.

The severe looking woman menacingly glared at her for some time before finally answering. "So, that means that you're treated better than the rest of us. See that prisoner being beaten over there?"

Ladha turned to see three guards kicking a whimpering prisoner, who was curled on the ground in a fetal position. "Yes."

"She's a C-class prisoner. They're treated the worst because they can't afford to bribe the guards, or have no influential friends protecting them. And see that prisoner with the disfigured arm?" Ladha gave a circular nod, despite not wanting to hear anymore. "The guards broke her arm two months ago so badly that an inch of bone was torn through her flesh," the severe-looking woman continued nonchalantly. "The guards said they would take her to the hospital only if she paid them. When she said she had no money, they left her in her cell."

"What about the prison doctor?" Ladha asked, appalled.

"He eventually applied some medicine and bandaged the wound, but allowed the bone to be exposed and the wound to become infected. There was even a journalist that visited the prison and discovered the truth, but the guards defended their action, claiming that the police were short staffed, and could not send an escort to take the prisoner to the hospital in time. Interestingly, the poor prisoner was sent to the hospital the moment the journalist left. The wound was tended to, but she will have that deformity for the rest of her life."

Although a part of Ladha was disturbed by the discrimination system within the prison, another part of her was grateful that she was an A-prisoner. She silently thanked Judge Seetha for fulfilling her promise.

Deciding it was time to change the subject, Ladha asked: "Once these little girls are auctioned off, what do they do?"

"Why, you interested?" the shorthaired woman asked, raising an eyebrow.

"Perhaps."

"Well, they can be anything you want. They can serve you, or clean your cell, but they're usually used for—"

"Companionship?" Ladha offered.

The two women looked at each other and snickered at Ladha's naivety.

"Sure, if that's what you want to call it," the severe looking woman said.

Suddenly understanding what she was implying, Ladha tried to mask her horror. "How old are these girls usually?"

The shorthaired woman shrugged. "Anywhere between nine to thirteen. They're usually homeless children living on the street, rounded up by the police at night and brought here. Their disappearance is rarely questioned by the public, who are pleased to be spared from being hounded by the daily nuisance of beggars."

"Don't forget that that adoption home also donates unwanted children," the severe looking woman added.

"And the police and guards are okay with this?" Ladha asked.

"Okay? Are you serious? They're the ones that organize it. The guards make a lot of money, and it keeps the prisoners happy. The police also make money, and the streets are cleared of beggars. For everyone it is a winning situation."

Except the poor girls, Ladha thought sadly.

"How do you bid for one?" Ladha asked, after they had moved three paces in the line.

"With anything you have. But soap and bidis are usually the currency of choice."

"Do you have one?"

"What, a girl? No. But, I've been saving for five years, so I imagine I'll have one within the next year," the severe looking woman said, her eyes sparkling with anticipation.

"But what if you two combined your resources," Ladha suggested. "Then you two could get a girl faster and share her. See, I'll help," she added, dropping a full bar of soap into the woman's hands.

The severe looking woman eyed Ladha suspiciously, trying to determine the motive for such generosity. "What do you want for this?"

"Just that if you win a bid, I shall meet this girl for one hour over the next two days. She can bring me my food, and clean my cell during that time. Two hours of her time is a fair exchange, no?"

The severe looking woman did not respond; it was her turn to use the latrine. She squatted and stared at Ladha, contemplating the offer. When she finished, and was being escorted back to her cell, she gave Ladha a circular nod in agreement.

During the rest of the first day, Ladha lay on her cot wondering how the auction had gone. Her first full day in Nillakoti had dragged on, despite being interrupted by a visit from Judge Seetha's personal aid, Mr. Kumar. Disappointed that the judge had not personally come to see her, she had accepted Mr. Kumar's explanation that recent circumstances made it impossible for the judge to personally visit. Mr. Kumar had further told Ladha that it was now his duty to ensure she was not being physically or mentally abused by the police or guards. Satisfied that Ladha was being treated well, Mr. Kumar had promised to return the following day to check on her again.

That evening when Ladha was escorted back to the latrine, she was unable to find the severe looking woman or her shorthaired companion that had taken her soap. She heard a couple of remarks about the bidding, but was unable to decipher the outcome. Disheartened, and reproaching herself for wasting such a valuable commodity as soap, she returned to her cell condemned to spend the night with her endless thoughts.

It was a few hours later when the eleven-year old girl had entered her cell with the tray of food, and began to take off her clothes. Appalled, Ladha stopped her, explaining she only wanted to talk, to hear Suma's ordeal so she could somehow help her. Suma was stunned by the request, but willingly complied. For the next hour, Ladha learned how Suma had grown up in a nearby Dalit village, and was kidnapped at the age of six in the middle of the night, like her own baby son. Suma explained how she was taken to an adoption home in Madurai where she would clean the place and serve her masters until a prospective couple—usually from a Western country like America, Australia, or England—would come to see her. That would be the only time she would be bathed, properly fed, and dressed in clean, fancy clothes. After five years of being rejected and having other children chosen instead of her, she was sold to the prison.

Hearing Suma's aching tale as she held the weeping child to her bosom, Ladha had instantly fallen in love, looking at the child like a daughter. Ladha promised Suma she would speak to Mr. Kumar the following day, and beg him to help her.

Just as Suma was leaving, Ladha was struck with a thought. She asked Suma the name of the adoption home. Once she was alone in the cell, Ladha locked the name in her memory, feeling a glimmer of hope that she may find her lost baby.

The sound of rattling keys in the lock to her cell door broke Ladha's reverie.

She stood up as the door swung open and Mr. Kumar walked in.

"Hello, Ladha," he said once the door was sealed behind him.

"Mr. Kumar, I'm glad to see you."

"What's wrong?" he asked, seeing her worried face. "Are they mistreating you?"

"No, no."

"Then, what is it?"

"It's another girl, Mr. Kumar. Her name is Suma. She's only eleven years old, and a slave like many others at this awful prison. They beat and abuse her. You must help me free her."

Frowning, Mr. Kumar took off his spectacles, wiping the lenses with his tie. "My responsibility is for your well being, Ladha. I don't have the authority or resources to help every woman or child in the Indian penal system."

"But they're raping her! She's an innocent child!"

Mr. Kumar sighed wearily. "I'll see what I can do. I can't promise you anything, but I'll try. Her name is Suma, you said?"

"Yes," she whispered, her eyes moist with gratitude. "Thank you, Mr. Kumar. May God bless you and your children."

"It's too soon to begin blessing me, Ladha. Now, you seem to be fine, so the only other matter is your discharge. You'll be released tomorrow morning. I'll meet you outside the gate to ensure everything goes smoothly. Understand?"

"Yes, thank you, sahib," she said, pressing her hands together in front of her forehead. "Thank you from the bottom of my heart. And thank Judge Seetha for me as well. She's a wonderful woman."

"I will. Good evening, Ladha," he said, knocking on the door to signal the guard he was ready to leave.

Once Mr. Kumar was gone, Ladha realized with distress that he had not asked what Suma's last name was, or what she looked like.

* * *

"Come on, Divya, we're almost there!" Aslam exclaimed, walking quicker.

Drenched with sweat, Divya's frown deepened as she tried to keep up.

They had been hiking up the dirt road for over an hour, and during that time she had become increasingly aware that the heat from the rising sun was growing in intensity.

And this is November. How the heck do these people survive in the summer? she wondered.

She adjusted her backpack, and tried to quicken her pace to catch up to him.

"How much further?" she panted.

"Another two or three kilometers," he said cheerfully.

"Oz, I don't think I can last that long in this heat."

"Oh, it's not *that* hot."

A shadow caught her eye, and she looked up to see a small shape plummeting towards them. Divya stepped back with alarm as it landed with a thud on the dirt road beside them. They exchanged uneasy looks before inching towards the object. Divya was shocked when she realized it was a bird.

"Shit, it just died from the heat and fell to the ground," she said.

"We don't know it's from the heat."

She looked at him incredulously. "Are you suggesting it died from a heart attack then? Oz, the bird fell from the sky!"

Aslam inched forward, and snapped his finger back when he touched the bird. "It's half cooked. Hungry?"

"That's not funny."

"Okay, perhaps we should take a break for a while."

They took refuge from the heat underneath a nearby tree. As Divya thirstily consumed half a liter of water, Aslam extracted a shiny cooking pan from his backpack.

"What's that for? Don't tell me you're seriously going to finish cooking that poor bird?" she asked apprehensively.

"No, silly! It's a gift for my mother. She has been using the same old pan for as long as I can remember. It's warped and partially melted, and she's always complaining about how she has trouble cooking with it. I've been saving up for some time to give her this. I can't wait to see her reaction. She'll love it. I did a lot of research, and this is definitely the most durable state-of-the-art pan on the market. It should last her twenty years."

"I'm sure she'll love it. You're a good son, Oz."

Aslam smiled, and packed the pan back into his bag.

After taking a much needed power nap, Divya felt rejuvenated enough to continue the arduous journey to Aslam's village.

"What time is it?" he asked impatiently after forty minutes.

She checked her watch. "Um...quarter to twelve."

"I can already see it now. Amma will be in the kitchen preparing lunch, and Appa will be sitting on the porch, helping my brother with his studies."

"And your sister?"

"The village is just over this ridge!" He quickened his pace.

"Wait up, Oz!"

Divya was relieved that he stopped at the top of the ridge. She panted up beside him, and was appalled at the sight below her.

The village of Desikapuram was in ruins.

"Oh dear God," she breathed.

243

Aslam dropped his bag and ran towards the scorched remnants of the village.

Divya chased him past charred huts and pyres until she found him weeping in a pile of ashes in front of a skeletal frame of a hut.

She fell to her knees and embraced him.

"They were my life," he whispered, scooping a handful of ash and watching it fall through his fingers. "Now they're dust."

Divya was speechless. She was still shocked at the destruction surrounding her. How could such atrocities still happen in the twenty-first century?

"Aslam?"

Divya looked up. An old man pulling a wagon was approaching them.

Aslam unsteadily stood up, and ran to the old man. "Murthy, where's Appa and Amma?" he desperately asked the village tutor in Tamil.

"Oh Aslam, it *is* you," Murthy said, tearfully. "I prayed that you'd never have to see this."

"Where is my sister and brother, Murthy? Where's my family? *Where?*"

"Aslam, I don't know how to tell you this," Murthy said, unable to meet his dreadful gaze. "Your father and siblings, the entire village, were slaughtered by the Zamindars."

"No!" Aslam cried, squeezing his eyes shut.

"I am very sorry, child."

"And Amma? You didn't mention her. Did she survive the attack?"

"Your Amma survived the attack, but..."

"But?"

"After the attack, she cremated your family, and then was arrested and taken by the district police."

"So, she lives. We must free her."

"It's too late for that, child."

"Too late? What do you mean too late?"

Murthy avoided Aslam's desperate stare.

"What is it, Murthy? Tell me!" Aslam demanded, shaking the old man.

Divya stared fearfully at the two men, wondering what was being said.

Murthy sadly motioned his head towards the rickety wagon he had been pulling. It was then that Aslam noticed the shape of a body underneath a white cloth.

Aslam let go of the old man and walked up to the wagon. He reached for the sheet but then hesitated, terrified of what he may see if he removed it.

A gust of wind blew across the village and the white sheet tore off the wagon revealing the battered, naked body of a middle-aged woman.

"Dear Allah!" Aslam screamed. *"Noooo!"*

Divya covered her mouth with horror.

"Guran died in Madurai prison," the old man said sorrowfully as he recovered the sheet and respectfully covered the body. "The police said it was from natural causes."

* * *

Divya watched Aslam lovingly place the new frying pan beside his mother. He kissed her bruised, cold forehead, and took the torch from Murthy. Fighting back his tears, Aslam set the pyre ablaze.

Despite the crackling fire, Divya shivered. She was surrounded by death. She thought about her brother's funeral.

Aslam stared dully as the flames consumed his mother. Divya wanted so desperately to comfort him, but she was lost for words, and stopped herself from holding him, justifying he needed to be alone.

Or is it that you are still too afraid of reaching out to him even though you know he needs you so?

Once the pyre was reduced to smoking ashes, Aslam walked up to Murthy and embraced him. "Thank you for bringing my mother back here, old friend. She would have wanted her ashes to nourish the soil of the village she helped build."

"She was a wonderful mother and friend, child. The honor was mine," said the old man, wiping the tears from his ancient eyes.

"Murthy, what happened to Punduthai's husband, my brother-in-law?"

245

"Butchered ruthlessly as he tried to defend the village from the Zamindars. T-They stuck his severed head on a stake, like any other man who fought them, as a warning. He fought bravely to defend his family, but there were too many...how can we fight with knifes and pitchforks against guns?" Murthy sighed heavily. "Guran cremated him along with your sister and their unborn child."

Aslam bit his lower lip, refusing to shed a tear. He was silent for a long time. "Murthy, my dear friend, can you do me one last favor?"

Divya watched as Aslam spoke gently with the old man in Tamil.

She was caught off guard when Aslam picked up his bag, and said to her: "Divya, Murthy here will look after you tonight, and take you to the adoption home in Madurai. He's a trusted friend who knew my parents before I was born. He'll make sure you return safely back to Bangalore."

"Where are you going, Oz?"

Aslam did not respond, but kissed her on the cheek.

She watched with disbelief as he walked out of the village, and disappeared over the ridge.

No, she thought, shaking her head. *I'm not letting him go.*

She ran after him, ignoring the calls from Murthy.

Divya climbed the ridge, and chased after the small shape in the distance.

"Oz! Oz!" she cried, breaking into a sprint.

Aslam stopped and turned to face her.

"Where are you going?" she demanded.

He did not answer, his face rigid and without emotion, his eyes dark and cold.

"Oz?"

"Go back to the village, Divya."

"I asked you a question."

"Just do it!" he shouted angrily. "*Go!*"

Divya stepped back, frightened by his fury.

"I'm going to find the people who did this. I'm going to torture each and every one of those bastards, tear them apart with my hands."

"Which people? Who did this?"

"The Zamindars. Those cowards butchered my family."

"Who are the Zamindars?"

"Divya, listen to me. This is not your fight or your concern. Get your adopted brother and return to your country. Do you understand me? Leave, now!"

"Oz, you can't do this. These people will kill you."

"I don't need to hear this."

Aslam turned and began walking down the road.

"Oz, I know what you're going through, but this is not the answer. I lost my brother as well. Please, Oz, listen to me. We can get through this together."

He ignored her.

"Please, don't go, Oz," she cried. "You promised you would never leave me."

He hesitated for a moment, but then kept on moving.

No, this can't be happening. I won't let him go. I can't lose him, again.

"Oz, I love you. I couldn't bear the thought of losing you."

He did not stop.

"I've come to a decision regarding your proposal!"

He froze.

"You kept asking how I learned to play badminton. As soon as I learned to walk my father taught me how to play. With patience and love we would play every Sunday. He trained me to become the female champion at my high school and University. God, I can still remember how proud he was. And now, I want you, the father of my unborn children, to teach them the same values that my father taught me. I want my husband to weep with pride when our children surpass our expectations. I want *you*, Oz. Mourn and remember your family, pass on their legacy, but swear on your unborn children, and to me, that you'll forget this suicidal crusade for revenge. Swear it, Oz!"

Aslam slowly turned around.

"Because I want to build a future with my husband."

He walked towards her, tears streaming down his face.

"Marry me, Oz."

He nodded and fiercely embraced her.

"Promise me you'll never go after those people," she wept. "Promise me you'll abandon all of these thoughts and create a life with me. Promise me, Oz. *Promise!*"

"I promise, Divya," he choked emotionally, holding her tightly. "I promise."

Chapter 13
Family Reunions
Sunday, November 18th, 2001

Ladha stepped out of the main prison gate, and waited for her eyes adjust to the morning sunshine. She noticed Mr. Kumar standing nearby in front of a shiny Ambassador, his crisp suit matching the color of the ivory car.

Mr. Kumar smiled, and motioned her over. He opened the back door for her.

She gave him an uneasy look, wondering if this was some sort of trap.

"It's okay, Ladha, you have nothing to fear. Please, have a seat," said a familiar voice from within the car.

Ladha warily bent forward to see Judge Seetha sitting in the back seat, still dressed in her black gown as if she were in court. Ladha smiled with relief, and sat down beside the judge. Mr. Kumar shut the door, got into the front seat, and instructed the driver to start the car.

"Where can we drop you, Ladha?"

"No, you've already done too much."

"Ladha, please. Your journey to search for your son will be difficult. Let me do this. Now, where would you like to go?"

"Priceless Child Adoption Home in Madurai."

"Kishore, did you hear that?" the judge asked her driver.

"Yes, madam."

"God bless you for your kindness," Ladha said.

"It is my honor to help someone so brave."

Ladha wondered whether to tell the judge about the little girl enslaved in the prison. The judge had already done so much for her, but Suma was doomed if she didn't ask for assistance. Ladha was unsure whether Mr. Kumar had fulfilled his promise. Only the judge could help Suma, and this was the only opportunity to ask.

Ladha sighed deeply. "Judge Seetha, did Mr. Kumar tell you about Suma?" Judge Seetha turned from Ladha, and looked outside the window. "Judge Seetha?"

"Mr. Kumar," said the judge, her voice distant.

Mr. Kumar turned around in his front seat, and handed Ladha a photograph.

Ladha gasped at the grisly sight of the naked girl lying on the dirty, cement floor.

"Is this Suma?" asked the judge grimly, continuing to look outside.

Ladha began crying, cursing herself for giving those two women her bar of soap. It was because of her that Suma was dead.

"I'm sorry, Ladha," Judge Seetha sighed wearily. "But you mustn't blame yourself."

"I was a fool thinking I could save her."

"Never believe her death, or your efforts, were in vain. I'll not rest until the atrocities happening at that jail are stopped. With the loss of this innocent child, those responsible will no longer be able to hide. Justice will be served, Ladha. Suma's death will lead to countless other children being saved, and none of that would've been possible without you bringing Suma's situation to my attention."

Ladha did not believe a word the judge said. The law had never done anything to protect the downtrodden, and the judge was naïve if she thought otherwise. Ladha suddenly wanted to be free from these people. She didn't want to be near anyone, and for an instant she yearned to be back in solitary confinement where she could be left alone in her sorrow and despair. The world was too dreadful to live in.

No one spoke as they drove into Madurai. As per Ladha's instructions, the driver parked the Ambassador a few buildings away from the Priceless Child Adoption Home.

The judge took hold of Ladha's hand, and placed ten thousand rupees in it.

Ladha stared at the stack of bills with disbelief. It was more money then she had ever seen.

Before Ladha could protest, Judge Seetha firmly said: "I don't blame you for not having faith in our justice system, but I want you to know Ladha that there's far more good than evil, beauty than ugliness, happiness than pain. Take this money, find your son, and start a new life. Just because we don't understand why things happen, doesn't mean there's no God or no purpose in the grand scheme of things. Some things are merely beyond our scope of understanding. But, one thing is certain—there's always a reason for everything. God is with you, Ladha, but if you need someone a little closer, you can call upon me at any time. Here's my card with all of my contact numbers."

Ladha was flabbergasted. Tears of gratitude and guilt for questioning the judge's sincerity spilled from her eyes. She hugged the judge.

"Now go, and may God guide you to your son," Judge Seetha said gently, closing Ladha's hand over the money.

Ladha wiped her eyes, and stepped out of the car.

* * *

Sub-Inspector Rao angrily watched as the Untouchable got out of the Ambassador and crossed the street, walking hurriedly towards the adoption home. He did not want to believe it, but his informants had been correct of her intentions. The woman was far more tenacious than he had anticipated.

Once the Ambassador was out of sight, he revved the engine of his motorcycle, and drove onto the sidewalk towards Ladha, ignoring any pedestrian or animal in his path. People cried out in alarm and dogs yelped in surprise as he sped past Ladha. He swerved the motorcycle in front of her, its tires screeching to a stop.

The sub-inspector felt a surge of satisfaction from the mortified look locked on her face.

She fearfully stepped back as Sub-Inspector Rao climbed off his motorcycle and menacingly advanced towards her.

He grabbed her by the arms. "If you're not outside the city by nightfall, I swear that not even your friend the judge will be able to save you," he seethed, squeezing her arms until she whimpered with pain.

The police officer threw her roughly to the ground.

"What's this?" he asked, noticing the wad of rupees clenched between her fists.

"No!" Ladha screamed as he wrenched open her hand and snatched the money.

"My, my, my. How does a convicted criminal get so much money the day of her release? No doubt you stole it!" he snarled, raising his hand to slap her.

Ladha cringed, but the sub-inspector caught himself, still afraid of the power his aunt the judge had in the city.

Breathing heavily, his eyes filled with rage, he pocketed the rupees. Never taking his eyes off Ladha, he slowly mounted his motorcycle. "Remember what I said. I'll be watching you. You have until sunset otherwise I'll burn you alive. And if you take one more step towards this adoption home, I promise your baby will end up like that Untouchable whore Suma."

Ladha shook her head, her hands covering her face, unable to comprehend the cruelty of the man.

"*Get out of here!*" he screamed.

Sub-Inspector Rao smiled maliciously as she tearfully ran away.

He started his motorcycle and roared down the street in the opposite direction.

* * *

Sitting underneath the metal awning of the roadside Punjabi fast-food stall, Divya watched with fascination and apprehension as the police officer cut the motorcycle in front of the woman, and began to harass her.

"Oz, are you watching this?" Divya asked.

She turned to Aslam who was gazing at the sprawling city in the valley below them, his mind elsewhere.

Divya turned back to the scene just as the police officer was getting back onto his motorcycle and the woman was running away.

I wonder what that poor woman did? Divya wondered.

As the police officer's motorcycle roared off, Divya looked compassionately back at her fiancé. The waiter arrived with their meals, but neither of them touched the food, each lost in their own thoughts.

They had barely said a word during their journey from the village to Madurai, and while she understood that he needed time to grieve, she still hated to see him seem so lost. She wanted to reach out and hold him, but again found herself resisting the urge. She thought back on the past week, and could hardly believe how quickly things had transpired. A week ago she was not even speaking to him, and now they were engaged. It was insane. She was going to be a wife! How could she take care of her husband if she barely knew how to take care of herself?

For an instant, panic and doubt surged over her like a tsunami. She felt as if she were drowning, struggling for breath, near the brink of hyperventilating. Divya forced herself to calm down and focus on the immediate task. If she thought too much of the future, she became overwhelmed.

Take it a moment at a time, Divya. You can do this.

A burst of frenzied clucking snapped Divya from her thoughts. The sound was coming within a cardboard box situated by a goat tied to a nearby post. Divya had assumed the box was empty. She leaned forward and peered into it, surprised to see three live chickens snapping at one another, their legs tied together. She realized with pity that the goat's neck was tied by rope to its right leg, preventing it from running away, and forcing its mouth to the ground where it was condemned to a life of eating grass or sniffing dirt.

Divya did not know what was worse—being trapped in bondage, or having one's head chopped off and being served for lunch.

"Oz, do you want some chicken or goat with your rice and yogurt?" Divya asked.

Aslam did not reply; he continued to absentmindedly toy with his food.

"At least we know it'll be fresh?" she joked.

He did not react. She sighed as she studied him, wishing she knew how to help ease his pain.

Divya took a few bites of her tasteless food, and admired the panoramic view of the noisy city and muddy Vaigai River below. The enormous Meenakshi Temple was especially enthralling, its twelve pyramid-like towers jutting spectacularly from the center of congested heart of Madurai. That morning on the bus to the city, an old Australian couple had told her that Madurai was founded over two and a half thousand years ago, becoming the cultural center of the ancient Pandya Kingdom. It amazed Divya that the temple—built in dedication to the consort of Lord Shiva—was erected before the birth of Christ.

Her eyes moved from the valley below to the two other prominent hills that surrounded the city.

Huh, interesting. Those hills do resemble an elephant and snake like that Aussie couple said. I wonder if the hill we're on looks like a cow.

Divya wanted to share her appreciation of the temple and view with Aslam, but decided against it. She continued to survey the city and surrounding area, unaware of the waiter replacing their half eaten plates with the bill.

Geez, the view is breathtaking.

She glanced at her watch, and a wave of uneasiness struck her—it was time.

"Oz, I'm going now...I'll be back soon...okay?"

Much to her surprise, he turned towards her and gently squeezed her hand. Before she could react, he let go of her hand, and turned back to the view of the hills and city.

It may not be much, but it's a start, she thought, encouraged.

Divya sighed and stood up. As she crossed the street, she examined the Priceless Child Adoption Home, which was under construction. Standing on bamboo ladders, several workers were working on restoring the front facade of the aged, three-story building.

Absorbed with the adoption home, she failed to notice a hunched figure shuffling towards her.

Although the woman spoke in Tamil, Divya could understand from her desperate tone that she was a beggar asking for money.

Still focused on the adoption home, Divya shooed the woman away with a hostile gesture. It took her a moment to comprehend what she had done. She turned, and was horrified at the gruesome sight before her.

The woman's face was so deformed that Divya did not know whether to scream or weep. It was as if her face had been melted from acid, carved up, and then set on fire. Her right eye was where her cheek should have been, her skin was scarred and raw looking, and she was missing her upper lip, exposing rotting teeth.

Divya could not begin to comprehend the anguish and suffering the beggar must have endured, and wondered what type of awful experiences had caused the poor woman to end up with such a deformity. Had she been born with such monstrous abnormalities, or were they man-made?

Her legs locked from shock, Divya helplessly watched the hunched beggar shuffle to the other end of the street and disappear into a narrow alley. She wanted to run after the woman and give her all her money, to beg for forgiveness for being so unkind and insensitive, but she did not move.

Guilt and sorrow consumed her.

I'm the ugly one, she shamefully realized.

Divya knew that the image of the grotesque looking beggar, and her own impotence, would forever be tattooed on her mind.

The driver of a bright yellow autorickshaw impatiently honked its horn, and angrily gestured at Divya to get off the center of the street.

Shaking with remorse, she crossed the street and hurried into the adoption home.

* * *

"And lastly, what about Valli?"

"Who?" Ramar asked, putting his feet on the table and studying the crusty corns on his toes.

"She's the girl who serves you meals and works in the kitchen," explained the impeccably dressed, longhaired man.

"What's her age?"

"Eleven."

"How long have we had her?"

"Um, seven years," the middle-aged man said, scanning the list.

"Bah, if no one is willing to adopt her, then perhaps someone will want her as a whore," Ramar sneered, fascinated with his feet. "Sell her to the Mumbai brothels for the best price you can."

"Have you seen what she looks like? We would insult our friends in Mumbai if we sent her. Besides, I've already heard rumors that she has been taken, which would considerably lower her value."

"Then send her with the next batch to Nillakoti Jail for the auction next month," Ramar yawned.

"Very good, sir. The prisoners or guards will pay a handsome price for her and are far less particular on her sexual history or preferences."

"Wait," Ramar said, forgetting about his feet and sitting up. "I want this one sent as a gift to the Head Jailer. No charge. He likes his girls especially young."

"Yes, sir." The man smiled as he made a note on his pad.

The black phone beside Ramar began ringing. "Yes?" he answered. "Who? Yes, send her in immediately."

"Is there anything else, sir?"

"I need those papers for the child I mentioned to you this morning."

The man opened his briefcase, extracted a file, and placed it on the table.

Ramar quickly flipped through the documents and grunted with approval.

"Now, leave me," Ramar commanded. "But if there's any problem, call me on my personal cell."

The man put away his notes, sealed his briefcase, and let the burly security guard open the door for him. He stepped aside as a lovely young woman walked past him. He hesitated for a moment to admire his boss' selection, and then closed the door behind him.

Ramar was on his feet, momentarily stunned by the young woman's beauty.

My God, she looks just like her mother. Sedhu, you bastard, it was a grave mistake to send her. You could have at least warned me.

Ramar dismissed the guard. The muscular man gave a quizzical look, wondering if he had heard right; he had never been ordered to leave his master's presence when there was a visitor. Ramar gave him an ugly look to confirm he had heard correctly. The bodyguard left the room.

Ramar pressed his sweaty palms against his white kurta pajama, and extended his hand to the apprehensive young woman. For the first time in years he felt nervous, a feeling he despised. He was glad there was no one else to witness it; much of his power stemmed from his ability to demonstrate cold, apathetic strength and conviction to his people.

The young woman hesitated for a moment, studying the face that somehow seemed familiar, before shaking his hand.

"Please, have a seat," he said in English, with only a trace of an accent. He warmly gestured her to the other wooden chair in the plain room.

"Thank you," Divya said anxiously, the sparse room reminding her of the countless, generic police interrogation rooms she saw in American movies.

"Would you like something to drink?" he offered, fascinated by her Canadian accent.

"No, no thanks."

"No? Come, you must have something. Mango juice, Limca, Fanta, Thums Up cola?"

"I'm fine, really."

Ramar picked up the phone and barked orders in Tamil.

"Are you hot?" he asked. "Let me turn up the ceiling fan."

He stood and fidgeted with the ceiling fan controls.

"Please, I really am fine."

Ramar sat down again and tried to calm himself. He felt as if he was staring at his newlywed wife over twenty years back.

My dear Rani, he thought wistfully.

Divya shifted in her chair, uncomfortable at how the adoption house director was staring at her.

"So, you and Papa went to the same school together in Punjab?" she asked, breaking the silence.

"What? Oh yes, Punjab."

"How did you two meet?"

"Um, in class."

"And you two were good friends?"

"The best."

Divya did not know what else to say.

"You look exactly like your mother," Ramar said.

"Oh, and how do you know that?"

Ramar leaned forward. "Because, Divya, I am your—"

The door to the room opened, and the serving girl Valli entered holding two glasses of chilled mango juice. Ramar glared venomously at her for the intrusion. Head bowed, she placed the drinks on the wooden table, submissively averting eye contact. Valli hurriedly left the room.

257

"You were saying?" Divya said.

Ramar hesitated.

Telling her suddenly did not seem right. He was not in control of his emotions, and felt uneasy of revealing anything that he may regret later. He needed to carefully plan things and consider the consequences. This was not the right time.

Ramar was a man obsessed with control. He never got intoxicated, terrified at the prospect of losing his inhibitions, even for an instant. Control was crucial for him, and the thought of losing it so quickly at the mere glance of his daughter was very unsettling.

After all these years, telling her won't solve anything...yet, he reasoned.

"Because I'm your mother's, I should say, *was* your mother's friend when she first met your fath...Sedhu in Punjab. Your resemblance to your mother is striking. When you first walked into the room I thought I was looking at her, over twenty years ago."

"So you introduced my parents?" Divya asked, intrigued at learning more about her parents' past.

"In a way," Ramar said, struggling to mask his remorse.

I should never have left you, Rani. I should have raised a family with you. Divya is such a lovely creature. I would be the envy of every man for having such a beautiful wife and daughter.

"Then it is a pleasure to meet you, for without you I would not be here," Divya said with a smile so dazzling that Ramar was momentarily speechless.

You have no idea how true that is, he thought.

Ramar felt as if his heart was breaking. Too many memories from the past were rushing back. He never anticipated that the sight of his daughter would unleash such pain, and he simultaneously cursed and blessed his brother for bringing Divya back to him.

"Let's get down to business, shall we?" Ramar said uneasily before she could ask him more questions about the past.

Divya nodded politely, and took a sip of her drink. "So, what do we need to do to finalize the adoption process?"

Ramar picked up the phone and punched the numbers. He said a few words in Tamil, and hung up. "It should only be a moment."

She nodded, and focused on sipping her mango juice to avoid meeting the eyes of the Director, who continued to gape at her.

Ramar realized that there was a melancholy aura around Divya; it made her further resemble Rani, especially during those last few months of their marriage before that fateful day. Ramar struggled to hold back his tears, and was relieved when the door to the room opened.

A grandmotherly looking woman with white, stringy, coconut-oiled hair walked in with a blanketed infant in her arms. As Divya stood up, Ramar took a moment to control his emotions.

"Divya, meet your adopted brother," he said.

She slowly approached the old woman with a gentle face. Her legs weakened from the sight of the sleeping baby.

"Oh my God!" Divya gasped, grasping the chair for support. "He, he—"

"Looks like your younger brother, no?" Ramar said proudly.

"Yes. Except for the mole on one corner of his mouth, it would be easy to mistake him as Rahul at two months," Divya stared at Ramar with disbelief. "How'd you do this?"

"Sedhu sent me a photograph of your brother. It was by chance we had such a similar match."

"But this is not right. Rahul's dead. We can't replace him with a virtual clone."

Ramar laughed, sending shivers down Divya's spine. It was a heartless, cold laugh. "You're exaggerating, my dear. Most infants look very similar at that age. There are similarities to your brother, no doubt, but that doesn't justify labeling him as a clone."

"But every time anyone looks at him they're going to think of Rahul. How can we focus on the future if we're constantly reminded of the past?" Divya sighed, suddenly realizing the futility of arguing with the Director. "What's the baby's name?"

"Rahul."

Divya stared at Ramar incredulously.

"You or I may not agree with this, but this is what Sedhu wanted," Ramar said.

"This is crazy...this can't be...it'll never work...how... why?"

259

"Your mother is very sick, and Sedhu is certain that this will help her."

Divya took a seat back in the chair, her head throbbing.

I can't believe Papa endorsed this.

Ramar told the old woman in Tamil to prepare the baby.

"Where's she going?" Divya asked.

"Just to get Rahul ready for his departure."

"I see." Divya realized she really didn't have much choice other than to follow her father's wishes, no matter how outrageous they seemed to her. "Do I need to sign anything before I go?"

"No. I've arranged everything. Just make sure you keep these documents with you at all times, and you'll be fine."

Divya opened the file and began studying the papers.

Something is wrong, a voice within her mind nagged. *It shouldn't be this easy.*

"Is all of this..." she tried to search for the right word without overly offending the Director, "...legitimate?"

"I understand your concern, Divya, but let me put your worries at ease."

"I'd appreciate that," she said, scanning the next document.

"You remember the man in the suit and long hair who passed you by the door when you walked in here?"

"Uh huh."

"He's my lawyer. He also works for the Madurai City Council. He personally filled out and delivered this paperwork. Just show these documents to the authorities, and I assure you that you'll have no problems."

"My father called you a few days ago and asked you to name this child 'Rahul?'"

"Yes, that was what he specifically requested."

"And, how old is the baby?"

"About two months."

"Then can you explain why Rahul is written on this birth certificate when my father's request came days ago?" Divya asked warily, dangling the paper in front of him.

Ramar did not say anything.

"All of this," she said, waving at the file, "the birth certificate, the immigration papers, parental consent forms, adoption papers, are all bogus, fake, aren't they?"

"Yes," he admitted, impressed.

Beautiful and intelligent. You raised her well, brother.

"My lawyer obtained the necessary and legitimate documentation through his connections with the city and state, and then I had forgers duplicate them to pass the scrutiny of immigration authorities. The occasional bribe also helps smooth the process," Ramar paused, carefully judging the reaction from his daughter. "You disapprove of my business?"

"Yes."

"Good, good. You speak boldly and from the heart. But let me ask you, Divya, what's so terrible that I do?"

"You steal children from their families. I can't imagine anything more atrocious and despicable."

She's quick, like her real father, Ramar thought with an inward smile.

"Divya, you have no proof of such an accusation. But even if I did, why's that so bad? When an impoverished family has several children who they can't feed, and especially have girls whose dowries they can't afford, I do them a favor. I give the family much needed money in exchange for the child. The child is then sent to countries in Pacific Asia, Europe, and North America to couples that can't have children. Tell me, what future does a poor and uneducated child have in a country of one billion? None. You've seen hundreds of children begging on the streets. I play a small part in alleviating that problem. Through my services, the impoverished family gains, the adopted child gains, and the childless couple gains. It is a win-win-win situation for all parties involved."

"And I have no doubt that you turn a handsome profit for your crimes."

"I also must make a living, true, but just because it is illegal doesn't mean it is wrong."

"It's evil."

"Then, based on that logic do you accuse your parents of being evil for not only sanctioning this, but asking me for a personal favor to bring them their new son by any means possible?"

"That's different," Divya said uneasily.

"Why, because you love them? Because, in your eyes, *they* are incapable of doing something wrong?" Ramar demanded with a piercing look.

Divya was silent, unable to defend her parent's actions.

"No response? Frankly, I am disappointed by your hypocrisy."

"I can't do this," she said, standing up.

"What if Sedhu is right, and this baby can bring your mother out of depression?"

"Why do you always call my father Sedhu, but do not call my mother by her name?"

Because I am your father, and saying Rani's name is too painful.

"Divya, listen to me carefully. Judge me, I accept that. But you have the power to save your mother, and I know deep down within your heart you'd never forgive yourself if you denied her this."

The door to the room opened, and the old woman with a kind face returned, holding Rahul in one hand and a bag of baby accessories in the other.

"Taking this baby goes against my morals," Divya protested. "Don't you understand that?"

"Stop being so *damn* selfish, Divya," Ramar said coldly. "Your mother's well being is far more important than trying to ease your own conscience. Now, stop preaching your *supposed* morality to me, take this infant, and bring him to his rightful mother."

Conflicted, Divya stared at the baby, wondering what to do.

* * *

As his daughter was escorted out of the room, Ramar wondered what life would have been like having a family with Divya and Rani. Since he had lost his wife and unborn child to his elder brother, Ramar had never loved another woman. No one had remotely caught his interest or captured his heart. When he was younger, he had slept with numerous women, but all of those affairs were shallow and had eventually ended.

To Ramar, the possibility of being betrayed by someone whom he was supposed to trust and share his soul with was far too risky for a heart badly scarred from the past. But, despite his ruthless exterior, Ramar still yearned for a family. He had no delusions of immortality, and wanted to have children to pass on his legacy and empire. Also, despite everything that had happened, and all the time that had passed, he still loved Rani, although he would rather die than admit it to anyone.

By pushing these feelings deep down, and abandoning his hollow affairs or any thoughts of marriage, he was able to focus and dedicate his life to his work. Nothing else had mattered to Ramar than to build financial and political power. His hatred for the Untouchables of Tamil Nadu was still tremendous, and he continued to make it his mission to methodically abolish the entire caste.

But seeing his daughter—a mirror image of his beloved Rani—made him question for the first time whether all of his efforts were worth it. Would he have been happier living a simple life and raising a family? For the first time in two decades he was filled with a wretched loneliness.

There was a knock, and Ramar looked up as his bodyguard opened the door. An irritated looking man in a police uniform entered, followed by Valli holding a tray.

"I am a busy man, Ramar, and I don't enjoy being summoned by your men when on duty."

"Have you forgotten *who* you work for, Rao?" Ramar asked callously, his face hard.

Valli placed two glasses of lime juice and a bowl of peanuts on the table before disappearing.

"No, of course not. Why was I summoned?" Sub-Inspector Rao asked with considerable more restraint.

"Was that Untouchable woman released from the prison today?" Ramar asked, reaching for several peanuts.

"Yes."

"And?"

"And nothing. I handled it."

"Is that so?" Ramar's eyebrow rose. He cracked the nuts' shells, popped the peanuts into his mouth, and crunched loudly. "Then why do my people tell me that you stopped her at the footsteps of this building?"

263

"It was nothing. Judge Seetha drove her straight from the jail, and I had to wait until she left before I could talk to that Untouchable. But I'm telling you, I handled it."

"Did she appreciate your handiwork of that prison girl slave?"

"I believe so," the policeman said with a sinister smile.

"Wipe that smirk off your face, Rao. I don't want anything to happen to that bitch, understand? We already have enough pressure from that meddling judge."

"I said it's been taken care of."

"I hope so, Rao, for your sake."

"Are you threatening me?"

"I merely want to emphasize that even though you're a distinguished police officer, it is *I* who make and enforce the laws in this city, *my* city. You're as expendable as...why, these peanuts." Ramar crushed the rest of the nuts in his hand until they were reduced to powder. "Understand?"

"You'll not see or hear from her again," Sub-Inspector Rao said quietly, his eyes on the pulverized peanuts spilling from the bottom of Ramar's clenched fist.

"Good, and don't dare try to keep anything from me again. I have eyes all over this city. Now, get out of my sight."

* * *

Divya stared at the little baby sleeping peacefully in her arms, spittle bubbling from his tiny lips. The uncanny resemblance to her late brother disturbed her. She had wanted to walk out of that dreadful room without the baby, but what alternative did she have? She disapproved of what her parents were doing, but she knew that if she had left the child—she could never call him Rahul—then she had sealed a dire fate for him. Ramar terrified her, and she could not leave an innocent child in his clutches.

He may be Papa's old friend, but that man is dangerous.

Cursing, the autorickshaw driver threw up his arms with frustration. Divya looked up, surprised at the congestion that encompassed their three-wheeler. She noticed that they were just outside the spectacularly carved south tower of the Meenakshi Temple.

Divya covered a blanket over the baby to protect him from the fumes spewing from the marred vehicles that surrounded them.

"Let me see what the problem is," Aslam said.

He began speaking in Tamil with the driver.

A shadow draped Divya, and she gasped with surprise as two palms appeared in front of her. She turned to see a woman in a ragged sari, begging for money in Tamil.

Images of the disfigured destitute she had rejected earlier that afternoon came rushing back. Divya guiltily reached for her purse.

The baby began stirring within the blankets, and released a piercing cry. His little arms pushed aside the blanket that covered his face.

Divya pulled out a hundred-rupee note, and turned to the woman.

The beggar stared at the child, ignoring the money. She glanced uneasily at the young woman in the autorickshaw, who smiled and encouraged her to take the money.

Divya cried out with alarm as the beggar snatched the baby from her lap and ran towards the curb. "Oz, the baby!"

"Stay here!" Aslam ordered.

He leaped out of the autorickshaw and chased after the beggar, maneuvering past each metallic obstacle.

The kidnapper darted through the snarled traffic and disappeared into the darkness of the closest alley.

Aslam ran down the garbage-strewn alley and stopped in front of a concrete wall.

A dead end.

Panting, he spun around, but heard or saw nothing out of the ordinary. Two stray dogs were sniffing a pile of rotten vegetables half way down the alley.

What the...? Where'd she go?

He wondered whether the beggar had somehow escaped through the door at the side of one building. He reached for the door. It was locked. He banged on the door, wondering if the beggar had locked it behind her.

He turned at the sound of a crying infant.

"Stop!" he cried in Tamil as the huddled figure in the distance jumped up from behind a pile of empty crates and ran out of the alley.

Shit, I ran right past her.

He chased after the kidnapper, running back into the blinding sunshine and down the block.

"Stop her!" Aslam kept shouting as he pushed himself through the sea of people, who were confused or irritated at being disturbed.

"Fresh sugarcane or coconut water, sahib?" asked a smiling kiosk vendor, blocking Aslam's path.

"Move!"

Aslam shoved the vendor into the fruit stand, his focus on the beggar.

The wooden kiosk collapsed, littering the sidewalk and street with fruit.

Nearby beggars ravenously swarmed over the scattered produce.

Realizing her pursuer was gaining on her, the beggar bolted into another alley. Aslam followed, ignoring the searing burning in his lungs, and willed his legs to move faster.

The woman desperately knocked a pile of empty crates behind her.

Aslam cursed as he tripped and fell heavily into a pool of stagnant water. Ignoring the pain from his lacerated knees and hands, he was back on his feet, even more determined to catch her.

The kidnapper stopped in front of a fence that dissected the alley.

Got you now! he thought with satisfaction.

She was barely able to squeeze through a hole cut at one corner of the wire fence.

Without hesitation, Aslam climbed to the top of the fence, swung his legs over, and jumped to the pavement on the opposite side.

He grunted as he landed heavily on his feet.

At the end of the alley, an autorickshaw screeched to a stop and Divya jumped out, blocking the opening.

The beggar cried with alarm as she realized she was trapped. She stopped, sobbing, protectively clutching the screaming baby, and praying incessantly in Tamil.

Aslam ran up to the beggar, grabbed her shoulders, and furiously whirled her around.

He gasped at the terrified face.

"Ladha?"

Chapter 14
A Proposal and an Ultimatum
Monday, November 19ᵗʰ, 2001

"Are you sure she's not some lunatic?" Divya whispered, warily eyeing the sleeping woman sitting across from them on the bouncing bus.

"Divya, I've known this woman most of my life. My mother was her good friend. She was our neighbor."

"I know, Oz, but who knows how the tragedy of losing her family during the massacre has affected her. How do you know for certain that that is Karuppan? You were studying at IIMB when the baby was born, weren't you?"

"Yes, but look how she holds the baby, even when she sleeps. Only a mother could hold her own child with such love. This woman is an honest and lovely person, someone incapable of deception."

"But—"

"Divya, I may not be able to help my family anymore, but I can help Ladha and Karuppan. That woman was the last friendly face my mother saw before she died. The least I can do is to make sure that they live in peace. They have suffered enough, and I'll do everything in my power to protect them."

Divya nodded. Although in her heart she believed Karuppan to be Ladha's child, admitting such a truth meant her father's friend, the Director of Priceless Child, was somehow connected to the butchering of the village.

So what does that make Papa? Divya asked herself. *Does he know about Ramar? Has he become so desperate to save Mama that he is willing to sanction such atrocities?*

She shook her head. *No, it can't be. Papa's desperation must be blinding him. Papa is incapable of supporting such crimes. He must not know what Ramar is involved in.*

She wondered how Ramar had gotten the baby from the Zamindars. Was he also ignorant in the entire affair like her father, just an innocent bystander oblivious to the source of his supplier? A nagging feeling made her think otherwise.

She knew Aslam could help bring some light to her questions.

"Oz, who are the Zamindars? And why do they do such things?"

His silence disturbed her, and she wondered whether she had asked him such a sensitive question too soon.

"The Zamindars, the landlord caste, are an upper-caste that have controlled most of the arable land for generations," he began quietly. "They force the lower-castes, especially the Dalits, to work on their lands as laborers for survival. The Zamindars use their birth into an upper-caste to justify their mistreatment of the downtrodden. They pay us just enough to sustain ourselves, and make sure that we're poor and dependent on them in every facet of life."

"How can they maintain such control?"

"Many ways. By keeping most of our children illiterate and ignorant, by preventing us from electing members of our own caste into power, often violently, and by constantly demeaning and threatening us. Oppression and racism are their weapons. Many Dalits simply tolerate and accept their place in society, believing they have earned their fate by some terrible deed they did in their past life, that this is their karma. They believe if they are good in this life, then they'll move up the social hierarchy when they are reincarnated, perhaps being reborn in upper-caste families themselves."

"Why don't the educated Dalits work together to change such archaic beliefs?"

"We're trying, but after thousands of years such beliefs are engrained in society. It'll take a long time to deprogram people. Also, many Dalits endure such atrocities and humiliations simply because they wish to live in peace."

"I had no idea.

"Did you know that on average three Dalit women are brutally raped, and two are killed every day? And these are only the *recorded* incidents. Through forced silence, fear, or denial, many other Dalit women do not report the atrocities they endure." Aslam sighed heavily.

"I can't believe stuff like this still happens. Professor Krishnamurthy said Hinduism was a tolerant religion."

"Divya, please remember that the Zamindars represent a small cluster of evil, power hungry individuals. The majority of Hindus are remarkably secular, resilient, and tolerant, especially in the cities. I love my country, and the fact that it is the only country in the world where every religion lives in relative harmony. And, to be honest, the government has put much effort to improve the lives of the downtrodden, but the Zamindars have much power and influence."

"But some Dalits are fighting back, aren't they?"

"Yes, but not in the conventional way. The Indian government has reserved quotas for Dalits in all educational institutions and given many scholarships. This has enabled many Dalits to be recruited to work in Gulf States, like the United Arab Emirates or Saudi Arabia, where the demand for skilled laborers is high. After a few years, Dalit children are able to send money home to their parents. Slowly, especially, over the past few years, the wealth of the Dalits has grown."

"Freeing you from the grip of the Zamindars?"

"Correct. Our community was able to gain some wealth and become less dependent on the Zamindars. They first ignored the trends, arrogantly assuming that we'd fail and return to them begging for help. They believed a handful of determined Dalits were no threat. But, when we didn't come back to their farms, and instead, demanded more rights, and began to purchase our own land, and organize and express our political voice, the Zamindars responded with what they know best—violence. Since the mid-nineties, thousands of Dalits from upper-caste dominated villages in Tamil Nadu were driven off their land and from their homes. My family was forced to leave with thirty other Dalit families in Rengappanaikkanpatti nine years ago..." he stopped, his eyes filled with anguish.

"Oz, you don't have to talk about this if it is too painful," Divya said gently, regretting broaching the subject with him.

"No, it's okay, I want my fiancé to know everything," he said, giving her a grim smile. His eyes glazed over as he recalled the past. "Before the Zamindar attack on Rengappanaikkanpatti we made up about a tenth of the village's population. The rest were upper-caste Hindus. My father's brother was an engineer who worked in Saudi Arabia for several years, and he sent us money. Combined with the income from my father, we became one of the wealthier Dalit families. Our little home was made from *brick* with two bedrooms, a kitchen, and a common room. We owned a four-acre coconut grove that was excellent for shade and profits."

Aslam smiled from the fond childhood memories. "The prosperity of the Dalits was a motivation for the attack by the Zamindars, who wanted to give a very simple message: there was no point in accumulating wealth. If we did not work on their lands for scraps, then we would suffer. The Zamindars stormed into our house one night without warning, dragged us out, and burned everything we owned to the ground. I watched everything we had worked for reduced to ashes for no reason other than hatred and jealously because we had accomplished something with hard work, and not stolen it like the Zamindars. God, if Amma hadn't held me back, I would have tried to kill all those bastards, especially their leader, who like a coward, covered his face with a black mask."

He paused, and Divya took hold of his hand and squeezed it with reassurance.

"They warned us that the next time they saw us they'd kill us," Aslam continued bitterly. "We were forced to flee to the neighboring village of Sholapuram. My father and a few other family heads boldly decided that they'd create their own village where only Dalits were welcome, and we'd not have to answer to any upper-castes or the Zamindars. They assumed that if we consolidated our resources and lived together, the Zamindars would be deterred from attacking us. My father had no faith in the government or police, and believed it was the only way for us to finally live in peace, dependent on no one other than ourselves."

"You actually founded and built a new village?"

"Yes, we did a little scouting and found a nice plot of land at the edge of the forest where there was a stream filled with clear, fresh water, and an abundance of fish. It was a government piece of land, but we didn't care. What had the government ever done for us? We took over, and no one ever bothered us about it. I was thirteen or fourteen at the time, and I remember how skeptical I was. But in time, when my father's dream materialized, I began to believe. As the Zamindars drove Dalits away from upper-caste

271

dominated villages, many more Dalits came and joined our village. Within two years, our village had grown to over a hundred families."

"Your father sounds like an amazing man," Divya said.

His face swelled with pride. "Yes, he was, but you saw how his dream has become a charred nightmare. And why? Because those butchers had to set an example, a deterrent for other Dalits. We were inspiring unrest across the region. We were providing hope and moral support to the surrounding Dalit communities, and they couldn't allow that, could they?"

"If the Zamindars hated the Dalits so much, especially the unrest your village was creating, they must have tried to destroy it earlier, right? Didn't you anticipate this? Didn't you have defenses?"

"Of course. There were enough of us to defend the village from one or two clans of Zamindars. Also, there has always been power struggles and bickering between the Zamindars in the state. The internal quest for power and leadership amongst themselves has always divided their forces, and kept us safe."

"Then how did this happen?"

Aslam's eyes widened, and he tightened his grip on her hand. "The landlords from the state must have finally united. Someone has taken leadership of *all* the Zamindars, and that person is responsible for destroying everything I loved."

"Oz, you are hurting me," Divya whimpered.

He released her hand, aghast. "Oh God, I'm *so* sorry. Are you okay?"

She looked at him anxiously. "Oz?"

"Divya, don't worry about me, okay?" he said, gently rubbing her hand. "I still have many things to sort out. I need time, but I haven't forgotten my promise to you."

Divya nodded, wishing she believed him. "I'm tired, Oz. I am going to catch a few hours of sleep."

"Perhaps that's best. We have a long day tomorrow."

Divya turned towards the window, and looked at the black world. In the distance, clouds flashed with lightning. There was a crack of thunder.

She soon heard Aslam breathing steadily as he slipped into sleep. But sleep eluded her. As she rubbed her throbbing hand, she prayed that she would have the strength to help him keep his promise.

* * *

"Are you sure this is going to work, Oz?" Divya asked uneasily.

"There's only one way to find out," Aslam said, knocking on the door.

"But he despises you."

"That's rather harsh, don't you think? Shhh, I hear him coming."

The door opened, and Divya restrained a chuckle at the red silk robe Chicken was wearing.

"Shit, look who's here? What do you want?" he asked suspiciously.

"I need a favor," Aslam said.

Chicken smiled arrogantly and waved them into his room.

Each student at the college received the exact same room with the standard desk, bed, and cabinet, and Divya was astonished at the renovated room she entered.

Halogen lamps were set up in each corner, casting warm light across the cream-painted room. The images of Keanu Reeves dodging bullets in the blockbuster *The Matrix* was playing on an enormous flat-screen television screen that hung on one end of the wall. Facing the television, a gorgeous, four-pillar bed dominated most of the room. Above the bed, a wall-unit air-conditioner hummed softly as it blew cool air. In another corner of the room was a customized wall unit that included a desk and state-of-the-art laptop computer. Between the bed and desk was a leather recliner that looked so comfortable that Divya was certain it could put an insomniac into a blissful slumber. Underneath the bed, Divya could hear the distinctive hum of a back-up generator that would preserve Chicken's tiny piece of heaven during the frequent power failures that plagued Bangalore.

This is not a University dorm, it's a luxury condo, she marveled.

Chicken took a seat in the recliner, and pressed a button on the armrest. Divya watched with amazement as the shutters automatically slid from the ceiling and covered the window. He pushed another button—the pounding music from the speakers set up throughout the room ceased, and the images on the television disappeared.

"So, how can I help you?" Chicken asked leaning back in his recliner, his fingers interlacing together.

"I have a friend who needs a job," Aslam said. "I'd really appreciate it if you could put in a word, a recommendation to your father?"

"Who's this person? What job did you have in mind?"

"She's from my village in Tamil Nadu. It was attacked by the Zamindars."

"Inter-caste wars, Oz? Come on," Chicken snorted with disbelief. "That's Dalit propaganda, man. That doesn't happen anymore. You know how the downtrodden will make up any story to advance their cause. The attacks are a fabrication, something that hasn't happened for decades. It's all bullshit."

Divya stared anxiously at Aslam, afraid he would break Chicken's scrawny neck.

With considerable restraint, his eyes sparkling with tears, Aslam said between clenched teeth: "My family was killed in that *fabricated* attack. I held my mother's broken body in my hands only two days ago."

Chicken's smirk vanished. "O-Oh fuck me, I'm sorry, man. Shit, I didn't know. I..." he stopped, lost for words.

Aslam sighed, realizing Chicken was not malicious but ignorant like many of the minority elite. "Chicken, I know this woman, and I beg you to help me. You'll not regret this decision. Ask your father to give her a job."

"Oz, I want to help, truly," Chicken said with sincerity as guilt consumed him for his foolish remarks. "But what would this woman do? You said yourself that she's from your village. What are her qualifications other than breeding?" Chicken winced as the words escaped his mouth. "Shit, I'm sorry, that was uncalled for. I can be an insensitive asshole sometimes." He sighed, wondering how much deeper he could dig his grave. "Look, Oz, I can't ask my father to pay her for nothing."

"Your Grandmother only speaks Tamil, correct?"

"Yeah, so?"

"I heard you complaining to your friends last week that your Grandmother is nearly blind and no one in your family has time to read to her."

"What's your point?"

"Ladha, this family friend of mine, can read to your Grandmother, and tend to her other needs."

Divya studied Aslam, impressed. Not only had he controlled his emotions, but he had also given Chicken a convincing argument.

Chicken cracked his knuckles, saying nothing.

"Come on Chicken, do me this favor," Aslam pressed.

"Listen, man, all I can do is to introduce this woman to my father," Chicken finally said. "Then it's up to her and you to convince him."

"Fair enough," Aslam said gratefully.

"And you'll return the badminton racket she won from me. I've been playing like shit since I lost it," Chicken said, unable to look at Divya.

"Agreed," Aslam said.

Chicken stood up. "Well, let's go then, man."

"What, now?"

"My father is flying to Singapore tonight. If you want to do this, then now is the only time."

"Thank you, Chicken," Aslam said, extending his hand.

Divya smiled broadly, pleased that the two rivals had set aside their differences for a common good.

"You're welcome, man," Chicken said, accepting Aslam's hand.

* * *

"Where's Oz, Divya?" Rekha called out.

Divya walked past the mess, and sat down on the stone wall between Naveen and Om.

"He's gone to Chicken's house."

"You are kidding, nah?"

"They've not spoken to each other since that badminton match," Naveen mused, smiling from the pleasant memory.

"That was true, until today," Divya said.

275

"What happened, Divya?" Naveen asked.

"I don't think it's my place to tell."

"We're all friends here," Naveen said, pulling out a cigarette.

"Yes, tell us, nah?" Rekha said, snatching the cigarette from his mouth and snapping it in half.

"Hey!"

"It is a filthy, disgusting habit, Naveen! Do not be stupid, nah?"

"But—"

"Shut it, Naveen, or I will smack you into tomorrow!"

Naveen stared gloomily at the remains of his cigarette lying on the ground.

"I guess there's no harm in telling you all," Divya said.

"And do not leave out any details," Rekha said as she slapped Naveen's hand, which was reaching for the ruined cigarette.

Divya explained the entire trip to Tamil Nadu, skipping anything that pertained to the loss of Aslam's family; she felt it was not her place to tell them. Divya explained Ladha's ordeal, and how the adopted baby was actually Karuppan, her kidnapped infant son. By the end of the story, Rekha was near tears, and Om and Naveen were visibly shaken.

"So, we approached Chicken to ask if he could find Ladha a job. They've all gone now to talk to his father," Divya concluded.

"Ladha actually witnessed the Zamindars butcher her children in front of her eyes?" Rekha asked.

"Yeah."

"That is so terrific," she said solemnly.

"What?" Divya asked with surprise, wondering if she had heard right. "Did you say it was 'terrific'?"

"Yes, of course. It is terrific."

Divya looked at her friend like she was crazy. "Rekha, do you know what that means?"

"Of course. It stems from the word terror, right Naveen?" she asked, looking at him for support.

"Well, um," he said, unwilling to tell her she was wrong.

"Do you mean it is *terrible?*" Divya asked.

"Areé, that's what I said, nah?"

"No, you said 'terrific' not 'terrible.'"

"It is the same thing!" Rekha said, exasperated.

Om snickered.

"What is so funny? This is a terrific story and I do not understand why you are laughing," Rekha said angrily.

"Rekha, 'terrific' has the completely opposite meaning to what you are trying to say," Divya explained. "'Terrific' means 'great' or 'wonderful.'"

"It does?" Rekha turned to Naveen, who gave a circular nod and hoped she would not hit him again. "No, it cannot be. I have heard my Papa say it all the time."

"Now that I think about it, I can understand the confusion, especially since 'horrible' and 'horrific' have the same connotation. But, I assure you that 'terrible' and 'terrific' have very different meanings in English," Divya said.

"How would you use 'terrific' in a sentence?" Rekha demanded.

"It's terrific to be engaged." Divya winced as she realized what she said.

"What? You're getting married?" Naveen said.

"No, wait—"

"No, it cannot be so!" Rekha cried.

"Let me clarify—"

"Divya, is it true?" Om asked.

"Yes, it is," Divya admitted. "Shit, Aslam and I wanted to tell you together."

"But this cannot happen!" Rekha protested.

"Why not?" Divya asked. "Aren't you happy for us?"

"I'm zapped!" Naveen said, embracing Divya. "And you should be kicked for them too, Rekha."

"Kicked means happy," Om clarified, noticing Divya's puzzled look.

I'm never going to understand Hinenglish slang, Divya thought.

"You don't understand. If you two get married everything will change, nah? You will get a home, get married, have lots of babies, and I will lose my buddy," Rekha wailed.

"He who rejects change is the architect of decay. The only human institution which rejects progress is the cemetery," Om quoted. "Harold Wilson."

277

"Om is right, Rekha. Things change. But nothing will ever come between our friendship," Divya said earnestly.

"You know I am kicked for both you and Oz. Just do not forget about us, nah?"

"I'll always be your buddy, and be there whenever you need me, Rekha. And that goes for all of you," Divya said.

"True friendship is like sound health; the value of it is seldom known until it be lost," Om said. "Charles Caleb Colton."

"You are awful chatty, Om," Rekha observed sourly. "Have you embraced a new religion today?"

"Um, Rekha, we better go, otherwise we will get late for our dinner reservations at Tandoor," Naveen said before Om could respond.

"Okay. Congratulations, Divya. I love you," Rekha said, hugging her friend fiercely. "And I want to hear all the details about how he proposed when I return."

"Congratulations again, Divya. We'll definitely celebrate soon," Naveen said, as he hooked his arm with Rekha's.

When Divya was alone with Om she said: "I need your advice, Om."

"I am honored you would seek my advice."

Divya sighed unhappily. "Om, I don't know how I'm going to tell my parents about my engagement. I'm expecting my father's phone call tonight, and I'm afraid he may take the news very badly. I feel that this isn't the right time to tell him. There are a lot of problems back home, and I just don't know how they'll react, particularly my father. I don't want to hurt or disappoint them, but I love Aslam very much. I'm sure this is what I want to do. I can't imagine being with anyone else. He's my soul mate."

"It takes a lot of courage to show your dreams to someone else," Om said. "Erma Bombeck."

"You think I should tell them, eh? But I'm so afraid of what they may say or do."

"Divya," Om said gently, taking her hands. "I don't have much experience in this, but as Mark Twain said: 'Courage is not the lack of fear. It is acting in spite of it.'"

Aslam drove up to them on his motorcycle, a large grin plastered on his face.

"Can I take it by your smile that Ladha was hired?" Divya asked.

"Yes, it was incredible. Hop on, and I'll tell you about it."

"May the love you share, so clear to view, come to bear, and make your dreams true," Om said. "Congratulations, Oz."

"You told him?" Aslam asked Divya.

"Are you angry?"

"Absolutely not! I'm thrilled," he exclaimed. He turned to Om. "Thank you for your warm wishes, my friend, but you didn't tell me who the author of that wonderful poem was."

"Frankly, I read it off a Hallmark card," Om admitted.

Aslam and Divya gave Om a strange look.

"Oh come now, smile! It's like an antidepressant without any adverse effects."

The three of them burst into a fit of laughter.

"Well, I'll leave you two alone. Remember Divya: The softest pillow is a clean conscience."

Divya smiled gratefully. "Thanks, Om. You helped a lot."

"What's that about?" Aslam asked as Om walked off.

"Oh, something between Om and I," Divya said with a cryptic smile. "Now, you really want me to get onto this death machine?"

"Yes, let's go."

"Can't we take an autorickshaw?"

"What?" Aslam studied her. "Divya, are you afraid of riding a motorcycle? Have you ever ridden a two-wheeler?"

"Yes, of course...No."

"I'll go real slow. Come on, if we're to be married then trust will be key for our relationship. Nothing will happen to you. Trust me."

"You better drive carefully, Oz, otherwise I'll kill you."

Divya awkwardly got onto the motorcycle, and tightly wrapped her arms around him.

"Ready?" he asked with a mischievous grin.

"Slowly and carefully, okay?"

"Hang on!"

Divya cried out with delight and fear as he revved the engine and throttled down the tree-lined campus road.

* * *

Grasping onto Aslam for dear life, Divya had never felt more terrified and exhilarated.

As he confidently accelerated past traffic, she had trouble keeping her watering eyes open from the wind blowing in her face. Soon the wonderful feeling of the wind raging through her black hair was replaced with the uncomfortable feeling of the vibrations numbing her bottom. Divya could feel every imperfection in the road, and she hoped they were close to their destination.

They stopped at an intersection at the request of the traffic policeman. As they waited for the officer to wave them through the bustling intersection, Aslam tapped Divya, and pointed towards a man sitting on a motorcycle in front of them. On the back of the man's T-shirt was imprinted:

If you can read this then the bitch fell off.

Divya was simultaneously shocked and amused by the audacity of the statement.

Blaring his whistle, the police officer waved them through the intersection.

After thirty minutes, Divya's thighs were cramping, and she could not stop coughing from the traffic's fumes; the pollutants emanating from the vehicles were choking her. Just as she was going to ask him to stop, Aslam drove through the entrance of the Bangalore Lal Bagh Botanical Gardens.

He parked the motorcycle, helped her dismount, and led her past the glass house that resembled a small replica of the famous Crystal Palace in London.

Hand in hand, they walked past a plethora of blooming roses and rare tropical plants.

"Oz, what are we doing here?" Divya asked.

"I just wanted to go for a peaceful walk with you."

"We could have walked around the campus."

"I wanted to be alone with you."

"We could've found privacy on the campus."

"Not complete privacy."

They followed the path past a beautiful flower clock and expansive lawns.

"So, what exactly happened with Ladha?" Divya asked.

"Oh, it was amazing, Divya. Chicken introduced Ladha to her father, Mr. Ravindra, as he promised he would, and explained her situation to him. Chicken even gave an excellent recommendation, saying Ladha would be perfect candidate to look after their grandmother and to read to her. Without hesitation, and this is the amazing part, Mr. Ravindra handed Ladha a Tamil newspaper and asked her to read it."

"He doesn't waste time, does he?"

"No, such a influential businessman doesn't have time for pleasantries. He got straight to the point. When he handed the newspaper to her, Divya, I swear I was more nervous than Ladha. She struggled at the beginning, and my heart sank. But it was just nerves, and soon she was reading through the articles quite well."

"That was it, then? She was hired?"

"Oh, no. Mr. Ravindra led Ladha to see Chicken's grandmother. Ladha spoke with the old woman in a private interview for over an hour. Afterwards, Grandmother Ravindra ordered her son to hire her immediately at any terms she wanted. It was amusing to see a powerful man as Mr. Ravindra become so tongue-tied in front of his mother."

"Does Ladha know how to negotiate?"

"No, this is where I took over. After all, it is my duty to act as her agent. And besides I don't have a business degree at the best Indian business management school for nothing."

"Oh, now you've become an agent, have you? And then?"

"Not only did he agree for a decent pay plus room and lodging for both Ladha and her son, but, if she does a good job, Mr. Ravindra agreed to pay for Karuppan's education."

"That's wonderful, Oz."

They made their way onto a quaint bridge overlooking a lake shimmering in the late afternoon sunshine.

"This was a good day, and I owe Chicken for helping us," he said as they admired the view from the center of the bridge. "Despite his arrogance and insensitive remarks, he's a good guy. He just needs to spend less time with servants and American movies, and more time at the temple or with his fellow students."

They stared at the reflection of the forest and falling sun, and enjoyed the antics from the multitude of wild birds that swooped through the air and leisurely swam in the cool pond.

After some time, Divya said: "Thank you for bringing me here. It reminds me of when you first took me to the roof."

Aslam kissed her deeply.

"What's that for?" she asked, breathless.

"That's what I wanted to do since that day on the roof, Divya. It was at that moment when I knew I loved you," he said, falling to one knee.

"Oz, what are you doing?"

"Proposing to you properly, my love."

* * *

"Divya, are you in there?" Rekha demanded, pounding on the bedroom door.

"Why are you shouting, I'm right here," Divya said, behind her.

"*Shit* man, you scared me," she gasped, clutching her heart. "Aslam," she said coolly, convinced their marriage would cause a rift in her friendship with Divya.

"What's the emergency?" Divya asked.

"Oh, you have a long distance call from your father."

"I'll give you some privacy then," Aslam said.

"Stop by my room later?" Divya asked, reluctant to let go of his hand.

"Sure. See you, Rekha."

"Uh huh," Rekha said, giving him cut-eye.

With a dreamy expression, Divya watched Aslam disappear down the flight of stairs.

Rekha cleared her throat loudly to bring Divya back to reality. "I will be in my room," she said crossly. "But if you have any trouble, come see me first, nah?"

"I will. Thanks," Divya said, apprehensively eyeing the phone receiver dangling from the wall.

Divya walked to the phone, trying to summon the courage to confront her father. She tried to simultaneously remember Om's wise words and reflect on the perfect afternoon she had spent with

Aslam, but neither memory surfaced. With trembling hands, and her mind void of a plan, she picked up the phone.

"H-Hello?"

"Divya, beta?"

"Hi, Papa."

"My God, I nearly hung up, I was waiting so long. Did you get the baby, beta?"

"Yes, Papa."

"And?"

"And?" Divya echoed stupidly, wondering how she could crawl into some dark corner and disappear into obscurity.

"Did you notice any...does he look like...well, you know, does he resemble..."

"Rahul?" Divya sighed.

"Yes, does he?"

Divya hesitated for a long time before deciding that the truth was the only approach she could take. "Yes, very much so, but Papa—"

"Oh, that's good news, beta. That's very good news."

"But—"

"But what? Did the Director of the Adoption Home, my friend, give you all the proper documentation?"

"Yes."

"And you said the baby is healthy, correct?"

"Uh huh."

"Then, what's the problem, beta?"

Oh dear Lord, how do I tell him when he's so emotional? He sounds so nervous.

"Hello? Hello, Divya? Are you there, beta?"

"I'm here, Papa, but listen to me, and please don't get upset, okay?" Divya winced as soon as she said those words. It was too late. The damage was done.

"Upset about what? What's going on?" he asked, near the verge of panic.

"Papa, the baby I was given was...stolen."

"What? Rubbish."

"It's true. I got the baby and then ran into his real mother, Ladha, who'd been searching for her son. Papa, that director, your friend, Ramar, is somehow involved with people that tore that child from his mother's arms during a raid on her village. A raid where hundreds were mercilessly slaughtered."

"Divya, you listen to me carefully. You must bring him to us," he said impassively.

Divya was speechless for a moment. "P-Papa, did you hear me? That baby belongs to his real mother who loves him and never consented to giving him up for adoption."

"Where's your proof? Where'd you find this woman?"

Divya was stunned by her father's reaction but tried to remain calm. "She was begging for money in Madurai, and then saw her baby when we were in the autorickshaw."

"She's a beggar?"

"That's not the point—"

"It's exactly the point. What's wrong with you? Can't you see that this woman has tricked you? She'll probably sell the baby for drugs or God knows what. How could you be so naïve?"

"She *is* his mother. You had to be there to understand."

"Did she show you a birth certificate?"

"No," Divya said miserably.

"Did you even take a blood test?"

"No," Divya said, realizing that her father would not accept the truth.

"So, you took her word based on intuition? Divya, I thought you were smarter than this. You've been in India for months and know people will desperately say or do anything to trick foreigners. How could you jeopardize your mother's health on gut instinct? How could you be so stupid?"

Her father's words stung, but Divya forced herself to remain calm. "Papa, a friend of mine knew this woman. They came from the same village. He said she's incapable of deception. That baby is hers. You should see how she loves him."

"And did this friend of yours see this woman's baby before?"

Dammit, Divya, if lying is the only way to persuade him then lie.

"No," she admitted, silently cursing her honesty. "He was studying here at IIMB when she had her baby."

"That's not good enough, beta, and you know it. Now, you get this child back and bring him to us where he'll be loved, and nurtured, and blossom. This child is the only way to save your mother and keep our family together. He needs us, and we need him."

"No, Papa, you're wrong."

"What did you say? *I'm* wrong? *I'm* your father and you have no right to do this to us!"

"I know what my heart says, and I trust my friend. *That's* enough. I'll not take a child from his real mother, Papa, and I can't believe that you'd ask me to do such a terrible thing."

"How dare you speak to me in such a manner? Have you gone mad? Have you forgotten who your parents are? We've done everything for you! Why are you doing this?"

"This is wrong, Papa. Don't you understand that?"

"Fine, if your misguided principles won't help your family, then tell me where this baby is and I'll get him."

"I can't do that, Papa."

"You'd betray all of us over your selfish conscience?" he said, trying to control his anger and despair.

"You always taught me to follow my values and heart."

"You foolish, thoughtless—" Sedhu caught himself, stunned at what he was uttering. This was his daughter, his Divya. She was naïve and needed guidance, not punishment. Sedhu tried to focus, thinking what he could do to salvage such a dire situation.

"Papa?"

"I'm sorry, beta..." Sedhu sighed. "There must be other children that look like..." He stopped and rubbed the bridge of his nose, trying to think clearly. "Okay, fine, so be it, beta. You'll go back to Madurai and get another baby. You still have three days."

"Papa, that place is not a proper adoption agency. We can go to another adoption agency. There must be hundreds in India."

"Impossible."

"Why, because those agencies are legal and would never permit a child to be smuggled to another country?" Divya asked angrily.

"Divya, I can understand if you don't like this man, but I've known him for many years and you must trust me. Please, do as I ask, beta."

"Papa, you haven't met him in over twenty years. People change, and he's not the man you think he is."

285

"I know exactly who he is!" Sedhu snapped. "Now, I don't want to hear any more about this."

Of all the problems he had anticipated in his plan, he had never suspected that his daughter would be his largest barricade. How could this be happening?

"That director, Ramar, is evil, Papa. He's a criminal, and he snatches children from their mothers. He may even be responsible for the butchering of many innocent Dalits. I'll have nothing to do with him, and I beg you to do the same."

"That's enough, Divya."

"What he's doing is wrong, Papa, and if you take a child from him, then you become just as bad as he is."

"Divya, if you say one more word, I swear..."

"Papa, why are you angry at me? I returned a baby who'd been snatched from his mother's hands, and I'm doing the right thing. Don't let your emotions cloud your judgment. Listen to your heart. I thought you'd be proud of me."

"Proud? *Proud?* You've brought us shame. I gave you a simple task and you have ruined everything!"

"Papa, please try to understand. Ladha has suffered so much. Her entire family was slaughtered just because she was a Dalit—"

"I don't give a *shit* who she is!" Sedhu erupted, holding the receiver so tightly that his knuckles were white. "You've *destroyed* our family. Do you realize that you've given away our Rahul?"

"His name is Karuppan, not Rahul," she said, her voice trembling.

"No, his name is *Rahul*, your *brother*, our *son!*"

"Rahul is *dead* and no other child will ever replace him!" Divya cried.

"Shut up!"

Divya flinched as if she had been struck. Never had her father spoken to her in such an abusive manner.

"Divya, I'm your father, and I know what is best for you and this family. Now, will you go back to the adoption house as I ask?" he asked coldly.

"No, I will not."

"I've never been so disappointed in you. Thank God your mother isn't hearing this."

"You leave Mama out of this."

"If you cared at all about your mother we wouldn't be having this conversation, and Rahul would soon be coming home to us!"

Divya began crying, filled with confusion and despair.

"Now, your flight is in three days, and I'll handle the mess you've created."

"No, I'm not coming home," Divya whispered.

"What? What did you say?"

"I'm not coming home," she said with more conviction, angrily brushing aside her tears.

"What nonsense are you talking about? Why?"

"Because I'm engaged!"

The following silence on the phone was deafening for her. The longer her father didn't answer, the greater her fear intensified. Divya wanted to say something but was too afraid to speak.

"I'll forget what you just said, Divya," Sedhu finally responded frostily as he struggled to restrain the volcanic fury building within him. "As you'll forget any deluded notions of marriage."

"I can't, Papa. I love him."

"Love?" He laughed hollowly.

Divya felt her blood turn to ice.

He sounds like Ramar, she thought.

"What do you know about love? How can you love anyone that I've never heard of, and whom you barely know? Have you gone insane, Divya? Who's this boy who has brainwashed you into marriage?"

"He's from a small village in Tamil Nadu. His name is Aslam," Divya said quietly.

"A *Muslim?*" he hissed.

"W-What does that matter?"

"Is he an Untouchable too?"

"What difference does it make what caste he is? You've always preached how Dalits should have equal rights, and how the caste system should be abolished."

"Has he touched you? Has he forced himself on you?"

This man is not my father.

"Are you pregnant?"

"N-No," Divya said uneasily, suddenly realizing that her period was two days overdue.

Oh dear God, I'm normally like clockwork.

"Don't you dare lie to me? Tell me the truth, dammit!"

"P-Papa, please understand that—"

"Answer me!" Sedhu roared. "He's taken advantage of you, hasn't he?"

Divya remained silent.

"So it's true," he spat with disgust. "Those bloody Muslims want to breed us out, and now my daughter has been desecrated."

"Papa!" Divya cried out, appalled by her father's bigotry.

"I feel like throwing up. Don't you realize that you're being used?"

"You're wrong, Papa. Aslam is not like that."

"Don't you dare mention his filthy name! This is an outrage!"

"I've done nothing wrong."

"Divya, you even try to defend your disgusting actions and I swear..."

"Just meet him, Papa. *Please.* Give it a chance. You may like him."

"Like him? That whoring Untouchable pig will *never* be good enough for you."

"No, I'll never be good enough for *him!"*

"Enough! Curse you for doing this to us. Curse you."

"Papa, no," Divya sobbed.

"You'll return immediately to Toronto, I don't care what the cost. If you don't obey me, you're no longer our daughter. You'll be stuck in India with nothing! You'll be penniless and without a family. Do you hear me?"

"Papa, you're emotional. Let's settle down, and talk about this. I want to tell you about how wonderful he is. Just keep an open mind. Give him a chance. *Please,* I *beg* you."

"This marriage will *never* happen," he ranted, not listening. "I forbid it! Do you understand?"

"Papa, please calm down. Is falling in love such a terrible thing? You should be happy for me," Divya said tearfully.

"Happy for *you?* You selfish, ungrateful *disgrace!* You make me *sick* and have brought *death* to your mother!"

"No—"

"Not another word, Divya. You will come home now and forget this revolting union. And you'll abort that animal spawn growing in you. Do you understand me? Yes or no?"

"Papa—"

"Don't call me that until I have an answer! I just want a yes or no. Think carefully because if I hear the wrong thing then you're dead to me like Rahul, and I'm childless. Now, you'll come home and salvage your life. Do you understand?"

"Yes, Papa, I understand" Divya said, wiping her tears. "I love and miss you and Mama very much."

"Good." Sedhu's voice softened. "And we love you too, beta. Now, *please*, come home."

"But until you're willing to meet Aslam and accept my decision I'll never come home."

"No, wait—"

"Goodbye, Papa," Divya said, hanging up on her father and burying her face in her hands.

PART III

Bangalore City
Karnataka, Southern India

Chapter 15
Kama and Artha
Friday, July 19ᵗʰ 2002

"Damn it, I hate those dogs," Divya grumbled.

She turned to her husband who continued to snore softly.

Even after being married for half a year, it amazed her how he could sleep through virtually anything. She hated to disturb him, but the constant snarling, howling, yelping, and barking outside their home was driving her insane, and she was certainly in no condition to deal with the matter herself.

"Oz? Oz, wake up. Can you please get those dogs to stop fighting?" she asked, gently nudging him.

"Huh? What is it, honey?" he mumbled sleepily, his eyes still closed.

"The dogs, Oz. They're making so much noise. I can't sleep."

"Honey, what do you want me to do? Chase them with a stick?"

"Yes, please," she said sweetly.

"Honey, you must learn to ignore them. I can spend all night trying to chase them away but they'll keep coming back. There are too many of them."

"And why is that? Why are there so many dogs in this city, and why do they all congregate in front of our home? Tell me, Oz, aren't there any dog-catchers in B'lore?"

"Of course there are," he sighed, sitting up.

"So why don't we call them? This is an emergency."

"Divya, if you were being mauled by those dogs not even an ambulance would come at this time of night."

She scowled. "Okay, we'll call them first thing in the morning."

"You can try, but it won't make a difference. People prevent the catchers from rounding up the dogs because they believe it's inhumane and cruel."

"You're kidding."

"No, I'm not, it's true."

"But, I always see people throwing stones or chasing dogs with sticks. I would think that people would support the dogs being taken away."

"Divya, if there are cows, goats, and pigs throughout the city then why should dogs be discriminated?" he asked, rubbing his eyes.

"But they're infesting the city, and are a nuisance to everyone."

"Yes, but those very people who chase dogs away don't want them to be rounded up and killed."

"I admire the beauty of dogs as well, Oz, but the way these animals reproduce. I mean, I honestly wouldn't be surprised if there are more dogs than people in this city, especially at night."

"I know..." he yawned loudly. "Excuse me...Divya, I'm just telling you how it is."

"You know every time you yawn it's like a slap in the face," she said angrily.

"What?" Aslam unsuccessfully stifled another yawn. "Honey, I'm only sleeping five hours a night. Don't take my yawning personally. I'm listening."

"Ah!" she exclaimed, grabbing her stomach.

"What is it?" he asked anxiously, suddenly awake. He turned on the bedside lamp.

"Oh!" Divya smiled with wonderment. "The baby just kicked. Here, feel it."

She put his hand on her swollen belly. "Does it hurt?" he asked.

"No, it's just a very strange sensation." Her eyes sparkled with life.

"Look at you. You're absolutely glowing."

Divya smiled warmly.

The baby kicked again, and Aslam gave a proud fatherly grin. "Wow, that baby has a kick. He's going to be a great football champion for India one day."

"How do you know we're having a son?" Divya asked, kissing her husband.

"Just like I knew I was going to marry you the first moment I saw you beating Chicken on that badminton court," he said, positioning his wife to lie on her side.

"Mmmm, that feels nice," she said, forgetting the dogs as he rubbed her back.

Despite the ruckus from the canine wars outside, Divya was soon asleep.

Aslam smiled and kissed his wife on the cheek. As he wrapped his arms around his family and drifted towards a peaceful slumber, he realized that there was nothing more in life he wanted.

* * *

"How much for these tomatoes?" Divya asked the vegetable wallah.

"For you madam, special price, only fifteen rupees."

"Rubbish! Are you mad? Last week they were ten."

"Yes, but due to the terrible, terrible droughts in northern Karnataka earlier this year, my scoundrel supplier has raised his prices, and alas I am unfortunately forced to put these modest increases onto my most loyal customers."

"*Modest* increases? This is robbery!"

"I am a humble man, and I too have a very large family to feed, madam."

"If what you say is true, then explain to me why the vegetable vendor on the other side of the market is offering tomatoes for twelve rupees a batch?"

The vegetable wallah feigned an expression of surprise. "Please, madam, I am a poor man trying to make an honest living. I swear on the lives of my unborn grandchildren that the price is most fair. This other seller you speak of is a crook, selling his rotten tomatoes below cost to steal my most loyal customers. I swear on the lives of my unborn grandchildren that you will not receive a better offer, madam."

"Okay, enough about your unborn grandchildren. I'll buy two batches for twenty-five rupees, and not a rupee more," Divya said firmly.

"If this is the only way I can retain my most best customer, then how can I refuse," the vegetable wallah said sadly, taking the rupees.

Divya watched carefully to ensure the vendor only bagged the best tomatoes. She had learned too many times in the past that whenever a customer was looking the other way, the vendor would slip a couple of over-ripe or rotten tomatoes in the bag that he hid on the bottom of the pile of tomatoes on display. But, of all the vendors she had encountered in the food market, this merchant had always treated her well and provided high-quality produce. The fact that he spoke excellent English was a bonus. These positives were well worth the additional few rupees Divya spent every day, although she never told her husband, certain he would reprimand her with a worried frown, stressing about their delicate financial situation.

Divya added the bag of tomatoes to her basket, and thanked the vegetable wallah who politely bowed a good-bye. She squeezed her way through the bustling market towards the poultry stall where she had agreed to meet Ladha.

Every weekday, Ladha and Divya would religiously travel together to the Bangalore Craft and Food Bazaar to do their grocery shopping. Ladha's employer, Mr. Ravindra, would have his driver drop Ladha at Divya's house where they would walk to the market together. If it rained, Mr. Ravindra's driver would drive them both to the market.

Holding her swollen belly with one hand, and the basket of produce in the other, Divya made her way through the vibrant bazaar until she was standing beside Ladha. Although she could not understand what was being said, she listened attentively to her friend speaking animatedly to the poultry wallah in Tamil.

Since a native Tamil woman ran the poultry stall Ladha was always left to haggle for the best pieces of chicken at the lowest possible price. Since the vegetable and fruit vendors spoke only Hindi and English, Divya was in charge of negotiating the produce.

But her improvement in English has been remarkable, Divya mused.

During months of reading Tamil books and letters to Chicken's grandmother, the old woman had become very close to Ladha, and insisted she learn English. Grandmother Ravindra dedicated two hours a day teaching Ladha how to speak English. In the past six months—much to the satisfaction and pride of Chicken's grandmother—Ladha had picked up an incredible amount of the language.

Buyer and seller continued to have a lively debate over the price of the chicken.

If you put these two into suits and a boardroom you'd think they were negotiating a multi-million dollar contract, Divya thought with an inward smile.

Ladha extracted the money as the poultry wallah expertly packaged several pieces of boneless chicken. Both seemed upset, as if they had been swindled, but Divya knew it was part of the act. Neither would have agreed to the price unless they were satisfied, and Divya had long ago learned how much Ladha loved to negotiate.

Ladha took the meat, and smiled when she noticed her friend standing beside her. She had been so focused on the negotiations that she had not noticed Divya.

"Finished?" Ladha asked in English.

"Yes, and look at the lovely cantaloupe I got."

"Can-taa-lope?" Ladha repeated, confused.

Divya held up the fruit, and Ladha smiled with recognition.

They walked past the craft section of the bazaar, enjoying the sights of the colorful handicrafts and handlooms, and the sounds of the vendors beckoning and enticing them to purchase their merchandise.

There was the distant clash of thunder, and Divya glanced uneasily at the gloomy, overcast sky. She hoped they would make it back to her house before the storm began. She wished they had gone to the market by car. Although she would never admit it, carrying the groceries when she was over eight months pregnant was exhausting.

At least your clothes are comfortable, Divya reminded herself, sympathetically eyeing an American, female tourist tugging uncomfortably at her sweat stained blouse.

Divya did not know how she had lived so long without Indian cotton. Not only did the local clothing make her feel more as if she belonged here, but it was practical. Since becoming pregnant, her entire wardrobe consisted of simple, yet colorful, loose-fitting shalwar kameezes. As her stomach had grown, she had especially appreciated the shalwar's expandable, elastic pants.

Like Indian clothing, her appreciation of Indian foods had also grown in the past half year. With Aslam working so many hours, she had learned how to cook a variety of North and South Indian dishes. She found the art of cooking to be fascinating, and treated her kitchen as her lab. She loved meticulously experimenting with a variety of ingredients. To her relief and delight, Aslam—her test subject—enthusiastically sacrificed his taste buds and stomach for her, often declaring her latest creation to be a culinary masterpiece, although there had been several amusing instants when her food would trigger a series of events that ultimately forced him to rush to the latrine.

"So how is Karuppan these days?" Divya asked, trying to distract herself from her aching back.

Ladha beamed at the mention of her son. "Very good. He crawls all day. Too curious, he is. Very tiring."

"He must sleep sometime?"

"Never wants to. I force him at night. But, never cries. Good baby."

"He'll grow up to be a strong man with the love you give him."

"Thank you, Mrs. Divya," Ladha said proudly.

On numerous occasions, Divya had asked Ladha to drop the formality, and simply call her Divya. But Ladha had stubbornly refused.

Ladha felt eternally grateful for the kindness Mrs. Divya and Mr. Aslam had given her, and dismayed at the thought of calling them by their first name. Although she had become more and more comfortable with Mrs. Divya through the months, the formal name remained.

"And how's work, Ladha? Is Mr. Ravindra back from Singapore?"

"Oh, yes. Sahib came home yesterday. When came, Karuppan crawled to him. Karuppan missed him much. Sahib very, very good man. He treat Karuppan like son, and Kurruppan love sahib. Sahib spoil him much. He busy man, but still find time for Karuppan. Treat me well, too. And sahib's mother cannot see, but always happy. Like reading to her much. She teach me good English, yes, Mrs. Divya?"

"Yes, she does," Divya agreed with a smile.

They turned off the main street, and into a twenty-foot wide, unpaved alley. As far as the eye could see, a seemingly endless series of doors were spaced every twelve feet apart on both sides. Although it was a relatively clean and safe neighborhood, the alley would turn into a muddy river during monsoon season.

Halfway down the alley, Divya stopped in front of a peeling, purple painted door. She unlocked the padlock, and stepped into the house. The size of a one car garage, and consisting of only two rooms and an outdoor lavatory in the muddy backyard, she still had trouble calling it a house, but it had definitely become her home.

Divya realized she had forgotten to make the bed and convert it back into a couch.

"Oh, I'm sorry, Ladha. How rude of me. Give me a moment," she apologized, hurriedly putting the groceries in the adjoining two-by-eight foot kitchen. She poured water into her battered kettle, and lit a match to ignite the tiny gas burner.

As the water began warming, Divya waddled out of the backdoor of the kitchen, and into the tiny patch of dirt that was her backyard towards the outdoor lavatory. Divya relieved herself, washed her hands, and returned to the kitchen to finish preparing the tea.

When Divya returned to the common room with a tray of biscuits, two steaming cups of tea, and three sticks of burning incense, she was surprised to find Ladha sitting on the couch.

"Ladha, you shouldn't have made my bed for me. That was unnecessary."

"Happy to help."

"And very kind. Please, have some tea."

297

"Good tea." Ladha approved after a sip. "Incense smells nice."

"Thank you. They're jasmine scented. Rekha discovered them and brought me some. I just love them."

"How Mr. Aslam?"

"Very busy with work. He was complaining how the commute to Infosys headquarters in Electronic City is very tiring, especially since there's so much traffic. But he loves his job, and the company treats him very well. Did I ever tell you that they actually lent the money for us to buy this house?"

"No, Mrs. Divya."

"Yes, Infosys is a wonderful company, and I'm sure they'll reward Oz soon for all the hard work and extra hours he's putting in."

Although Divya was amazed and grateful at how quickly Aslam had found them a home, she worried for her husband. She would often wake up and notice him staring at the ceiling, his forehead wrinkled with concern as he worried how he would provide for his family. She never had complained about their living conditions, proud and happy for all they had, but she knew he stressed constantly for improving their lifestyle, often taking on additional projects and overtime to gain further favor with his superiors.

"Mr. Aslam work hard for family."

"Yes, he does."

"Pain?" Ladha asked, gesturing at Divya's belly.

"No, not at all. The baby's kicking a lot, but it's a wonderful sensation. Oz insists that it's a boy, although I've no idea how he can possibly be so certain."

Ladha did not say anything, enviously staring at Divya's pregnant frame. She yearned to be pregnant again with another one of Raja's children. She sighed despondently, missing her husband and other children. She focused her thoughts back on Karuppan—her life.

There was a honk outside, signaling Ladha's driver had arrived.

"Must go," Ladha said, putting down the teacup.

"See you tomorrow?"

"No. Tomorrow is sahib's son's birthday. Two-day event. Much work."

"It's Chicken's birthday tomorrow! Our invitation must have got lost in the mail," Divya chuckled, standing.

Despite Aslam and Chicken reconciling their differences and animosity towards one another, neither would consider the other a friend. As soon as school had ended, Chicken had quickly immersed himself back into the elite circle of the opulent. He distanced himself from any student that had come from a meager background in fear of being criticized by his wealthy friends. Although Divya would have loved to see them become friends, she grudgingly accepted that her husband and Chicken lived in different worlds dictated by a different set of societal rules.

"Invitation lost? Not understand," Ladha said as she collected her groceries.

"Wish him a happy birthday from us, Ladha, and I'll see you on Monday to go to the market," Divya said, changing the subject.

"Okay, Mrs. Divya. Namasté," Ladha said, putting her hands together to signal goodbye.

"Namasté, Ladha," Divya said, returning the gesture.

Divya stepped out of the house and waved as the honking car drove out of the alley. Fat drops of rain began to hit her, and the darkened sky was suddenly ablaze with jagged streaks of lightening. As she re-entered the house, the lights flickered. She quickly lit the house with candles in anticipation of an imminent power failure.

Divya glanced at her watch.

Shit, it's late! I have to get prepared for class.

Grumbling at how her condition slowed her down from performing even the simplest of tasks in a timely manner, Divya collapsed onto the couch and flipped open her books, examining what lessons were scheduled for today.

* * *

"Anita?"

The little girl stopped playing with her ponytail, and cast her big, brown eyes at her teacher.

"Can you tell me what the national bird of India is?"

299

"Peacock," said the seven-year old.

"Very good!" Divya smiled warmly. "You're dismissed for today. And don't forget to do your homework over the weekend."

"I won't," Anita said. She stood up from the carpet and ran out of the house.

"Amit, tell me the national fruit of India?"

"Um, mango, Mrs. Khan?"

"Yes, good. See you tomorrow."

She watched the little boy scamper out of the family room before she turned to her next student. "Sapna, what is the national animal of India?"

"Tiger!" she shouted out excitedly.

"Wonderful. You may leave. Have a good weekend."

Divya turned to the last child sitting cross-legged on the floor before her. She hoped he had done his homework for a change. She hated making him stay after-class, and she really had to use the bathroom.

"Vijay, did you do your homework last night?"

"Yes, Mrs. Khan."

"Alright, tell me, what is the national flower of India?"

Vijay's face screwed with concentration. "Rose?"

"No, Vijay," Divya said with disappointment. She wanted him to guess again, but she was beginning to cramp. "It's the—"

"Wait, lotus!" he declared triumphantly.

Divya smiled with relief and nodded. "Excellent. Good night, Vijay, and keep up the good work."

"Thank you, Mrs. Khan," he said, grabbing his bag and bolting out of the room.

Divya heaved herself out of her seat as Naveen, Rekha, and Om walked in.

"Hey, fatso!" Rekha cried, embracing her friend.

"Oh, it's so good to see you," Divya said, waddling out of the common room. "Have a seat, and I'll just be back in a moment."

Although the backyard was muddy, Divya was pleased that the rain had stopped and the sun was peaking through the clouds. She hated using the latrine when it was raining.

Once she had gone to the bathroom and made them tea, Naveen said: "Divya, we have a confession to make. We were outside the door and listening to you teach."

"What?"

"Yes, and we believe that you were far too hard on your students with those questions. They're only little children."

"And so adorable," Rekha said, dreaming of the children she would one day have.

"Children learn a tremendous amount at that age," Divya said. "They just need a little discipline. Don't underestimate their capabilities, Naveen."

"Very well, do you believe in the premise that all should be treated equal?" Naveen asked.

"Certainly," Divya said with a smile, knowing where this was going.

"Good, since you asked your students questions about India, I'll do the same. Let the teacher be tested. Agreed?"

"Agreed."

Naveen selected the closest textbook to him, and flipped through the pages. "Tell me...what's the population of India?"

"According to last year's census, it was over one billion."

"Number of states?"

"Twenty-eight states, and seven centrally administered union territories."

Naveen frowned, and flipped the pages. "Uh huh. Okay, and the number of major languages spoken?"

"Seventeen languages, and eight-hundred and forty-four dialects."

Naveen glanced at Om who agreed with a circular nod.

Naveen paused for some time, taking several sips of tea, and then closed the book. He closed his eyes, thinking of the perfect question to stump his friend. He suddenly snapped his fingers. "Okay, which nations or empires has India invaded before or after the British rule?"

"Nice try, Naveen, but I'm not falling for that trick. India has *never* invaded another nation in its ten-thousand-year history. And since you mentioned the British, may I also add that before the British invasion in the seventeenth century, India was the richest nation in the world."

Rekha whistled, impressed. "She's good, nah?"

"India is also the birthplace of calculus, the number zero, and chess," Divya continued.

"Now, you're just showing off," Naveen laughed. "Okay, I give up. You're a good teacher."

Rekha jabbed him in the ribs, "No, she is a *great* teacher."

"I admit that I was apprehensive of teaching such young children at the beginning," Divya said. "I have a business degree, not a teaching degree. And Professor Munde offered such a wonderful opportunity for me to be his teacher's assistant once Oz got hired at Infosys. But, I didn't want to travel to the campus and back in my condition, and we needed the extra money. Fortunately, Oz knew several people that wanted their children to improve their English, and now I can't deny how much I love it. The children are so innocent and wonderful, and I've also learned so much about India. But God, although it can be lovely, it can be such a frustrating place to live. Do you know that when I went last week to apply for a driver's license, I actually had to bribe the official just to get the application form?"

"Like cancer, corruption is killing this great nation," Naveen agreed solemnly.

"I cannot imagine living anywhere else," Rekha said. "This is our home."

"So far as I am able to judge, nothing has been left undone, either by man or nature, to make India the most extraordinary country that the sun visits on his rounds. Nothing seems to have been forgotten, nothing overlooked. Mark Twain," Om said with a proud smile.

"Om, you're beginning your job at the Indian Consulate in New York next week. America will soon be your home," Divya pointed out.

"India is the cradle of the human race, the birthplace of human speech, the mother of history, the grandmother of legend, the great grandmother of tradition. Our most valuable and most instructive materials in the history of man are treasured in India only. Also, Mark Twain," he added.

"For an American, Mark Twain certainly had much love for India," Naveen remarked.

Om raised his teacup in salute.

"Enough about India and America, nah? I want to hear how my friend's pregnancy is coming along. Are those pesky dogs still keeping you awake at night?" Rekha asked.

Divya frowned and nodded. "They're driving me mad!"

"Look at the bright side, Divya. They're just prepping you for when you have a child screaming throughout the night. This is good practice. For the next five years sleep will be a luxury for you and Oz," Naveen said.

Divya snorted. "Oz can sleep through anything."

"There is an African Proverb that says: 'However long the night, the dawn will break,'" Om added with a laugh.

"Thanks for all of your sympathy," Divya said sarcastically. "What great friends I have."

"Are you excited about being a mother?" Naveen asked.

"Oz is zapped...I am terrified," Divya admitted.

"I remember how afraid you were just before the wedding, and you persevered. Having a baby can't be that different," Naveen said.

"Actually, this may sound superficial, but I'm really worried about getting back into shape after the delivery," Divya said. "There are a lot of women who have these terrible looking stretch marks that never go away."

"Think of stretch marks as pregnancy service strips," Om said. "Joyce Armor."

"Yes, I've a feeling that having a baby is like going to war, and I certainly will have the scars to prove it. But I hope it isn't *too* many scars or *too* much pain." Divya sighed anxiously.

"Forget about that, nah? Imagine what your baby will become, and how he or she will improve this world."

"I'm sorry, Rekha, but I've never thought that far ahead for his future," Divya said.

"How do you know it's a he?" Naveen asked.

"I don't, but Oz is certain it is going to be a boy, and I've been corrupted by his thoughts."

"Come on! You are telling me that you never think about your baby growing up?" Rekha demanded.

"I do sometimes wonder what features he'll have of me or Oz, or what he'll sound like when he learns to talk."

"First you have to teach a child to talk, then you have to teach it to be quiet. Prochnow," Om said.

"Om, how were you as a baby?" Rekha asked.

"When I was born, I was so surprised I couldn't talk for a year and a half," Om said. "Gracie Allen."

"Too funny!" Divya laughed.

"And very appropriate, nah?"

Om looked at his watch, frowned, and stood up.

"You're leaving?" Divya said, crestfallen. "Stay for one more cup of tea?"

"I've many things to do before my flight tomorrow, and little time," Om said. All three in the room were surprised he had not quoted someone. "Sorry, I couldn't think of an appropriate quote," he added with a grin.

"We'll miss you terribly, Om," Divya said sadly. "Please write often otherwise I'll never forgive you. If you write enough, I may even consider naming my baby after you, if he is a boy."

Om was touched. "I no doubt deserved my enemies, but I don't believe I deserved my friends," Om said, embracing Divya. "Walt Whitman."

Om said goodbye to Naveen and Rekha, giving each of them a fierce hug. At the front doorway, he gave them a mischievous smile. "By the way, congratulations on your engagement you two." He walked out of the door, relishing the look of surprise on their faces.

"How the hell did he know that?" Naveen sputtered.

"That devil!" Rekha exclaimed.

"Is it true?" Divya asked, studying her two friends with a mixture of surprise and joy.

They both looked at each other, and nodded.

"And you didn't tell me earlier? What were you waiting for? When did this happen?"

"Two days ago," Naveen said.

"We wanted to wait until we told our parents first," Rekha explained.

"You haven't told them yet?" Divya asked.

"It's not that easy, nah?"

"Why not?"

Rekha uneasily glanced at Naveen for guidance.

"Show her, Rekha," Naveen said.

"Because of this," Rekha said, extracting a newspaper clipping from her purse.

Divya took the clipping and read the circled excerpt:

<u>ALLIANCE</u>
<u>INVITED FOR BRAHMIN GIRL</u>
<u>WELL SETTLED IN BANGALORE</u>

Suitable match
(Pretty good-looking, fairly bright, home loving, meritorious, fertile, educated, 23 yrs, 5'4", having a few minor white spots inside body not apparent)
Daughter of renowned, respected, cultured family

FOR TALL, PROGRESSIVE, EMOTIONALLY ATTRACTIVE,
EMPLOYED, PROFESSIONAL, DRAWING HANDSOME SALARY,
SLIM, FAIR, SOBER, NON-SMOKING,
MIN 6'0", MAX 30 YRS,

Caste no bar and large dowry.
Reply with Biodata, Photo and Horoscope
To Box No. A628C Times of India
Bangalore - 550005

"It's terrible, nah?"

"I can't believe this," Divya breathed, reading the advertisement again.

"I know!" Rekha cried miserably. "Can you believe how they had the nerve to write that line about the dowry and caste? It is like they are willing to give any amount of money to get rid of me."

"I thought caste wasn't an issue with you?"

"It isn't, but the entire advertisement insinuates that my parents are desperate to find anyone to take me."

"I took you," Naveen said, squeezing her hands.

"But they don't think that, nah?"

"Rekha, that's not true. You're making too many assumptions. Your parents adore you, and I think you're the most beautiful and special person in the world," Divya said.

"Then why am I 'pretty good looking' and 'fairly bright,' nah?"

"Those were just typos. I think they meant to say that you're 'pretty, good looking, fair, and bright,'" Naveen explained. "You know how the newspapers often make mistakes. Why would your parents ever say that, Rekha?"

"Then why did they write about my white spots? I mean they are only two little dots on my chest that are merely a slight discoloration of my skin. You would need a magnifying glass to find them. Oh, this is so humiliating," Rekha moaned.

"I'm sure they had good intentions when they wrote this, Rekha," Naveen persisted.

"No, no. This is my father's revenge for peeing on his good suit when I was two."

"Well, look at the bright side, Rekha," Divya said.

"And what is that?"

"At least your fertile," Divya said, bursting into a fit of laughter.

"Ha, ha, very funny," Rekha said, frowning.

"Rekha, I think you're missing the big picture about this advertisement," Naveen said. "You have to tell your parents about us."

"I know, Naveen. But this is a nightmare."

"No one knows that this advertisement is about you. It's okay, Rekha. You don't need to freak out," Naveen said.

"Is it okay, Naveen? You are definitely not six feet tall, although you are fair and sober," Divya said, laughing harder. "And Rekha did get you to finally quite smoking."

"I am very happy this is amusing you." Rekha slapped Naveen across his arm. "Why did you make me show her this, nah?"

"'Renowned and cultured family'?" Divya laughed, tears rolling down her cheeks.

"Disgusting, isn't it?" Rekha said. "My father's factory manufactures cricket equipment, and he considers himself to be *cultured* even though he knows nothing about music and cinema, and scratches his enormous stomach every chance he gets. He's the Indian version of Al Bundy!"

"No more, please!" Divya begged, gasping for air.

"And do you know why the word 'meritorious' was used? My father's friend taught him that word a few weeks ago. He uses it every chance he gets, even though he barely understands what it means."

"I'm going to pee in my pants!" Divya cried, clutching her cramping side.

"Good! You deserve it for laughing in my hour of need," Rekha said, smiling.

"Just tell me one more thing," Divya asked, once she had regained her breath, and wiped the tears from her face. "Why do they want a horoscope?"

"My mother is very superstitious, nah? Oh my God! Naveen is the wrong sign," she exclaimed, covering her mouth, her eyes wide. "What are we going to do?"

"It's okay, buddy. Your parents both love me, and I'll talk to them, if you wish. I'll convince them that Naveen is a wonderful man, and how much he loves you," Divya said.

"Would you really?" Rekha asked. "Oh Divya, my parents respect and love you so. Your words have such an influence on them. Can you speak with them early next week before I introduce them to Naveen?"

"It'd be my pleasure, Rekha."

Rekha hugged her friend with gratitude.

"Thank you, Divya. That would mean a lot to us," Naveen said.

"It's the least I could do for such good friends. Now, tell me how Naveen proposed?" Divya asked.

"Oh, I am glad you asked. I have been dying to share this story. It is very romantic," Rekha gushed, her face blushing from the warm memory.

The rest of the afternoon was spent discussing the future. It was one of the more enjoyable afternoons Divya had had in a long time, and she felt guilty kicking her friends out despite how exhausted she felt.

Divya collected the teacups, and decided to wash the dishes after a late-afternoon nap. She pulled the coach out into a bed and collapsed.

When Divya awoke, she was surprised to find herself in darkness.

What time is it? How long have I been asleep?

She sat up and gasped at Aslam sitting on a chair beside her, a serene smile on his face.

"Geez, you startled me. How long have you been sadistically watching me sleep?" Divya asked.

"Sadistically? That's a rather harsh thing to say to your husband who was admiring his beautiful wife. And it was only for a few minutes. I just got home."

"What time is it?"

"Nearly eight."

"You're home early today," Divya observed.

"Shall I go back to work?"

"No, this is a nice surprise, don't be silly. But, I haven't made dinner yet. I slept far longer than I wanted."

"That's expected considering how little sleep we get because of those dogs."

"You can help me make dinner, and then we can catch up on each other's days."

"I brought food," he said, turning on the bedside lamp.

"What? You never bring home food. Is this a subtle hint about my cooking?"

"This is hardly a *subtle* hint, honey," he said. Divya frowned as he laughed. "Come on, I'm just kidding. You know I love your cooking. This is a special occasion," he said, walking into the kitchen.

"Are you going to tell me you're finally fed up of me waking you up at night, and that you're leaving me and our unborn child for a sexy secretary at work?" she asked, catching the delicious scents wafting from the kitchen. She suddenly realized how famished she was.

Is that Chinese food I smell? she thought, salivating.

Aslam walked back into the bedroom, and placed a plate piled high with Chinese delicacies beside his wife.

"Keep spoiling me like this, and you can sleep with the entire company," Divya said gleefully, stabbing a piece of garlic shrimp with her fork.

"How was your day?" Aslam asked as he dipped his oily spring roll into some plum sauce. "Did those three buggers come over?"

"Yes, and they all asked about you and send their best. It's sad that Om is leaving tomorrow for New York."

"I'm going to miss him, too. But let the Americans deal with his eccentricities for some time."

"Oh, you'll never guess what else happened?"

"Rekha and Naveen are engaged."

"What? How'd you know that?"

"I just know these things. I have a sixth sense."

"Om told you didn't he?" Aslam shrugged as he scooped a spoonful of egg-fried rice into his mouth. "I knew it!" she said, slapping his arm.

Aslam spit out grains of rice and pieces of egg as he laughed.

"Stop making a mess!" she said, hitting him again. "Now, look what I have to clean up."

"You're the one hitting *me!*" he laughed harder. "Yes, Om told me. You know I can't keep anything from you."

"And that's why I love you." Divya kissed him. She smiled at the sweet taste of plum sauce on his lips. She wanted to kiss him again.

"Tell me more about their visit. What else did I miss?" he asked, glancing fondly at the portrait on their wall of the five of them standing in front of Mysore Palace. He loved that picture, and often found himself staring at it; the photograph reminded him of the solidarity of friendship he shared with them. Aslam suddenly wished he had been able to take some time off work to see them today. He wondered when they would all be together again, reminiscing and laughing about their past adventures, and excitedly discussing and sharing their bright futures.

"Hmmm, what else did you miss?" Divya said, trying to remember the afternoon. "Oh my God, Oz, Rekha's parents put out this advertisement in the *Times of India* to find a prospect for her. It was the funniest thing I've ever read..."

After they had eaten, they cleared the plates and got ready for bed.

"So?" Divya asked as she got into bed.

"So, what?"

"Are you going to tell me?"

"Tell you what," he said with a cryptic smile. He pulled the covers over them and wrapped his arms around her.

"Stop it, Oz! What's the special occasion you mentioned?"

"I got promoted."

"Are you serious? That's wonderful!" Divya exclaimed, hugging him.

"Yes. My presentation and proposal to the clients was an enormous hit. We got the Hindustan Lever account, and they want me to be the project manager. That means an extra five thousand rupees a month, a guaranteed two year stint in B'lore, and my own cabin."

"Cabin?"

"Yes, how do I describe it? It's a step up from a cubicle. It has a lot more space and privacy with four walls."

"An office?"

"Yes. I have an office now. But, we call it a cabin."

"There's still so much to learn. I associate a cabin with a room on a boat. I still have trouble understanding you at times."

"Divya, your Hindi has improved considerably since we were married, and I'm working hard to speak your style of English."

"Yeah, you're right."

"Hey, I still haven't shared the rest of my surprise, and it'll cheer you up."

"What, there's more? What surprise?"

"Tomorrow I'm taking you to Hogenakkal Falls."

"Isn't that in Tamil Nadu?"

"Yes. It's a four to five hour drive from here. Honey, what's wrong? You don't look happy."

"It's a sweet gesture, but I can't ride in my state on your motorcycle, and public transportation would take forever to get there. I go to the loo every thirty minutes!"

"I've thought of that. And that's why I have a car."

"We can't afford to rent a car."

"Who said anything about renting?"

"You didn't steal it, did you?"

"No, no. My boss was so happy that we got the account that he asked if there was anything he could do for me. I asked for his car for the weekend so I could treat my wife to a proper honeymoon."

"Honeymoon?"

"Yes, we never had one, as you've reminded me a thousand times."

"I was only kidding. A honeymoon meant nothing to me. I just wanted to be married to you."

Aslam smiled and kissed her.

"So your boss agreed to give you the car?" Divya asked.

"Without hesitation. And, Divya, the car is a brand new Ford Ikon. It's spacious, luxurious, with ample power, and air-conditioned."

"But I'm over eight months pregnant," Divya said half-heartedly, though her husband's excitement was becoming increasingly contagious. "What if something happens?"

"You are still three weeks away from your due date. Oh, come on, Divya. With it being the rainy season, the falls are supposed to be spectacular. It'll only be for one day. We'll leave early tomorrow morning, and reach there by lunch. And, if we leave early afternoon, we'll return to B'lore by night."

Divya thought for some time, wondering if there was any other reason not to go.

"Well?" he asked anxiously.

She broke into a smile. "Exactly how early are we leaving tomorrow morning?"

Chapter 16
Hogenakkal Falls
Saturday, July 20th, 2002

Divya admired the spectacle with awe. The orange orb rose with increased intensity over the horizon, its heat slowly dissipating the mist that blanketed the sodden, verdant rice paddies.

For the first time since they had left the empty streets of Bangalore in the cool pre-dawn morning, Divya was glad that Aslam had dragged her into the car.

It had been months since she had left Bangalore, and the sights, smells, and sounds of the countryside enthralled her. She smiled at they drove past several buffaloes wallowing serenely in a nearby pond, and frowned at the countless clusters of dilapidated one-room homes—made of mud walls and rusty corrugated-iron roofs—that littered the edge of the state-highway.

As they passed mile after mile of lush landscape, her sleepiness lessened, and once they crossed into Tamil Nadu, she was fully awake, practically pressing her face against the window like an overly excited child.

Aslam also remained silent during the drive, thoroughly enjoying the feel of driving his supervisor's powerful vehicle.

Together, wife and husband passed the first half of the journey in a comfortable silence.

Aslam slowed the six-cylinder Ford as they approached a crowd of spectators.

"I wonder what's going on?" he said.

"I don't know, let me find out." Divya lowered her window. "Excuse me—holy smokes!" she exclaimed, seeing the crumpled van, its fender wrapped around an enormous tree just off the edge of the road. The van and tree were engulfed in flames.

A blast of heat struck her as the Ikon passed the flaming wreckage. Afraid of getting burned, she quickly put up the window.

"Impatient, reckless drivers," Aslam muttered.

"I hope the passengers got out," Divya said.

She wondered why no one in the crowd seemed to be doing anything about the inferno, and why no emergency personnel had arrived on the scene.

Aslam maneuvered the Ford Ikon past the crowds and parked vehicles and accelerated down the state highway. A mile later, Divya was shocked to find several police officers sitting underneath a banyan tree outside a police station, laughing and oblivious to the fiery accident only minutes down the road.

Maybe they can't see the fire? she thought as they drove past the police officers.

She looked back, and saw black churning smoke rising over the trees in the distance.

No matter how long I live in this country there'll always be things I don't understand.

They drove past a great, muddy river where women squatted by the banks, and vigorously rubbed their soapy clothes against the flat slabs of stone. Children splashed in the river to relieve themselves from the heat, an irritant that the Ikon's air conditioner spared Aslam and Divya from suffering.

"Divya, can you pass my goggles?" Aslam asked.

She turned towards her husband and blinked with confusion.

"They're in the glove compartment," he added.

"Oz, what are you talking about? Goggles?" Divya opened the glove compartment.

"Yes, it's bright outside."

"Oh, *sunglasses*." She grabbed the shades, and locked the new term into her mind.

In the distance, Divya noticed several dozen locals spreading hay across the center of the road.

What the hell?

Her jaw dropped as Aslam accelerated and drove through the center of the mound, scattering hay in all directions. She glanced in the rear-view mirror to see the locals dashing back into the center of the road and quickly re-piling the hay.

Ten minutes later, she glared at Aslam as he drove through a second mound of hay gathered in the center of the highway. Oblivious to her cut-eye, he began humming a song from the most recent Bollywood hit.

313

As they approached a third group of people spreading hay over the asphalt, Divya said: "Oz, drive around the hay."

"Sorry, what?"

People rushed out of the way as the Ikon sped past them, creating a wake of hay.

"Oz, what's the matter with you?"

"What do you mean?"

"Why are you so driving over those poor people's hay?"

Aslam laughed.

"What's so damn funny, eh? These people slog all day in the blistering heat only to have their work destroyed by duffers like you crashing through their hay just for a thrill."

"Divya, those laborers *want* me to drive through the hay," Aslam said, laughing harder.

"What?"

"That's how the locals get their rice separated. It's far more efficient than having the ox stomp through it, as was the traditional practice. Now they let the traffic on the state highways do the laborious work for them, and leave the ox for other mundane tasks."

"Oh...I thought they were spreading it over the highway because it was the most flat area they had to dry it. You're not pulling my leg, are you?"

"No, I'm not. Why do you think Indian rice sometimes tastes so rubbery?"

"Really?"

"Of course," Aslam said, struggling to keep a straight face.

"You dog!" she cried, realizing he was teasing her. She slapped his arm.

"Ouch," he said, feigning pain.

"Snake," Divya muttered, turning to conceal her smile.

* * *

Sedhu awoke with a groan as dull pain shot from the base of his spine. Although a necessity, sleeping on the wooden hospital chair was beginning to cause more harm than good.

He kept his eyes closed, wishing he would forever remain in a state of slumber where his dreams were filled with the smiling faces of his beautiful Rani and children. Life was so much more bearable asleep. He did not want to get up. Living for the past months with his hospitalized wife lost to the living world, and the painful awareness that his remaining child had abandoned her family and eloped with a worthless Muslim Untouchable, had sent him to the brink of suicide.

He vividly remembered the feel of the serrated blade on his wrist. A moment before he had slit open his arteries, an image of his wife and dead son had filled his mind. Why should he allow his enemies to win by giving up? he had wondered. With that thought, his despair had transformed to rage. He was enraged at the hand fate had given him, and he hated all those responsible for taking what he loved. For the first time in his life, he had a glimpse of his brother's mind. He understood what true hatred felt like, and like the waters of a warm bath, he had allowed it to encompass him—an endless surge of blinding fury. He hated the faceless Muslim terrorists that had crashed those Boeings into the World Trade Center, and he despised the faceless Muslim Untouchable that stole his daughter. Refusing to be defeated, Sedhu had put down the knife. Rage gave him the will to fight. He still had to keep going for the sake of his wife.

With each passing day, Sedhu somehow found the strength to continue in the hope that his wife would someday come back to him. When he was not at work destroying his career—his once promising research was in disarray, he had alienated all of his colleagues, and his once jam-packed classes were now empty due to his incompetence and indifference—he was at the hospital with Rani. But despite holding her hand, talking to her, and tending to her needs, he never felt more alone. Rani's mind continued to detach itself from reality and drift into oblivion. All those lonely hours with his wife—who barely showed any recognition or desire to live—gave him too much time to think of his daughter, and how she had been manipulated by that worthless Untouchable, the man responsible for everything he had lost.

The overwhelming feelings of despair and impotence he had felt when Divya hung up on him all those months earlier remained raw. And Sedhu sought the aid of powerful sedatives to find some solace. The little, white pills became the source of his sanctuary, permitting him six hours of uninterrupted, coma-like sleep.

Shaun Mehta

Certain that any remnants of his dream and slumber were
gone, he sighed. It was time to start another day of battling his
conflicted feelings, endlessly switching between utter hopelessness
and relinquishing optimism that Rani would recover from the
chronic depression that held her spirit imprisoned.

Sedhu stretched, opened his eyes, and gasped.

Rani was gone.

For nearly a year, he would open his eyes every morning to
find his wife asleep in the hospital bed. Rani's state had continued
to deteriorate to the point of semi-coherence. She would only leave
her bed to relieve herself, bathe, or be pushed in the wheelchair, all
acts that only occurred with the assistance and encouragement of
a nurse or Sedhu. Last week, Rani had even begun to lose control
of her bladder in bed, an act that had brought Sedhu to tears.

But now the bed was empty, crisp sheets tucked tightly over
the mattress. Looking at the clock hanging over the bed, he knew
at this time of the day the nurses were changing shifts. So where
was his wife?

Waves of panic surged through him. He stood, and nearly
cried out with surprise.

Rani was sitting on a bench by the window, gazing at the sun
soaked forest that encompassed much of the hospital.

"R-Rani?" he whispered.

She turned towards him, her face brightening into a warm
smile.

"I didn't want to wake you," she said gently, her eyes
sparkling.

"You look so beautiful," he breathed. "Am I dreaming?"

She shook her head. "No."

"Are you okay?"

She nodded and smiled again.

Sedhu began crying. He had prayed for so many months,
begging God to let him see his wife smile at least one more time.
And now that his wish was granted, he selfishly yearned for the
moment to never end.

"How...I can't believe...thank you God...oh..." the words were
lost as Sedhu's emotions poured from him.

Rani extended her arms, and embraced her weeping
husband.

316

"Sedhu?" she said softly, stroking his peppered colored hair. "Where are my children? Where are Divya and Rahul?"

* * *

"How do you feel, Oz?" Divya breathed, peering over the cliff and staring at the raging water flowing into the narrow gorge.

"Zapped!" Aslam exclaimed. "I feel woolly headed."

"What? I know you're speaking English, but I have no idea what you just said," she laughed.

"Woolly headed means, um, like I'm light headed. I feel like I'm floating, as if this is all surreal...Um, honey, what are you doing?"

"I want to try something." Divya carefully turned around, praying she would not slip on the slick rock.

"Be careful."

Now I know why our guide wanted his money in advance! Divya thought morbidly.

She sat back down and dangled her legs off the side of the cliff. She smiled as he sat beside her and wrapped his arm around her. Together they silently watched the frothy water jettison into the abyss from both sides of them.

The deafening roar of the water, the warmth from the sun and the spectacular view of dozens of falls plummeting into the canyon brought a peace to her mind she had never felt before. She mused how insignificant Niagara Falls—so close to her family home—appeared in comparison.

And there's no way I'd be allowed to dangle my feet of the side of the Falls. Hmmm, I wonder if this is part of India's population control policy?

"What are you thinking?" Aslam asked.

"This is absolute, untapped beauty, Oz," Divya sighed. "Thank you for bringing me here."

"So, it was worth it?"

"Yeah."

"Hiking over all those burning rocks and stagnant muddy streams in your bare feet?"

"Definitely."

317

"Taking the coracle boat across the river, even though it made you feel nauseated?"

"Absolutely."

"Having our coracle semi-sink when our intoxicated rower rammed the boat into that jagged rock, piercing the waterproof hide and cracking the wicker frame?"

"Yes, yes, and *yes!*"

"Excellent. Happy anniversary, honey."

"W-What?"

"We got married exactly six months ago to this day. Since you never got a proper honeymoon after our marriage, I thought we'd celebrate both occasions today."

"That's very sweet, Oz." Divya kissed her husband. "I'll always remember this day."

"So, you really like this?"

"Of course I do, silly."

"It's not too sappy?"

"Oz, I love it. Thank you."

He smiled. "I'm glad. I've always wanted to bring you here."

They enjoyed the view for some time before he said: "Did you know that many distressed lovers jump from this point to their deaths?"

"Are you insinuating something?" Divya laughed.

"No, no, I just found it romantic. Almost like the Indian version of Romeo and Juliet."

She rested her head against his chest. "Yes, it is, my Romeo."

* * *

"Why dear brother, what a pleasant surprise. I haven't heard from you since that debacle with the adoption," Ramar said in Tamil.

"How are you?"

"You don't give a *fuck* how I'm so spare me the pleasantries."

Sedhu squeezed the receiver of the phone.

You've already sold your soul to this monster. Nothing matters anymore but Rani.

"I need your help, and I need it now," Sedhu said quietly.

318

"Who do you think you *are?*" Ramar roared. "I answer to *no* one, especially *you.*"

"Rani has come out of her depression."

If not for the static on the phone, Sedhu would have been certain that the phone line had gone dead. He could not even hear his brother breathe.

Ramar cleared his voice. "Is she...?"

"The doctor says that there is a great chance of full recovery."

Although it was barely audible, Sedhu was certain he heard a faint sigh. "And what does this have to do with me?"

"There are some complications."

"What type of complications?"

"Apparently, Rani has blocked out all events after September tenth. It is some type of mental defense mechanism. I don't know how else to explain it."

"She remembers nothing that happened after?"

"Nothing. She lost some of her memory during the ECT, but nothing like this. Now, as far as she is concerned her daughter is still studying in India, and her son is alive with our old friend in New York."

"Doesn't she wonder why she was in the hospital for the past ten months?"

"No, she doesn't. Deep down she knows something is wrong, but she refuses to confront it."

"Hasn't anyone told her the truth?" Ramar asked incredulously.

"No. The doctor says that shattering the delicate fantasy her mind has created could devastate her. She has to come to terms herself. No, for the sake of Rani we have to keep as many elements that existed before September tenth intact."

"What are you suggesting?"

"Ramar, she's asking to see her children."

"Have you gone insane? I'm a powerful man, but just because I've the power to take life doesn't mean I've the power to bring it back. Your son is dead, Sedhu."

"I know that. I was thinking of something else. It's a long shot, but it may work."

"I don't care. I helped you once and you made a mess of that. What if that infant boy you lost grows up and seeks vengeance for the death of his family?"

"That'd never happen! He's just a baby. He has no idea who you are."

"But that Untouchable bitch of a mother may know. And Divya is the one who reunited them."

"Ramar, if you ever touch one hair on her, I'll—"

"Are you threatening me?"

"No, I mean, I—"

"You bastard. I may be many things, Sedhu, but I would never harm my own daughter."

"I'm sorry. I'm emotional about Rani's recovery. Please, help me, Ramar. I don't know what I'll do if I lose her again."

"Stop it. You sicken me. I foolishly helped you once and it was a grave mistake. I will not do so again."

"Even when the fate of your daughter is involved."

"How dare you try to manipulate me by using Divya? Just because you can't take care of the problems that *you've* created you expect me to? The brother who you so cowardly *abandoned!* The brother whose family *you stole!*"

"Ramar—"

"Enough! It would be unwise to upset me, Sedhu," Ramar said, struggling to control his anger.

"Just hear what I propose. Give me one minute, and I swear that I'll never bother you again. I swear on our mother's life."

"Don't you dare mention her name. *Ever!* She died broken hearted because of *you.*"

"Please—"

"Shut up. Just be quiet. I don't want to hear anymore. Why don't you come here and solve your own problems? Huh? Answer me!"

"I am a wanted criminal in India and you know it."

"I never asked for your help," Ramar hissed. "And we are *even* as far as I'm concerned. I assure you that you'll not be adopting any more children from my agency."

"I don't want to adopt any more children. Listen to me."

"Good bye, Sedhu."

"Ramar, just one minute. *Please.* I'll never bother you again. I swear on Rani's life. Please. She still means something to you, I know she does."

"Rani is nothing to me. As far as I'm concerned you both can rot in hell. She's a whore."

"No."

"An immoral, ungrateful whore!"

"No, no, you're wrong."

"A bitch who'd fuck any dog for a rupee!"

"Shut up, Ramar, shut up! She was *raped* by Kaddar that day in the village!"

Sedhu squeezed his eyes with remorse. *What have I done?* he thought. *After all these years I've revealed the truth that I swore to Rani to preserve.*

"You're a desperate liar," Ramar finally whispered, his voice shaking. "Rani had shared Kaddar's bed for months."

"Who told you that, Kaddar? No, Ramar, you're a fool."

"I don't believe you."

"Rani loved you. Rani caught Kaddar's eye the day you were married. For months he kept insinuating that he wanted her, but she ignored him, never believing he would have the nerve to commit such an atrocious act, especially since he was married with children."

"Why didn't she tell me?"

"She knew you, Ramar. She knew that you would butcher Kaddar and his entire family if you ever learned the words he had uttered to her. She was terrified of the blood you would shed. You were so happy after marriage, especially when you learned you were going to be a father. The thought of disrupting that peace you had was unbearable for Rani. Remember how miserable she was for months? You just assumed it was because of her pregnancy. But, no, the conflict within her was tearing her apart. Do you remember, Ramar?"

Ramar did not respond, but Sedhu knew he remembered.

"That day, Appa beat Kaddar because he found a stain on one of his leather sandals. Appa beat Kaddar with that very sandal, screaming at him for his incompetence, until it snapped in half. Then Appa said he would take the cost of new sandal from Kaddar's wages. It was the final straw for Kaddar. He had hated our family for years for how we treated him, and he knew that the most fitting retribution for an Untouchable was desecrating the beloved wife of his upper-caste master. The house was empty, and Kaddar approached Rani, threatening to slit your throat at night if she did not sleep with him immediately. She resisted, but was overpowered and raped. That was when you discovered them, and assumed that your wife was unfaithful."

"If this is so, then why didn't she tell me then?" Ramar whispered, although he already knew the answer.

"She tried. In your rage you kept beating her. Kaddar kept screaming that she desired him and had been with him for months, and you believed him! You never gave her a chance, Ramar, your own wife. And then, later, when I learned the truth, she promised me never to mention it to anyone. She wanted to start a new life, to forget the past. I respected her wishes until now because I need your help."

There was silence on the other end. Sedhu's mind was racing but held no thoughts. He felt ill yet relieved for finally sharing the truth with his brother. But he also felt fear for what terror his truth would unleash.

"What did you have in mind?" Ramar finally said, his voice quivering with emotion.

Sedhu explained his plan to Ramar.

"*You're* insane," Ramar said with a hollow laugh. "I'll never help you with such madness. I should kill you for even suggesting I sacrifice everything I've worked towards for something so preposterous. It's your incompetence that has driven Divya to remain in India, and get married and pregnant."

"I can't change the past, Ramar. But you must listen to me. This is your daughter's life and future at stake."

"It makes no difference. It's her life. I'll not help you, even if it is for Rani. I have enough problems to deal with, and it has taken me too many years to put you all in the past."

"I beg you, Ramar, *please.*"

"Control yourself! You're such a pathetic, groveling swine. Take what dignity you have, and scuttle back to the woman you snatched from me for there is nothing you can say to make me help you."

Sedhu closed his eyes again, and begged God for mercy. "Even if the man Divya married is an Untouchable Muslim?"

With a fury that would haunt Sedhu for the rest of his life, Ramar unleashed a barrage of profanity. "*Lies!*" he cried with deadly rage.

"That's right, Ramar. Your daughter, your blood, is mixing with the very filth you have dedicated your life to eradicate."

"I'll take care of this," he hissed.

"Thank you, Ramar. And please, hurry."

"But, on one condition. And it's non-negotiable," Ramar said with a sudden calm that sent shivers of ice through Sedhu.

"What condition?"

"Your failure towards my daughter and wife is appalling. I'll do what you suggested, but you'll now answer to me and only me. Things will be done my way, no questions asked."

"W-What things?"

Ramar ignored his question. "If you ever question any requests I demand of you in the future, I swear to you that I'll never leave you alone until I'm dead. There is no city, town, or hole on this Earth where you can run and hide."

Sedhu stopped breathing, his heart frozen in mid-beat.

"I know what you are thinking, Sedhu, and you're right. I *am* the Devil and you *have* sold your soul to me. You brought me back into your lives, and now *I'll* decide how and when *I* choose to leave it. Do you understand?"

Sedhu was too petrified to answer.

"*Understand?*" Ramar screamed.

"Yes," Sedhu whimpered.

Ramar slammed the phone down and beckoned his guard to summon his men.

* * *

After treating themselves to an oil massage from one of the hundreds of masseurs that practiced their trade on the shaded islands that dotted the Kaveri River, Divya and Aslam descended a staircase chiseled along the side of the slippery cliffs. After negotiating a fair price, Aslam hired a more sober boat wallah to take a coracle down the river.

"Where are you taking me, Oz?" Divya asked with anticipation.

"You'll see."

Divya soon forgot about the surprise as the coracle drifted past a series of impressive cataracts. She was pleased that the water was not too turbulent; it minimized her nausea.

Aslam tapped the boat wallah on the shoulder, and pointed to the shore. Divya smiled as she saw two magnificent stallions grazing beside two guides.

They reached the rocky shore and disembarked from the coracle. As they approached the horses Divya suddenly felt apprehensive.

"I don't know if I can do this," she said uneasily. "What if I fall? I'm worried about the baby."

Aslam effortlessly mounted his chestnut horse. "The guide will help you get on, and will never release the reins of the horse."

"I don't think this is a good idea," she said half-heartedly, stroking the back of the black stallion.

"Come on, Divya. You've told me many times that this has been a dream of yours. Everything will be fine. Trust me."

She nodded, and with much grunting, and the help of both guides, got onto the horse.

For the next hour, she could not wipe the grin off her face. They rode along a trail that led along the side of the river until they finally came to a secluded cove where a narrow waterfall was pouring into an azure pond.

Aslam dismounted, and helped his wife safely reach the ground. He handed one of the guides some money in exchange for a basket.

"What's that, Oz?"

"Lunch. Freshly fried fish and rice, and some bananas for dessert."

She embraced him. "You've thought of everything."

"The guides will be back in two hours. I thought we could enjoy the scenery and privacy."

"It's perfect."

Aslam set up the picnic. Divya waited anxiously as she was served, her stomach rumbling from the wonderful aroma of the fried sturgeon. She devoured the tasty fish.

"You're hungry," Aslam remarked.

"I'm sorry," she said with embarrassment, her mouth full of food. "I didn't know how famished I was."

"It's okay. I'm glad you like it, and there's nothing to be ashamed of. You barely eat at all when you really should be eating for two."

They finished the meal in silence, savoring the food.

"Would you like some bananas?" she asked.

"The sun is very hot. I think I'll cool off in the water and then have my bananas later. Do you want to join me?" Aslam began undressing down to his boxers.

"No, I think I'll just enjoy the scenery from here," she said, admiring her husband's wiry physique.

Aslam dove into the cool water.

Divya unpeeled a banana, and screamed with surprise at the figure suddenly sitting beside her.

With lightening quickness the monkey grabbed her banana, and threw the fruit with perfect accuracy to his comrade sitting on a lower branch of a nearby tree.

Divya stood up and glared at the monkey. "You little monster!"

"Divya, look!" Aslam laughed, running out of the water.

A third monkey appeared behind her, and stole the remaining unpeeled bananas and dashed up another tree. With a mixture of frustration and fascination she watched the monkey leap to a neighboring tree and bounce on the branches with his companions, as if mocking her.

"I hate those wretched beasts," she chuckled.

"But you have to admit they're incredibly intelligent."

"And cunning. What are we going to do about dessert?"

"Well, we do have each other," Aslam said.

He kissed her, the water from his hair dripping on her.

"Oz, stop. It's the middle of the day and I'm over eight months pregnant."

"Hey, it's our honeymoon," he whispered hoarsely. "And there's no one here."

"You are a bigger beast than those monkeys."

He grinned, and then kissed her even more deeply.

"You're soaking me," she said, fighting hard to resist the temptation to return her husband's passionate kiss. "Besides, I can't with those monkeys watching and eating our food. It's like we're their entertainment."

"Let them watch."

Aslam began rubbing her back just as she liked it.

Ah, that feels so good...no, no, be strong.

"Tonight," Divya said firmly, pushing him away.

"Tonight?" he repeated, his eyes dancing. "Hey!"

"Stop being a baby," Divya laughed as she covered his head with a towel, and furiously rubbed his wet hair.

Excited voices of laughing children, and images of elaborate water slides twisting haphazardly into the cloudless sky, suddenly filled her mind.

She released the towel and stared at the innocent face of Rahul.

"Divya, why are you crying?"

She blinked furiously as the image of her baby brother transformed back to her husband, and the background of waterslides morphed into the surrounding cliffs. The laughter of children changed to the excited shrieking of monkeys leaping from branch to branch.

"W-what? Oh, Oz, it's you."

"Of course, it's me. Who else would it be?"

Her tears blurred Aslam's concerned face. "I was thinking of Rahul."

"I'm sorry, honey. I know you must miss him dearly."

"I can still feel the heat of the sun from that day," Divya said more to herself, her eyes glazing as she reminisced. "Gosh, it was such a great day. It was at this water amusement park north of Toronto, Wild Water Kingdom. Papa was in the wave pool, Mama kept switching between the hot tub and sunbathing, and Rahul and I kept going up and down the waterslides until we couldn't stand anymore. By the end of the day, we were both asleep before Papa left the parking lot."

"It sounds wonderful."

"It was," Divya nodded, wiping her tears. "Did you know that once we got home he carried me to bed? Oz, this was only last year, and he pulled his back doing it. I only found out the next morning, but he never complained about the pain."

"He loves you very much."

"Papa is a good man. He's always taken such good care of us, especially Mama. He adores her. Even twenty years after their marriage, they would tease and tickle and kiss each other constantly as if they were infatuated teenagers. I always pretended it bothered me, but I was delighted by the love they shared. Oz, there was so much laughter in our home before all this happened. Oh, God, why did this happen?" she sobbed, covering her face with her hands.

"I think you should call him, Divya."

"I told you that I never wanted to talk about that."

"Divya, please listen—"

"It's a beautiful day, Oz. Don't ruin it by broaching this subject."

"I've been silent long enough. You're missing them so much. I only want to talk about something already consuming your thoughts."

"I told you how he feels and what he said."

"No matter what he said, he's your father. He was surprised, emotional, and angry. I'm sure he didn't mean it, and is full of regret and remorse. No parent can remain angry at their child, Divya."

"My family is as dead as yours."

"Divya, don't say that."

"They haven't tried to contact me once in the last eight months, despite the wedding invitation I sent. I was foolish to get my hopes up then. Remember how upset I was when they didn't reply? I could be dead for all they know."

"Call him, Divya. Let him see his grandchild. If he is half the man you say he is then I know he'll accept us. And think of your mother. She has already lost one child. Now, she could gain a grandchild. You are all they have. And they are all you have. You all have suffered such a grave loss with Rahul. Nothing is worth you all suffering any longer. You should be supporting each other during these times, not fighting."

"Oz, no."

"Divya."

327

"I just can't."

"Or *won't*," Aslam countered angrily. "Don't be so goddamn selfish, Divya. Listen to yourself. You miss them and I know they miss you. Your stubbornness is causing nothing but pain and misery. And why? What do you have to lose by trying?"

Divya was stunned. Since their marriage, Aslam had never raised his voice. She felt as if he had slapped her.

"My parents are dead and I can never see them again," he said with a softer voice. "But it's not too late for you, Divya. Both your parents are still here. Resolve your differences. Put this in the past before it is too late. I swear to you that once they're gone you'll regret not sharing what precious time is left with them. Trust me, I know."

"I don't know, Oz."

"Just one call, Divya. Just call them once. That's all I ask. I know things will be better after that. If not for you, then at least do it for our child. He deserves to have grandparents that will spoil him with love."

Aslam's tender words brought a lump to Divya's throat. "Okay," she whispered, tears spilling onto her shalwar kameez.

"You'll call him as soon as we get home?"

"First thing tomorrow morning."

"Divya, you can't stall any longer."

"Oz, I'm not. The best time to reach them is late evening in Toronto."

"Promise, you'll do this?"

Divya nodded, her eyes filled with hope and despair. "Please, hold me."

He embraced her tightly.

Chapter 17
Delivery
Sunday, July 21th, 2002

Aslam tried to ignore his wife trying to shake him awake. "Oh, come on, Divya, not again," he groaned. It's the middle of the night."

"No, Oz—"

"Let the dogs bark, honey. I need some sleep. Lots of things to do tomorrow."

"My water broke."

"I'll fix it in the morning," he murmured, embracing the waves of sleep that washed over him. His eyes fluttered open and he bolted up. He stared at his wife. "Is this is a ploy to avoid calling your parents in the morning?"

She shook her head with a smile.

His eyes widened with a mixture of fear and panic.

"Oh shit!" he cried, leaping out of the bed.

"Oz, chill." Divya said calmly, watching her husband run around the room. "Everything will be fine."

"Really?"

She nodded reassuringly.

"Then why are *you* comforting *me?* And *where* is your suitcase?"

"In my lap. I'm ready, my love. Just get into the car, and drive me to the hospital, okay?"

Still in his pajamas Aslam grabbed the keys to the Ikon and ran out into the humid night, screaming at the packs of dogs to move out of his way. "You damn mangy mutts, out of my way. You, stop pissing on my boss' car! Shoo!"

So, that's how I could have got him to get rid of those dogs, Divya thought with a smile.

She waddled outside, and winced as Aslam kicked a dog away from the car. She felt a twinge of guilt for the scrawny animal.

Whimpering, its tail between its legs, the dog followed its companions and disappeared into the shadows.

Once he was sure the path for his wife was clear, Aslam got into the car and gunned the engine.

With a marker and scotch tape, Divya scribbled a note and taped it to the front door.

Aslam jumped out of the car to help his wife. "Divya, what are you doing?"

"I'm writing a note to put on the front door."

"What for?"

"Ladha is coming Monday morning to grocery shop with me. I want her to know that I'll be in the hospital delivering the baby so she doesn't have to worry or wonder where I am. Ouch!" Divya grimaced with pain and hunched over.

"Oh my God, are you okay? Is it a contraction?"

"Uh huh."

"Can you make it to the car?"

"Give me a sec, Oz." She tried to take deep breaths, but her cramps worsened.

"Should I call an ambulance?"

Divya would have laughed if she had not been in such pain. "Didn't you tell me that you could be lying in the center of M.G. Road bleeding to death and it would be days before an ambulance ever reached you?"

"Things aren't that bad," Aslam said unconvincingly, stroking her back. "Should I pick you up?"

"You could barely pick me up when I wasn't pregnant," Divya said, her sweaty face contorted with pain. "It's okay. I can make it to the car."

Panting and leaning heavily on her husband for support, she managed to get into the car.

Aslam threw the suitcase into the trunk, and ran into the house to grab his cell phone. He prayed his wife and child would make it through the night unscathed.

Aslam slammed the car door shut, and looked at his beautiful wife, his lovely Divya.

She is so beautiful, he thought. *Allah, don't take her away from me.*

"Oz, I'm scared," she said anxiously, clutching her swollen belly, her hair and brow dripping with sweat. "Something doesn't feel right."

Aslam smiled and squeezed her knee. "I love you, Divya."

She stared at him, her eyes searching his for hope.

"And everything will be alright. I promise," he added, kissing her.

She closed her eyes. "Okay, but hurry. This baby is suddenly in a rush to meet his parents."

Aslam put the car into drive and slammed the accelerator. He hoped his boss would not be too angry at the amount of damage he was about to inflict on the vehicle.

* * *

The Ford Ikon skidded to a stop in front of the Mallya Apollo Hospital in the heart of Bangalore.

Aslam was relieved that two attendants were waiting by the main entrance. The receptionist he had spoken to on his cell—as he carelessly sped and veered through the empty streets of Bangalore—had heeded his pleas.

Aslam jumped out of the car, and anxiously watched the attendants assist Divya onto the stretcher.

"Sir, please move your car," one of the attendant's commanded in Kannada.

"But my wife!"

"Oz!" Divya cried with pain, reaching out for her husband.

"She's in good hands. Park your car properly and meet us in the maternity ward," the attendant ordered sternly.

"I love you, Divya. Be strong. I'll be with you in a moment."

Aslam squeezed her hand reassuringly and kissed her pasty forehead so she couldn't see the concern on his face. He let go of her hand.

"Oz, don't go!"

He hesitated, watching his wife be carried into the hospital, and then got back into the Ikon. He thanked Om for advising him to register Divya at a private hospital. Although they could scarcely afford the bill, the quality of treatment was unmatched to any other medical facility in the city.

His mind void of thoughts, Aslam mechanically parked the car down the street. Entering the hospital, the beauty of the main reception area awed him.

It looks more like a hotel than a hospital, he thought, admiring the wood paneling, marble floor, and granite counters. He was impressed that even the receptionists were smartly groomed and dressed in crisp, bright uniforms.

The reception area was jammed with people, and Aslam forced his way to the front of the receptionist desk. Several people standing in line glared and cursed.

"Excuse me, miss, but where's the maternity ward? My wife, Divya Khan, was just brought in," Aslam said to the young receptionist.

"The maternity ward is on the third floor, sir. Go to the back of the building, past that security guard, and take the elevators." The young woman turned to the next person. "Yes sir, how may I help you?"

Using his elbows, Aslam shoved his way through the crowds to the back where a large Sikh security guard was blocking the walk-through metal detector that led to the rest of the hospital.

"Visitor pass?" the guard asked sharply, stepping in front of Aslam.

"Excuse me? No, I'm not a visitor."

"Medical personnel pass then?"

"No, you don't understand. My wife is in labor with our first baby. Could you please let me through?"

The bulky Sikh did not move. He pointed to the sign above him.

No entrance permitted without authorized visitor's pass. One visitor permitted for each patient at one time. Maximum five minutes per visitation. Zero tolerance for offenders.

"But my wife is in there!" Aslam said.

The guard stepped aside to let an elderly gentleman pass by.

"Why did *he* get through?" Aslam demanded.

"He had a visitor pass," the Sikh replied impassively.

"Look, the line up to the receptionist is enormous, and this is an emergency. Can you please make an exception?"

"Get a visitor pass from the receptionist."

"The receptionist told me nothing about a pass. She told me to go to the third floor. Now, can you please step aside?"

"No visitor pass, no admittance."

"I can't believe this," Aslam exclaimed angrily. He had not expected this to occur at a private hospital. He pulled out his wallet and extracted a hundred rupees. "Is this enough?"

"How dare you!" the Sikh growled.

"What, not enough? How about two hundred?" Aslam asked, pulling out another bill, and beginning to curse Om for suggesting they go to this hospital.

"I suggest you get a proper visitor pass or I'll have you removed from this hospital."

The Sikh stepped forward and towered over Aslam.

"How much money do you want?" Aslam asked, exasperated.

"None! Get a pass or I'll throw you out like a dog!"

Aslam stared at the Sikh, completely dumbfounded.

A security guard unwilling to accept a bribe? What's this country coming to?

Aslam sighed, and turned back to the mass of people swarming the receptionist. He nudged his way to the proper line, and anxiously waited his turn, his mind focused on his wife and soon-to-be-born child.

He noticed a bronze bust of the venerable Sai Baba by the main entrance. The sculptured face stared serenely at him. He leaned forward and read the inscription on the plaque beneath the bust; it stated Sai Baba had funded and blessed the hospital during its inauguration.

Although he had always questioned the legitimacy of a man who claimed to be a visionary of God, and who was worshipped by tens of millions, he began praying to the bronze bust.

Please let my wife and baby survive this unharmed. I'll always be grateful if you grant me this one request.

"You must leave a piece of identification if you want a visitor's pass, sir."

Aslam looked up at the pretty receptionist smiling at him.

How much time has passed? How did I get to the front of the line?

"Sir?"

He numbly nodded and handed her his driver's license. He turned back to the benevolent looking bust, searching for some sign.

"Here you go, sir," she said kindly, handing him the pass.

Aslam grabbed the pass and made his way back to the Sikh security guard, who dismissively waved him through as if the earlier encounter had never happened.

Too impatient to wait for the elevators, Aslam bounded up the staircases to the third floor. Unlike the main reception area of the hospital, the rest of the building was far less lavish. The white paint on the walls was peeling and bubbling, and the lighting was dull. Not much money and renovations had been put into the hospital since its auspicious, Sai Baba blessed, inauguration.

In the maternity ward, Aslam asked the first nurse he ran into to escort him to his wife. Instead, he was led to the main waiting area, and told a doctor would come to him as soon as there was anything to report.

The hours slowly passed, and the waiting drove him to the brink of emotional exhaustion. He wished to be with her.

He remembered how Divya had told him how a husband was permitted to stay by his wife during delivery in North America, a practice that was unheard of in India.

Divya had asked him several times if there were any circumstances where he could be with her during the delivery, but he had balked at the idea for months. Such a suggestion was so strange to him. Only after consistent pleas from Divya, he had conceded, and reluctantly made an appointment with the head of the maternity ward at Mallya Apollo Hospital. Aslam remembered how he had met Dr. Stewart a month earlier at his beautiful home outside Bangalore, and how impressed he had been by the articulate fifty-year-old Australian.

"Is there anyway my wife's request could be granted, doctor?" Aslam had asked.

"I've been trying to implement such a policy in this hospital for years, mate, but the bloody bureaucracy...I am sorry," Dr. Stewart sighed.

Aslam had left that day satisfied that he had done his best. Now, he cursed his compliancy. If he had pushed hard enough he could be helping Divya rather than being useless and trapped with his fears and anxiety. For the umpteenth time, Aslam stood up and began pacing around the small waiting area, his eyes on the floor. As he paced, he tried to think of happier times in his life to distract his mind. He became oblivious to the hours that passed, his mind filled by pleasant memories of his wife.

He came to a sudden halt. Two immaculate, designer dress shoes had replaced the familiar gray, granite floor in front of him.

"Mr. Khan?" said an Australian accented voice.

Aslam looked up to meet the gaze of Dr. Stewart who was dressed in surgical garments.

"I was the doctor who assisted your wife in the delivery."

Aslam tried to decipher Dr. Stewart's face for a hint of his wife's situation. But the doctor was unreadable, completely poker-faced.

Questions inundated Aslam's mind. *Doctor, how's my Divya? Is everything okay? Did she have the baby? Is it a boy or girl? Are there any problems? Is she okay? What happened? In the name of Allah, please answer me!*

But the words failed to form. All Aslam could do was desperately stare at the man who had all the answers to his questions, his anxiety increasing as macabre thoughts of every complication occurring during the delivery seized him.

"Mr. Khan..."

Aslam began to shake.

"You're the father of a healthy, bouncing son."

Aslam burst into tears. "A father? A boy?" he whispered with disbelief.

"Yes, that's right."

"Thank you!" Aslam cried, heartily embracing the man.

The doctor laughed. "Congratulations, mate!"

"And my wife?"

"Fine, just fine. Both are fine."

"Oh, thank you, doctor," Aslam exclaimed emotionally, hugging the man again.

"Please, I did nothing. Your wife is a very strong, young woman."

"Yes she is," Aslam laughed, wiping back his tears. "May I see my wife and son?"

Dr. Stewart's smile vanished into serious professionalism. "No, not yet. Your wife had a tough delivery and she needs her rest. We're currently cleaning up the baby and making sure everything is fine, just a precaution," he added to alleviate the look of concern on Aslam's face. "Don't worry, Mr. Khan. There were some complications during the delivery but both your son and wife are past any danger. They're perfectly healthy and will recover. They just need some time to rest. Why don't you go for a walk? You can see your family in an hour."

"Perhaps I should wait here."

"Nonsense. I have a suggestion. There's a flower shop down the street that sells the most spectacular bouquets, flowers that are fitting for a wife as lovely as yours. This shop gets new flowers delivered to them every morning at four-thirty. You have half an hour. I'm sure your wife would appreciate it. They're two blocks east of the hospital on the main street."

"That's a wonderful idea. I'll do that. Thank you very, very much, doctor."

"Please, it's because of these moments that I decided to go into this profession. Now, go get some air and those flowers, mate. Doctor's orders."

* * *

Aslam was struck by a blast of heat as he emerged from the air-conditioned hospital. He noticed with irritation that cars and autorickshaws were blocking the hospital's two ambulances parked in front. A security guard was playing cards with an autorickshaw wallah on the hood of one of the ambulances.

No wonder it takes so bloody long for medical personnel to get to an emergency!

Aslam dismissed his anger. Now was not the time to worry about the inefficiencies of his country. His beautiful Divya was okay, and he was a father.

Praise Allah, I have a son!

He grinned.

I told Divya that it would be a boy. I sensed it. I better purchase a football for him later today. He can never start too soon, especially if he's going to play for India one day.

His thoughts remained on the bright future as he walked down the street away from the hospital, searching for the flower stall.

How many blocks away did Dr. Stewart say the flower shop was? Two? Three?

He noticed a figure examining his parked car in the distance. It appeared to be a police officer.

Oh shit, I better not be getting a ticket! My boss will crucify me.

"Hey!" Aslam cried out in Kannada as he ran towards his car. "What's the problem?"

The police officer turned around and waved at the Ford Ikon. "Is this your vehicle?"

Aslam froze at the familiar face. The hairy tumor-looking growth on the left cheek was bushier and darker than he remembered, and the paunch was more pronounced, but he was certain this was the police officer that had stopped his motorcycle and asked him to pay a bribe to the storekeeper nearly a year ago. The glistening, betel-leaf stained teeth confirmed his suspicion.

"Yes, this is my car," Aslam said warily, hoping that the policeman did not remember him.

"Do you have a pollution license for this vehicle?"

"Pollution license? This is a brand new car, sir, and all new models meet government pollution regulations."

"Pollution license," the police officer repeated, extending his hand.

"Look at the other vehicles." Aslam pointed at the line of rusted, pollution spewing vehicles parked along the street. "Why aren't you examining them?"

"Pollution license, *now*."

"But—"

The police officer swung his lathi and smashed the closest headlight to him.

"What are you *doing?*" Aslam screamed.

The police officer destroyed another headlight on the Ikon. "I'll not ask you again for the license."

"Stop it! Okay, okay, don't cause any more damage. It's in the car."

Aslam unlocked and opened the door. He reached across the driver's seat and popped open the glove compartment, praying his boss had the proper documentation in order.

Aslam looked up with surprise as the cold metal of handcuffs snapped against his wrist. "Hey, what are you doing?"

The police officer snapped the other half of the restraints to the steering wheel. "Be silent."

"I asked you a question!" Aslam demanded, awkwardly standing back outside.

The police officer jammed his lathi into his gut.

Aslam fell to his knees with a painful grunt, the wind knocked out of him.

"I said, *shut* up," the police officer said harshly.

"I've done nothing wrong," Aslam gasped, trying to stand.

"Is that so? Do you think I'm a fool that I wouldn't remember the young bastard on the motorcycle who tried to deceive me last year at Infosys Circle? Do you know how much trouble you caused me with that shopkeeper? I first suspected he was cheating me. I nearly cut off his balls before I saw that beggar woman with all that booze you gave her. After a little beating, she eagerly told me what happened." His mustache curled upwards as he smiled, his blackish-red teeth glistened. "Oh, I've waited anxiously for this moment."

"There must be a mistake. I never tried to deceive you."

The police officer did not reply, studying his watch.

"Please, let me go and I'll explain everything. I'll pay you for all the trouble I caused. Look, sir, my wife just had our first child tonight. *Please,* be merciful."

The police officer looked down the street, and then struck Aslam across the face with his lathi. Blood exploded from his broken nose. The police officer grabbed Aslam's hair and stood him back up.

"Congratulations," the police officer said, spitting tobacco juice on his face.

Aslam bite his lip to avoid crying out in pain as the police officer punched him again in the stomach, determined not to give his tormentor any more satisfaction. Visions of Divya flashed through his mind.

"Muslim pig," the policeman hissed, his face inches from Aslam.

Aslam gagged from the police officer's reeking breath.

The police officer released his hair and threw him to the ground. Whistling, he turned and walked down the street, playfully swinging his lathi.

Breathing heavily, and drenched with blood and sweat, Aslam fearfully watched the police officer walk away. He thanked Allah for being spared from any more punishment. He grimaced as he stood up, wondering how to free himself from the handcuffs.

A black maruti van suddenly screeched in front of him. Aslam looked up with terror as the side door slid open.

A hail of bullets erupted from the shadows of the van and slammed into the Ford Ikon and Aslam. Glass exploded, and Aslam screamed in pain as blood gushed from the hundreds of fatal wounds that littered his body. As Aslam slumped onto the bloodied pavement—his lifeless body leaning against the Ford's punctured metal—the van tore down the street towards the police officer.

"Hurry up, let's go!" he cried, running to the braking van.

The police officer's eyes widened with surprise as the smoking muzzle was shoved into his chest.

"No, wait—"

Bullets ripped into the police officer, hurling him to the cement.

Before the side door was slammed shut, the black van recklessly turned at the end of the block and vanished.

* * *

Sedhu pulled out his ringing cell phone and answered it.

"Yes?" he whispered so he would not wake up Rani; she was sleeping in the adjoining bedroom.

He stared at the moonlight shining on the polished bathroom tile.

"The delivery is complete," said a digitally scrambled voice.

The line went dead.

Sedhu closed the cell phone, and turned on the tap to the sink, avoiding his reflection in the mirror. He splashed his face with cold water until he was numb.

He turned off the tap, and stared out of the window at the quaint neighborhood, oblivious to the water that dripped onto his clothes and blemished the shining floor.

Falling to his knees, Sedhu covered his face and wept.

Chapter 18
Revelations
Monday, July 22nd, 2002

Divya groaned and opened her eyes.

Where am I? she thought drowsily as her eyes adjusted to the harsh florescent light.

Then she remembered the excruciating agony of the delivery, and the joy of Dr. Stewart placing her screaming newborn son in her arms.

I have a healthy baby boy, she thought, sighing happily. *Where's my husband? Where's my Oz?*

Divya's smile widened as she saw a shape in the corner of the room stand up and move towards her.

"Oz?" she asked gently, turning her head.

She gasped with fear and surprise as the fuzzy image cleared into the stern face of the Director of the Priceless Child Adoption Home.

"What are you doing here?" she demanded harshly, trying to sit up.

Divya suddenly realized that her arms were restrained to leather tethers attached to the hospital bed.

"What's going on here?" she asked anxiously. "Why am I bound?"

Ramar sat calmly on a stool beside the bed, but remained silent.

"I asked you a question, *dammit!* Why are my arms restrained?"

"For your own protection."

"From whom?"

Ramar's eyes feigned surprise. "From yourself, of course."

Divya was stunned, but quickly masked her surprise. "That's ridiculous. Get out of here. I don't want you here. Where's my husband?"

"Your husband?" Ramar echoed.

341

"Aslam Khan. Where is he?"

"Oh, are you referring to that Untouchable Muslim?" he asked with distaste.

"I want to see him immediately."

"That will be quite impossible."

"Impossible?" Divya paled. "What have you done to him?"

"It was a most unfortunate incident."

"No, God, no," she whispered.

"A random act of madness that constantly terrorizes this great nation."

"No, this can't be happening."

"Apparently, a police officer was the target."

"No, no, lies. All lies."

"And Aslam was in the wrong place at the wrong time."

"I don't want to hear anymore."

"It happened on the street outside the hospital."

"*Please*, stop."

"He was shot several times," he said, reaching into his pocket.

"Shut up, shut up, shut the *fuck up!*"

"He's dead, Divya," Ramar said impassively, dropping Aslam's wedding ring on her lap.

"You bastard *murderer!*" Divya screamed, trying to lunge at him.

"Control yourself."

"*I'll kill you!*"

"Such hysterics are not useful for anyone. You need your rest and to calm down," he said, standing.

"You *sonofabitch!*"

"We'll talk more when you are in a better state of mind."

"Noooooooooo!"

Ramar picked up the ring, and walked out of the room.

* * *

Ladha studied the note taped on the purple door.

Since her English was poor, she slowly read the note a second time to make sure she understood the message.

Ladha,
Sorry, that I can't come to the market with you,
but I am at Mallya Apollo Hospital having the
baby!
Wish me luck!
Love Divya.

Mrs. Divya and Mr. Aslam are having their baby! she thought, grinning with delight.

Ladha hurried past a sari-clad mother bathing her squirming, naked baby underneath a rusty water tap.

She emerged out of the alley and jumped into the waiting Zen hatchback. Ladha slammed the door to the car, and in rapid Tamil ordered Mr. Ravindra's driver to take her to Mallya Apollo hospital.

* * *

Divya opened her eyes to find Ramar sitting on the stool studying her. A burly security guard stood beside the entrance of the hospital room, his menacing face partially hidden in shadows.

So it wasn't a nightmare, she thought dully. *Oz is dead. I have no one.*

Divya was still bound to the bed. She now understood what Ramar meant by the restraints being there for her own protection. If she could, she would slit her wrists in an instant. She did not want to live anymore.

For several moments, they both stared at each other—one with curiosity, the other with hatred.

"Divya," Ramar finally began, leaning forward, "there's not much time and there's much I need to tell you. Do you understand me?"

She did not respond. Her mind screamed for death.

"Your mother has asked for you and Rahul."

Divya looked at the ceiling.

"And Sedhu asked me to bring both of you to him."

Shaun Mehta

Although dozens of questions tormented her, she pushed them aside. She blankly studied the swiveling ceiling fan.

"Divya, did you hear me?" he asked, his voice rising.

Ramar sighed and studied his daughter. He suddenly despised himself for causing her so much pain. He had no regrets for ordering the Muslim Untouchable to be killed, but he wished that he could make her understand why it was necessary.

None of this would have ever happened if I'd raised her myself. Then she'd understand, he thought bitterly. *But, what if it isn't too late?* another voice reasoned. *What if, with time, she'll understand why you did what you did? If you tell her the truth, then maybe she'll forgive rather than loathe. What do you have to lose?*

Ramar suddenly felt nervous. It was a feeling he despised. It made him feel weak—impotent. He turned to his guard and dismissed him, ordering him to return in fifteen minutes.

The guard obeyed without protest, wondering what powerful hold the young woman had on his master.

Ramar glanced back at Divya, sighed, and cleared his throat. "Divya, the first time we met in Madurai at the Adoption Home you asked me why I always called your father Sedhu, but never referred to your mother by her first name. You found that strange, and I intentionally avoided answering that question. Do you remember that?"

Don't acknowledge him, Divya. He's a monster. He wants you to respond to him. It's a trap.

She continued to stare at the ceiling.

"I think it's time to answer that question," he continued, intently studying her face for a reaction. "You see I can't call Sedhu your father, because he isn't."

Her heart skipped a beat, but she remained expressionless.

He's lying, Divya, he's lying. Don't give him the satisfaction of upsetting you. Ignore the sonofabitch.

"You see, Sedhu is my brother, and your mother and I were married before you were born."

Divya clenched her teeth and dug her nails into the palm of her hands.

"And that makes me your legitimate father, Divya. It was *I* who suggested your name to Rani before you were born," he said,

344

his voice cracking from emotion and his eyes welling with tears. "I know you may have difficulty believing me, but it's true. Sedhu stole my family away from me and fled to Canada, and I foolishly let him. You're my daughter, Divya, and I love you with all my heart."

"*Liar!*" she screamed, lunging at him. "I'll kill you, you *fucking* cockroach! Release me coward and I'll tear you *apart!*"

Ramar flinched as if he had been struck. He had exposed the truth to her, and this was how she reacted? He was flabbergasted.

"D-Don't you see that everything I've done has been in your best interest?" he stammered.

"You kill my husband, destroy my life, and claim to love me? You sick *fuck,* you're not my father!" she cried, spitting on his face. "*Fuck you!*"

All emotion disappeared from Ramar's face. He stood up, wiping his face. His eyes burned with fury.

"You can say or do anything you want, but the truth will always remain!" he thundered, his voice rising with each word. "You're my daughter. Your son is my grandchild. You don't believe me?"

"I'll *never* believe you!"

"Then explain these DNA tests that prove I speak the truth?" he asked, extracting a sheet a paper and dangling it in front of her to read. "I had them done on you and the baby right after the delivery."

"Impossible! Counterfeits!"

Ramar pulled out photographs from his jacket pocket and tossed them on her lap. "And are these counterfeits as well?"

Divya stared at the photos with disbelief. The first was undeniably her mother—over twenty years younger—being married to Ramar. In one corner of the picture was a young Sedhu, sitting cross-legged, and watching the ceremony with a large smile on his face. Although she did not want to, she studied the second black-and-white photograph. In it were two teenagers and a middle-aged couple. In the corner of the picture was written: *Mangalum family portrait, December 1975.*

"Those are your grandparents, and Sedhu and I." Ramar said quietly.

"Mangalum?" she whispered with dismay, shaking her head.

"Yes. That's your real name. My brother changed your family name to Ambani when he fled to start his new life in Canada."

Could it be possible? Has my entire life been a lie? she wondered. *No, it can't be! These photos are fake, created by a computer.*

"Divya, listen to me," Ramar said with urgency. "No matter how hard this is for you, you can't escape the truth. Didn't you ever wonder why you never met your cousins, or uncles, or grandparents?"

"I had an uncle in New York," she whispered.

"Oh, yes, Uncle Sebastian. The man who perished with your little brother during the World Trade Center disaster, correct? No, I am afraid that he was only your uncle in name. You see, your Uncle Sebastian is a Roman Catholic who was born in Goa. He and Sedhu began the same program at the University of Toronto and became good friends. He certainly loved you and treated your family well, but I assure you that he was no uncle. No, your family was waiting *here* for you. Your grandparents died unable to ever see their grandchildren."

"Then it was *their* fault, not Papa's! Papa explained to me that he and Mama fell in love and were forbidden to marry. I know how they were forced to run away from Punjab and change their names to Ambani. Papa never lied to me."

"If this is true, then have you ever heard your parents speaking Punjabi?" Ramar asked, sitting down beside her.

She was silent, desperately trying to recollect even one moment when she had heard them speak Punjabi. She couldn't. She eyed Ramar, whose mouth curved into a smile.

"They always told me that they never wanted to ruin our English," she said defensively, but with far less conviction than before.

"Nevertheless, isn't it strange that they *never* spoke their mother tongue, even between themselves?"

"They could have spoken Punjabi when I wasn't there."

"Perhaps, but I am sure they would have unconsciously reverted back to their native tongue from time to time in your presence."

Divya suddenly had a flashback of her parents having an intense argument in the middle of the night. She had awoken to

346

go the bathroom, and had heard their heated words in a strange language that she was certain was not Punjabi; she had several Punjabi friends at school. Had they been speaking Tamil?

"You can't manipulate me with such speculation," she cried, unwilling to accept the possibility of Ramar's words.

"Even if you dismiss the Punjabi, you can't dismiss the dozens of other signs that have been around you for some time. Think back to all of the things you once found strange but ignored or forgot, and they'll now fit into place and make sense. Think back and remember, Divya. Yes, it's possible to fabricate DNA tests and photographs, but even I don't have the power to alter your memories. Think back, Divya, and the truth will come out."

Divya tried to shut out the memories that came flooding back to her, but couldn't. Ramar had triggered the past, and she suddenly remembered her conversation with her father when he had requested her to go to Madurai to adopt a child. For someone who claimed to have never visited Madurai, she had found his extensive knowledge of the city unusual.

"Yes, that's it, look into the past," Ramar whispered with encouragement.

Sedhu's exact words of how to get to the Priceless Child Adoption Home resonated in her mind: '*Madurai is a sprawling city, so it's very easy to get lost. From the bus or train station take Vilachery Main Road up the slope of Pasumalai Hill to Sourashtra College, which is about six kilometers away. From there, you can see the Meenakashi Temple and the Vaigai River.*'

Sourashtra College! Where have I seen that before?

With a growing feeling of dread, she eyed the black-and-white Mangalum family portrait lying on her chest. Sourashtra College was emblazoned on a young Sedhu's T-shirt.

Tears of betrayal fell on the photograph. "No, it can't be."

"Yes, it's coming clearer, isn't it?" Ramar whispered, his eyes wide. "Never underestimate the power of denial."

"Why are you destroying everything I love and believe in?"

"Because nothing is more important than the truth. Your entire life has been fiction and the least I can do is make you realize this. You need to understand the truth so you know that I'm not a villain. I, too, am a victim of terrible circumstance. I lost

347

my daughter and wife, Divya, and I understand how you must be suffering."

"Why would he lie? You said he *fled* to Canada?"

Ramar nodded solemnly. "Yes, for *murder*."

"Murder?" Divya covered her face, shaking her head. "No. No, Papa couldn't hurt a fly. He's so peaceful, so good."

"I'm sorry, Divya, but it's true. Why'd you think your father has never once visited his homeland? He'd be arrested if he took one step on Indian soil. Ask him. He can't deny the truth. I have proof. I can show you the warrant for his arrest, if you wish." Ramar's watch suddenly beeped, and he glanced at it to confirm the time. "Divya, I'm afraid it's time for you to return to Canada."

"Why are you doing this?" she sobbed. "Just leave me and my baby alone."

"You'll never see me again, I assure you, Divya. I have no place in your life. But at the same time, you needed to know the truth."

"I don't care about the goddamn truth. I just want to see my baby. *Please,* let me see him."

"For the sake of you and your mother, I must let you go," he continued, ignoring her pleas. "You have come back in my life, but I understand that you belong with your mother. That's the sacrifice I am willing to make for you. You may not realize it, but one day you will, now that you know the truth."

"I'll never go back to Canada! I'm not going anywhere!" she shouted, trying to break her restraints.

"Have you heard a word I said?" Ramar demanded. "Do you understand the sacrifices I've made for you and your mother?"

"*Fuck you, pig!*"

"No one insults me. *No one!*"

"There's nothing more you can do to me!"

"Is that so?" Ramar said coldly, struggling with his emotions. "Since my daughter seems to be so ungrateful, perhaps I'll just focus my energies on raising my new grandson?"

All the fight from Divya instantly dissipated. "Oh God, not my baby. Please don't take him away from me."

A smile of satisfaction crossed his face. "I must admit that I do admire your tenacity, Divya. Even the sniveling fool of my brother couldn't diminish the fire of your father. Your blood boils like mine! You make me very proud."

"Please, let me see my son."

"You mean your brother, Rahul, don't you?"

"No, no, he's my baby, my son. Rahul is dead!"

"You're emotional and confused, child, and that's understandable."

"No! I want to see my baby! You can't do this!"

"Don't you see that I can do anything I want? Now...*Rahul* is resting, and will soon be reunited with his mother, who is anxiously waiting for both of you. You've all been apart far too long."

"Why are you doing this?" Divya asked, breaking into tears again.

"I'm a man of my word, Divya, and now your father and I are even. He once saved my life and now I'm saving his. You'll understand when you're older. You have your whole life ahead of you. Soon you'll be married and have children, and all of this will be forgotten. Trust me. Things will soon be much better. You were confused and misguided, and no one blames you for this."

"But *I am* married, and I *have* a child."

"No, Divya. That was all a bad dream. The next time you wake up, you'll be in the comfort of your bed back in your home, reunited with your perfect family. And in time you will thank me for this."

Divya spat angrily at Ramar. "You disgust me!"

"I'd be careful what you do for the sake of that bastard you spawned with that Muslim Untouchable!" Ramar roared, his teeth bared and his fist clenched. "You'll *respect* me!"

"What's going on here?"

Ramar and Divya turned with surprise to find Dr. Stewart standing at the doorway.

* * *

Ladha admired the bouquet of flowers she had purchased at the small flower shop two blocks from the hospital. The flowers were blooming and freshly picked. She hoped Mrs. Divya would like them.

With her flowers in one hand, and her visitor's pass in the other, she walked past the formidable Sikh security guard, and took the stairs to the third floor. Although Mrs. Divya had repeatedly tried to get Ladha onto an elevator, she had refused. She trusted her two legs over standing in a box being lifted by a cable any day, and no one was going to persuade her otherwise.

On the third floor, Ladha studied the room numbers, searching for Mrs. Divya's room. She noticed a white-faced doctor enter a hospital room at the end of the hallway.

The way the room numbers were ascending, Ladha realized Mrs. Divya's room was the one the doctor had entered. She decided she would wait in the hall until he finished his examination before visiting her friend.

An unforgettable voice suddenly reverberated through the empty corridor: "I'd be careful what you do for the sake of that bastard you spawned with that Muslim Untouchable! You'll *respect* me!"

Ladha dropped the flowers, her face locked in terror. She whimpered as images and voices from that nightmarish night flashed through her tormented mind. As if it was happening again, she witnessed the masked man ruthlessly execute her daughter and son with his pistol. She was certain it was the same voice that had ruthlessly committed those atrocities and kidnapped her baby. And now that monstrosity was in Mrs. Divya's room!

"What's going on here?" came the voice of an English-man from within the hospital room. It was the doctor's voice.

Her hands trembling, Ladha edged to the door, and peaked through the crack. Although she knew the risk was great, she had to see the face of the man responsible for murdering her family. Although the white-coated doctor blocked most of her view, she saw the hateful face of the masked man that had haunted her dreams for the past year.

The face permanently branded in her mind, Ladha looked away and pressed her back to the hallway wall, tears of pain and fear pouring down her face.

What's he doing here? Is he looking for my baby and I? Has Mrs. Divya told him where my baby is without knowing who he is? Oh dear God, what if his desire to punish my family is not complete?

Panicking over the safety of Karuppan, Ladha trampled over the flowers and dashed down the hall.

As she disappeared down the staircase, the doors to the elevators opened and Ramar's bodyguard emerged. He stopped, frowning at the crushed flower petals scattered across the hallway.

* * *

"Oh, Dr. Stewart, thank God!" Divya cried with relief. "This man murdered my husband and wants to take my baby from me. Please stop him. Call security. *Quickly!*"

Her mouth fell with horror as Ramar stood and warmly shook the doctor's hand. "Hello David, good to see you."

"And you too," David Stewart said. "Is my patient ready for her injection?"

Ramar's bodyguard entered the room, and tapped his watch.

Ramar nodded. "Yes, proceed, doctor. We're behind schedule."

Defeated, Divya began crying uncontrollably.

The doctor pulled out a syringe and smiled at her. "No need to cry, dear girl. This won't hurt too much."

"H-How could you betray my baby and I?" she stammered. "We put our lives in your hands. My husband was a guest in your home. He *respected* you!"

"For the money, of course, dear girl," Dr. Stewart said, searching for a good vein. "My son got accepted at Wharton to do his MBA, and my daughter wants to take violin lessons. Do you have any idea how expensive it is to get a good violin instructor in India? Ah, here we go. Don't struggle, dear girl, otherwise this will hurt more."

Ramar motioned his bodyguard to hold Divya's arm in place.

"Good, that's it," the doctor said as he injected the medicine.

Divya was instantly overcome with sleepiness.

"You'll burn in hell for this," she said drowsily.

"Temper, temper, Mrs. Khan."

"*Miss. Ambani!*" Ramar snapped.

"Yes, of course," the doctor said quickly, eyeing Ramar fearfully. "My apologies. As I was saying, *Miss. Ambani*, you've had a very trying day, so I can understand your frustration. So, just relax, dear girl. This'll help you rest as you'll need your

351

Shaun Mehta

stamina and full wits so you can be strong for...what have you named him?" he asked Ramar, afraid he would say something else wrong.

Aslam, Divya tried to say, afraid at the sudden loss of her voice.

"Rahul," Ramar replied coldly.

"Right, lovely name," the doctor said with approval. He turned to Divya. "Yes, as I was saying, Rahul's healthy and will need your support now more than ever after that unfortunate tragedy regarding your husband. My deepest condolences."

"Can she travel in this state?" Ramar asked impatiently.

She strained to hear the doctor's answer, but his words became incomprehensible.

Divya tried to fight the powerful medication and stay awake, but within a few moments the images of the doctor, Ramar, and the bodyguard blurred and faded into darkness.

Chapter 19
Homecoming
Tuesday, July 23rd, 2002

Divya watched with reverence as the holy man tied her sari to the groom's shirt, symbolizing their sacred union.

Bride and groom exchanged garlands and rings, and holding each other's adorned hands, slowly circled the sacred fire, which represented the divine witness.

Divya placed her hand on the groom's chest, and recited the Vedic hymns that prayed for the union of their hearts and minds.

The next few moments were a blur for Divya as she numbly went threw the motions she had memorized, her thoughts elsewhere.

Am I doing the right thing? she asked herself for the thousandth time. *Can I tell all my friends and God that this is the person I want to share my heart and soul with? What if Papa was right, and I'm about to make a tragic mistake?*

As soon as she thought of her father, painful stabs of regret and sorrow filled her. Ever since she was a little girl, she had dreamt of her father giving her away to the groom. And now not a single member of her family was present.

Realizing they were entering the Seven Steps stage of the ceremony, she focused her attention back on the wedding. Nothing was more important than this rite in the ceremony, and she was determined to do it correctly. Questioning her decision or her parents' absence did not matter now. She was about to recite vows in front of God, vows she would preserve until she died.

As they took each step, both bride and groom sang a promise in Sanskrit to each other: "With God as our guide, let us take the first step—to nourish each other in any circumstance. Let us take the second step—to help each other grow together in spiritual, mental, and physical strength..."

Fresh tears filled her eyes. Aslam was singing with such passion and conviction, saying the words from a ceremony that was not even part of his religion. She had never been so touched.

Shaun Mehta

Any doubts she had vanished, and she realized that there was no other person in this world she would rather spend her life with.

"Let us take the third step," they both continued. "To preserve our wealth for the benefit of our family and loved ones. Let us take the fourth step—to share our joys and sorrows together and harmoniously..."

As Divya stepped past Om—who was performing duties on behalf of her family—she smiled. She blessed her good friend for finding such a wonderful interfaith priest to marry them both in a fashion that emphasized spirituality, the beauty of both their faiths, and avoided religious dogma. The interfaith priest was wonderful, and had helped her and Aslam develop a customized marriage ceremony that satisfied them and offended no one.

"Let us take the fifth step—to promise to care for our children and to ensure they exemplify everything good in this world. Let us take the sixth step—to be together forever, no matter what the obstacles and challenges...."

Keeping her head down, Divya shifted her eyes to catch a glimpse of the crowd watching the ceremony. Despite her obscured vision—the cherry red silk of her sari covered her head—she saw Rekha weeping with a large smile in front of the congregation of students that surrounded the sun soaked IIMB college amphitheater.

"Let us take the seventh step—to vow to each other that we shall remain lifelong friends, the perfect halves to make a perfect whole."

They stopped circling the fire, and faced each other. Divya admired how handsome Aslam looked in the simple silk kurta and turban he was wearing.

Aslam's voice cracked with emotion as he said: "With these seven steps we have become friends. Let me reach your friendship. Let me not be severed from your friendship. Let your friendship not be severed from me."

Aslam's brown, watery eyes were filled with love. He touched her heart and said: "I hold your heart in serving fellowship, your mind follows my mind. With my words, you rejoice with all your heart. You are joined to me by God."

As dictated by Hindu traditions, Divya and Aslam became husband and wife as they fed each other a piece of sweet date.

354

Om and Naveen—sitting around the periphery of the fire—stood up and walked beside Divya and Aslam to a small table where the nikaah-nama lay.

The interfaith priest began speaking in Arabic, reciting marriage-related verses from the Qu'ran that both Divya and Aslam had selected together. Every word the holy man spoke was translated into English in Divya's mind. She was thankful that Aslam had stubbornly forced her to learn the meaning of the words during the weeks leading to their wedding.

"I don't want you just to agree to something that you don't completely understand," he had calmly reminded her whenever she grew frustrated in trying to memorize the Arabic translations.

The priest began to explain the details of the nikaah-nama. As he recited each sentence, Divya and Aslam thrice repeated: "Qubool," accepting the terms that were being read from the nikaah-nama.

Before the wedding, Aslam and his young Muslim lawyer friend had explained to Divya that the nikaah-nama was a civil contract under Islamic law, necessary to be completed in order for their marriage to be valid. Other than the nikaah-nama, Aslam explained that there was no other uniformity or standard ritual at a Muslim marriage, a concept Divya had found surprising.

The priest paused and smiled approvingly at the bride and groom.

"Qubool, qubool, qubool," Divya said in unison, her eyes locked on Aslam.

I accept, my love. Wholeheartedly and forever, I accept.

The interfaith priest signed the contract, and then nodded at Aslam, Divya, Om, and Naveen to do the same. Bride, groom, and the two witnesses signed the nikaah-nama.

Divya looked apprehensively at Om, who circular-nodded with encouragement.

"I, Divya, offer you myself in marriage in accordance to the love of God," she said in perfect Arabic, her eyes brimming with tears. "I pledge, in honesty and sincerity, to be for you a faithful and helpful wife, swearing to Allah to love no other."

Aslam was stunned by Divya's Arabic, and wondered how she had learned those words. He looked at Om, who was unable

355

to conceal his mischievous, sparkling eyes. Aslam shook his head with disbelief, and turned back at his beautiful bride.

"I pledge, in honesty and sincerity, to be for you a faithful and helpful husband," he said in Arabic. "I swear to Allah that I'll love no other. You're my life, my family, my soul, and my heart."

Under Islamic law, Divya and Aslam became husband and wife as they fed each other a piece of sweet date.

Divya held her husband's hands and squeezed them tightly, amazed at how warm they felt. She never wanted to let go of them. They were one.

She suddenly felt the heat from Aslam's hands begin to dissipate. Puzzled, she looked down to see his flesh and muscle peel and shrivel into exposed bone. Horrified, she looked at her husband to find a skull grinning at her.

"Divya, what's wrong?" it asked.

She screamed herself awake.

A bedside lamp flicked on, and Divya tightly embraced the familiar figure sitting beside her, relishing the heat emanating from her mother.

"Don't cry, beta. Don't cry. Shhhh, it was only a nightmare," Rani soothed her.

"Oh, Mama, it was terrible. I was getting married and my husband turned into a skeleton."

"It was just a nightmare, beta. There's nothing to fear. You're safe, back in your home."

Home?

Divya let go of her mother, staring at her with anxiety and confusion.

"I shouldn't be here," Divya whispered, studying the dark shapes in her room. A faint light was shining from the borders of her curtains.

Why am I asleep in the middle of the day? This is my bedroom, but somehow this doesn't feel like home. It feels foreign and strange—cold.

"You're exhausted and famished from your journey, beta. You need some rest," Rani said with a kind smile. "Lay back down, and I'll get you some soup. You've had a difficult journey."

"What day is this?" Divya asked, trying to clear her mind. "How'd I get here?"

"Tuesday, July twenty-third, beta, and you flew, of course."

With the time difference, I've been unconscious for two days, Divya calculated.

"No, how did I get into my bedroom, Mama?"

"I picked you up from the airport and you fell asleep in the car," said a deep voice from her bedroom doorway. "You asked where Mama was, and I told you she was getting your room ready and cooking your favorite foods. But, you were *so* exhausted that I had to carry you to your room, like I did when you were a little girl, remember?"

"Papa?"

"Yes, beta, I'm right here. How are you feeling?" Sedhu asked warmly, walking towards the bed.

"I think she may have a fever," Rani said with concern, placing her cool hand on Divya's forehead. "Look, Sedhu, she's shaking."

"Why don't you get a damp cloth and that soup you just made," Sedhu suggested to his wife. "Traveling such a distance can be quite strenuous. She needs to eat something."

"No, don't go," Divya said, clenching her mother's hand; she stared at Sedhu with growing terror, remembering everything that had happened over the past few days.

Rani glanced anxiously at Sedhu for guidance. "Don't worry, everything will be fine, dear. Go get her some food," Sedhu said, studying his daughter.

Rani nodded, and kissed her trembling daughter on the forehead. "I'll be back in a few moments, beta."

"No, Mama, don't go, please."

"I'll just be downstairs, beta. Mama isn't going anywhere. I promise," Rani said, standing up. She smiled reassuringly, and then walked out of the bedroom, closing the door behind her.

Divya sat up and pressed her back against the headboard as Sedhu took another step towards the bed. She hugged her knees to her chest, her eyes wild as if he was a monster that had suddenly appeared from beneath the bed.

"Are you okay, beta?"

She did not reply, struggling to bring form to the snippets of hazy images that circled her mind. She glanced at the prick marks and bruises on her arm from multiple syringes and the markings on her wrists from the restraints. She suddenly remembered

357

awakening in an airplane and being injected with another dose of sedatives.

Divya shivered as she thought of the resources and influence Ramar must have utilized to transport her across the world and past customs in her drugged, unconscious state.

"Are you cold, beta? You've nothing to fear," Sedhu said. "You're home with your family."

"I have my *own* family."

"Yes, you have a mother, a brother, and your father. It's me, Papa, beta."

"My mother's in denial, my brother's dead, and you're a lying murderer."

"Silence!" Sedhu exploded, stepping forward and grabbing her by the arms. She winced as he painfully squeezed her shoulders. "There'll be no shouting in this house. *Ever!* Do you understand me! *Do you?*"

"You're hurting me."

Sedhu released her and stepped back, breathing heavily. "I-I'm sorry," he stammered, aghast at his outburst. "We just can't get your mother upset. She's in a very fragile state. We mustn't raise our voices. The doctor says it'll distress her. Okay?"

Divya rubbed her throbbing shoulders, her eyes never leaving the man that she had once loved.

"You were quite exhausted from the journey," he said, trying to sound casual as he stepped back into the shadows. He began to straighten the teddy bears she had arranged on her bookshelf years ago. "You were asleep for nearly two days."

"You mean *drugged*, don't you?"

His shoulders sagged, his back facing her. "I'm not proud of what was done, but you left me no choice."

"Left you no choice? You sanctioned the murder of my husband," she cried, bursting into tears.

Sedhu swept his index finger across the dusty shelf. "My, my, we really should dust this room. This is very unhealthy."

"Admit it. You killed him," Divya said coldly, wiping her tears. "You're a killer. You killed your son-in-law."

He sighed sadly and turned around. "Divya, he was manipulating you. He was against us. He stole you from us when we needed you the most. Don't you see that? I had to get you away from him in order to make you realize that we're the ones who love you. You belong with us, your family."

"No, you're wrong. He persuaded me to call you, to make contact. It was *I* who resisted, who was stubborn. He finally convinced me to call you, and I was going to, but I went into labor that night...if only I had called earlier perhaps this would have been avoided...oh, how could this happen?" she bewailed.

Sedhu was shocked. *Is it possible? Did I misjudge him? What have I done?*

"Divya, please listen to me," he said desperately. "I only wanted him out of the way, not killed. It was all a misunderstanding. You know I'd never do anything to harm you. I'm your father, your Papa."

"You're nothing to me," she said, her voice filled with agony and anger. "You've destroyed me."

"Divya, how can you say that? We're flesh and blood."

"Liar! My father is your brother. Ramar told me everything."

Despite the darkness, she watched his face turn a shade paler. And with a sinking feeling she knew everything Ramar had told her was true. But did that mean Sedhu was also a wanted murderer who had fled India to escape persecution?

Her head was spinning. She felt overwhelmed and nauseous. Everything was happening too fast.

"No, that's not true," Sedhu whispered with denial.

"It is. He showed me the blood tests and old photographs of his marriage with Mama. It's true, isn't it? Admit it. Or will you hide behind more deception? Answer me, dammit!"

Sedhu did not say anything. He didn't know what to say. Although he had assumed the slightest possibility of Ramar revealing the truth to Divya, he had dismissed it as an acceptable risk in order to save Rani.

"You've been deceiving me from the very beginning, haven't you?" Divya pressed relentlessly. "You're nothing but an imposter. You sicken me!"

Sedhu was silent for a long time, listening to Divya crying and carefully considering what to say. Finally, he said: "Listen to me, *I am* your father, Divya. Perhaps not by blood, but I've dedicated my life to preserving the well being of this family. I am your father a thousand-fold more than Ramar will ever be.

359

You can't deny this. I've always loved you and your mother. This is *our* family. *I am* your father and *you're* my daughter. And not even a dangerous, warped man like Ramar can change that. Yes, it's true. He's your biological father. You have the right to know, and I'll hide no further. There's been enough deception. But, if we are speaking of the truth, then you should know the *entire* story of what happened, and not Ramar's *version*. Did he explain how I saved your pregnant mother before he was ready kill her?"

Why would Ramar try to kill his wife and unborn child?

"He told me you're wanted for murder, that you stole us from him and fled India."

"No, that's not true. He murdered an innocent villager, and I took the blame to protect him. He was insane with rage, Divya, and he was going to kill your pregnant mother too. I saved your lives, and took you both to Toronto because I had received a scholarship to begin my doctorate."

"More lies. You'll say anything to deceive me."

Sedhu stepped back into the light cast from the lamp, his eyes blazing with anger. "Then ask your mother. If you don't believe me, then ask her. She was there, battered and bruised from his beatings, pregnant with you. Ask her how Ramar stripped her naked and beat her in front of the entire village until she was near the brink of death. Ask her how I risked my life to bring her to Toronto where we would be safe. Ask her before you condemn me. I left my entire family and life behind to save both of your lives. *Ask her!*"

Divya searched Sedhu for any hint of deception. All she could sense from him was the truth.

Is it true? Did he honestly save Mama and I from Ramar? she wondered. *Maybe he really does want what's best for us. What if he's a victim of all of this like I? No, it does not matter. He contacted Ramar and wanted to break up my marriage to Oz. He's been against me from the beginning. Whether directly or not, he's responsible for the destruction of my family. Oh Lord, what's happening? I don't know what's real anymore.*

"Divya, talk to me. Say something," Sedhu said, sitting on the edge of the bed.

"Why lie to me about Ramar?" she asked, a part of her still searching for the truth.

"At first, your mother asked me never to repeat a word. Then, there was no sense in drudging up the past, something both your mother and I had worked hard to forget. We were all one family and none of that mattered. We were happy and that was in the past. What was the point to remember such atrocities? Divya, we were happy once. We can be happy again."

Divya shut her eyes, wishing for some answers or direction. But she found neither guidance nor solace.

Oh God, I don't know what to do or think. Please help me. Save me from this insanity. Bring my Oz back to me. Let Ladha appear at the doorway so we can go to the market for the day. Oh, why did this happen? I was so happy. Why?

"Do you remember when I took you to the zoo?" he asked, interrupting her tortured mind.

She looked at him for a moment before shaking her head.

"You were seven years old. It was a beautiful summer day."

The memory came rushing back to her as if it was yesterday.

"I was very distracted that day," Sedhu continued. "I'd been spending a lot of time working on some research papers, and my deadline was quickly approaching. I'd been living in my office and spending very little time at home. I only took you to the zoo because you had cried and cried that morning over how I'd promised to take you. You clung to me desperately, refusing to let me go to work, and I finally conceded. Do you remember, beta?"

"Yes."

"Although I consented to take you, I was agitated, my mind completely absorbed in my work. And when you excitedly tried to show me the gorillas or the giraffes, I'd barely acknowledge them. You finally got fed up with me, and sulked for the rest of the afternoon. Do you remember, Divya?"

She nodded, reliving the memory.

"That night as I was tucking you into bed, you told me that you wanted to share something with me. But I was very upset that the entire day was wasted, and I was anxious to get a few hours of work before I went to bed. So, I sternly told you that it could wait until tomorrow, and that you should go to sleep. My mind was preoccupied with returning to my research, and I was completely oblivious to how insensitively I'd spoken to you."

"I remember how angry I got," Divya said, reminiscing. "I told you that you always made promises you never kept. And then... then I did something when you left...what was it?"

"I'll tell you, beta. I turned off the light and went to my office. But I couldn't concentrate on my work. I felt guilty for how I'd treated you, and realized how little time I'd been spending with you. I returned to your room to see if you were still awake, hoping you would share your surprise with me. You were asleep, but I noticed several torn pieces of pink construction paper by the base of your bed. When I picked them up and put the pieces together I had tears in my eyes. That day I swore that nothing would be more important to me than my family."

"The card," she whispered, remembering.

Sedhu pulled out the heavily taped, heart-shaped card from his inner jacket pocket, and handed it to her. She read the card written in bright red marker:

I am   the
luckiest daughter in the
whole wide world.
I love you,
Papa.
D.

"You saved it all this time," Divya murmured, guilt consuming her for having such terrible thoughts about her father.

He has always been gentle to Rahul and I. He couldn't possibly be part of such monstrosities. How could I think such things of him? He has always loved us, provided for us, kept this family together.

Sedhu nodded. "Yes, I've always kept it close to me, beta. You taught me how there was nothing more important than the love a child has for her parents."

"Oh, Papa."

"I swore on that day that I'd never put my work before my family. Even when I received several offers to be the dean of science schools across the country and in the U.S., I declined. Why? Because it was *my* duty. It was my *Dharma*, my obligation as head of this family to be the best husband and father I could be. Nothing else mattered."

"No one asked you to make such sacrifices."

"Don't you see, beta? They weren't sacrifices. It was my responsibility to do everything in my power to ensure the happiness and safety of all members of my family. Just like it is *your* responsibility to be a dutiful, loving daughter...and *sister*."

"No, I can't, Papa, *please*."

"It's your *Dharma*."

"He's my son," she sobbed, shaking her head.

"No, he's *our* son. And you'll be *his* sister. You must accept this, beta. Think about your mother. Think about our family. Don't destroy us, beta. *Unite* us. Fulfill your duty and Dharma for this family, as your mother and I have. Nothing is more important."

"I can't."

Sedhu placed his hands on top of hers, his eyes gazing steadily into hers. "Yes, you can. Beta, you must listen to me and trust me. I had nothing to do with what happened to Aslam. I swear on your mother's life. That was all Ramar's doing. I only wanted to speak with you. But Ramar's hatred consumed him because Aslam was part of a lower-caste *and* a Muslim. Ramar has so much hate for Untouch...er...Dalits. That's why he nearly killed your mother and murdered those Dalits before you were born. He caught her with one of them and went mad with rage. I can prove it to you. I swear."

"What do you mean 'he caught her with one of them'?"

"The Dalit was my family's servant, Kaddar. He tried to rape your mother, and Ramar caught them. He assumed his wife was being unfaithful and refused to listen to reason. He burnt Kaddar alive in front of the village and beat your mother until she was near death. I saw it all. It was horrible. The entire village, including your Grandfather, cheered and encouraged him to do it. I intervened, and was banished from my village and family. I escaped with your mother to Canada. But since that day, Ramar's hatred for Dalits has only grown. He has crusaded his life to destroying them."

Divya felt as if she was hearing a tale from a Bollywood movie.

Do such things still happen? she wondered.

363

She then remembered the charred remains of Aslam's village, and the explanation her husband had given her about the Dalits and the Zamindars. She thought about what Ladha had told her about the raid, and how her children were slaughtered and her baby kidnapped. Divya trembled, and wrapped her arms around herself.

"Beta, please listen to me," Sedhu said, interrupting her thoughts, his eyes filled with sorrow and remorse. "I admit that I never embraced Aslam, and I was irrational and foolish not to make contact with you. I swear that when I received your wedding invitation I picked up the phone a hundred times. But I was weak, scared. I should've tried harder, for you. But I didn't, and I'm sorry. But that doesn't mean that I am a killer. You must believe that I abhor any form of violence. You know your Papa. I've made many terrible mistakes in the past, I admit it, and this is by far the worst. I'll never forgive myself for bringing Ramar back into our lives. Oh God, I am *so* sorry I spoke to Ramar about this. I should have known better, but I thought he had reformed. This was all a tragic, tragic mistake."

"Mistake?" she echoed, rubbing her throbbing head.

"It was stupid. I'll never forgive myself," he said tearfully. "But now we have to move on, and this is the only way to save your mother. *Please*, Divya, you must believe me. What can I do to make you believe me, beta?"

"But it's all a lie. How long can Mama deny the truth that my baby is not her son, but mine?"

"It doesn't matter. She's well again. The woman we both love is happy and healthy. It's the most important thing. Everything else is trivial. It'll all work out."

"But even with my support, these lies can't continue. What will her friends say or think? Everyone knows Rahul died last year. We can't bring back the past. This is insane, Papa."

"I've spoken to everyone already. They believe that you've returned from India with our new adopted son, Rahul. They all know that Rahul is not the same Rahul, but they've been told to be very careful and sensitive in how they talk about him in front of your mother. Everything has been taken care of."

"But he's *not* adopted!" she cried. "He's *my* son!"

"And he's now in a loving home where all of his needs will be looked after. He will have a university fund established, and have both his sister and parents loving him. You'll be involved in every aspect of his life, and will watch him grow into a wonderful man. Tell me, Divya, if he was back in India with you what opportunities would he have now that he has no fa..." Sedhu trailed off.

"I'd have managed," Divya whispered.

"How? You could barely manage your meager lifestyle with two incomes and no child. How would you manage on one? What future could you possibly build for him?"

"At least we'd not be living a lie. You talk about Dharma, and you are right. I have a duty to be a *mother* to my baby."

"No, no, you're wrong, beta. Your first responsibility is keeping this family together. And without your mother, there's no family. Remember how sick your mother was after Rahul's funeral? Remember?"

Consumed with anguish, Divya thought back to her mother's vegetated state after Rahul's funeral. "It was horrible. She lost her will to live."

"Yes, and I suffered watching her condition deteriorate despite the drugs they pumped into her and the horrible treatments she endured. But now look at her. She is like the vibrant and loving woman who relished every aspect of life before the tragedy. It's as if the past year was some terrible nightmare. And without the return of her children, she would've never awoken. Don't you see? You and Rahul saved her! You two gave her the desire and will to continue to live."

"This is madness. I'm sorry, I can't do this. I can't pretend to masquerade as something I'm not. No matter how much I love Mama, you ask for the impossible."

"Ever since that fateful phone call with you, your mother's few words were always the same. She kept asking: 'Where are my children?' But Rahul was gone and you never came or called. What could I tell her? That her son was dead? That her daughter had willingly disappeared when she needed her the most? How could I sever the only hope she had left? So when all options had run out, I did what I had to do. If only you had called or come home, beta."

"I thought of her everyday."

"That didn't help her, beta. She was on a suicide watch for months. She had no reason to live except for her children, and her only remaining child had abandoned her."

"No, I never abandoned...I-I had no choice."

"Yes, you *did*. You *did* have a choice. You knew exactly what was happening here and you *chose* to ignore it. You failed in your duty as a daughter when your mother needed you the most. Anytime you were ill your mother wouldn't rest until you recovered, tirelessly worrying and tending to your needs. And where were you when *she* got sick, Divya. Where?"

"Papa, please don't do this to me. I want to see my baby."

"Now, you have a chance to redeem yourself. And you must. This is your second opportunity. *Please*, beta, I can't keep doing this without you. Don't you understand that? I have no more strength to fight this struggle alone. *Please*, help us, beta. I beg you, for the sake of your mother. She has already suffered through so much. Bring this family back together," Sedhu wept, dropping his head into her lap.

Guilt and confusion swelled her heart. "Please, don't cry, Papa."

"I am sorry, beta, I am so sorry. Please, forgive me for all the pain I caused you."

Divya bit her trembling lip. "I-I forgive you."

"And do as I ask. *Please!*"

"No, I can't."

"Beta, listen to me, listen to your Papa," he said looking desperately at his daughter. "There's something else. Ramar."

"What about him?"

"He's still in love with your mother."

"What? You told me he nearly beat her to death."

"Yes, it's true. But on some level he still loves her, and is obsessed with reclaiming the family he falsely believes I stole from him. He resents me and is deluded. He's never told me this directly, but every fiber of my being screams this when I speak to him."

"But it makes no sense. Why would he return me to you, then?"

"It doesn't have to! He's insane," he said, his watery eyes wide with fear. "Divya, he has given me little time to help your mother, otherwise he has threatened to take her, Rahul, and you back to India. If I can't help Rani then he believes he can. He's completely irrational, beta. Think about it, why else would he tell you who he was? Why would he tell you that I killed that Dalit and I stole your mother from him? He's trying to turn you against me. He's searching for any remote excuse to finish me and take you all back. He blames me for losing everything."

"But how could he get Mama? He's on the other side of the world. You're safe here in Toronto, right? Isn't this why you came here in the first place?"

"He now has the means, beta. I didn't think he could bring *you* here, but he did without any difficulties, and at a moment's notice. He is a very powerful and dangerous man. You've met him. I'm sure you've seen what he is capable of. He has powerful connections."

She thought back to her confrontation with Ramar in the hospital, and the rage she had seen on his face. Another shiver passed through her as she saw the terror in Sedhu's eyes.

"There's no telling what he'll do, beta. *Please* help us," he persisted desperately. "Or he'll destroy us."

There was a knock on the door. "The soup is ready," came Rani's muffled voice. "And I made a nice sandwich. Can I come in?"

"For your mother," he whispered.

"I'll do as you ask," she said quietly, hanging her head.

"Oh, God bless you, beta, God bless you!" he cried, embracing her tightly. "Thank you." He quickly wiped the tears from his face as he stood up. "Yes, Rani, come in."

The door to the bedroom opened, and Rani walked in with a tray. "Here you go, beta, hot, homemade soup. Your favorite."

Sedhu put his finger to his lips as stepped into the shadows behind Rani.

Divya smiled weakly as her mother put the tray over her legs. "Smells wonderful, Mama."

I've sold my soul, she thought miserably.

With Sedhu and Rani smiling and nodding with encouragement, Divya forced herself to sip the bland soup.

367

Chapter 20
The Pilgrim
Wednesday, July 24th, 2002

Divya studied the tiny, sleeping figure below her, tears rolling down her cheeks.

Moonlight streamed through the nursery's blinds and onto the peaceful face. When Divya had first sneaked into the nursery, she had promised herself to take no more than a minute to see her baby. But she had lost track of time, captivated by the life she and Aslam had created together.

"You have a son, Oz," she whispered. "I hope you knew that before..." she trailed off, painful loneliness and emptiness swelling within her.

As Divya examined her baby, the ache to lift him far surpassed the ache of her milk-filled breasts. But, she resisted; touching Rahul would shatter any control she had over her fragile emotions.

The baby began to stir as his mother's tears fell on his face. He began to squirm restlessly and his face scrunched up.

"No, no, no, don't cry," Divya whispered urgently.

Terrified that her parents would find her in the nursery, she closed the door and switched off the baby monitor moments before Rahul began to cry.

"Please, stop," she begged.

Filled with panic, Divya picked up the baby and held him up to her shoulder.

"Shhhhhh."

Rahul's crying intensified.

"What's wrong? Do you need your diaper changed?" she asked softly, sniffing his bottom. "No, that's not it. Are you hungry?"

Divya sat down on the rocking chair and instinctively began to lift her shirt. She froze, realizing what she was about to do.

Oh, dear God. How can I pretend to be something I'm not?

She anxiously strained to hear any movement or sound in the house. There was none.

Afraid that any moment of hesitation would change her mind, she put her wailing baby to her swollen breast.

The baby stopped crying and intuitively rubbed his mouth against her breast until he felt the nipple. Rahul started sucking on her milk vigorously.

It was a sensation Divya could never have described to anyone, something only a nursing mother could understand. At that moment, an everlasting and indestructible bond was created between mother and her baby. All her pain and loss temporarily dissipated. Time stood still. Divya's world became no larger than the nursery's four, colorfully painted walls—nothing else existed or mattered.

"Whatever happens, we'll always have this time together," she murmured, rocking the chair slightly. "This'll be our time. They can't take this away from us. I'll always be here to give you the nourishment that God has provided me."

A peace overcame Divya as she watched her baby feed himself to sleep. Reluctantly, she wiped the milk from his chin, put him back in the crib, and covered him with the blanket that only a year ago had belonged to her baby brother.

Divya studied her son for another hour before she forced herself to turn on the baby monitor. She kissed her sleeping son on his forehead, and quietly returned to her bedroom.

* * *

Wide-awake, Divya lay underneath her covers, listening to the familiar sounds of the house awakening. Those sounds gave her mixed feelings of nostalgia and horror. She could hear her father humming as he shaved and showered, and she could hear the banging of pots and pans in the kitchen as breakfast was being prepared.

It's as if nothing has changed, as if India never happened.

She closed her eyes, visualizing everything that was about to occur.

Once Sedhu was dressed in his suit, he would knock on her door to signal that it was time to wake up. He would gently ask her through the door to get ready, and then go downstairs to the kitchen. He would read the newspaper as her mother cooked an omelet laced with Indian spices, burnt toast, and Earl Gray tea. Divya would then force herself out of bed, and go into her bathroom to get ready. As she brushed her teeth, she would hear her father downstairs angrily flipping the pages of the newspaper, complaining about the bureaucracy of the Canadian government, the terrible state of the Indian cricket team, and how poorly his stocks were performing. As he would finish eating, her mother would urge Divya to hurry up as she was getting late for school. As Divya would run down the stairs—her hair still wet—Sedhu would be by the front door, putting on his shoes. She would peck him on the cheek and wish him a good day, and he would leave for work. In the kitchen, Divya would grab a strawberry yogurt, banana, and a multi-vitamin. As she ate her breakfast, and made a sandwich and salad to take with her to school, her mother would be trying to feed Rahul, who would be covered with food.

This was the routine her family had perfected for years, and now blood had been spilled to re-establish and preserve it. Divya felt a wave of nausea hit her.

There was a knock on her door. "Beta, get up. It's time to start the day," Sedhu said through the door.

Divya managed to wait until he descended the stairs before she dashed into the bathroom and threw up in the toilet.

Heaving, her hands still wrapped around the lip of the porcelain bowl, she heard Sedhu greet his wife, play with Rahul for a moment, and then turn to his breakfast. Divya flushed the toilet to drown out Sedhu complaining about India losing to Pakistan in yesterday's cricket match.

Wake me from this nightmare.

Another surge of vomit splashed into the toilet.

"Divya, hurry up, beta. You'll be late for school!" Rani shouted from the kitchen.

I graduated from school last year! Divya wanted to scream.

Divya closed the lid to the toilet and sat down, determined to wait until Sedhu left so she would not have to face him in the foyer. She wanted to do everything in her power to break the routine that her father had diligently tried to reconstruct.

After what felt like an eternity, she heard the front door slam shut. Divya sighed, feeling she had won a minor victory. She showered slowly, turning the water as hot as she could bear. Soon the pain of the searing water on her skin blocked out all thoughts. She brushed her teeth, combed her hair, and dressed, forcing herself not to think beyond each moment. As she descended the stairs, she was shocked to find Sedhu standing in the foyer, watching her.

He must have waited there for nearly an hour, Divya realized, shaken. *This is a nightmare that can't be altered. I can't wake myself up or escape. He'll never let me go. I'm too big a piece in his warped puzzle.*

"Have a good day, beta," he said with a smile, his wary gaze devoid of affection.

Like a zombie, Divya walked up to him and pecked him on the cheek.

He smiled with approval, and walked out of the front door, leaving her standing alone in the foyer.

Divya turned towards the kitchen doorway, which was ablaze with sunshine. She numbly entered the kitchen to find her mother trying to coax her son to accept a bottle of warm milk.

Get away from him! Divya thought, consumed with jealous rage.

The dark feelings within Divya disappeared when she saw the jovial expression on her mother's face.

"Good morning, beta. How are you?" Rani asked warmly.

"Fine, Mama."

"Did you sleep well?"

"Yes, Mama."

"I'm glad to hear that. You're feeling better?"

"Uh huh."

"Oh, yes, *good* boy!" Rani smiled with encouragement as Rahul finally began sucking from the bottle.

Divya looked away, unable to bear the sight of her baby in another's arms.

On the counter her yogurt, banana, and vitamin sat on a plate. Twenty dollars lay beside it—her spending money for the day. Sedhu had thought of everything, she realized. With limited access to money, he could keep her from running away. She had no choice but to stay. She was trapped.

"Do you have time to talk with your mother?" Rani asked, her attention still focused on the baby. "We've much to catch up on.

I want to hear all about your trip to India. Did you meet any nice Indian boys? A handsome doctor or lawyer, perhaps?"

"No, Mama," Divya replied, a painful look washing across her face.

"Come now," Rani persisted, still focused on Rahul. "Tell your mother, beta. I won't get upset. You're a beautiful, young girl, and soon it'll be time to get married and bring me grandchildren! I am not getting any younger, you know?"

"I'm late for school," Divya whispered, pocketing the money, and heading out of the kitchen.

"Yes, of course, beta, but *we're* going to finish this conversation later. Oh, before I forget, try to be back before seven o'clock for the party."

Divya froze. "Party?"

"Yes, didn't your father tell you?" Rani asked, looking up.

Divya shook her head.

"Of course he did. He must have. It's to celebrate Rahul's birthday, of course. Divya, I'm disappointed in you. How could you forget? You haven't even wished him a happy birthday," she scolded gently, turning back to the squirming baby.

Divya looked at the calendar hung beside the fridge. Sure enough it was July twenty-fourth. Her brother would have been four today. She glanced at her mother, who was wiping the milk that was dripping down the baby's chin.

This isn't the same Rahul, Mama. This isn't your son and this isn't his birthday. He's my son, your grandchild, and he was born on July twenty-first in Bangalore, India, where I fell in love and married my Oz. Your son died nearly a year ago. He was a good boy unjustly taken from us. You can't live this lie, Mama. And neither can I.

"You're such a good boy," Rani laughed, holding the baby against her shoulder and trying to get him to belch.

"Can I hold him, Mama?" Divya asked softly, yearning to embrace and protect him for eternity.

"No, not now, beta," Rani said, patting his little back. "You're late for school, and I have to bathe him. Say goodbye to your sister, Rahul. Say goodbye to your didi."

The baby belched, his round, dark, brown eyes—the same hue as Aslam's—staring at Divya.

372

Rani began to laugh. "Remember how Rahul always used to get didi and your name mixed up, beta?

"I remember," Divya said, teary-eyed.

"Come on Rahul. Say bye, bye, to divi. Bye, divi. Say *divi, Rahul.*"

Rani did not notice her daughter walk out of the kitchen and quietly close the door behind her.

* * *

With her father working at the University of Toronto, Divya's home was only a fifteen-minute subway ride to the downtown core.

Divya took the underground train downtown to the Eaton Centre, the largest shopping center within the heart of the city. The enormous complex was always jammed with people, the perfect place to disappear into obscurity for several hours. When Divya was studying at the University, she had often come to the mall during her spare time, window-shopping and fantasizing about the things she desired but could not yet afford. It had always brought her comfort. Now, it all seemed trivial and insignificant.

Divya found herself in front of a pay phone and dropped a quarter into the slot. She mechanically dialed the number she had memorized so many years ago, and prayed for someone to pick up the phone on the other end.

"Wai?" answered an oriental-accented voice.

"Oh, I'm sorry, I must have the wrong number. Is this four-one-six, eight-one-zero, one-zero-seven-six?"

"Yes, right number. Who speak with?"

"Tatyana Tully. Is she there?" Divya asked, desperate to talk to her oldest friend.

"Tully? No longer here. Mr. Tully, nice man, got good job. Sell house good price. Family move to Hong Kong six months ago."

"Do you have their address or phone number?"

"No, sorry."

"Thanks."

Disappointed, Divya hung up the phone. She could not believe that even her friend was gone. But she could not blame Tatyana. Divya had not contacted her once since she had been married, absorbed in her new life. Guilt and remorse filled her. She truly was alone.

Divya walked in a daze through the mall, trying to distract her anguished mind. But she did not find solace. She thought about how her life had been shattered. And she thought of Aslam.

She fondly remembered the past year they had shared, and dreamt of the life they should have spent until their children had children, and their devotion to each other had strengthened from decades of growing old together. She imagined her and Aslam still in deep love despite their old age, constantly laughing and making love in their small, cozy home.

Divya walked out of the mall, oblivious to the blast of summer heat that slammed into her, a dreamy expression on her face.

Her mind turned to the present, and she wondered what they would be doing right now if nothing had changed.

Oz would be getting ready for work, anxiously searching for a clean, ironed shirt, she thought. *And I'd be sipping my tea and teasing him as I waited for Ladha to come so we could go to the market.*

Screeching tires and blaring horns snapped her back to reality. Like a deer frozen in headlights, Divya stared at the car skidding to a stop a few feet from her. Hundreds of pedestrians were staring at her standing in the middle of the intersection as if she was insane.

"What the heck are you doing?" screamed the driver of the emerald Lexus.

"Get off the road!" shouted another driver.

"Do you *want* to get killed?" demanded a third driver, shaking his fist.

Shaken, Divya quickly crossed the street, wondering how she had ended up in the middle of a busy intersection.

Stop these senseless thoughts about Oz, Divya! You're going mad imagining a world that doesn't exist. He's not going to work ever again, and you'll grow old alone. Oz is gone, and there's nothing you can ever do to change that. Oz is dead.

Divya sat down on a bench outside a picturesque Catholic church, and buried her head in her hands. For the first time since discovering the tragic truth, she cried and mourned for the loss of her husband and the life they were supposed to spend together.

Through her despair, she tried to think of her options. How could she escape her predicament? No solution came to her mind. She had no money, no passport, and only a handful of distant high school and college friends who would certainly be endangered if they helped, even if she were somehow able to convince them of her dire situation. Although she could not explain it, she felt as if Ramar was even watching her now. She and her baby were trapped forever, condemned to live a lie that would eventually destroy them both.

"When tears are on the outside, healing is in the inside."

Divya looked up and stared at the figure as if he was an apparition.

Impossible.

"Om?" she gasped.

Om sat down beside her with a saintly smile.

"What are you doing here?" she whispered in shock, grabbing his hand to make sure she was not hallucinating.

Om pointed towards the church behind them where swarms of young people were emerging from the main entrance.

"You're Christian?" Divya asked with surprise.

"Going to church doesn't make you a Christian any more than going to the garage makes you a car. Laurence J. Peter."

"What are you doing in Toronto? You're supposed to be in New York."

"World Youth Day. The Pope arrived to the city today, and my starting date for work was postponed a week. This was an opportunity I could not resist. So, I decided to come here from New York like the hundreds of thousands of other pilgrims who've congregated here from every country on the planet. Divya, the love these people have for each other and life is overwhelming. In fact, we were all about to spread across the city to perform good deeds."

"But you just said you aren't Catholic."

"Do you know what Voltaire said on his deathbed in response to a priest asking him to renounce Satan?"

"No."

"He said: 'Now, now my good man, this is not the time for making enemies.'"

Divya laughed. She could not remember the last time she had laughed.

Suddenly, she was filled with remorse for exhibiting joy.

"Where's the baby?" Om asked, his eyes dancing.

"How'd you know?"

Om smiled, and pointed to the sky.

Divya blinked with surprise.

He laughed, and pointed to her flatten belly. "Actually, I knew before I saw you. I received an e-mail from Rekha this morning. She told me."

"How does she know?"

"She wrote that she and Naveen stopped by your home on Monday—"

"Oh, my God! I was supposed to talk to Rekha's parents about Naveen," Divya moaned.

"Don't worry about that. Once Rekha read the note on your door, she confronted her parents on her own, and after they met Naveen, her parents approved and blessed the engagement. Divya, Rekha is euphoric. They're having an engagement party next week. Half of B'lore is invited!"

"That's wonderful!" Divya cried happily.

Her smile vanished as she thought about what Om had just said. The only note she had written had been addressed to Ladha. Another thought struck her. Why hadn't Rekha or Ladha visited her at the hospital after she had had the baby?

"Om, what note did Rekha read on my door?"

Om curiously studied her. "The note *you* wrote addressed to Rekha and Naveen that said you'd gone into labor and given birth to a healthy son, of course."

"Did the note say anything else?"

"Don't you remember?"

"Remind me, *please.*"

"Okay...um, what else did it say? Oh yes, it stated that in an effort to repair the rift with your parents, you and Oz were flying to Toronto to show your parents their new grandchild. Frankly, I know how important your parent's support is to you, Divya, but isn't it a little too early to be traveling with your baby, especially since he was born prematurely?"

She did not reply, her mind whirling. Ramar must have implanted the false note. And if he had done that, then she was certain he had meticulously covered all loose ends in India. Aslam's work at Infosys and her classes had all been dealt with to prevent any questions from being raised. Ramar had effectively and permanently wiped the Khan household.

Her eyes widened as she thought of Ladha. She prayed Ramar had not found her; she had no doubt that he would ruthlessly dispose of Ladha and Karuppan if he had the opportunity.

"Actually, I apologize for criticizing," Om continued, oblivious to the fear on her face. "I am sure you wouldn't jeopardize the health of your baby if it was unsafe to travel."

"Did Rekha's e-mail say anything else?"

"Divya, what is going on?"

"Please, Om, tell me. It's important."

"Ummm...yes, let's just say that Rekha was very upset that you gave birth and left without even calling her. You should e-mail her as soon as possible, especially to congratulate her on her engagement. God, speaking of which, I haven't actually congratulated you for the baby, have I? Let's all go out for dinner tonight, my treat, if you're available, of course. Where's Oz? Is he with the baby and grandparents? He must be very happy to be a father. Is he helping you change diapers? If not, tell me. I've been experimenting with voodoo, and with some success."

She shook her head, struggling to contain her tears from the mention of her husband's name.

"Divya?"

She remained silent, her lips trembling.

"Areé, what's wrong? Why were you crying earlier?"

Divya looked away from Om, eyeing the C.N. Tower jutting far above the other skyscrapers as she tried to fight back her tears. The concrete tower looked magnificent in the cerulean sky.

"Divya, please tell me. Where's Oz?"

She burst into tears and wrapped her arms around him. "Oh, Om, he's dead. They killed him. My Oz was murdered."

Om's face drained of color. "Murdered?"

For the first time he did not know what to say. Face ashen, he held her tightly as she wept.

"Tell me," he eventually said.

Om listened as Divya told him the entire story from the moment she had gone into the labor to when he had found her on the bench outside the church.

"I hate them both," she said, referring to Ramar and Sedhu, her voice cracking with anguish.

"Gandhi always said: Hate the sin and not the sinner."

"Did you hear a word I said?" she demanded.

"The weak can never forgive. Forgiveness is the attribute of the strong. Gandhi also said this."

"I don't give a damn what Gandhi said!"

"Although the world is full of suffering, it is also full of the overcoming of it,'" Om intoned mechanically. "Helen Keller."

"Stop quoting dammit! *Stop it!*"

Om was silent, shaken.

"Oh, Om, I'm sorry," Divya wailed, burying her head against his chest.

"No, Divya, it's I who must apologize. You're right. I'm shocked that Aslam is...I can't believe it," he sighed sadly, his eyes welling with tears. "When I don't know how to deal with my emotions, I begin reciting quotes. And you're right, sometimes words can't make the pain go away."

"Om, what do I do? I'm so afraid and lost."

"We have to get you and your baby out of here," Om said with resolve, wiping his tears. "There's no other alternative."

"No, I can't. It's too dangerous."

"You can't escape your destiny, Divya. You can't pretend to be something you're not. You're the mother of that baby, not his sister. Your parents are delusional. This is madness. Everything that child is, and will be, is from *you* being his mother. How long can you continue this farce? Look how you already agonize."

"Om, no. It's too risky. They've already killed Oz. If they discover I can't continue this charade, or that I'm even considering running away, they'll take my baby away from me forever. I'd kill myself if something happened to him. Oh my God," she gasped. "I shouldn't even be talking to you. Om, you don't understand how dangerous these people are. They have eyes and ears everywhere. I've put you in grave danger. I must go."

Divya stood up, her surroundings suddenly feeling very ominous.

Om grabbed her arm. "Divya, wait a moment. Please, sit down, just for a moment."

She sat down on the bench, her eyes darting in every direction.

"Good. Thank you." Om extracted a card and pen from his red backpack, and scribbled on the back of it. "I'm staying at the Consular General of India's private residence. He's a close, family friend. My address and phone number is written on the back of my business card. If you need anything, or change your mind, please contact me anytime. Believe me, Divya, I'll take care of everything. All you have to do is call. You're no longer alone."

Divya fiercely embraced her friend. She squeezed her eyes shut, wishing never to let go. She desperately wanted to escape with Om, dreading the thought of facing her parents again. Reluctantly, she released her friend. She could not abandon her baby.

"One more thing, Divya. Take comfort and strength from your baby. Through him you'll know what to do. You'll both be in my prayers," Om said, his eyes filled with warmth and compassion.

She nodded with gratitude, and wiped away her tears. Bravely standing and turning away from her only refuge, Divya walked hurriedly back to a nearby subway station.

"God bless you and your baby," Om whispered as he watched her descend the concrete stairs to the underground.

* * *

Divya sat cross-legged on her bed in her pajamas, holding her old favorite teddy bear for comfort. The house shook from the laughter and clamor of the party downstairs.

The celebrations for Rahul's 'birthday' had begun an hour earlier, and Divya was unable to muster the will to face her parents or their friends.

After speaking with Om, she had aimlessly ridden the subway for hours. She had come home late to find her parents scrambling to make sure all the arrangements for the party were flawless before the first guest arrived.

Sedhu had hired a reputable Indian cuisine caterer and a bartender to ensure his guests were well looked after. He had employed a maid during the day to clean the house to a sparkle. Sedhu did not want Rani to worry about anything except tending to Rahul's needs. He was nervous; tonight would be a pivotal test for his wife and how she interacted with Rahul in front of others. Although he was confident that Rani would persevere, he was uncertain how Divya would react. She was sullen and unpredictable, and it made him apprehensive. As Divya had entered the house, Sedhu had criticized her for being tardy, and ordered her to hurry up and get ready.

For the umpteenth time, Divya sighed as she studied the lavender shalwar kameez draped over her desk chair. She did not want to wear Indian clothing, but Sedhu was persistent, arguing there was nothing else loose enough to hide her swollen breasts. Without her mother's knowledge, she was even wearing one of her bras; Divya's bras no longer fit her.

Divya ignored the knock on the door.

Sedhu opened the door and entered the room. Divya could not help but notice how handsome he looked in the suit he was wearing.

As he sat down on the bed beside her, Divya hugged her teddy bear, her eyes on the floor.

"Divya—"

"Don't bother saying what you were going to say, because I can't do this. I can't go down there and pretend to be something I'm not."

"I know this is a very difficult time for you, beta, and I'm sorry I snapped at you when you came home. I'm very apprehensive about tonight, and it was insensitive of me to take out my frustrations on you. I realize how much we're asking from you, especially so soon." Divya looked at him with surprise. "Yes, I'm not *that* selfish that I don't empathize with the suffering and pain my daughter is enduring."

"If you understand what I'm enduring as you *claim,* then let me be. I need to be alone. Everything is happening too fast."

Sedhu shook his head. "No, you must learn to move on. Trust me, in time everything will become less painful. You need time to adjust. Remember that..."

Divya stopped listening, her mind on Om's business card safely hidden underneath her mattress. Knowing that Om was nearby gave her strength and comfort.

Om's words filled her mind: *'Take comfort and strength from your baby. Through him you'll know what to do.'*

"Please, beta, you must come downstairs, just for a few moments. It'll make your mother very happy. Everyone is asking about you, and I made sure to order your favorite foods. Come, say hello, eat something, and then you can come back upstairs."

Divya put the teddy bear aside and stood up.

"That's my girl!" he enthused proudly. "Go change, and I'll wait for you in the hallway."

When Divya stepped out of her room a few minutes later, Sedhu smiled broadly. "You look beautiful, beta. Now, can you give your Papa a smile?"

Divya forced herself to smile.

"Good! You look lovely, beta, just like your mother," he said, leading her down the stairs.

For the next half an hour, she mingled with old and new faces. She did not hear a word they said, but somehow responded to their questions appropriately. For the entire time, her thoughts were focused on Om, wishing he was with her now.

Divya heard her mother laughing at the opposite end of the living room, but refused to look at her. She intentionally stayed as far as possible away from her mother, who was proudly displaying Rahul to a group of women.

When Divya felt she had made a long enough appearance to appease her parents, she began to make her way up the stairs, relieved that she had somehow survived the ordeal.

"Divya, where are you going?" Sedhu called out. "We're about to cut Rahul's birthday cake. Come here, beta." Divya ceased her ascent in mid-step, her shoulders sagging. "Come on, hurry up, beta. Your mother is lighting the candles."

Divya followed her father into the dining room where everyone was gathering around a spectacularly decorated chocolate ice-cream cake. Glittering in a golden colored, silk sari, her mother stood by the cake with Rahul in her arms.

Divya's heart ached at how adorable her baby looked in the new clothes he was wearing. She miserably thought of all the clothes she had knit for him over the past few months in her home back in India, never to be used. She remembered how Aslam always got angry with her for sacrificing her sleep by knitting throughout the night.

Divya sighed sadly. She missed him so much.

She stayed at the periphery of the room as Sedhu dimmed the lighting.

Sedhu motioned her to come stand beside them. She shook her head, but an angry frown from her father prevailed. Divya made her way through the murmuring crowd until she was beside her mother.

"He only drinks bottled milk," Rani was telling an old woman whom Divya had sporadically seen over the years. "Our pediatrician claimed that iron-fortified, Vitamin D enriched formula is just as nutritious as mother's milk."

"Is that so?" said the old woman, whose thick make-up was unable to conceal her intensely wrinkled face. "Well, Rani, I must say that you're fortunate to have such a precious son. He's *too* lovely. I've always wanted to have a son, but God had other plans for me, giving me *six* daughters. Does the baby keep you up at night?"

"Oh no, he's an angel. He gives his mother zero grief," Rani said, kissing him on the check.

"A perfect gentleman indeed," cackled the old woman.

Divya felt as if her heart was being ripped out watching her mother interact with her baby.

The old woman turned to Divya and smiled. Divya could not help but notice the large gap between her front yellow teeth.

"Divya, my child, how are you? How was India?" the old woman asked.

"Good, auntie," Divya said vacantly. Although she could not remember her name, it did not matter. All of her parent's friends were either referred to as 'uncle' or 'auntie.'

"You know, you've grown *too* much. I remember you when you were *this* big," the woman said, holding her hands three feet apart.

"Uh huh."

"Doesn't your brother look *too* cute?"

Can't you see that all of this is an elaborate farce! Are you all blind? Wake up! I am his mother!

"Yes, auntie," Divya said, jealously scrutinizing her mother and son.

"And your mother looks very happy. It's good to finally see her happy, isn't it, dear?"

Divya blinked. She suddenly saw her mother differently. Rani's face was glowing more from her beautiful smile than from the lighted birthday cake candles. Divya could not remember her mother ever looking so radiant. Her father was right. Rahul had given her mother a reason to embrace life.

"Yes, she is looking happy, isn't she?" Divya murmured, the conflict within her tearing her apart.

"Oh dear, I think you've spilled something on your lovely dress," the old woman said, curiously staring at Divya's chest.

Divya was horrified to find two stains growing around her leaking breasts.

"Did you spill something, beta?" Rani asked, her attention on Rahul, who was squirming restlessly in her arms.

Shocked and humiliated, Divya was lost for words.

"Everybody it's time to cut the cake for the birthday boy!" Sedhu cried out to break the awkward moment. He quickly handed Rani the cake knife.

"You'll have to forgive my daughter," Sedhu chuckled to the old woman. "She's always spilling things all over her clothes. She is quite clumsy and absentminded at times. She definitely got those traits from *my* side of the family."

"Oh, Sedhu!" the old woman cackled.

"Go change *now*," he hissed in Divya's ear.

"Actually, that's quite understandable, Sedhu. As you know, I have *six* daughters of my own," the old woman said, still suspiciously eyeing Divya. "And all of them are *too* absentminded, their minds always soaring in the clouds. They never listen. It really can be *too* frustrating. God knows how they'll manage their homes when they find nice Indian boys."

"Yes, I know exactly what you mean," Sedhu laughed loudly, his eyes glaring at Divya to leave.

"Excuse me," Divya mumbled, struggling to escape the dining room.

Tears blurring her vision, Divya quickly made her way upstairs and locked herself in her bathroom as the guests began singing 'Happy Birthday.'

Chapter 21
Dharma
Thursday, July 25th, 2002

Divya lowered her shirt over her breast, and wiped the drops of milk off her baby's tiny, pink lips.

She gently rocked the chair to lull her baby to sleep.

Am I doing the right thing? she wondered.

Divya had remained in her bathroom long after the last of the guests had left and her parents had gone to bed. Thankfully, neither of her parents had tried to approach her after the party.

During those hours locked in the bathroom, Divya knew that she could no longer endure a deceptive life entrapped in this house. She would no longer submissively endorse the evil that Ramar had created and Sedhu had accepted. With each round of laughter from the party below, Divya's anger intensified.

Why should I allow Ramar to eclipse my son's future? she had thought with growing fury. *Why should I resign myself to the tyranny of the monster that killed my husband? Sedhu may have conceded to Ramar's control over his life, but I'll no longer be his marionette. No, Ramar, no, I've severed my puppet strings. As long as I have breath in me, I'll fight. Your evil shall not prevail.*

An hour after she was certain her parents were asleep, she had emerged from the bathroom and changed into a T-shirt, jeans, and running shoes. Moving quickly, she had packed her old school backpack with any jewelry she owned. She had briefly contemplated tossing her own wedding ring into the bag, before dismissing that idea. No matter how dire her financial situation, she would never sell her wedding ring. It was a symbol of her union with Aslam, and even though he was dead, she knew his soul remained close to her.

Divya had then packed her bag with essential baby supplies. She spent a few moments searching the house for her passport but soon gave up, realizing her father had probably locked it in his safety deposit box at the bank as another means of ensuring she remained at home.

I'll show them, she had thought.

But now, with Rahul in her arms, she questioned her decision.

What if I get caught? What if they take my son away from me forever? What should I do? What is my Dharma?

The mantra she had heard in her Spirituality class suddenly came to her mind. Looking at her baby, she began to sing the prayer:*"Heý ishvarā dayā-nidheý bhavat-krypāā anenā japo-paasanā-dikarmnāā-dharmāā-arthāā-kaamāā-mokshāā-naam sadyah siddhiir-bhavennāh."*

Rahul peacefully fell asleep in her arms.

Yes, I am doing the right thing.

Filled with resolve, Divya carefully stood up from the rocking chair, and gently put her son on the change table so she could wrap him in the warmest blanket she could find.

Despite having it memorized, she put her hand in her back pocket to feel Om's business card. She pressed the thick paper of the card between her fingers for reassurance. The card was something tangible. It was her key to break away from her prison. The card made her believe that the words Om had spoken were not empty promises but her salvation.

Divya prayed Om would have enough connections at the Indian Consulate to help her, especially since she did not have a passport for herself or her son. But doubt continued to creep into her mind. Terrible images of being caught and punished by Ramar and Sedhu consumed her.

Stop it, Divya, stop it. Clear your head and focus. You can do this. Have faith in yourself.

Lips pressed tightly together in determination, Divya focused her mind on her goal.

She put on her backpack, and carefully picked up her son, hoping he would remain asleep until she left the house.

"Oz, my love, I know you're nearby watching over us. Give us strength and guidance," she whispered, cuddling her baby.

Divya smiled as the baby nuzzled against her shoulder.

Okay, time to go.

As she turned around, her backpack nudged the baby monitor off the table. It landed on the carpeted floor with a soft thud.

Terrified, she held her breath and tightly held her son. She stared wild-eyed at the closed door to the nursery, waiting for Sedhu to charge in and snatch her baby from her.

There was no movement in the house. All was silent.

Divya exhaled slowly.

She silently made her way past her parent's bedroom, and crept downstairs to the foyer. Divya hoped Sedhu had not changed the security alarm since she had left for India. She typed in the six digits representing her mother's birthday, and sighed with relief as the red light on the security panel turned green.

Divya opened the front door and walked outside.

Enthralled by the silent night, she forgot to close the front door. Everything seemed so peaceful and surreal. Even the crickets had ceased chirping. She felt as if she and her baby were the last two people on Earth. Only part of the crescent moon was exposed from the clouds. The strong warm winds brought minor relief from the humid night, but she did not care. She breathed deeply, as if she had finally broken the surface of the dark waters she was drowning in to get a lung full of precious air.

Divya looked at her sleeping baby for encouragement and strength. She could do this.

She cuddled her baby against her to shelter him from the wind, and quickly walked down the sidewalk towards the subway entrance.

* * *

A soft thud awoke Sedhu. For a few moments he lay in a sleepy daze, his mind reflecting on the successful evening.

Rani had looked glorious, laughing and smiling the entire evening. He could not recall the last time his wife had seemed happier. The entire party had gone extremely well. The guests had been full of praise, despite the small incident with Divya. Nevertheless, the damage was minimal, and whatever had happened was not his daughter's fault. She was trying, he reminded himself, and that was what mattered. In time, India would become a distant memory for her, and she would soon become absorbed in her life here. She was merely going through an adjustment period, he reasoned, which was natural. She would find interests, a job, and in time, remarry and properly start a family.

Eyes closed, Sedhu smiled at that thought. He imagined how all the guests would be brimming with admiration at his beautiful daughter, and how the community would gossip for generations about the dazzling wedding he had organized and hosted.

Soon their nightmare would be completely behind them, and everything would be fine again, just as it had been before. Their family would become so happy that not even Ramar would be able to intimidate him.

With a thunderous bang, the wind slammed the front door shut.

Sedhu sat up and instinctively grabbed the baby monitor. He put the device to his ear, straining to hear any sound. He heard nothing.

He turned to Rani who was snoring softly, the flawless features of her oval face fixed in an expression of serenity. He kissed his beautiful wife on the cheek. A faint smile crept on her lips. Sedhu relaxed, and leaned back into bed.

Was I imagining things? he wondered, eyeing the baby monitor again. *I should check on the baby, just in case.*

Sedhu sighed and got out of the bed.

Putting on his slippers, he yawned and scratched his head. He walked out of the master bedroom and into the nursery.

Sedhu felt as if he had been punched in the stomach as he stared with disbelief at the empty crib.

Oh dear God, no!

He ran into Divya's room—empty.

He looked out her bedroom window, desperately surveying the front yard and street. In the distance, by the intersection, he saw a silhouette moving quickly towards the subway station.

In his pajamas and slippers, Sedhu sprinted downstairs and rushed out of the house.

* * *

Divya watched Rahul sleeping peacefully.

She anxiously looked around the underground station. Nothing had changed. She was alone on the center platform, which divided the northbound and southbound tracks. The tunnel where the northbound train would emerge from was still in darkness. On the opposite side of the platform, the doors to the southbound train were open, and the only passenger—a vagrant dressed in torn, dirt-clad clothing—laid spread out across the plastic seats, unconscious in a blissful, drunken stupor.

As she impatiently waited for the northbound train, Divya studied the posters plastered on the walls across the tracks. In front of her was an advertisement by the Ministry of Tourism boasting the wonders of Niagara Falls. A huge photograph of the famous waterfalls dominated the poster.

She smiled wistfully as a series of pleasant images from that gorgeous, sunny day at Hogenakkal Falls came back to her—the aggressive monkeys stealing her bananas, her pregnant frame struggling to get onto the horse, and the intoxicated boat wallah smashing their coracle into a cluster of rocks jutting from the river. It had been the perfect, belated honeymoon.

That had happened less than a week ago, but it seemed like years had passed. That was a different world, a different life.

Divya sighed deeply, and tried to fight back the tears. Everything had been so perfect. How could so much change so quickly?

She suddenly remembered what Aslam had told her about the waterfalls as they had sat at the top of the cataracts overlooking the swirling chasm below.

'Did you know that many distressed lovers jump from this point to their deaths?'

Divya looked at her son. Tiny spittle was bubbling between his lips.

Oh dear Lord, what am I doing?

"Your attention, please, your attention. The southbound train to Union Station will be leaving this station in two minutes. Thank you for riding the TTC," said a pre-recorded voice over the intercom.

How much can Om possibly help me? she thought with despair. *But without Om's help, how can I do this on my own? And even if he does, how can I live with the fact that I've condemned my son's future?*

389

She glanced at the destitute sprawled within the parked southbound train.

Is that my son's fate?

She could not endanger Om with Rahul. It was far too risky. Enough people had perished. She removed his business card from her jeans with her left hand and threw it onto the railway tracks.

What was I thinking? This can't possibly work. I've no money and nowhere I can safely go. And even if we do escape, we'll always be on the run, afraid of being caught. We'll never have peace.

The conversation she had had with Ramar in the hospital room came to her mind, and then she remembered what Sedhu had later told her in her bedroom.

They'll never rest until they have Rahul. They'll always be chasing us as long as I have him. He's the key to their twisted plans.

There was a distant sound of a train. The northbound train was finally arriving.

And what about Mama? She's so happy now, and has nothing to do with this. She loves Rahul so much. What will happen to her if she loses another child? She never once asked anything from me, and now how can I bear the responsibility of destroying her fragile state? She looked so happy tonight—glowing. What if she goes back into depression, or something worse happens because of me? What if Papa is right and this is my Dharma?

She glanced down the tunnel. In the distance, the darkness was retreating from a faint, yellow light of the approaching northbound train.

But I can't live another moment in that prison back home, watching my baby grow to consider his mother to be another. I can't bear to witness it. I just can't do it. I won't do it. I'll never be his sister. I'm his one and only mother. My brother is dead and I can't live this lie.

Like the glowing eyes of a cat in a shadowed alley, two yellow dots pierced the darkness of the northbound tunnel.

But what will they do to me when they realize I can't continue this hoax? What will they do when they realize I'm an impediment to the success of their plans? How do I alleviate the suffering for both my baby and I? What do I do? What do I do?

Aslam's words came back to Divya: '*Did you know that many distressed lovers jump from this point to their deaths?*'

Divya thoughts shifted to the last words Om had told her in front of the church: '*Take comfort and strength from your baby. Through him you'll know what to do.*'

She looked at Rahul. And suddenly, it all became so clear. She knew what she had to do.

There is only once choice, she realized, studying his innocent face.

Slapping footsteps of someone quickly descending the staircase of the platform echoed through the station.

Divya kissed her baby gently on the forehead. "I love you," she whispered. "And I'll always be watching you."

"Divya!"

Divya glanced at Sedhu, who was staring wildly at her from the bottom of the stairs, gasping to catch his breath. She moved up to her father, placed the sleeping infant into his hands, and stepped back. He stared at her with disbelief.

"Thank God!" Sedhu examined the baby to make sure he was unharmed. "Let's go home, Divya," he sighed, his eyes still on Rahul. "We can sort this out tomorrow, okay, beta?"

The headlights of the northbound train had grown into a blinding intensity.

"Divya?" He looked up and his eyes widened. "Divya, come back here!" he shouted over the ruckus of the arriving train.

Divya moved closer towards the edge of the platform.

Sedhu stared at Divya, suspended in shock.

A blast of air swept through the station as the first of the train cars emerged from the tunnel.

Divya looked at Sedhu and smiled sadly. *Take care of my baby,* her eyes conveyed.

"*Stop!*" he cried in horror, realizing what was about to happen.

The brakes from the northbound train resonated through the chamber.

The doors of the southbound train began dinging.

Divya turned, crossed the platform, and leaped between the closing doors of the southbound subway.

The northbound train screeched to a halt.

391

Divya pressed her back against the sealed doors, trembling at the thought of what she had almost done. The vodka-reeking bum across from her groaned, his brown-bagged bottle nestled protectively in his arms. He muttered incoherently in his slumber.

As the southbound train began to pick up speed, Sedhu pounded the plastic windows with his one free hand, screaming for the train to stop.

Eyes glistening, Divya did not look back.

* * *

Sedhu chased the train to the end of the platform. He cursed as the rear, red lights of the southbound train disappeared into the tunnel darkness.

The northbound train doors dinged and shut, and it rushed out of the station, leaving Sedhu alone on the platform with Rahul.

As discarded paper and trash whirled around the platform from the rush of wind caused by the train's departure, Sedhu studied the little baby. He was pleased that Rahul was still asleep, despite all the noise and commotion. He kissed him on the forehead, and sighed with fatigue.

With no money or passport your sister couldn't have gone far, he silently spoke to the baby, stifling a yawn. *Don't you worry, Rahul, I'll find her in the morning. But, first, I need to bring you back home before your mother begins to worry, don't I?*

Sedhu turned around and gasped as three rapid flashes suddenly illuminated the shadows from one end of the platform. He grunted with pain as three bullets struck his chest.

Sedhu fell to his knees, wheezing for air. He stared at the man in the trench coat emerging from the shadows, walking slowing towards him. Smoke emanated from the silencer of the pistol clutched in the man's gloved hand. The gun disappeared into the trench coat.

The stranger gently took the baby, and leaned forward until he was inches from Sedhu's ear. "Your brother sends his deepest condolences of your imminent death."

Sedhu blinked at his murderer, his eyes beginning to glaze.

"But, he assures you that your family will be well looked after," the assassin added, with a devilish smile.

The man stepped back as Sedhu fell to the ground, struggling to take air from his collapsed lung.

Blood bubbled from Sedhu's mouth.

"Send my regards to that Muslim, pig, son-in-law of yours I slaughtered," the assassin chuckled as he strolled out of the platform, the sleeping baby in his arms.

EPILOGUE

Madurai City
Tamil Nadu, Southern India

Moksha
July 2012

With his entourage of assistants, bodyguards, the newly appointed Superintendent of Police, and a personal advisor, Ramar walked into the Ponnuswamy Barber Shop in the heart of Madurai. A triumphant smile plastered his face. Although the election was not until tomorrow, he had just been told that there was no question he would be the next MP of the Madurai Constituency.

Shri Ramar Mangalum, Member of Lok Sabha Parliament, he thought to himself, savoring the sound of his imminent title.

Ramar glanced around the tiny barbershop, surprised that it was empty. He always came once a month on the same day and time to have his faithful barber give him a thoroughly enjoyable haircut and shave.

Where is he? Ramar wondered with irritation.

The sound of rummaging from the storeroom in the back answered his question.

Ramar took a seat on the red, fake leather chair, and cried aloud in Tamil: "Hey, Mohan, hurry up! I don't have all day!"

A young boy emerged from behind the curtain. He was dressed in a creased white shirt, and a frayed pair of beige trousers.

"Where's Mohan?" Ramar demanded. Swiveling the barber chair around, he suspiciously eyed the boy.

Unable to meet Ramar's intense glare, the boy looked humbly to the floor. "Forgive me, sahib. He's gravely ill, and apologizes for not being able to serve you today."

"Who are you?"

"I am Mohan's nephew, sahib. He has been teaching me his trade for some time now, and if you'll allow me, I'll serve you today."

Ramar had not allowed another person to cut his hair for fifteen years. But, as his assistant had constantly reminded him, the next twenty-four hours were filled with speeches to the public, press conferences to the media, and meetings with the powerful few that controlled the district. This was the only time Ramar could cut his hair and get a professional shave if he wanted to look good in front of the cameras.

"Come here, boy!" Ramar commanded. "Look at me!"

The boy took a few steps forward, and anxiously glanced up.

"How old are you?"

"Twelve, sahib."

"And how long has your uncle been training you?"

"Nearly three years."

"And Mohan trusts you to serve me?"

"Yes, sahib."

"With his *life?*" Ramar demanded. The boy did not answer, his eyes filled with terror. "Do you know who I am?"

"Y-Yes, sahib."

"Good. Be warned that if I'm in any way displeased with how you cut my hair, or if you so much as knick me when you shave, I will *kill* your entire family in front of you, starting with your Uncle Mohan. Understood?" The boy nodded fearfully. "Good. Now, do you know *how* I want my hair cut?"

"Yes, sahib. Uncle Mohan was very clear on how to serve you."

"Excellent."

"May I begin, sahib?"

Ramar consented with a curt circular-nod. He watched the boy carefully examine the neatly arranged pairs of scissors on the table.

The young barber selected the pair that best fit his needs, and lowered the barber chair to the ground so he could reach Ramar's head comfortably.

One assistant took a seat on a tattered coach and grabbed a magazine to flip through, and the other assistant pulled out his mobile phone to verify Ramar's upcoming appointments.

Ramar's personal advisor was examining his Palm Pilot, and his bodyguards remained standing by the entrance to the barbershop, preventing any other patrons from entering. Superintendent of Police Rao took a seat on the couch, and unrolled the newspaper he was holding.

"Poor Auntie Seetha," he chuckled remorselessly as he read the main title on the front page.

Dalit-Loving Judge Murdered at her Madurai Home

The little barbershop was congested, and only three fans provided any relief from the terrible heat. Two of the fans were pointed towards Ramar.

Looking at the mirror in front of him, Ramar watched the boy expertly cut his graying hair. Satisfied that he would not have to kill the boy's family and end up wearing a headpiece to cover any damage the boy inflicted, Ramar shut his eyes and began to relax.

He thought about how much easier the election campaign had been than anticipated. He had actually enjoyed bribing officials and tampering the votes. By spending years ensuring his allies controlled the police and every major position of power in the district, Ramar's campaign had been relatively painless.

Ramar smiled maliciously as he thought about how the Untouchable community had pitifully tried to protest his candidacy by staging a peaceful demonstration in front of Madurai City Hall. With one phone call, Ramar had ordered Superintendent of Police Rao to send his forces to fire tear gas and rubber bullets at the crowd. The main Untouchable leaders responsible for organizing the protest were arrested, beaten, and left for dead in the local jail, their trials indefinitely postponed. And with his influence with the press, Ramar was delighted to read, listen, and watch through the local media how the Untouchables were accused of provoking the police.

Ramar made a mental note to find an appropriate, loyal judge to preside over the Untouchable leader's case. With the meddlesome Judge Seetha out of his way, Ramar would make sure that each of those Untouchables was condemned to spend the rest of their miserable existences rotting in prison. With Ramar's influence, the Untouchable leader, of course, would meet his untimely death once he was transferred to the local penitentiary.

Ramar only wished his father and mother were still alive to witness his greatest achievement. For a brief moment, his thoughts fell to his older brother. Even the presence of Sedhu would have made Ramar's moment of triumph more special. For the first time in a decade, Ramar felt a hint of regret. He quickly brushed the thought aside.

You're getting sentimental in your old age, Ramar thought, studying his wrinkled face and sunken eyes that looked every bit of their fifty-one years of age.

He closed his eyes, his mind inescapably drifting to the past.

Following Sedhu's death, everything had gone according to Ramar's plan—except for finding Divya. Despite all of his resources, he had never managed to locate her, eventually concluding with sadness that she was probably dead.

Despite the disappearance of his daughter, Ramar had traveled to Toronto to dutifully cremate his brother, and then bring Rani and Rahul back to India. He had grieved with Rani, and tried to help her overcome the tragedy of her husband's unfortunate murder. After six impatient months of mourning, Ramar had proposed. He was delighted when Rani agreed to marry him, and had unleashed the most spectacular wedding that Madurai had ever experienced. The entire city had celebrated for days during the auspicious event. Although Rani appeared sullen during the wedding, Ramar had assumed she was still mourning for Sedhu. More time was needed, he reasoned, and his love would help Rani move forward. But after the wedding, things between the new bride and groom remained unchanged, and Ramar's fury had grown as Rani refused to reciprocate his love for her.

For years he denied the fact that she had merely married him for the security of Rahul. He kept telling himself that she needed a few more months to mourn, but with each passing year, his patience to capture Rani's love dwindled, and he eventually accepted the fact that the bottle provided her far more solace and comfort than he ever could.

But there was still Rahul.

Ramar's chest swelled with pride at the thought of his son, the descendent to continue his legacy. Rahul was growing into a wonderful boy, far smarter, handsome, and stronger than any of the boys his age. Although a part of him still knew that Rahul had the blood of an Untouchable coursing through him, years of denial had made him ignore that terrible fact and push it to the deepest recesses of his mind. As far as Ramar was concerned, Rahul was *his* son, a virtuous, Zamindar-caste Hindu created between him and Rani. That was the only truth he was willing to accept.

"Sahib?"

Ramar opened his eyes and admired the barber's work. Although his face remained expressionless and his eyes devoid of emotion, Ramar was delighted with how his hair was cut.

With a proper suit to disguise my paunch, I'll look ten years younger tomorrow, Ramar thought, imagining how he would appear on stage in front of his supporters as he celebrated his victory.

"Did Mohan tell you how I like my tea, boy?"

The young barber nodded enthusiastically, eager at the prospect of further pleasing his master.

"Then get some for me and my men!" Ramar ordered sharply.

The boy brushed past the guards, and ran outside to instruct the tea boy across the street on how to prepare the tea.

The young barber re-entered the barbershop, and used a jasmine scented, powdered brush to wipe off any traces of hair around Ramar's neck. The boy pulled out a mirror to show Ramar the back of his head.

A circular-nod signaled Ramar's approval.

"A shave, sahib?"

"Yes, and be careful."

As the boy began preparing for the shave, Ramar beckoned his chief advisor.

"Sir?"

"Call my wife and tell her that I want her ready by eight o'clock for the reception with the mayor," Ramar instructed. "And tell Rani that I expect my son to join us during the celebrations tonight."

"Yes, sir." The advisor stepped outside to make the phone call.

The boy retrieved a new blade and carefully examined its sharpness with his eye and finger. Dissatisfied, the boy pulled out a long strip of leather and began to meticulously sharpen one edge of the blade.

You better be careful with that blade, boy, or I'll cut your throat with it.

It had been many years since Ramar had killed another with his own hands, but the thought of it still thrilled him. Regrettably, such acts were too risky for his political career. He now had an army of eager men willing to do it for virtually no pay, but just for the honor of serving him and his cause.

Although tempting, killing this boy won't be the best thing for publicity, Ramar thought with an inward smile. *Besides, he's a promising barber, and Mohan is getting old and won't be here forever.*

The advisor returned and nervously whispered to Ramar: "Sir, your wife is feeling tired and ill, and says she'll not be attending the reception tonight with the mayor. As for your son, his tutor has taken him for a field trip to some waterfalls for the day, and has forbidden him to attend the ceremonies due to his upcoming examinations."

"How can a child of ten be too preoccupied with exams to attend his own father's inauguration?" Ramar exploded, clenching his fists. The advisor cringed with fear, and stepped back. "His alcoholic mother and that overprotective tutor are behind this! I've barely seen him in the past six months because of these elections! I should never have agreed to have him educated by that quote-spewing moron!"

Suddenly conscious that he had said too much about his private life, Ramar tried to relax, and urged himself to enjoy the shave.

"I don't even know what that pompous, philosophical bastard is saying half the time," he muttered, sighing heavily.

I'll deal with them both after my triumph tomorrow. Rahul is old enough to begin to learn my business. I'll enroll him in the best school when we move to the capital, and tutor him privately in the evenings. Rani and that damn tutor can rot in Madurai.

The barber began to generously apply creamy lather to Ramar's face, and the soon-to-be elected MP's anger dissipated. He sighed and closed his eyes, his new plan calming him.

First MP and then Chief Minister, Ramar envisioned, turning his mind to more pleasant things. *And then I'll make the lives of the Untouchables in Tamil Nadu so miserable that they'll either be forced to leave or be eradicated.*

The tea boy entered the barbershop, precariously holding a tray filled with steaming glasses of tea. He placed a glass beside Ramar, and placed the tray on the magazine table.

The young barber began shaving Ramar, wiping the cut stubble and cream on a towel draped over his left shoulder.

With shaking hands, the tea boy lifted a glass of tea for the Superintendent of Police. Tea spilled over the edges of the chipped cup.

"Be careful, boy!" Superintendent Rao barked.

Startled, the tea boy dropped the cup of tea. Glass shattered at the feet of the policeman.

"Incompetent fool!" Superintendent Rao snarled.

Ramar opened his eyes and smiled, amused at the scene. He closed his eyes again, beginning to recite his victory speech in his head.

"I-I'm very sorry, sahib. I beg for forgiveness," the tea boy pleaded, crouching to pick of the pieces of broken glass.

The Superintendent of Police grabbed the tea boy's stained shirt and lifted him up angrily. "Who'll pay for my shoes to be cleaned, worm? *Who?*"

"Sahib?" the barber asked Ramar.

"What?" Ramar snapped, irritated that his few moments of peace were disturbed. His eyes opened with a flash of anger.

Superintendent Rao gaped with pain as the tea boy jammed a shard of broken glass deep into his throat.

"This is for the death of my family and all innocent Dalits!" the barber cried, slitting Ramar's throat from ear to ear with the razor blade.

The last thing Ramar saw through the reflection of the blood-splattered mirror was a familiar looking mole on one corner of the young barber's upward curved mouth.

401

* * *

With his small hands firmly clasped by the middle-aged woman with gray streaks of hair, and his tutor with the shaved head, the ten-year old boy navigated up the sun-soaked rocks and across the countless tributaries. The roar of the waterfalls became increasingly louder, intensifying the little boy's excitement.

The boy ascended a large border and gasped. A hundred feet away, he was captivated with the sight of a young woman, her long black hair and gorgeous silvery-white sari fluttering in the wind. She stood at the edge of the waterfalls, her back to them.

"Who's that, Mama?" the little boy asked as they continued to carefully walk over the rocks and streams.

"You remember what I explained to you earlier, beta. I'm *not* your mother. It took me many years to figure that out." She gratefully smiled at the tutor who had helped her escape the entrancing allure of whiskey, and made her discover the truth. "Remember, *I'm* your Grandmother."

"Is she an angel, Grandma?" the little boy asked, amazed at how the sun shimmered off the young woman's sari.

Both adults laughed.

"No, beta, that's not an angel," Grandma replied gently, brushing the bangs from his large, brown eyes.

"Then who is she?"

"I've explained to you several times whom you were going to meet today, beta."

"That's her!" he exclaimed.

"Yes."

"What's she doing?"

"My, you're one with many questions. She comes here every year on this very day to remember."

"Remember what?"

"To remember and celebrate your real father's life. She misses him terribly. He was a very good man."

"My *real* father? What'd he look like?"

"You, beta. He looked very much like you. In fact, I believe a large part of him lives through you," she said, placing her hand over his heart.

402

"Is that why I'm to be raised as a Muslim?" the boy asked, his eyes wide. "Because my father was a Muslim?"

"Yes, that's your mother's decision, and you must fully accept that. It would make your father very happy," the grandmother said gently.

"I understand," he said, looking at his tutor who had already begun secretly teaching him the ways of Islam over the past half year.

They stopped twenty feet away from the edge of the falls. There were no more streams to cross. The little boy and young woman stood at opposite ends of a flat slate of rock. The current whisked the frothy water surrounding the rock over the cliff. It was a majestic sight.

Temporarily out of questions, the little boy stared at the young woman who still faced the edge of the cataracts. He was unsure what to do or say next.

"Go on, beta," the grandmother urged him above the roar of the waterfalls.

"What if she doesn't like me?" he asked apprehensively.

"That will not happen, beta."

"But if she doesn't like me, will you be my mother again?" he asked hopefully.

"A pessimist sees the difficulty in every opportunity; an optimist sees the opportunity in every difficulty," the tutor recited. "Sir Winston—"

"Churchill. Yes, yes, you've told me that a zillion times," the little boy said impatiently.

The tutor smiled with approval. "Allah-u-Akbar," he praised, raising his hands into the air.

"My daughter has loved you since the moment you were born, beta," the grandmother said. "You have nothing to worry about. She has sacrificed much for you, and loves you unconditionally. Now go, but be careful, beta. You've nothing to fear. We're right here."

The little boy let go of their hands, and began to slowly make his way towards the young woman. Although scared, he refused to turn back and show his fears. He bravely moved forward towards the edge of the waterfalls.

The young woman turned and looked at the little boy. She crouched to her knees, her lovely face breaking into a warm smile, her eyes brimming with tears.

All of the boy's fears disappeared at the sight of the tender face that was somehow familiar to him. He ran towards her.

Mother and son embraced.

Glossary

areé: "hey."

Artha: a Hindu theological life goal of accumulating material wealth. A means of getting comforts and enjoyments in life.

beta: son or daughter, my child.

bidi: leaf-wrapped tobacco.

bhajan: a collective prayer, song.

chhee: "yuck" or "gross."

dandia raas: a dance performed by a group who move in circles in measured steps, marking time by the beat of sticks (dandia). The dance comes from the Indian state of Gujarat.

didi: sister.

Dharma: a Hindu theological life goal of fulfilling one's social obligations as a student, father, mother, daughter, sister, etc. It defines a set of rules to regulate our ethical and societal code of conduct. Dharma represents the conscience.

dhoti: a long, cotton loincloth worn by Hindu men.

diyas: tiny, clay lamps with cotton wicks soaked in clarified butter or cooking oil.

Diwali: the festival of lights, representing the new year on the Hindu calender.

duffer: a fool or moron.

karma: the effects of a person's actions that determine one's destiny in one's next incarnation. Karma is an act, or course of activites, that will consequently shape one's future.

Kama: a Hindu theological life goal of fulfilling one's desires. Kama is the experience of attaining pleasure through the senses.

kurta pajama: a loose, comfortable shirt without a collar that extends to the knees and matching loose pants. Generally worn men on the Indian subcontinent.

lakh: a hundred thousand.

lathi: a heavy stick, often bamboo, bound with iron, and used by Indian police officers.

Maharaja: a Hindu king.

Maharani: a Hindu queen, wife to the Maharaja.

mantra: a religious prayer, often chanted or sung.

Moksha: a Hindu theological life goal meaning liberation. Moksha is the pursuit of seeking liberation from insecurity, fear, and finding peace from within.

motti: a fat female.

murgi: chicken.

namasté: "hello" or "goodbye."

nah?: "eh?"

Om: In Hinduism, Om represents infinite peace and love, the absolute, and the super-conscious. Om is beyond the senses and intellect. It is to become one with a higher power.

pooja: worship, offering.

pundit: a Brahman priest versed in the Sanskrit language and the ritual practice of Hinduism.

rangoli: a traditional art of decorating courtyards and walls of Indian homes or places of worship. Colorful paint, chalk, or paste is used to draw intricate and ritual designs. Usually motifs of plants, animals, or geometric shapes are created.

rupees: Indian currency.

sahib: sir.

samosa: a deep-fried pastry filled with vegetables or meat.

sari: an outer garment generally worn by women on the Indian subcontinent. A sari consists of a length of light weight cloth made from cotton or silk, with one end wrapped about the waist to form a skirt, and the other end draped over the shoulder or covering the head.

shalwar kameez: light, loose trousers with a tight fit around the ankles, and a long tunic worn with a scarf. Made of cotton or silk, and worn by women on the Indian subcontinent.

sitar: a stringed, lute-like musical instrument that is played with the hands. The sitar is used to play classical Indian music.

tabla: an Indian tuned drum, usually in a pair of two sizes, that is played with the hands.

tharki: pervert.

yaar: friend.

wallah: a person who specializes in that trade

Zamindars: a group of upper-caste landlords.